ISABEL WOLFF

Forget Me Not

HarperCollins*Publishers*

HarperCollins*Publishers*
77–85 Fulham Palace Road,
Hammersmith, London W6 8JB

www.harpercollins.co.uk

Published by HarperCollins*Publishers* 2007
1

A catalogue record for this book
is available from the British Library

ISBN-13: 978 0 00 717829 2
ISBN-10: 0 00 717829 8

Set in Sabon by Palimpsest Book Production Limited,
Grangemouth, Stirlingshire

Printed and bound in Great Britain by
Clays Ltd, St Ives plc

This book is proudly printed on paper which contains wood
from well managed forests, certified in accordance with
the rules of the Forest Stewardship Council.
For more information about FSC,
please visit www.fsc.org

Mixed Sources
Product group from well-managed
forests and other controlled sources
www.fsc.org Cert no. TT-COC-2139
© 1996 Forest Stewardship Council
FSC

ACKNOWLEDGEMENTS

I am grateful to a number of people for help in the planning and research for this book. I would particularly like to thank the garden designer Charlotte Rowe who gave very generously of her time and knowledge; I am also indebted to the garden designers Clare Mee, Helen Billentop and Duncan Heather: any horticultural gaffes or infelicities are mine. I would also like to thank Sam Diment of Hammersmith and Chiswick Landscapes, Mike Gill of Bee Plus Ltd. for enlightening me about urban beekeeping; Sarah Anticoni for advice about family law, John Causer for information about aspects of criminal law and Neil Robinson of MCC Library. I am also grateful to Kate Williams and Holly Pope.

As ever I would like to thank my brilliant agent Clare Conville and everyone at Conville and Walsh. I owe a huge debt of gratitude to Maxine Hitchcock at HarperCollins for her brilliant editing, her generous encouragement and her patience with me when progress was slow. I am also grateful for the excellent additional editorial input I have had from Rachel Hore and Lynne Drew. At HarperCollins I would like to thank Amanda Ridout, Katie Fulford, Leisa Nugent, Cassie Browne and Bartley Shaw. Finally I am indebted, as ever, to Greg for his love and support during the writing of this book.

PERMISSIONS

For Alice and Edmund.

Show me your garden, and I shall tell you what you are.

Chinese proverb.

ONE

'It's hard isn't it?' said Dad. 'Saying goodbye.' I nodded, shivering slightly in the mid-February air. 'It's sad seeing it with everything gone.' We gazed at the back of the house, its windows glinting darkly in the late-afternoon sunlight. 'Maybe you shouldn't have come.'

I shook my head. 'I wanted to see it one last time.' I felt Milly's tiny hand in mine. 'I wanted Milly to see it one last time too.'

I'd been down several times to help Dad pack up, but this was the final goodbye. The following day Surrey Removals would arrive and our long association with the house would cease. As I stood there, memories spooled across my mind like the frames in an old cine film. I saw myself in pink shorts, on the swing; my parents, posing arm in arm under the cherry tree for their silver wedding photo; I saw Mark throwing tennis balls for Bob, our border collie; I saw Cassie doing cartwheels across the lawn.

'I'll just go round it once more,' I said. 'Just to check . . . you know . . . that I haven't left anything.' Dad nodded understandingly. 'Come on, Milly.'

We went inside, picking our way through the expectant crates, our footsteps echoing slightly over the bare floors.

I said a silent goodbye to the old-fashioned kitchen with its red and black quarry tiles, then to the big, bay-windowed sitting room, the walls stamped with the ghostly outlines of pictures that had hung there for thirty-eight years. Then we went upstairs to the bathroom.

'Starbish!' Milly announced, pointing at the curtains.

'Starfish,' I said. 'That's right. And shells, look, and seahorses . . . I used to love these curtains, but they're too frayed to keep.'

'Teese!' Milly exclaimed. She'd grabbed Dad's toothbrush. 'Teese, Mum!' She was on tiptoe, one chubby hand reaching for the tap.

'Not now, poppet,' I said. 'Anyway, that's Grandpa's toothbrush and we don't use other people's toothbrushes, do we?'

'*My* do.'

I opened the medicine cabinet. All that remained were Dad's shaving things, his toothpaste and his sleeping tablets. He said he still needed to take one every night. On the shelf below were a few of Mum's toiletries – her powder compact, her dark-pink nail varnish, streaked with white now through lack of use, and the tub of body crème I'd given her for her last birthday, hardly touched. I stroked a little on to the back of my hand, then closed my eyes.

How lovely, darling. You know I adore Shalimar. And what a huge jar – this will keep me going for ages!

'Mum! Come!' I opened my eyes. '*Come!*' Milly commanded. She'd grabbed my hand and was now leading me up the stairs to the top floor, her pink Startrites clumping against the steps.

'You want to go to the playroom?'

'Yes, Mum,' she panted. 'Paywoom!'

I pushed on the varnished door, inhaling the familiar musty smell of old dust. I'd already cleared most of the toys, keeping a few that weren't too wrecked for Milly. But there was still a stack of old board games on the table, a jumble of dressing-up clothes in a basket and, scattered across the green lino, a selection of old comics. The debris of a happy childhood I reflected as I picked up an ancient *Dandy*.

Milly reached inside a little pink pram. 'Look!' She was holding up one of my old Sindys with the triumphant surprise of an actress with an Oscar.

'Oh . . . I remember *her* . . .' I took the doll from Milly's outstretched hand and it gave me a vacant stare. 'I had lots of Sindys. Five or six of them. I used to like changing their clothes.' This Sindy was wearing a frayed gingham shirt and a pair of filthy jodhpurs. Her once luxuriant nylon tresses were savagely cropped, thanks, I now remembered, to Cassie. As I ran my thumb over the bristled scalp I felt a stab of retrospective indignation.

I know Cassie annoys you, darling, Mum would say. But try to remember that she's six years younger than you and she doesn't mean to be a nuisance.

'She's *still* being a nuisance,' I breathed. I held the doll out to Milly. 'Would you like her, sweetie?'

'No.' Milly shook her dark curls. 'No, no, no,' she muttered. The severe coiffure was clearly a turn-off. She thrust it back into the pram.

I quickly gathered a few things into a bin liner. As I did so a stray Monopoly note fluttered to the floor.

'Five hundred pounds . . .' I turned it over in my hands. 'Shame it's not real – we could do with some more cash right now – and this' – I held up a battered Land Rover – 'was Mark's.' Its paint was chipped and it was missing a wheel. 'You know Uncle Mark? The one who sent you Baby Annabelle?' Milly nodded. 'He lives a long way away – in America.'

'Meika,' Milly echoed.

'You've only met him . . . once,' I realised disconsolately. 'At your christening.' I looked around the room. 'Mark and I used to play here a lot.' I remembered changing the signals

3

on his Hornby train set and arranging the little fir trees by the side of the tracks. 'He and I were great friends, but we hardly see each other now. It's sad.'

Especially for Milly, I thought. She doesn't have many men in her life. Not much of a dad; no brothers, just one grandfather, and Mark, her only uncle, had been living in San Francisco for the past four years.

'OK, darling – let's go. Bye-bye, playroom,' I added as I closed the door behind us.

''Bye, paywoom.'

Then we crossed the landing into my old room. As we sat on the bed I looked up at the frosted-glass bowl light fitting in which I now noticed the hunched corpse of a large spider. It must have been there for months. Then I glanced at the window-panes, the lower left one visibly scored with large, loopy scribbles. 'I did that,' I said. 'When I was six. Granny was a bit cross with me. It was naughty.'

'Naughty,' Milly repeated happily.

'You'd have loved Granny,' I said. I lifted Milly on to my lap and felt her arms go round my neck. 'And she'd have adored you.' I felt the familiar pang at what my mother had been deprived of.

''dored . . .' I heard Milly say.

We stood up. I said a silent goodbye and closed my bedroom door for the very last time. Then I glanced into Mark's room, next to mine. It was almost empty, the dusty white walls pebbled with Blu-Tack. He'd cleared it before he left for the States. He'd stripped it bare, as though he was never coming back. I remember how hurt my parents had been.

Now we went downstairs and I stood in the doorway of their room.

'I was born in here, Milly . . .'

You arrived three weeks early, Anna. But there'd been heavy snow and I couldn't get to the hospital so I had to have you at home. Daddy delivered you – imagine! He kept joking that

4

he was an engineer, not a midwife, but he told me afterwards that he'd been terrified. It was quite a drama really . . .

Their mahogany wardrobe – along with other unwanted furniture – was being sold with the house. I opened Mum's side – there was a light clattering as the hangers collided with each other. I visualised the dresses that had hung on them until only a few months ago – it had been two years before Dad had gone through her clothes. He said the hardest part was looking at her shoes, imagining her stepping into them.

Now Milly and I went downstairs to say goodbye to the garden – the garden my mother had nurtured and loved. It was only just emerging from winter mode, still leafless and dormant and dank. But as we stepped outside I remembered the flowerbeds filled with phlox and peonies in high summer; the lavender billowing over the path; the lilac with its pale underskirt of lilies of the valley in May; the lovely pink Albertine that smothered the arch. Every tree, shrub and plant was as familiar to me as an old friend. The *Ceanothus*, a foamy mass of blue in late April; the Japanese quince with its scarlet cups. I remembered, every autumn, the speckly green fruit with which my mother made jelly – the muslins heavy with the sweet, stewed pulp.

Chaenomeles. That's the proper name for quince, Anna – Chaenomeles. *Can you say that?*

My mother loved telling me the proper names of plants and started doing so when I was very young. As I trailed after her round the garden she'd explain that they weren't just pink flowers, or yellow shrubs, or red berries. They were *Dianthus*, or *Hypericum*, or *Mahonia* or *Cotoneaster*.

'That purple climber there,' she'd say. 'That's a clematis. It's called *Jackmanii*, after the person who first grew it. This pale gold one's a clematis too – it's called *tangutica*. They're like fairies' lanterns, aren't they?' I remembered her pinching open the jaws of snapdragons, and showing me the fuchsias, with their ballerina flowers. 'Look at their gorgeous tutus!'

she'd say as she'd wiggle the stems and make them 'dance'. In the autumn, she'd gently rub open the 'coins' of silvery Honesty with their mother-of-pearl lining to show me the flat seeds within. Gradually, with repetition, the names sank in and I'd acquired a botanical lexicon – the lingua franca of plants. As I got older she'd explain what they meant.

'The Latin names are very descriptive,' she'd say. 'So this little tree here is a magnolia, but it's called a *Magnolia stellata*, because *stellata* means star-like and the flowers do look like white stars – do you see? This plant here is a Hosta tardiflora – a late-flowering *Hosta* – it's "tardy"; and that big buddleia over there's a *Buddleia globosa*, because it's got spherical flowers like little globes. And this thing here is a *Berberis evanescens* which means . . .'

'Disappearing,' I heard myself now say. 'Quickly fading from view.' I thought, bitterly, of Xan.

Then I remembered again the advice my mother had given me, at twenty, when I'd first had my heart broken. 'Jason seemed very . . . pleasant,' she'd said carefully, as I'd sat on my bed, in floods. 'And yes, he was good-looking, and well dressed – and I suppose he had that lovely car.' I thought, with a pang, of his Lotus Elise. 'But he really wasn't right for you, darling.'

'How can you say that?' I'd croaked. 'You only met him once.'

'But that was enough for me to see that he was, well, what I'd call – to use a gardening analogy – a flashy annual. They make a great impression, but then they're gone. What you really want, Anna, is a hardy perennial.' I'd had a sudden image of myself marrying a *Forsythia*. 'A hardy perennial won't let you down. It will show up year after year, reliable, and trustworthy – and safe. Like your father,' she'd added. 'Always there for me. Whatever . . .'

I picked Milly up. 'I didn't do what Granny advised,' I whispered. 'But it doesn't matter, because it means I've got

6

you. And you're just' – I touched her nose with mine – 'the sweetest thing. The bees' knees.'

'Bizzy nees.' She giggled.

I hugged her, then put her down. 'Now look at these little flowers, Milly. They're called snowdrops. Can you say that? Snowdrops?'

'Snowtops . . .'

'And these purple ones here are called crocuses . . .'

'"Kisses.' Her breath came in tiny pillows on the frosty air.

'And this, you may be interested to know, is a miniature wild cyclamen.'

'Sick . . .' Milly giggled again.

'Granny used to say they had windswept little faces, as though they'd stuck their heads out of the car window.' As we stood up, then walked across the lawn, I imagined myself, as I often did, years hence telling Milly what had happened to my mum.

You had a wonderful granny, I could hear myself say. She was a lovely, vibrant person. She was interested in lots of things and she was especially interested in gardening. She knew a lot about it and was very good at it – she'd taught herself the names of all the plants and flowers. And she would have taught you them, Milly, like she taught me, but sadly she never got the chance, because a year before you were born she died . . .

I heard a step and looked up. Dad was coming through the french windows, holding a cardboard box. Like the house, he had an air of neglect. He used to look well-preserved for his years, young, even. At nearly seventy, he was still good-looking, but had been aged by grief.

I never thought I'd be without your mother, he'd say for months afterwards. She was twelve years younger than me. I simply never thought it. I don't know what I'll do.

Now, after three years, he did. He'd finally felt able to sell up and was moving to London, just a mile away from Milly and me. 'I've loved this house,' he said as he came and stood next to us. 'We've been here so long. Nearly four decades.'

I imagined what the walls had absorbed in that time. Talking and laughter; weeping and shouting; the cries of child-birth, even. I imagined us all embedded into the very fabric of the house, like fossils.

I heard Dad sigh. 'But now it's time to uproot and move on.'

'It's for the best,' I said. 'London will be distracting. You'll feel happier there – or, at least, better.'

'Maybe,' Dad said. 'I don't know. But it'll certainly be nice being so near to you and Milly.' I noticed the silvery stubble on his jaw. 'I hope you won't mind me dropping in from time to time.'

'I wish you wouldn't say that,' I protested gently. 'You know you can come whenever you like. I've encouraged you to do this, remember?'

'I won't be a nuisance.' I rolled my eyes. 'And I'll babysit for you. You should take me up on that, Anna. Babysitting's expensive.'

'That's kind, but you'll need to get out yourself – see your friends – go to your club, plus I've got Luisa now, haven't I?'

'That's true.'

I reflected gratefully on what wonderful value for money au pairs are. I could never have afforded a part-time nanny – especially with the fees for Milly's new nursery school. But for seventy pounds a week, I get up to five hours' help a day from Luisa, plus two babysits. She's a godsend.

'Not that I go out that much,' I told Dad. 'I usually work when Milly's asleep. I can get a lot done then.'

'You should go out more,' he said. 'It would be good for you. Especially in your situation.' He set off down the garden – Milly and I following – then he stopped to hold back an overhanging spray of winter jasmine. Everything looked so unkempt.

'Thanks for all the sorting out you've done over the past month,' he added as we walked on. 'I know I've said it before, but I've really appreciated it.'

'All I did was a few runs to Oxfam, and I didn't clear everything.'

'Well, it was wonderful just having you here. I'd have got very down doing it on my own.'

I thought, irritably, of my siblings. Mark's in the States, fair enough; but Cassie could have helped. She only came once, to clear her own room. Not that Dad seemed to mind. But then he indulges Cassie, as though she's nine years old, not twenty-nine. Being the 'baby', she's always been spoilt.

Our feet crunched over the gravel as Milly and I followed Dad down the long, narrow path, past the silver birch and the greenhouse. I had a sudden image of my mother in there, in her straw hat, bent over a tray of seedlings. I imagined her glancing up, then waving to us. We walked on, and I assumed that Dad was taking the box to the garage to put in the car. Instead, he stopped by the bonfire patch and began to pile bits of wood on to the blackened earth with a fork.

'I saw Xan yesterday,' I heard him say as he splintered an old crate underfoot.

My heart stopped for a beat, as it always does at Xan's name.

'Where was that, then?' I smiled a bitter little smile. 'On the nine o'clock news? The one o'clock? *Panorama?*'

'*Newsnight.*'

'Oh.' A solitary magpie flew overhead. 'What was he talking about?'

'Illegal logging.'

'I see . . .'

'Poor you,' Dad said. He leaned on the fork. 'You cope very well, Anna, but being a single mum's not what your mother and I would have wished for you.'

What you need is a hardy perennial. Someone who'll always be there for you. Whatever . . .

'Don't misunderstand me,' Dad added quickly. 'I love Milly so much . . .' He reached out to stroke her head and I noticed how frayed the cuffs of his shirt were. I made a mental note to take him shopping for some new ones. 'But I wish you had a better set-up, that's all.'

'Well . . . I wish I did too.'

'It can't be easy.'

'It isn't.' In fact, it's hard, I reflected grimly. However much you love your child, it's hard bringing them up on your own. It's hard not having anyone with whom to share the daily anxieties, or the responsibility, or the joys, let alone the long, lonely nights when they're tiny babies, or the naked terror when they're ill. 'But this is the set-up I've got. And there are plenty of kids who have *no* contact with their fathers.' I thought of Jenny, my friend from NCT. 'And at least Milly does have *some* sort of relationship with her dad' – I bit my lip. I had uttered the dreaded 'D' word.

'Daddy!' Milly yelled, right on cue. '*Daddy!*' She's only met Xan six times in her two and a half years, but she adores him. 'Dad-*dy*!' she repeated indignantly. She stamped her feet, dancing on the spot with frustration, then threw back her head. 'Dad-*deee*!' she yelled, as though she thought she might summon him.

'It's all right, darling,' I soothed. 'You'll see Daddy soon.' This wasn't so much a white lie, as a neon-flashing Technicolor one, as I hadn't the slightest idea when we'd next see Xan. Milly has to make do with seeing him on TV. She's elated for the few moments he's on-screen, then she bursts into tears. I know just how she feels.

'Dad-*eee* . . .' Her face had crumpled and her big grey-blue eyes had filled. My father distracted her by getting her to help him pick up leaves. I stooped to pick some up too and, as I did so, my eye fell on the cardboard box, which seemed to be full of old papers. On one yellowing envelope I saw my mother's neat italics.

'Good girl,' I heard Dad say as Milly scooped up twigs in her mittened hands. 'Let's pick up these leaves over here, shall we – they're nice and dry. That's it, poppet. Now, go and stand next to Mummy while I light the fire.'

'I always thought I'd be just like Mum,' I said, almost to myself now, as Milly wrapped her arms round my knees. 'I thought I'd have a completely conventional family life – just like she did.' Dad didn't reply. He was trying to strike a match, but they kept breaking. 'I thought I'd have a husband and kids. I never imagined myself bringing up a child alone, but then . . .' I shook my head.

'. . . then life happened,' Dad said quietly. The match flared and he cupped it, then put it to the pile.

'Yes. That's what happened. Life.' We heard the crackle of burning leaves and a thread of pewtery smoke began to curl upwards, scenting the air.

Dad straightened up. 'Have you taken absolutely every-thing you want from the house? Because what doesn't go in the removals van will be disposed of by the cleaners. I left out a pile of your mum's gardening books I thought you might want. Did you see them?'

'Yes, thanks. I just took three, and her trowel and fork – I wanted to have those.'

'That would make her happy,' he said. 'She'd be so pleased at what you're doing. Not just because she loved gardening so much, but because she thought the City was too hard for you – those long hours you had to do.'

'I do long hours now.'

'That's true.' Dad began to fan the fire with the rusty lid from an old biscuit tin. 'But at least you're not a wage slave any longer – it's all for you and Milly. Plus you enjoy what you're doing more.'

11

'Much more,' I agreed happily. From the holly we heard the chittering of a wren. 'I love being a garden designer.'

'A fashionable one according to *The Times*, eh?' That unexpected bit of coverage had really lifted my confidence; Sue, my former PA, had spotted it and phoned me. 'And those appearances on GMTV must have helped.'

'I think they did.' I'd recently done five short pieces about preparing the garden for spring.

'And what happened with that big contract in Chelsea you were hoping to get?'

'The one in The Boltons?' Dad nodded. 'I've done the survey and I'm taking the designs over on Saturday. If it goes ahead it'll be my biggest commission by a very long way.'

'Well – fingers crossed. But if you're ever stuck for money you know I'll lend you some. I could be a sleeping partner in the business,' he added with a smile.

'That's kind, but I budgeted for the first two years being a bit tough and you know I'd never ask you for help.' Unlike Cassie, I thought meanly. She's always touching Dad for cash. Like that time last year when she simply *had* to go and find herself on that Ashtanga Yoga retreat in Bhutan – Dad had 'lent' her most of the three and a half grand. 'Anyway,' I went on, 'things should be a little easier this year.' There was a soft pop as sparks burst from the fire, like lava from a tiny volcano.

'Well . . .' There was a sudden, awkward silence. Dad cleared his throat, then I saw him glance at the box. 'I . . . imagine you'll want to be getting back now, won't you?'

'I . . . guess so.' I looked at my watch. It was only 3.30. I still wasn't quite ready to say my final farewell, plus I was enjoying the warmth of the fire.

'I know you don't like driving in the dark.'

'That's true.'

'And then it'll be Milly's bedtime.'

'Mm.'

'And I've got things to do, actually.'

'Oh.' Dad wasn't usually in a hurry for us to leave – quite the opposite. 'OK, then . . . we'll be on our way.' I looked at the cardboard box. 'Are you sure you don't need help with anything else before I go?'

'No. I've just got to deal with this before the light goes.'

'What is it?'

'Just . . . old correspondence.' I suddenly saw that a red stain had crept up Dad's neck. 'Valentine cards I'd sent your mum – that sort of thing.'

I didn't remind him that today was Valentine's Day. Not that I'd received so much as a petal, I thought ruefully. I was a romance-free zone.

'She never threw them away,' I heard Dad say. 'When I finally went through her desk I found them.' He shook his head. 'Every Valentine card I'd ever sent her – thirty-six of them,' he went on wonderingly. 'She was very sentimental, your mum. Then I sorted through some old letters that she'd sent me.'

I did up Milly's top button. 'But why would Mum write to you when you were married?'

Dad fanned some smoke away. 'It was when I was in Brazil.' He looked at me. 'I don't suppose you remember that, do you?'

'Vaguely . . . I remember waving you off at the airport with Mum and Mark.'

'It was in 1977, so you were five. I was out there for eight months.'

'Remind me what you were doing.'

'Overseeing a big structural repair on a bridge near Rio. The phone lines were terrible, so we could only keep in touch by letter.'

Now I remembered going to the post office every Friday with our flimsy blue aerogrammes. I used to draw flowers on mine, as I couldn't write.

13

'It must have been hard for you, being away for so long.'

'It was,' Dad said quietly.

'So that was before Cassie was born?'

He snapped in half a small, rotten branch. 'That's right. Cassie was born the following year.'

I looked at the box again – a repository of so much emotion. 'Are you sure you don't want to keep them? It seems a pity.'

'I will keep them.' Dad tapped his chest. 'Here. But I don't want to sit in my new flat surrounded by things that make me feel . . .' His voice had caught. 'So . . . I'm going to look at them one last time, then burn them.'

'I understand,' I said. 'We'll be on our way, then. But ring me when you've got to London and we'll pop over.' Dad nodded. 'Say bye-bye to Grandpa then, darling.'

Milly tipped up her face to be kissed.

'Bye-bye, my little sweetheart.'

I hugged him. ''Bye, Dad.' *Damn*. I'd done it again.

'*Dad*-ee!' Milly cried.

By the time I'd strapped her into her car seat, and we were turning out of the drive, Milly was chanting 'Dad-dy! Dad-dy!' with the passion and vigour of a Chelsea supporter.

'It's OK, darling,' I sang. 'We *will* be seeing Daddy, but not for a little while, because he's busy at the moment.'

'Daddy. Bizzy,' she echoed. 'Bizzy. Daddy!'

'Oh! Look at that horsy,' I said.

''Orsy! Dad-*dy*!'

'And those lovely moo cows. Look.'

'Moo cows. Dad*eeeee* . . .'

As we idled at a red light, I glanced in the mirror and Xan's eyes stared back at me – the colour of sea holly. I often wished that Milly didn't resemble him so much. And now, as her lids closed with the hum of the engine and the warmth of the car, I recalled meeting Xan for the first time. Not for

14

a moment could I have imagined the shattering effect that he would have on my life.

As I released the clutch and the car eased forward, I remembered how cautious I'd always been until then. I was like Mark in that way – sensible and forward-looking. Unlike Cassie.

'You need to have a life plan,' Mark would say. He was two years older and we were close in those days, so I listened to him. 'I'm going to be a doctor.'

By fourteen, I had my own plan mapped out: I'd work hard, go to a decent university, get a good job and buy a flat. In my late twenties I'd find myself that nice hardy perennial, get married and have three children, going back to work when the youngest was at school. My salary would not be essential, but would pay for a seaside cottage somewhere, or a house in France, which said hardy perennial and I would ultimately retire to, enjoying frequent visits from our devoted children and grandchildren, before dying peacefully, in our sleep, at ninety-nine.

For years I'd followed my plan to the letter. I read History at York, then got a job at a City hedge fund, where I joined the Equity Research department, gathering intelligence on investment ideas – analysing 'fundamentals across multiple sectors' as they called it. The work wasn't always thrilling, but it was very well paid. I bought a small house in Brook Green, paid the mortgage and pension; then, with the rest, I enjoyed myself. I went skiing, diving and trekking; I joined a gym. I went to the opera, where I sat in the stalls. I spent time in my garden, and with family and friends. I was on track to reach my personal goals.

When I turned thirty, I started on the treadmill of engagement parties, hen nights and weddings. Feeling I ought to make more of an effort to meet someone, I joined a tennis club, gave parties and went on dates. With these I kept in mind my mother's old-fashioned precepts: 'Wait before returning their calls,' she'd often say. 'Make them think you're too busy to see them. Never, *ever* throw yourself at them, Anna. Try and retain a little "feminine mystique".' I'd groan at all this, but she'd retort that there was a little dance of courtship that needed to be danced and that it was her duty to give me 'womanly' advice.

'All mothers should,' she once said with a vehemence that took me aback. 'My mother never told me anything,' she'd added bitterly. 'She was too embarrassed. But I wish she had done, because it meant I was hopelessly unworldly.'

Which probably explains why she married Dad when she was twenty.

'It was a whirlwind romance,' she'd say coyly whenever the subject came up.

I'd discreetly roll my eyes, because I've always known the truth.

'A tornado,' Dad would add with a wry smile. They'd gone up the aisle two months after meeting at the Lyons Corner House on The Strand.

'It was raining,' Mum would say, 'so the café was full. Suddenly this divine-looking man came up to me and asked if he could share my table – and that was that!'

But it used to amuse me that my mother, whose own romantic life had been so happily uneventful, should seem so anxious to educate me about affairs of the heart.

The men I dated were all attractive, clever and charming, and would have been 'husband material', were it not that they all seemed to have major drawbacks of one sort or another. Duncan, for example, was a successful stockbroker – intelligent and likeable – but his enthusiasm for lap-dancing clubs was a problem for me; then there was Gavin who was still getting over his divorce. After that I dated Henry, an advertising copywriter, who avoided traffic jams by driving on the pavement. The second time he was cautioned I called it a day. Then I met Tony, a publisher, at a wedding in

16

Wiltshire. Tony was clever and fun. But when after six months he said that he didn't want anything long-term I ended it. I couldn't afford to waste my time.

'You've still got ages, darling,' my mother had said consolingly afterwards. We were sitting on the garden bench in Oxted, under the pear tree. It was her birthday, the tenth of May. She put her arm round me, wrapping me in the scent of the Shalimar I'd given her that morning. 'You're only thirty-two, Anna,' I heard her say. My eyes strayed to the little blue clouds of forget-me-nots floating in the flowerbeds. 'Thirty-two's still young. And women have their children much later now – thank goodness.'

I suddenly asked her something I'd always wanted to know: 'If you could have your time again, Mum, would you have waited longer before starting a family?' She'd had Mark when she was just twenty-one.

'Well . . .' she'd said, blushing slightly, 'I . . . don't think having a child is ever a mistake.' Which wasn't what I'd meant. 'But yes, I did start very early,' she'd gone on, 'so I never really worked – unlike you. But you're lucky, Anna, because you're of the generation that can have a fulfilling career, fun and independence, and *then* the happiness of family life. And you're not to worry about finding that,' she repeated, stroking my hair. 'Because you've still got lots of time.'

Which was something that she herself didn't have, it seemed, because less than a month later she'd died.

Now, as I turned on to the motorway I remembered – as I often do when I'm driving and my mind can range – that awful, awful time. I was so shocked I could barely breathe. It was as though the Pause button had been pressed on my life. What would I do without my mother? I felt as though I'd been pushed off a cliff.

And what if *I* only had twenty-three years left, I had then begun to wonder, as I lay staring into the darkness, night after night. What if I only had ten years left, or five, or *one*?

Because I now understood, in a way I could never have grasped before, how our lives all hang by a thread.

I had a fortnight's compassionate leave, which I needed, as I had to organise the funeral as Dad could barely function. Going back to work after that was a relief in some ways – though I remember it as a very strange time. My colleagues were kind and sympathetic to begin with, but as time went on, naturally, they stopped asking me how I was, as though it was expected that life should now carry on as normal. Except that nothing seemed 'normal' any more. And as the weeks went by I felt increasingly dissatisfied with the life I'd been leading – the fact-finding about investment opportunities that were of zero interest to me – the number-crunching and the daily commute. I now 'analysed the fundamentals' of my own existence and realised that the goals I'd striven to achieve seemed trivial. So I made a decision to change my life.

I'd often daydreamed about giving up the rat race and becoming a garden designer. I could never go to someone's house without imagining how their garden would look if it were landscaped differently or planted more imaginatively. I'd already designed a couple of gardens as a favour – a Mediterranean courtyard for my PA, Sue, at her house in Kent; and a cottage garden for an elderly couple over the road. They'd been delighted with its billowing mass of hollyhocks and foxgloves, and doing it had given me a huge buzz.

So I signed up for a year's diploma course at the London School of Gardening in Chelsea. Then I went to see my boss, Miles.

'Are you quite certain?' he asked as I sat in his office, heart pounding at the thought of the security – and the camaraderie – I was about to sacrifice. He rotated his gold fountain pen between his first and second fingers. 'You'll be giving up a lot, Anna – not least the chance of a directorship in maybe two or three years.' I had a sudden vision of my name on the thick vellum company stationery. 'Don't think I'm trying to dissuade you,' Miles went on, 'but are you sure you want to do this?' I glanced out of the window. A plane was making its way across the cobalt sky, leaving a bright, snowy contrail. 'You've been through a lot lately,' I heard him say. 'Could it just be a reaction to your mother's death?'

'Yes,' I replied quietly. 'That's exactly what it is. Which is why I *am* sure I want to do it – thanks.'

I worked out my notice; then, in early September Miles gave me a leaving party in the boardroom. Seeing the big turnout, I was glad I'd put on my most glamorous Prada suit – I'd been thrilled because I'd got it half price – and my beloved Jimmy Choos. I wouldn't be wearing these heels for a long time, I thought, as I circulated. I wouldn't be buying any more either – I'd have zero income for the next year. Nor would I be drinking champagne, I thought, as I sipped my third, nerve-steadying glass of fizz.

Suddenly Miles chinked his glass, then ran his hand through his blond curls – he looked like an overgrown cherub. 'Can I have everyone's attention?' he said, as the hubbub subsided. 'Because I'd just like to embarrass Anna for a moment.' A sudden warmth suffused my face. Miles flipped out his yellow silk tie. 'Anna – this is a very sad day for all of us here at Arden Fund Management – for the simple reason that you've been a dream colleague.'

'And a dream boss!' I heard Sue say. I smiled at her. 'I'm regretting egging you on to do this gardening lark now!'

'You've been a real team player,' Miles went on. 'Your meticulous research has helped us do our jobs with so much more confidence. You've dug away painstakingly on our behalf. And now you're set to do spadework of a different kind.' I smiled. 'Anna, we're going to miss you more than we can say. But we wish you every success and happiness in your new career – in which we hope that these small tokens of our huge appreciation will come in useful.'

19

I stepped forward and he presented me with a large, surprisingly heavy gift bag, from which I pulled out a silver-plated watering can – engraved with my name and the date – and a pair of exceptionally clumpy green wellies. I laughed, then made a short thank you speech, just managing not to cry, as the reality of it all finally hit me. Then, clutching my presents and having tipsily – and tearfully now – hugged everyone goodbye, I went to have supper with Sue.

It felt strange going through Arden's revolving doors for the last time, giving the guys on security one final wave. Sue and I went round the corner to Chez Gerard for our valedictory dinner. As we ordered, I looked at Sue who was only seven years younger than my mum; in some ways she was like the aunt I'd never had.

'You know, Anna . . .' Sue lowered her menu. 'I've worked for you for five years and not had a single bad day.'

'You've been much more than a PA, Sue.' I felt my throat constrict. 'You've been a true friend.'

She put her hand on my arm. 'And that's not going to stop.' Then she opened her bag and took out a gift-wrapped package. 'I've got something for you too.' Inside was a beautiful book about Alpine flowers, which I've always loved, with stunning photographs of dainty gentians, Edelweiss and *Dianthus* growing in the Carpathians, the Pyrenees and the Alps.

'Thank you,' I murmured. 'It's lovely.' I turned to the title page and read Sue's inscription: *To Anna, may you bloom and grow* . . . 'I hope I do,' I said anxiously.

'Oh, you will,' Sue said.

Later, as our coffee arrived she mentioned that she'd arranged to meet her friend Cathy for a late drink. 'Why don't you come along?' she suddenly suggested.

I sipped my espresso. 'Oh . . . I don't . . . know.'

'You've met Cathy before – at my forty-fifth birthday drinks, remember?'

'Yes, I do – she was nice.'

'We're meeting at this new club near Oxford Circus, then we'll get the train back to Dartford together. Say yes, Anna.'

'Well . . .'

Sue glanced at her watch. 'It's not even ten. And you're not doing anything else tonight, are you?' I shook my head. 'So?'

'So . . . OK, then. Thanks. Why not?'

'I mean today's your last day in the City after *twelve* years,' she added as we emerged on to the street.

'Twelve years,' I echoed. 'That's more than a third of my life.' I felt unsteady from all the champagne.

'You don't want it to just . . . fizzle out, do you?'

'No. I want it to end in a memorable way.'

'With a bang – not a whimper!'

'Yes!'

But as we stepped on to the escalator at Bank tube station, my right heel got stuck in the metal slats. It was wedged. As we neared the bottom, I began to panic. Then, as I wrenched it free, it sheared off.

'Oh, *shit*,' I moaned as I hobbled off. Sue's hand was clapped to her mouth in horrified amusement. 'There's a metaphor in this,' I said grimly as I retrieved the amputated stiletto. 'I'm leaving the security of the City, so I'm going to be down at heel.'

'That's nonsense – you're going to be a big success. But there's only one thing for it . . .'

'Yes, Superglue,' I interjected. 'Got any?'

'On with the green wellies!'

'Oh *no*!'

'Oh yes.' Sue giggled. 'What else are you going to do? Go barefoot?'

'Oh God.' I laughed as I pulled them on, attracting amused looks from passers-by. I stared at my legs. 'Very fetching. Well, I'm suited and booted all right. At least they fit,' I added

21

as I clumped along the corridor. 'But they make my feet look massive.'

'You look delightfully Boho.' Sue laughed.

'I look bizarre.'

'Well, you did say you wanted a memorable evening.'

'That's true.'

Five stops on the Central Line later and we'd arrived at Oxford Circus, where Cathy was waiting for us by the ticket barriers.

I registered her surprised glance. 'My heel snapped off.'

'Never mind,' she said sympathetically. 'With a smile like yours no one's going to notice your feet.' I could have kissed her. 'The Iso-Bar's just up here.' Two thick-set bouncers stepped aside to allow us through the purple rope.

'This place hasn't been open long,' Cathy explained as we went down the steps into the vaulted interior. 'I saw Clive Owen in here last time. He actually winked at me.'

'Lucky you,' I said. 'But let's have some more champagne. I'll get it while you two find a table.'

I went up to the crowded bar. I felt self-conscious in my wellies, though it was, mercifully, quite dark – but I couldn't seem to catch the barman's eye. And I'd been standing there for a good ten minutes, feeling irritated by now, and annoyed by the spinning spotlights which were making my head ache, when I became aware that the man standing on my right was gesticulating extravagantly at the barman, then pointing at me with both index fingers, thumbs cocked. He saw me looking at him and smiled.

'Thanks,' I said to him, as I placed my order. I looked at him properly, then felt a sudden thump in my ribcage. He had dark curly hair that spilled over his collar and his eyes were a smoky blue. He was mid thirties, tall and slim, but his shoulders were broad. 'That was kind of you,' I added. 'I couldn't get the barman to notice me.'

'I don't know why,' the stranger replied. 'You're very

22

noticeable. You look like . . .' Gwyneth Paltrow I hoped he'd say. Or Kirsten Dunst. People do say that sometimes – if they've had enough to drink.

'. . . an iceberg,' I heard him say. 'You look so tall, and pale and . . . cool.'

'And of course I have hidden depths.'

'I'm sure you do.' To my annoyance, this made him glance at my feet. Puzzlement furrowed his brow. 'Been on a countryside march, have you?'

'No.' I explained what had happened.

'How inconvenient.'

'You're telling me.' I paid for the bottle of Taittinger. 'But I always carry alternative footwear around with me.'

'So I see. How practical.'

'Anyway, thanks for your help there. You're a gent.'

'Sometimes,' he said wistfully. 'But not always . . .'

Now, as I overtook the car in front, I thought how different my life would have been if I had left it there – if I had simply said a polite goodbye to the handsome stranger, then gone to find Cathy and Sue. Instead, I'd filled a glass with champagne and handed it to him. As I'd done so, I looked at him more boldly – the alcohol and my odd, heightened mood had made me feel uninhibited. I felt his interested glance in return.

'Are you here with anyone?' I'd asked, half expecting a glamorous female to zoom up to us and lead him away.

'I came with a friend, but he's gone outside to phone his wife.'

'And where's yours?' I asked with a directness that amazed me.

A look of mild surprise crossed his face. 'I don't . . . have one.'

'Do you have a girlfriend?'

'No . . .' he replied slowly, 'since you ask. But tell me' – he chinked my glass – 'what are you celebrating?'

I thought of my mother. 'Nothing. But I'm about to start a new life.'

'A new life?' He raised his glass and I watched the slender columns of bubbles drift upwards, like waving fronds. 'Well, here's to that new life of yours. So what are you doing? Emigrating? Getting married? Going into a nunnery? Joining the circus?'

'None of those things.' I explained that I'd just had my last day in the City and would start my garden design course on the Monday.

'So you're going from hedge funds to herbaceous borders.'

'I am.'

'From shares to . . . scented stocks.' I smiled. 'From Wall Street – to wallflowers. Shall I go on?'

'No.' I giggled. 'I had enough horticultural jokes at my leaving party just now.'

He leaned against the bar. 'So what happens when you finish the course?'

'I'll start my own consultancy – Anna Temple Garden Design.'

'Anna Temple . . . ? You should be worshipped with a name like that. Do you have a large and devoted following?'

I shook my head. 'Tragically not.'

'I find that surprising.'

'And what's your name?' I asked. 'I can't chat you up properly if I don't know it.'

He smiled again. 'It's Xan. With an "X".'

'Because you're X-rated?' I was enjoying my new-found brazenness. Only two hours into my new life and I seemed to be uncovering fresh aspects of my personality, I reflected. Cassie – a born flirt – would be impressed.

'No.' Xan laughed. 'It's short for Alexander.'

I had another sip of champagne. 'That's a bit classier than Alex, isn't it?'

'I think that's what my mum thought.'

Then Xan's friend appeared and said that he had to leave; so I invited Xan to join me at the table that Sue and Cathy had now found. He chatted politely to us all at first, then he and I began to talk one on one. He told me that he'd spent ten years in Hong Kong, in banking, but had given it up to work for the BBC.

'Are you enjoying it?' I sipped my champagne.

'It's wonderful. I only wish I'd taken the plunge before. Life's too short not to be doing something you love.'

'That's just the conclusion I'd come to,' I said feelingly.

'I'm a news trainee – luckily they let in the odd late starter.'

Sue and Cathy were putting on their coats. 'We've got a train to catch,' Sue said. She picked up her bags, then bent to hug me. 'You seem to be having a *very* memorable evening,' she whispered. 'Maybe it *will* end with a bang after all.' She giggled and straightened up. 'See you on Monday, then, Anna – oops! – no I won't!' She hugged me again. 'But I'll phone you.'

'Please do, Sue – and thank you for the book.'

Xan was politely getting to his feet, but Sue motioned for him to sit down. 'No, no, no – you stay put, you two.'

So that's what Xan and I did – for how long I don't remember; then I saw him glance at his watch. 'I'd better go,' he said. 'It's midnight.'

'Oh.' I felt a spasm of regret mingled with panic. 'Pumpkin time, Mr Cinders?'

'Bedtime. I've got a busy day.'

'Well . . .' I stood up, aware, by now, that I'd had a lot to drink. 'I'll make my way too. But I'm glad I've met you.' I held out my hand. 'Today's been a big day for me and it wouldn't have been the same without you.'

'Really?'

'Yes. I'm not quite sure why. In fact,' I added as I picked up my bags, 'I've got the peculiar feeling that I was *meant* to meet you.'

Xan was staring at me. 'Where do you live?'

I felt a jolt of electricity. 'Brook Green.'

'Well, I'm in Notting Hill. I'm getting a cab back – I'll give you a lift. If you like,' he added diffidently.

A cloud of butterflies took flight in my stomach. 'Yes. I would like that. Thanks.'

We stepped out on to Oxford Street, where we were buffeted by reeling, ululating drunks. Xan put a protective hand on my arm and my skin tingled with pleasure. A gentle rain was falling, so taxis were scarce. Suddenly we saw a yellow light. Xan stepped into the road and flagged down the cab; it drew up beside us with a diesel chug.

'Brook Green, please,' Xan said, opening the door for me. 'Then Notting Hill.'

I stepped in. 'You'll drop me off first?'

'Of course.'

'You *are* a gent,' I said as we pulled away.

'I try to be,' Xan replied. He looked out of the window. Raindrops beaded the glass, refracting the neon lights from the shops. 'But I'm sometimes tempted to be very ungentlemanly.'

'Really?' I watched two raindrops snake down the window then merge into each other with a tiny shudder. 'And are you tempted now by any chance?'

There was silence, except for the churning of the engine and the swish of wet tyres.

'Yes,' Xan said softly. 'I am.'

At that I slipped my arm through his, edging a little closer, feeling the warmth of his thigh against mine. We sped down Bayswater Road, through Notting Hill and along Holland Park Avenue where the sentinel plane trees were already shedding their huge leaves.

'Not much further,' I murmured. Xan's profile was strobing in the street lights. 'We'll be there in five minutes.' Daringly, I lifted my hand to his face and tucked a stray curl behind

26

his ear. 'You can take me home any time,' I murmured. At that Xan looked at me, locking his gaze in mine. I traced the curves of his mouth with my fingertip, then we kissed. His lips tasted of salt and champagne.

'Anna,' he breathed. I could smell the scent of lime on his neck. 'Anna . . .' We kissed again, more urgently, then I dropped my hand to his lap, feeling his jeans straining against his hardness. By now I felt almost faint with desire.

'What road, mate?' we heard the driver bellow.

'Oh . . .' I said. 'It's Havelock.' My face was aflame. 'It's at the very end there, on the left. The corner house.' I fumbled for my bags as we drew to a halt. Xan opened the door and we both stepped out – my heart pounding with apprehension. But instead of paying the driver, Xan just stood there awkwardly, looking at me.

'Well . . . thank you,' I murmured. 'For the lift . . . and . . .' Why was he hesitating? Perhaps he'd lied about being single, I thought dismally. Or maybe he was shy and didn't want to presume. Yes – that was it, I decided. He was shy. So I uttered the words that would change my life. 'Won't you come in?' I said quietly. 'For a . . . I don't know . . . cup of coffee or something?'

'Coffee?' Xan echoed with an air of surprise, as though I'd said 'gazpacho'.

'Yes. Coffee.' I turned up my collar against the thickening rain. 'Ethiopian or Guatemalan. Decaff – or extra caff. You can have an espresso – or a latte. You could have hot chocolate – I've got some very nice organic stuff – Fair Trade of course,' I added with a tipsy giggle, 'and I *think* there's some Horlicks.' I could see that the driver was impatient to go. 'Ovaltine?' I tried with a smile. But still Xan stood there. I'd got it wrong. He wasn't interested. Disappointed, I turned away.

I heard the click of the cab door, then the chug of its engine as it drove off.

27

But as I turned the key in the lock, there was a sudden step behind me, then Xan's voice: 'I don't suppose you've got any PG Tips?'

Now, as I turned off the motorway in the gathering dusk, I remembered, with a stab of regret, the elation I'd felt as I'd fumbled with the door, then jabbed at the beeping burglar alarm. I'd registered, with relief, that the house looked fresh and welcoming. There was a jug of tiger lilies on the sitting-room mantelpiece and everything was tidy. On the dining table was a shoebox containing the sympathy cards I'd had and to which I was finally replying. I covered it and went into the kitchen, slinging my jacket on to one of the ladder-back chairs.

Xan followed me in, and as I filled the kettle I saw him glance at the framed photo of my parents on the dresser. I hadn't told him about my mother as I didn't like saying it, because if I said it, that made it seem true.

'So what will it be?' I asked him as I opened the cupboard. 'I don't have PG Tips, but I do have Kenyan, Darjeeling, Ceylon, Assam, Green tea, Camomile tea – or if you want something really fancy, this –' I held up a box of Jasmine and Lavender. 'So what would you like?' I repeated with a smile.

'Nothing,' he replied.

'Surely you must want *something*,' I whispered seductively.

'Well, yes, I do, actually . . .' He looked away, slightly shyly, then returned his gaze to mine. 'I'd like you to . . . take something off . . .'

I felt goosebumps stipple my throat. 'And what might that be?' Xan nodded at my feet. 'Oh. There . . .' I giggled as I pulled off the wellies.

'That's better,' he said quietly. He was staring at my legs. 'You know, Anna, you have very attractive ankles.'

'Thank you. My elbows are quite nice too.'

Xan didn't reply. He just stood there, looking at me, as if

assessing me. So I took a step towards him and we kissed. Then, without saying a word, I gently loosened his tie and led him up the white-carpeted stairs to my bedroom. I unbuttoned his shirt – his chest was broad and smooth – then slid my hand down. I'd never taken the initiative like this in my life. I unzipped him, gently pushed him on to the bed, then lifted off my top in one upwards sweep as his hands caressed my bare hips. I was possessed by a physical longing for him that I'd felt for no man. I wanted him. I needed him.

'*Now*,' I whispered as he eased himself into me. His eyes widened, then we moved slowly, deliciously together. He eventually came with a great shuddering spasm and we lay, encased in one another, in the dark. Xan fell asleep quickly, but I lay awake, intoxicated with excitement and champagne. I gazed at the line of his jaw, lightly stubbled with shadow, and the way his lashes curled over his cheek.

This could be the start of a new relationship, I thought happily, to go with my new life . . .

I fell asleep too and dreamt of my mother. But it was an upsetting dream because she was walking towards me, through the garden, and I longed for her to hold me but I knew that she wasn't going to. And then I wasn't even sure that it was her, because her face was morphing and changing, her features becoming indistinct and unfamiliar. I awoke feeling sad and confused.

What would she have thought of this scene, I wondered, as I glimpsed the grey light of early morning slanting through the blind? She'd be disappointed.

Oh Anna – how could you? You'd only just met. What have I always told you? That if you like a man it's much better to wait . . .

I felt a sudden stab of panic. Xan's side of the bed was empty. I sat up, staring at the indentation his head had made on the pillow, then swung my legs out of bed. He must be in the bathroom. But I knew, from the resonating silence, that he wasn't. His clothes, which had strewn the carpet, had gone.

I glanced at the clock. It was only 6.30. I hurried downstairs in case he'd left a note for me – but there was nothing to indicate that he'd ever been in the house except for his scent on my sheets and skin.

I sank on to the sofa, the house piercing me with its emptiness. My head ached and my mouth was sour. From outside came the whine of a milk float. Why did Xan have to go?

That wasn't what I'd imagined at all, I thought now, as I drove through south London in the gathering dusk. I glanced at Milly in the mirror. She was fast asleep, thumb in mouth, her forefinger curled over her nose.

Before I'd drifted off to sleep that night I'd fondly imagined that Xan and I would spend the morning in bed, and that we'd then have a leisurely soak in my big Victorian bath. After that we'd go to my local deli, where we'd chat over organic bacon and eggs as though we'd known each other for ever, then we'd go for a walk in Holland Park. We'd date for three blissful months, at the end of which he'd whisk me off to Florence and propose. We'd have a summer wedding in the Belvedere the weekend after I'd finished my course.

Why couldn't he at least have woken me to say goodbye? I'd thought angrily. Why couldn't he at the very least – the very gentlemanly *least* – have left a note, saying that he didn't want to disturb me and that he'd ring me later and PS, was I doing anything that night?

But Xan had done none of those things. He'd just fled – as though he'd made some dreadful error of judgement. As I'd sat there, my throat aching with a suppressed sob, I'd thought of how seductive I'd thought I'd been – but in reality, how eager and crass.

'I went to bed with a man I'd known for *two hours*,' I moaned. I buried my head in my hands. How could I have been so reckless? He could have been a murderer, or a nutcase – or a thief. Except that I knew he wasn't any of those things – he was engaging, and clever, and nice – which was the worst thing about it.

'I liked him,' I groaned. 'I really *liked* him.' But he'd obviously seen it as a one-night stand. He'd got what he'd wanted and vanished in the time-honoured way. My mother's old-fashioned advice had been right.

By now it was still only seven. I ran a bath and soaked myself in it, fat tears of disappointment mingling on my cheeks with the film of condensation from the steam.

I didn't leave the house all morning in case he phoned, but he didn't, and by lunchtime I was delivering deranged monologues to Xan in which I pointed out that my behaviour the previous night was quite uncharacteristic, and that contrary to what he might have thought I was not in the habit of leaping into bed with men I'd only just met, thank you!

By late afternoon I was radioactive with indignation . . .

Xan was a rude bastard, I told myself furiously as I ripped the sheets off the bed. He thought he could just sleep with me and disappear, did he, as though I were . . . *cheap*? I yanked a pillow out of its case. Or maybe he'd been lying when he said he didn't have a girlfriend. How could a man that attractive *not* have one? That was why he'd hesitated, I now saw – out of guilt. And that was why he'd left so early, so that she wouldn't know he'd been out all night.

She was probably someone from work. I conjured her – a leggy brunette, with big brown eyes and a fabulous figure. Or maybe she was someone he'd met in Hong Kong. Now I imagined a slender Chinese girl with golden skin and a sheet of hair so shiny you could see your face in it. I felt a stab of jealousy – an emotion to which I knew I was not entitled, having known him for less than twenty-four hours.

He wasn't worth a second thought, I decided, as I stuffed the duvet cover into the washing machine. I turned the dial

31

to '90' to scorch him off my linen. He'd said that he wasn't always gentlemanly, I remembered as I slammed the door. Well, at least he was telling the truth about that.

Dring!

I straightened up at the sound of the doorbell.

Drinnnggg!!

Heart banging, I peered down the hall. A tall figure loomed through the panels of coloured glass. I checked my reflection in the circular mirror at the bottom of the stairs, took a deep breath and lifted the latch.

Misery washed over me – then hope.

'Miss Temple?' A man was standing there, holding a bouquet.

'Yes?'

'These are for you.'

'Oh. Thank you,' I said weakly as he handed them to me. '*Thank* you.' I thought I might weep with relief. Then I hated myself for being so silly about the whole thing: I was thirty-two, after all, not sixteen.

I carried the bouquet down to the kitchen and laid it on the worktop. It was a hand-tied bunch of bronze chrysanthemums, yellow roses and cream gerbera. I snipped the gold ribbon and it slipped to the floor. There was an envelope pinned to the tissue but I put it aside. I wanted to defer the pleasure of reading Xan's card.

I found a white jug and put the flowers in it, adding a two-pence piece as my mother had taught me, because the copper makes them keep longer and I wanted these ones to last for ever. Then I picked up the envelope. It felt thicker than normal, I realised, as I slid my thumb under the flap, but that was because there wasn't just a card inside it, but a letter. I unfolded it with trembling hands.

Dear Anna, I read. His handwriting was untidy. *I'm sorry I had to leave so early, but I was on an early shift this morning which I've only just finished . . .*

32

'Hurrah!' I shouted. Then I remembered what he'd said – that he had a 'busy day' ahead. I slapped my forehead, hard, with the palm of my hand. I'd been so uptight – and hung-over – that I'd forgotten. I might have behaved like a femme fatale but I was far from being one, I realised. I simply couldn't keep my cool.

I would have called you, but I don't have your number and you seem to be ex-directory. I gave my brow another hard slap. *Anyway, it was wonderful meeting you –*

'Yes!'

– and I'd love to see you again.

'YES!'

But I think we need to talk first.

'Oh . . .' I felt a sudden sagging sensation.

Are you free tomorrow night? Xx.

I should have followed my mother's advice and told Xan that I had a prior engagement – but it was too late for such manipulation. The horse had bolted, plus I was sick with anxiety about what he would say. So we met at the Havelock Tavern, a gastro-pub not far from me. I'd found a quiet table while he got us some drinks. A deliberately demure Virgin Mary for me and a bottle of Stella for him.

He lifted his glass and gave me a wistful smile. 'It's . . . good to see you again, Anna. You look lovely.'

'Do I? Oh. You too,' I added nervously, disconcerted by the fact that I found him even more attractive sober than I had done drunk. My knees were trembling so I slid my left hand over them. 'Anyway . . .' I took a deep breath. 'You said we needed to talk.'

Xan's expression darkened. 'I think we should.'

My heart sank. 'That's fine . . . but I'd like to say something first.'

He looked at me quizzically. 'What?'

'Well' – I sipped my tomato juice – 'that . . . what happened on Friday night wasn't . . . typical of me. I wouldn't like you to think that.'

He shrugged. 'I didn't . . . think anything in particular.'

I stared at the tiny island of ice in my drink. 'I wouldn't like you to assume that I'm in the habit of jumping into bed with men I've known for five minutes, just because I did that with you.'

'But . . .'

'So I just wanted to say that that's not how I am. Far from it. In fact, I'm normally quite shy with men.'

'Really?' His surprise annoyed me. 'Erm . . . you weren't very shy on Friday, Anna.'

I felt myself blush. 'Well, as I'm trying to explain, that was a complete aberration. I'm not quite sure why,' I added, still wondering what on earth it was that had gripped me. 'Usually I go out with a guy for at least a month before anything can happen on *that* front . . .'

He sipped his lager thoughtfully. 'I see . . .'

'Or a minimum of ten dates. Whichever is the greater.'

He nodded slowly. 'Right. And does that have to mean dinner, or can the dates include lunch and breakfast?'

'Could you be serious about this, please?'

'And what about afternoon tea?'

'Look, Xan, if you could just listen for a minute, I'm trying to explain that I acted totally out of character – I really wasn't myself for some reason – and so I feel . . .'

He'd laid his hand on my arm. 'Relax.' I noticed how beautiful his hands were: large and sinewy, with strong, straight fingers. 'There's no need to be so intense. This is the twenty-first century – and we're adults, aren't we?'

'Of course – but I'd had far too much to drink – because of my leaving party – then I had loads more champagne after that – and I think that's the reason why I leapt into bed with you actually. In fact, I'm sure it is.'

'Oh.' He'd withdrawn his hand. 'Thanks.'

34

'I'm sorry,' I stuttered. 'All I meant is I don't normally have casual sex.'

'What *do* you have then – formal sex? You wear a ball gown and tiara, and the guy wears a DJ?'

'Don't be silly.'

Xan put down his glass. 'I'm not. I just don't understand why you feel you have to justify what happened. You don't, Anna. We were very attracted to each other.'

I stared at him. 'Yes . . .' I whispered. 'We were.'

'And we still *are*,' he said tentatively. 'Aren't we?'

My heart was pounding like a kettle drum. 'Well . . . yes,' I repeated. 'But you said we needed to talk, which sounded ominous, as though you've got something unpleasant to tell me.'

'Such as what?'

'Well . . . that you're already seeing someone, for example, or that you're engaged, or married, or cohabiting, or that you take drugs, or think you might be gay. As we don't know each other it could be *anything* – erm . . . that you murdered your father and slept with your mother for all I know, or that you once had an affair with a sheep – not that I remotely think you look the type to engage in anything as sordid as inter-species congress but . . .'

'*Anna* . . . ?' Xan was shaking his head in bewildered amusement. 'All I said was that I thought we should talk first – as in' – he turned up his palms in a gesture of helplessness – '*talk*.'

'Oh. Oh I see. About what?'

'Well – anything – because we didn't exactly talk much on Friday night, did we? But I obviously didn't express myself very well – the flower shop was closing and I was in a hurry.' He shrugged. 'All I was trying to say was that I'd like to' – he shrugged again – 'get to know you.'

'Oh. So . . . why did you hesitate before coming in?'

'Because you'd clearly had a lot to drink and I wasn't sure

that I should. As I say, I do *try* to be gentlemanly.' He sipped his beer. 'Happy now?'

I nodded. 'Yes.'

He lowered his glass and peered at me. 'Are you always this complicated?'

I smiled at him. 'No.'

So, over dinner, we talked. The relief of knowing that Xan didn't appear to have some hideous drawback restored my confidence. I waxed lyrical about my garden design course, which was due to begin the next day.

'It's based at the Chelsea Physic Garden,' I explained. 'It's a wonderful place – like the Secret Garden – full of rare trees and medicinal plants. I'll be studying horticulture and planting design, hard landscaping, technical drawing, garden lighting; how to use decorative elements such as statuary and water features . . .' I shivered with apprehension. 'I can't wait to get started.'

Then Xan told me about his two-year BBC traineeship, which was just coming to an end. He picked up his knife. 'I'm in the process of applying for jobs. It's rather nerve-racking.'

'Which bit of the Beeb do you want to work in?'

'I'm not sure. I'm in the newsroom at the moment, which I like, but there are some reporting jobs coming up, which would be great as I've done quite a bit of on-screen work for *BBC World*. Or I might go for something at the business unit to capitalise on my financial background. There are various options, although the competition's always stiff.'

Then he told me about his family. His father had worked for the British Council, so as a child he'd lived all over the world. 'We were nomads,' he explained. 'Always packing and unpacking. Moving's in my blood.'

'How glamorous,' I said wistfully, feeling suddenly dull and suburban. 'I'm afraid staying put's in mine. We've lived in the same house for thirty-five years.'

'We being . . . ?'

'My parents – well, parent now.' I felt a stab of loss. 'My mother died three months ago. Three months ago today,' I suddenly realised. 'On Saturday June the eighth.' As I said this I felt the familiar pressing sensation on my sternum, as though someone had left a pile of bricks on my chest.

'Was she ill?' Xan asked gently.

I shook my head. 'She was very fit. Her death was totally unexpected. A bolt from the blue,' I added bitterly.

'So . . . what happened?'

I stared at the single pink rose in its slender vase. 'She sprained her ankle.' Xan was looking at me quizzically. 'Dad said that she'd slipped coming down the stairs before lunch. Her ankle was badly swollen so he took her to hospital, where they bandaged it. And that evening she was lying on the sofa, complaining about what a nuisance it was, when she suddenly began to feel ill. She thought it must have something to do with the painkillers she'd been given, but in fact something terrible was happening to her – she'd got a blood clot in her leg, which had travelled round her body and reached her lungs. Dad said that she was struggling to breathe . . .' I felt myself inhale, as if in a futile attempt to help her. 'He called the ambulance and it came within ten minutes, but it was already too late – she'd died in his arms. She'd sprained her ankle and a few hours later she was dead. We couldn't believe it,' I croaked. 'We still can't.'

'How terrible,' Xan murmured after a moment. He laid his hand on mine. 'You must feel . . . I don't know . . . derelict.'

I looked at him. 'Derelict . . . ? That's *exactly* the word.' And in that moment I knew *that* was why I'd behaved so recklessly two nights before. It was so much more than physical lust. It was because for three months I'd been curled into myself – half dead with grief – and I'd wanted to feel . . . *alive*.

'How old was she?'

37

His features were blurring. 'Fifty-five.'

'So young . . .' Xan was shaking his head. 'She could have expected another twenty years at least.'

'None of us can expect it,' I said quietly. 'We can only hope for it. I know that now in a way that was only abstract to me before.'

We sat in silence for a moment or two.

'What about the rest of your family?' Xan asked, so I told him a bit about Cassie and Mark. 'And your private life? Boyfriends?'

I shrugged. 'I haven't been out with anyone for quite a while.'

'But you're very attractive – in a glacial sort of way – so you must get offers.'

'Thank you. Sometimes I do. But not from anyone I've been that interested in.' I fiddled with my napkin. 'And what about you?'

'I *was* seeing someone, but we broke up in May.'

'What was she like?'

'Rather lovely,' he said regretfully. I felt a dart of jealousy. 'Cara was very intelligent. Very attractive. Very successful . . .'

'She sounds heavenly,' I said joylessly. 'So what went wrong?'

'She just expected too much from the relationship too soon. We'd only been together three months, but she was already pushing to move in with me – but it just didn't feel right.' He shook his head. 'She was constantly demanding to know where things were going. In the end I couldn't stand it.'

'Well,' I said, 'I'm not like that. I'll admit that I was, before my mother died, but that's changed everything and my biological clock is now firmly on "snooze". My course is going to take nine months, then I've got to get my business up and running, so my priorities now are professional ones.' I glanced at my watch. 'In fact, I'd better go – I have to be at the Physic Garden by nine tomorrow morning. Thanks for dinner.'

Xan got to his feet. 'Can I walk you home?'

I smiled. 'Sure.'

'I'd love to see you again, Anna,' Xan said as we stood by my gate. The wisteria which smothered the house was in second flower and the scent was lovely. He stroked my cheek. 'Would that be OK?'

I felt a sudden burst of delight – like the explosion of a seed pod. 'It would be . . . fine.'

'But . . . no . . .'

'Strings?' I suggested wryly.

He shook his head. 'Pressure. Just no . . . *pressure*. OK?' He kissed me, set off down the narrow street, turned and waved.

'No pressure?' I repeated quietly. 'Of *course*.'

TWO

As I eased the car into the usual space outside my house, I thought of the lovely autumn I'd spent with Xan. It was a time of liquid sunshine and lengthening shadows, somehow suited to the intense sadness I felt about my mother, but also the near euphoria at being with him.

'It's thanks to you,' I'd said to Sue over the phone. 'If you hadn't persuaded me to come with you that night, I'd never have met him. You were my fairy godmother!'

'I'm delighted to have been,' she replied. 'He's good-looking, he's clever and it'll be great for you to have some romance in your life after so much sadness. But it's early days,' she cautioned. 'So don't fall for him too hard, will you?'

'Of course I won't.'

But I already had.

Xan and I got into a pattern, early on, of meeting at least twice during the week, to see a film or play, or we'd just hang out together, either at my place, or at his flat in Stanley Square. It was full of exotica from his nomadic childhood: a suit of antique armour from Japan; colourful textiles from Guatemala and Sumatra; a piece of delicate fan coral that he'd picked in Belize.

'I feel bad about it,' he said, 'but that was thirty years ago and no one gave much thought to conservation then.'

There were a lot of travel books and an antique globe that his parents had given him for his eighteenth birthday. They'd retired years before and lived in Spain.

'They lived abroad for so long they couldn't settle here,' Xan said as we strolled through the communal gardens at the back of his flat a week or so after we'd met. The leaves were beginning to turn bronze in the mid-September sunshine. 'My sister Emma's the same. She teaches English in Prague. And what about your siblings? Tell me more about them.'

'Well . . . Mark's an eye surgeon – as I told you. We used to be close . . .' I felt a wave of sadness. 'But he's distanced himself from us all over the past year or so.'

'Why's that?'

'Because . . . he had this awful row with my parents – over his new girlfriend.'

'What was the problem?'

'They just thought she was completely . . . wrong. He'd only known her a month but I knew how excited he was about her, because he rang me to tell me that he'd met someone really special. So I asked him about her, and I must say it didn't sound that great because he said she was eight years older – forty-one – divorced with two teenagers. But Mark said that he just felt this incredible affinity for her. He said he didn't care about her age, or even the fact that she didn't want more kids. He said he just knew that he wanted to be with her for the rest of his life.'

'What did she do?'

'She's an actress.'

'Is she well known?'

'I don't think so – her name's Carol Gowing.' Xan shrugged. 'I'd never heard of her,' I went on, 'though I've since spotted her on TV a couple of times – usually in small parts on things like *Holby City* or *The Bill*. Then in April I saw a photo of her in *Hello!*. She was at the BAFTAs with her brother, who's an artist, and her father, Sir John Gowing, who owns Northern TV – he was up for some lifetime achievement award. The article underneath said that Carol had been successful in her twenties but that her star had faded. But she's certainly beautiful and Mark was smitten.'

'So he brought her home to meet your folks . . .'

'No – it was still too early for that. But he took her to Glyndebourne for her birthday, and by chance my parents were there too that night and they bumped into each other as they came out for the long interval. So they had their picnics together, and apparently Mum and Dad just . . . loathed her on sight.'

'Because of the age gap?'

'I guess so. Plus Carol let slip that she didn't want any more children, so I can understand Mum feeling disappointed, but on the other hand . . .' My voice trailed away.

'It was Mark's life.'

I heaved a sigh. 'Yes. My mother was wonderful in many ways but . . .' I felt a stab of disloyalty. 'She could be . . . interfering. In a benign way,' I added guiltily. 'She only ever meant well. She believed she knew what was best for her children – long after we'd all grown up. She didn't seem to accept that we had to make our own mistakes.' I thought of all the advice she'd given me. 'The next day Mum went to see Mark at his flat in Fulham and apparently there was this dreadful scene, in which she told him point blank not to get involved with Carol. I don't know the details because Mark wouldn't discuss it; but shortly after that they split up. Perhaps Carol wasn't that keen on him anyway – I'll never know – but I'm sure my mother's coldness would have put her off.' I suddenly wondered whether, if and when I met Xan's family, *his* mum would take against me. 'Mark blamed my parents,' I continued, 'especially Mum. He was so angry with her – he said he'd never talk to her again – and after that he became distant with us all. The next thing we knew, he'd got a job at a hospital in San Francisco.'

'And does he come home?'

I felt a pang of regret. 'No. He came for Mum's funeral, of course, but he only stayed one night. He looked so . . . *terrible*. His face was a mask. But he must have felt even worse than we all did, because of the rift he'd had with her.'

There was a rustle overhead as two squirrels chased each other along a branch, then suddenly turned and faced each other, backs arched, their tails aquiver.

'Have you been over to see him?'

I shook my head. 'I don't think he'd want me to go. In fact, he barely communicates with us now – apart from the odd e-mail, or dutiful birthday card. I've tried e-mailing him, telling him how sad I feel, and asking him to keep in touch, but so far I've had a cold response. It's as though he's punishing us all.'

'That seems unfair.'

'I talked to my dad about it but he just looked sad and said that he thought Mark was "finding himself". Then he added, very regretfully, that he thought he and Mum had handled things "terribly badly".'

There was more rustling from above, as a conker fell through the leaves, landed with a light thud and bounced away, the impact splitting its spiny green shell.

'And what about Cassie?' I heard Xan say, as I stooped to pick it up. 'Is she like you?'

I prised the chestnut out of its soft white casing, admiring its mahogany perfection. 'No,' I replied. 'Not at all. She's the physical opposite – short, curvy and very dark – you'd think she was Spanish or Italian.'

'Whereas you could be . . . Icelandic. Your skin's so pale, I can see the veins at your temple; and your hair . . .' He tucked a lock behind my ear. 'It's so blonde it's almost white.'

'Mark's very fair too, as was Dad when he was younger.

43

Cassie's a bit like my mum, but bears no resemblance to the rest of us, in looks or personality.'

'What does she do?'

'That's a moot point – not much; or rather she does lots of things, but none of it adds up to anything.' We sat down on the wooden bench that encircled the base of the tree like an anklet. 'She mostly temps – flitting from job to job. She's twenty-six now so I try to persuade her to have some sort of career plan. But she just spouts that bit in the Bible about the lilies of the field and about how they toil not neither do they spin.'

'Is she religious?'

'Cassie?' I snorted. 'Not in the least. She's also worked as a lingerie model – my parents never found out about it, luckily – and then as a croupier; they were horrified, but she said the money was great. She's forever short of cash.'

'Why's that?'

'Because she's always lived beyond her means. She rents a flat in Chelsea – it's very small but it costs a fortune. I said she should try and buy somewhere in a cheaper area but she won't compromise on postcode; plus she has very expensive tastes – designer clothes, luxury holidays, smart restaurants – things that I, on my City salary, would have hesitated over, Cassie just goes for.'

'So she's a hedonist, then.'

'Completely – and she's got this old MG that's continually breaking down. She's always running to Dad to pay her garage bills.'

'Does he mind?'

'He doesn't seem to. He's always indulged her – all her life.' I felt the familiar stab of resentment. 'Almost as though he were trying to compensate her for something,' I suddenly added, although I'd never had this thought before.

Xan stretched out his long legs, crossing them at the ankles. I stared at his pale suede desert boots.

'And how's your dad been coping since your mother died?' I heard him ask.

I heaved a deep sigh. 'Not well.'

I went down to the house every weekend. Dad didn't talk much, so we'd watch TV and do practical things – the shopping and gardening, his washing and ironing. He stopped listening to music because it made him cry. He'd left all Mum's things just as they were. It had taken him three weeks to wash the wineglass she'd been using. It still had her pink lipstick marks.

I couldn't console Dad, any more than he could console me – but I did my best to distract him. I'd encourage him to ring his friends, or go to the golf club.

'Not yet,' he'd say quietly. 'I just . . . can't.'

During the week I'd spend my free time with Xan. I'd wake in his arms, feeling excited but at the same time intensely comfortable. It was as though we'd known each other years before, but had recently met again and were keen to resume the relationship. Yet the truth was I hadn't known him that long.

How long? I wondered one morning in late October as I sat in one of my horticulture lectures. The tutor was asking us to devise a planting plan for dry, shady conditions. *Anemone japonica*, I wrote down and *Helleborus argutifolius*. *Acanthus mollis* thrives in shade, as does *Pulmonaria* – that does wonderfully in dark corners and the dappled leaves are still pretty when the flowers have faded. It was a month since I'd met Xan. I looked out into the garden below, admiring the Indian bean tree beneath the window. No, I realised, it was more. We'd met on Friday the tenth of September so that was – I discreetly glanced at my diary – nearly seven weeks. I flicked back through my diary again, then forward, then a little further back. And now I saw that there was a red ring round a date in late August.

A sudden jolt ran the length of my spine . . .

45

I'd been late before, I told myself as I walked briskly up Flood Street on to the King's Road at lunchtime. My cycle had probably changed due to stress. Shock can do that, I reflected as I went into the chemist's. I looked at the range of tests.

'We've got these on 3 for 2 if you're interested,' the pharmacist said benignly.

'Erm . . . no thanks,' I replied as I paid. One would be more than enough, I thought as I half walked, half ran back to the Physic Garden, my heart pounding.

I wasn't pregnant, I told myself as I peed on the stick. If I were I'd know, because you're supposed to get symptoms pretty early on, aren't you? I tried to remember what they were. Nausea, obviously. When did that start? Wasn't the taste of metal said to be an early sign? I slotted the stick back into the cartridge to await the result, which would take two minutes. I flushed the loo, then washed my hands. And wasn't a bloated feeling a giveaway? I wondered as I yanked down the towel. Well, I didn't feel bloated. Another minute to go. Engorged breasts? A perfunctory feel suggested nothing out of the ordinary. Twenty seconds now . . . Did I *look* pregnant? I peered into the mirror. No. Right then . . . Holding my breath, as though about to dive underwater, I picked up the test . . .

It was as though I'd stepped into a crevasse.

A blue cross in the second window means that you are pregnant.

I stared at the blue cross in mine – so strong it seemed almost to pulsate. With trembling hands I retrieved the carton from the paper bag and reread the blurb. Then I sank on to a chair and closed my eyes. Now I suddenly remembered what I'd said to Xan the night we met: *I'm about to start a new life . . .*

Xan . . . I've got something to tell you . . .

I couldn't tell him something so huge over the phone. But

he was filming in Glasgow and was then going to Spain to see his parents, so I wouldn't get to see him for five days.

In the interim I tried to imagine his reaction. He'd be shocked. Not least because he'd said no pressure. I laughed darkly. No *pressure*? So, no – he was hardly going to be overjoyed. But if he could just be accepting – however grudgingly – that would be more than enough.

But what would I do about my course? I'd wonder, and my new career. The anxiety would make me feel sick. Then my mood would lift and I'd be entertaining a pleasant fantasy in which Xan was putting his arms round me and telling me that although, yes, it *was* rather soon, it would all be fine and we'd buy a house together a bit further out, with a nice big garden. And I was mentally landscaping said garden with a glorious play area complete with swing and slide, and a tree house – yes, a really great tree house – when the phone rang. My heart surged.

'Anna . . . ?'

'*Xan* . . .' I sank on to the chair with relief.

'I'm back and, well . . .' He sounded tired but then he'd been travelling.

'I missed you, Xan.'

'I missed you too,' he said, with a kind of surprised sadness. 'But . . . look . . . I need to see you. Can I come over?'

'Yes . . . Yes, I'll cook. Come at eight.'

He arrived at half past, carrying a huge bunch of pink roses. He kissed me on the cheek, which struck me as oddly formal. He seemed remote, but I put it down to fatigue.

'You've gone to a lot of trouble,' he said, almost regretfully, as we ate our risotto.

I looked at his plate. 'But you've eaten so little.'

'Yes . . .' he said distractedly. 'So have you.'

'Well . . . that's because . . .' Adrenalin burned through my veins. '*Xan* . . .' I put down my fork. 'There's something I have to tell you . . .'

So I did.

Xan froze, as though someone had poured liquid nitrogen over him. In the ensuing silence all I could hear was the hum of my computer.

'You're *pregnant*?' he whispered. 'But *how*?'

'Well . . .' I shrugged. 'In the . . . conventional way.'

'But . . .' He was shaking his head. 'We've been so careful.'

'Not the first time. We weren't careful then.' I remembered rummaging in my bedside table, mid-passion, for a stray condom that had been at the back of the drawer for ages.

'The first time?'

'I think that's when it happened. In fact, I'm sure.'

Xan had gone white. 'Oh. *God* . . .' He was blinking at me uncomprehendingly. 'Are you saying you got pregnant the night we *met*?' He emitted a burst of mirthless laughter. 'But – we'd known each other *two hours*!'

'Yes . . .' I nodded nervously. 'I suppose we had.'

'So that was . . . ?'

'Seven weeks ago.'

'Seven weeks?'

'That fits with what my GP said. And I had an early scan on Monday. I don't think there's much doubt. They date it from two weeks before, which means I'm actually nine weeks.'

Xan's grey-blue eyes were staring wildly. 'But . . . this is . . . terrible.' My heart plummeted. 'It couldn't be *worse*.'

'Well, actually, Xan, it could be – it really could,' I stuttered, taken aback by his hostility. 'Because, OK, it's very serious – I'm not denying that for a minute – but far worse things happen every day, don't they, really terrible things that people can never get over, like what happened to my mother for example, there's no getting over that. But with this at least . . . at least no one's . . . *dead*, are they?'

'No,' Xan said grimly. 'But someone's *alive*!' He got up and walked over to the window. 'Oh *Jesus*, Anna . . .' He

48

turned and stared at me, his smoke-blue eyes blazing with wounded fury.

'Look,' I said, 'I . . . understand that you're . . . shocked. I was incredibly shocked myself.'

'*Were* you?' He was staring at me with naked scepticism.

'Yes. I was! I didn't do it deliberately if that's what you mean! But' – I lowered my voice, anxious to keep the conversation as calm as possible – 'I've had five days to think about it all and I believe it'll be OK. I really do.'

'No, it *won't*! It'll be a *disaster*!'

I was taken aback by his vehemence but tried to stay calm. 'Look, Xan, I've thought it all through and of course I don't expect you to marry me or even live with me if you don't want to.'

'Well, that's big of you,' he said bitterly. 'Because I can tell you right now I'm not going to be doing either!'

I felt a stab to the stomach. 'All right,' I breathed. 'If that's how you feel.'

He threw up his hands. 'Of course it's how I feel – I've known you for less than two months! And how do I even know that it's mine?' At that I felt a pain in my chest, as though Xan had physically injured me. 'You say it happened the night we met. But how do I know that you hadn't thrown yourself at some other poor sod the day before?'

I stood up. 'There's no need to insult me. Of course it's yours.'

'How the hell do I *know*?'

'Because for one thing I wouldn't lie about it.'

'Why not?' he spat. 'Plenty of women do!'

'And for another I hadn't slept with anyone for six months before I met you. But we'll do a DNA test if you don't believe me.'

Something in Xan's softening expression told me that he did. He dropped on to the sofa, his head sinking into both hands. I heard him inhale deeply, as if trying to steady himself.

49

'An iceberg,' I heard him murmur. 'I said you looked like an iceberg, Anna, the night we met. And I wish I'd been more wary. Because now I've been holed by you and this will sink me.' I heard him emit a low groan.

I came and sat on the chair near to him. 'Please don't be like this, Xan,' I tried again, my voice catching. 'There's no need. We're both in our thirties, we both have resources and I repeat that you don't have to make any kind of commitment to me. But the reason why I feel reasonably optimistic about the situation – although I agree it's not ideal and I've been sick with worry myself – is because we live so near to each other and . . .'

'Anna . . .' he interjected wearily.

'Please let me finish – and that's the key thing, that you'll be close.'

'But . . .'

'As for the responsibility,' I went on, 'I won't expect you to go halves with me on that, or even on the money. I've always been independent and that won't change. All I'd want . . .' My throat was aching now. 'All I'd want', I tried again, 'is for you just to be there. To play *some* part, however small. To be a *father* . . .' I felt my eyes fill. 'Even if our relationship ends, which, judging by your very angry reaction I think it might . . .' I pressed my left sleeve to my eyes. 'You only have to *be* there.'

'But I *can't* be,' I heard Xan say. I looked at him. He seemed stricken now, rather than hostile. 'That's the whole problem.'

I stared at him non-comprehendingly. 'Of course you can. We live less than two miles apart.'

'Yes,' he said. Hope rose in my chest. 'We do now. But as of next week . . . we won't.'

I stared at him. 'What are you talking about?'

Xan heaved a profound sigh. It seemed to come from his very depths. 'I've got a job, Anna. That's what I was steeling myself to tell you this evening.'

50

'You've got a job? Oh. But that's . . . *great*.' I stared at him. 'Isn't it?'

'Not in every way.' He sighed. 'No. Because this particular job means I'll be leaving London. In fact,' he added quietly, 'I'll be leaving the UK.'

I suddenly felt as though I was slithering down an icy incline. 'You'll be leaving the UK?' I repeated. 'But *why*?'

'Because I'm going to be a foreign correspondent.'

'A foreign correspondent?' I echoed blankly. 'Where?'

Paris? I wondered in the two seconds before the axe fell. Or Rome? Rome's not that far. We could have weekends together if he went to Rome. Madrid would be OK too – or Dublin for that matter.

'Indonesia,' I heard him say.

From outside I caught the distant wail of a police siren.

'Indonesia? *Oh*. But that's . . . far.'

'Yes. It's very far, Anna. I'm sorry.'

'But . . . Indonesia's nearly Australia.'

'Yes. And that's why I won't be there for you – if you go through with this.'

If you go through with this . . .

I stared at Xan. 'For how long?'

'Two years.' He sighed. 'Renewable. Or what's more likely is that I'll be posted somewhere else after that.'

'And when do you go?'

'Next Thursday. They're arranging my work permit now.'

'But . . . you didn't tell me you were applying for jobs overseas.'

He shook his head. 'Because I wasn't. This has come completely out of the blue. The guy who was due to go has had to pull out because of family difficulties. They needed to fill the post quickly, preferably with someone who knows the region well – and they knew that I do. I lived there when I was a teenager – my parents had a posting in Jakarta; and I did business there when I was based in Hong Kong.'

51

'Oh,' I said faintly. 'I see.' I went over to the table, picked up our plates and carried them into the kitchen.

'And I told you, Anna – I'm a nomad. I could easily live abroad.'

I banged down a bowl on the worktop. 'But I want you to live here. Near me. I'm going to need you, Xan. *We're* going to need you.' Tears were streaming down my cheeks.

'I'm sorry,' he groaned. 'I can't do that.'

'Say you can't take it,' I wept. 'Tell them your circumstances have changed. Tell them *you've* got "family difficulties"!' I sank on to the chair.

'But it's agreed – and the point is I want to go.'

I pressed a napkin to my eyes. 'You came here tonight to break up with me,' I whispered. Xan looked out of the window. 'That's why you brought me the flowers.'

'I'm . . . sorry, Anna, but don't you see? I'm lucky to have got this – it's a fantastic break. But yes, I knew it would spell the end for us, so I'd been bracing myself to tell you because I really like you and I felt sad at the thought of not being with you, but now . . . *this* . . . ?' He was shaking his head. '*Please*, Anna,' he said. 'Please *don't* do it. We've been together for less than two months. It's not long enough.'

'It is for me!' I shouted. My hands sprang to my face. 'It's more than long enough for me to have fallen in *love* with you!'

Xan emitted a frustrated sigh.

It was more than long enough for my parents too, I reflected. The same thing happened to them, in much less liberal times, but my dad had just done the right thing.

'Let me come too,' I croaked. And in the split second before Xan replied, I saw myself rocking a wickerwork cradle on a veranda, on a hot, humid night, beneath a slowly rotating fan.

'No,' I heard him say softly. 'It's out of the question.'

I stared at a tiny mark on the carpet. 'Yes,' I whispered

after a moment. 'You're right.' I'd only just started my course and my father needed me – I couldn't abandon him now. I looked at Xan. 'I can't possibly go. Even if you wanted me to, which you probably wouldn't.'

'Anna – we haven't been seeing each other long enough to make any plans – let alone have a child together. A *child*?' he repeated. 'Jesus Christ!'

I thought of my parents' wedding photo – my mother's conspicuously large bouquet of red roses not quite concealing her burgeoning bump.

'And what if you weren't going abroad?' I asked. 'How would you feel about it then? If you were staying here?'

Xan looked at me. 'Exactly the same.'

'Oh,' I said quietly. 'I see.' I stared at the carpet again, scrutinising the little mark. I now saw that it was shaped like an aeroplane.

'Don't do this, Anna,' I heard Xan say. 'You'll wreck both our lives – and the child's . . .' – he seemed unable to say the word 'baby'. 'It's so unfair on it, not having a father from the start. Children have the right to be born into a stable family unit, with two parents to love them.' I stared at him. 'Please, Anna. Don't. I do want children one day, but I want to be a father to them – not some absent stranger.' His eyes were shining with tears. 'It's still early days and you have a choice. Please, Anna, *don't* do this. *Please* . . .' he repeated quietly.

I stared at Xan, too shattered to reply. Then he picked up his bag and walked out of the house, closing the front door with a definitive click.

THREE

The private clinic I'd booked myself into a week later was called the Audrey Forbes Women's Health Centre and was in a rain-stained sixties office block in Putney High Street, next to a bookshop. I glanced in the window at the colourful pyramid of children's books: *We're Going on a Bear Hunt*; *The Gruffalo*; *The Very Hungry Caterpillar*. I wasn't in the least hungry myself, I realised, even though I'd been told to have nothing to eat or drink.

I gave my name to the receptionist on the ground floor, then pressed the button to summon the lift. To my disappointment it arrived straight away. The interior smelt of stale cigarette smoke and cheap scent, which added to my nausea, which had been increasing daily. I arrived at the fifth floor with a stomach-lurching jolt.

There was a faint smell of antiseptic mingled with the odour of plastic chairs as I entered the huge waiting room. There must have been about eighty seats or so – a good half of them occupied by women, some as young as children, others as old as grannies. Perhaps they were grannies, I thought. It was perfectly possible to be a granny and pregnant – even a great-granny, come to that, if you'd got started young enough.

To my left two women, one early twenties, the other late

thirties, were chatting in a subdued way. As I queued at the desk I caught fragments of their conversation.

Oh, you'll be fine . . . about two hours . . . don't cry . . . left you in the lurch, has he . . . ? Don't upset yourself . . . I haven't even told my husband . . . well, he'd kill me if he knew . . . no, not really painful . . . don't cry.

'Name, please?' said the nurse.

'Anna Temple,' I whispered. I felt a wave of shame.

'And how will you be paying today? We take Mastercard, Visa, Maestro, American Express, cheque with a valid guarantee card – or cash,' she added pleasantly.

I handed her my credit card.

'That'll be five hundred and twenty-five pounds,' she said as she slotted it into the machine. 'Which includes a 1.5 per cent handling charge.' This somehow made it seem like excellent value. I wondered if she was going to offer me a 3 for 2, like the pharmacist, or maybe a discount voucher, for future use. She handed me a clipboard. 'Please fill out this form.'

I stepped to one side, filled it in and returned it to her. She handed me a plastic cup to fill, and told me I'd be called within the hour.

As I walked to the Ladies I ran through my mental list, for perhaps the thousandth time in the past seven days, of the Eight Good Reasons for not proceeding with my pregnancy. I listed them again now, in descending order of importance.

I am heartbroken about Xan. If I have his baby I will never be able to get over him.
Having Xan's baby when he doesn't want me to feels wrong.
I do not wish to bring a baby into the world with no father in its life.
It will make it so much harder for me to find someone else.
Having a baby now will wreck my new career.

I will have no income for a very long time.
I will be too engrossed in my own problems to help my
dad, who needs me.
Being a single mother will be lonely and hard.

As I washed my hands, a girl came out of a cubicle. She looked about fourteen. Her mother – who looked no older than me – was leaning against the basin, arms akimbo, an expression of pained resignation on her face. As I followed them back to the counter with my cup I wished that I had someone with me – but who would it have been? Not Xan, obviously, even if he weren't on a plane, crossing five time zones to reach the other side of the world. Not Cassie. She'd be no comfort at all. Would I have wanted my mother? No. Not least because she'd been there herself but had worked it all out. I had a sudden hankering for Granny Temple, who was always practical and kind – but she'd died in 2001.

As I took my seat again, near to a wall-mounted TV – *This Morning* was on: they were cooking something revolting-looking with red lentils – I remembered my consultation with my GP. It was already too late for the method where you take a pill; so it had to be the early surgical technique.

'It takes five minutes,' my doctor had said reassuringly. 'And the recovery time is quite short – just a couple of hours. Now, are you sure about it?' she asked, as she signed the letter which would state that my mental health would be impaired by my proceeding with the pregnancy.

'Yes. I'm quite sure,' I lied . . .

I am heartbroken about Xan, I repeated to myself now, like a mantra. If I have his baby I will never be able to get over him. Having his baby when he doesn't want me to feels wrong. I do not wish to bring a baby into the world with no father . . .

What was my fourth reason? I couldn't remember. What *was* it?

'Anna Temple!' I heard. I stood up. 'You'll be going down to the ward next,' said the nurse, 'but first go to the locker room, take everything off, put your belongings in a locker, put on a paper gown and wait.' I did as I was told. Then, clutching the back of the gown, which felt uncomfortably breezy and exposed, I sat down with two other women in the waiting area. I felt suddenly self-conscious about my bare feet. The polish on my toes was chipped and there was a ridge of hard skin on my heels. But the thought of prettifying my feet in preparation for an abortion made me feel even more sick than I already did.

I picked up a leaflet about contraception so that I wouldn't have to catch the eye of either of the other two women who were waiting with me.

'Anna Temple?' said another female voice now, after what seemed like a week but was probably twenty minutes.

I followed the doctor down the draughty corridor into a cubicle.

'OK,' she said as her eyes scanned my form. 'We'll just run through a few things before I perform the procedure.'

'Could you tell me how it works,' I said.

'Well, it's quite simple,' she replied pleasantly. I noticed a speculum lying on a metal tray on the trolley next to her and some syringes in their wrappers. 'You'll be given a local anaesthetic, into the cervix, and once that has worked, the cervix is gently stretched open, and a thin plastic tube is then inserted into the uterus, and the conceptus . . .'

'Conceptus?'

'That's right. Will be eliminated from the uterus.'

'The conceptus will be eliminated from the uterus,' I echoed.

My head was spinning. I closed my eyes. I was ten weeks pregnant. The 'conceptus' was over an inch long. It had a heart that had been beating for five weeks now – a heart that had suddenly sparked into life. It had limb buds, which were sprouting tiny fingers and toes, which themselves had even tinier nails. It had a recognisably human little face, with nostrils and eyelids; it even had the beginnings of teeth . . .

The doctor began to tear the wrapper off a syringe. 'If you could just hop up on to the bed here . . .'

I stood up. 'I need to go.'

She looked at me. 'You need to go?'

'Yes.'

'Well, there's a bathroom at the back, by the fire exit.'

'No,' I said weakly. 'That's not what I mean. I need to go as in "leave". I can't do this. I don't know how I thought I could. It's . . . not the right thing – at least, not for me. My boyfriend – ex-boyfriend now – doesn't want me to go ahead. And when I told him I was pregnant he was very upset, and he said that a child has the right to be born into a stable family unit with two parents to love it, and that may very well be true. But now I'm here I realise that more important than that, a child has a right to be *born*.'

She looked at me. 'So you've changed your mind?'

'Yes. I'm sorry,' I added, as though I thought she might be disappointed.

'That's quite all right.' She sighed. 'You're not the first.' She crossed my name off the list and gave me something to sign. 'Good luck,' she said as I left.

I retrieved my clothes from the locker and got dressed, and walked past reception, not even telling the nurse on duty that I was going, not asking – or even caring – whether I'd get my money back.

I didn't wait for the lift but ran down the four flights of stairs and stood outside the building for a moment, inhaling deeply, feeling my heart rate gradually slow. Then I went next door into the bookshop, found the parenthood section, pulled out a copy of *What to Expect when You're Expecting* and took it to the counter.

'I'm going to have a baby,' I said.

*   *   *

58

I sent Xan a long e-mail that night, explaining my decision.

He wrote back one sentence: *I will never forgive you for doing this.*

I hit Reply: *I will never forgive myself if I don't.*

The next morning I drove down to see my father.

'Well . . .' he said after a moment, as we sat at the kitchen table. 'This is a . . . surprise, Anna. I can't deny it.' He was shaking his head in bewildered disappointment, as though I'd just had an unexpectedly poor school report.

'I hope you don't disapprove,' I said in the awkward silence that followed. 'I don't really see why you should,' I went on, 'because first of all loads of women go it alone these days, and secondly the same thing happened to you and Mum.'

I saw a look almost of alarm cross Dad's face, but he and Mum had always glossed over their shotgun wedding; absurdly, I'd thought, given that it had been screamingly obvious that there was a two-month gap between their marriage and the date of Mark's birth.

'Sorry, Dad,' I said. 'I didn't mean to embarrass you.' There was another silence in which I found myself wondering whether he and Mum had had terrible rows about her unplanned pregnancy, or whether Dad had just accepted that he should do the 'right' thing.

'I'm sorry,' I repeated. 'But I'm just so . . . upset.'

'It's OK,' I heard him murmur.

'And I'm acutely aware that I'm in the same position as Mum was thirty-five years ago. But she was lucky – because she had you. And you didn't abandon her, or berate her – like Xan has done with me. You just dealt with it, then made a happy life with her' – my throat was aching – 'for nearly forty years 'til death did you part. And although it may sound strange to be envious of one's own parents, I am envious of you and Mum.' I felt my eyes fill. 'Because I know your sort of happiness is not to be my lot.'

What you need is a hardy perennial.

59

'I'm going to bring up this child on my own. It's not what I would have hoped for.' I felt a tear slide down my cheek. 'It's going to be lonely, and hard.'

'Yes, it is,' Dad said, handing me his hanky. 'But it's going to be a joy too – because children are; and when they come along, I believe that you just have to accept it.' He looked out of the window.

'What are you thinking?' I asked quietly.

'I'm thinking that maybe this new life has started because your mother's ended.'

I felt the hairs on my neck stand up.

I've got the peculiar feeling that I was meant to meet you.

'Yes,' I murmured. 'Maybe it is . . .'

Dad put his hand on mine. 'You won't be on your own, Anna. I'll help you, darling. So will Cassie.'

I doubted that Cassie would help in the slightest – but she was at least thrilled by my news. 'I'm delighted,' she said when I phoned her that night and told her that she was going to be an aunt. 'Good on you, Anna! Congratulations!'

'Well, thanks,' I said, genuinely touched by her enthusiasm. 'But can I just repeat that I'm not with the father – Xan. He's gone to Indonesia. He doesn't want to know about the baby. He didn't want me to have it. He's effectively abandoned me and I'm extremely upset.'

'Yes, I know,' Cassie said matter-of-factly. 'I heard you say all that.'

'Then why are you quite so happy about it?'

'Because I think it's great that you're to be a single mum. Good for your image. You've always been far too . . . I don't know . . . organised about everything – always planning ahead – and now you've been bowled a googly.'

'Well, I'm glad you approve,' I replied crisply. 'Do let me know if you'd like me to develop a drug habit or get a criminal record, won't you?'

'I'm going to start knitting for the baby at my Stitch 'n'

Bitch group,' she went on, ignoring me. 'Bootees first, then a couple of matinée jackets. I wonder whether it's going to be a girl or a boy . . . ? Maybe you could find out when you go for your scan. Or no – *I* know – I'll make everything in yellow. Do you like moss stitch?'

My director of studies was very understanding. Most of our course was project work – in addition to the daily lectures we had to produce designs, to professional standards, for four different gardens. Then in June there'd be two Horticulture exams to test our plantsmanship, and the baby was due a week after these. I'd carry on with the course, as normal, but would just have to pray that I didn't give birth early. I was cheered by stories of first babies arriving late. So, to my surprise, my life didn't descend into turmoil, as I'd thought it would, but went on more or less as before: except that now Xan wasn't in it, but his baby was – as though they'd swapped places. From time to time I'd pick up Sue's book and reread her unwittingly prophetical inscription. I was blooming and growing all right.

I was aware, each day, of the baby unfurling inside me like a fern. When I went for my ultrasounds I'd watch in silent awe as it did underwater twirls and turns, or waved at me with its petal-like hands. I could see its profile, as it rocked in its uterine cradle; I could see the filigree of its bones, no bigger than a bird's; I could see the arc of its vertebrae, like a string of seed pearls.

'I love you,' I'd whisper to it each night, as I lay, hands clasped to my swelling abdomen, feeling it jump and dance. 'I'm sorry you're not going to have a dad, but I'll love you five times as much to make up for it.'

I e-mailed Xan an update but got no reply. His attitude wounded me, but it also helped me, because it enabled a carapace of scar tissue to form over my heart.

Seeing him on TV was hard though. The first time it happened I cried. Suddenly there he was, on the screen, looking dismayingly attractive, talking about some economic summit or other in Java. A couple of days later he was on again, talking about *Jemaah Islamiah* and the threat they posed to Indonesian democracy. He began to appear more and more – hijacking my emotions: so much so that I took to watching the news on ITV. I couldn't risk an unexpected sighting of him wrecking my day.

In mid April I went to the first of my antenatal classes in the local church hall in Brook Green.

I felt nervous as I arrived, my despondency increasing as one cosy-looking couple followed another into the large draughty room. I'd prepared myself for this by putting a large aquamarine ring of Mum's on my fourth finger; this also made me feel closer to her in some small way. If she hadn't died, I reflected, she would have come with me to these classes and I'd have felt so much less alone.

I discreetly glanced round the seated group: the other women all had their menfolk in tow, and sported gleaming gold bands and showy engagement rings that flashed and sparkled in the strip lights.

There was a twenty-something blonde with her husband. They clutched hands the whole time, like infatuated teenagers. There was a brisk-looking brunette, with her bespectacled spouse. There was a woman in her late thirties who looked as though she was about to pop there and then. And then there was a large woman with long red hair, bulgy blue eyes and an almost perfectly round face, like a plate. She looked familiar, though I didn't know why. Perhaps I'd seen her in the local shops. But she was clearly the oldest of us – mid forties – and was twice the size of her husband who, with his red cheeks and fixed grin, reminded me of a ventriloquist's puppet.

The woman suddenly stifled a burp and patted her chest. 'Wind,' she explained with a little smile, as though she thought we might be interested.

By now we all seemed to be here, chatting in low voices, or swigging Gaviscon to ease our indigestion. I was the only single mother, I realised; my heart sank to the soles of my shoes. Then the teacher, Felicity, began handing out an assortment of paperwork on breastfeeding, pelvic floor exercises, what to pack for the hospital etc. But just as she was about to start the class another woman, a year or two older than me, walked in alone. I breathed a small sigh of relief.

'Is this seat free?' she asked me pleasantly.

'Yes it is.' I beamed at her. 'Hi.'

The newcomer was dressed all in black, she was wearing Doc Martens and her dark hair was cut in a boyish crop. Her neat, regular features were unadorned by make-up. She wore an engraved silver ring on her right thumb, but her left hand was bare.

'Right,' said Felicity. 'Now that we're all here, let's introduce ourselves.'

'We're Nicole and Tim,' said the lovey-dovey couple in unison, then they laughed.

'I'm Tanya,' said the brisk-looking brunette, 'and this is my husband Howard.' Howard smiled abstractedly, as though he wished he weren't there.

'I'm Katie, this is my fiancé Jake and we're expecting twins.' A shiver of sympathy went round the room.

Then it was the turn of the large red-haired woman. She waited until silence had descended, a patient little smile on her lips. 'I'm the journalist, Citronella Pratt.' Now I realised why she looked familiar. She wrote a weekly column in the *Sunday News*. 'And this is my husband, Ian Barker-Jones,' she added unctuously.

'I'm an investment banker,' he said.

I was so taken aback by the Pratt-Barker-Joneses' self-satisfied introduction that I forgot it was now my turn. Felicity prompted me with a little cough and I felt all eyes swivel towards me.

'Oh. I'm Anna Temple,' I began. 'My baby's due on the eighteenth of June and . . . erm . . .' There was an air of expectation – so I did this cowardly and, as it was to turn out, stupid thing. 'My other half' – I swallowed nervously – 'Xan . . . works overseas, as a TV reporter. In Indonesia,' I added, aware that my voice sounded an octave higher than normal. 'In fact, he'll be out there for a few months, and so . . .' I twisted my ring back and forth. 'I'll be coming to these classes on my own.'

I looked up and saw Citronella cock her head to one side and smile at me, but it was a shrewd, knowing sort of smile that made my insides coil.

Then the woman who'd just arrived spoke up.

'My name's Jenny Reid,' she said confidently, in a soft, Northern Irish accent. 'My baby's due on June the fifth. And I'm here on my own because I don't have a partner – but I'm fine about it.'

I saw Citronella's eyes widen with something like excitement; then she collapsed her features into an expression of conspicuous solicitude.

In the coffee break she waddled over to Jenny and me. 'How *brave* of you,' she said to Jenny, clasping her fat, spatulate fingers over her massive bump. 'I just want to say how much I *admire* you.'

'For what?' Jenny asked with a brittle smile.

'Well.' Citronella shrugged. 'For going through such a *momentous* thing as childbirth alone.'

'Thank you for your concern,' Jenny replied evenly, 'but as I said at the beginning, I'm perfectly fine.'

'No really,' Citronella persisted. 'I think you're marvellous – honestly – *both* of you,' she added, nodding at me. I struggled to think of some retort, but a suitably sharp put-down eluded me.

'Well, I think *you're* brave,' I heard Jenny say.

Citronella's nostrils clamped shut. 'Why?' she demanded.

'Well – having a baby so late. I think that's very brave,' Jenny went on pleasantly. 'But, you know, hey – good for you!'

As Jenny turned back to me, her flushed cheeks only now betraying her emotion, I made a mental note never to offend her.

For her part, Citronella looked as though she'd been slapped. Then, determined to recover, she smiled, revealing large square teeth the colour of Edam and walked away. And though nothing was said about it by either Jenny or me, we both knew that a bond had been formed between us that day.

Over the next six weeks of the classes Jenny and I became natural allies. We'd do the exercises together and chat in the breaks: but though she was always friendly, Jenny seemed very self-protective, never revealing anything personal. When, after a month, I confided that I wasn't really with Xan and that I found it very hard, she touched my hand and made sympathetic noises, but offered no confidence in return. All I knew about her was what she'd told me at the first class – that she'd grown up in Belfast, had moved to London in her teens and until last year had taught History at a 'very tough' comprehensive in north London, but had given it up to train as a counsellor.

Jenny seemed so resolutely single that I wondered if, like me, she'd become pregnant after a short relationship and the man had gone off. But she didn't radiate the air of disappointment and vulnerability that I knew I did – instead she projected a determined calm that bordered on defiance. This made me wonder if she'd got pregnant deliberately, by a friend, or on a one-night stand, or even by donor sperm, though at thirty-four she seemed young to have made such a choice.

Citronella, on the other hand, I soon knew all about, both from her boastful pronouncements at the birthing classes and from her columns, which a kind of horrified curiosity prompted me to look at on-line.

I was struck, most of all, by their vulgarity. No detail of Citronella's life seemed too personal – too disgusting even – for her to share with her readers: that her breasts were already 'leaky', that 'sex was uncomfortable' and that her bowels 'could do with some help'. The overall theme of Citronella's weekly bulletins, however, seemed to be how 'fortunate' she was. That she was 'fortunate enough' to have a ten-year-old daughter, Sienna, for example, who, 'fortunately' was 'extremely intelligent, popular, and beautiful' and who 'fortunately' was *thrilled* at the prospect of a new brother or sister. I learned that Citronella's first marriage to a nappy manufacturer had sadly ended eight years before, but that she had then been 'fortunate enough' to meet her 'banker husband, Ian' shortly afterwards, with whom she was 'much happier', she'd added smugly.

Fertility treatment was another favourite theme. 'Ian and I would *never* have had IVF,' Citronella wrote in early May. 'We both think it *quite wrong* that something as sacred as life should begin in a jam-jar of all places! And then of course there's the cancer risk . . .' I hoped that Katie and Jake hadn't read it – they'd happily admitted to having had help in conceiving their twins. 'And yes, I know there's no actual *proof* of a link,' Citronella had gone on. 'But one instinctively feels that such hormonal interference *must* be doing *irreparable* harm. *Fortunately* I conceived naturally,' she'd continued, 'though I admit I never expected the *enormous* blessing of another child. But being pregnant now, at forty-four, does make me *feel* for my single women friends. They are all roughly my age and must increasingly be aware that they are unlikely now ever to marry, or have children and are therefore bravely facing up to the prospect of a lonely old age.'

With opinions like these it seemed incredible that Citronella had any friends, single or otherwise. In the following week's column, headed IS IT REALLY RIGHT TO GO IT ALONE? her theme was single mums.

So far so clichéd, I thought as I scanned it; then I read the next sentence and felt as though I'd stepped into a sauna. *There are no less than two single mothers in my antenatal group*, she'd written. *Let me say that* no one *admires them more than I do* – Citronella liked to dress up her horrible pity as generosity of spirit. *But one does wonder – quite apart from the social slur – how their children will fare in life without the firm, loving hand of a father to guide them . . .*

'Did you see what she wrote?' I whispered to Jenny as we waited for our next birthing class. We were the first to arrive and the room was empty but for us.

Jenny rolled her eyes. 'Yup! Doesn't she know it's "no fewer than", rather than "no less than"? The woman's an ignoramus.'

'But her comments about single mothers . . .' I swigged some Pepsodent. 'As though you and I were the lowest of the low.'

'Well . . .' Jenny gave a philosophical shrug. 'At least she didn't name us.'

'No – but what she said – about our children. *What* "social slur"? How *dare* she! She's evil,' I added darkly.

'Evil?' Jenny looked surprised, affronted almost. 'Oh no, Citronella's not evil,' she said, with a strange kind of authority which puzzled me, until I remembered that she'd grown up in Belfast, where she'd said it was nothing out of the ordinary to hear gunfire and explosions. 'But you could certainly rearrange the letters and say that she's vile. Don't let her get to you, Anna,' Jenny went on calmly. 'You're going to have a baby. That's all that matters. Your life is about to be filled with unimaginable love . . .' Jenny said this with an almost Messianic fervour that intrigued me. 'And at least we won't have to see Citronella after tonight.'

At that I felt a frisson of liberation, but at the same time a sadness that the classes were now at an end.

'You will keep in touch, won't you?' I said to Jenny, as everyone left. 'I'd like to be . . . friends.'

Puzzlement clouded her features. 'But we already are,' she said and I felt suddenly, unaccountably happy. She picked up her bag. 'I'm due first – so I'll let you know.'

'I'll come and see you,' I offered.

'Yes – do come and see me – or rather us.' She smiled and then to my delighted surprise, she hugged me. 'Good luck with your exams.'

I grimaced. 'Thanks.'

In the event my exams were fine – I even managed to enjoy them in part, though every time I felt a twinge I'd panic that my waters were about to break – the baby was due in less than ten days.

In the absence of an Other Half, I'd decided not to have a birthing partner. There was no one I'd want to see me in such a state. It was bad enough for your husband to see you down on your hands and knees, bellowing like a bull, without inflicting that on a friend. I was happy just to have a couple of midwives – I knew many of them from my pre-natal visits – and some Mozart. As I packed my hospital bag I resolved to stay relaxed and to put my faith in Nature. But in the event Nature got completely squeezed out.

On the Sunday morning after my last exam I woke with a terrible headache and a peculiar buzzing sensation in my upper body, as though there was a swarm of bees in my chest. I waited for the sensation to subside, but it didn't. I staggered to the bathroom and was sick. Knowing that something was wrong, I called a minicab and went to the hospital. The midwives said that my blood pressure was high.

'How high?' I asked the nurse as I sat in a treatment room.

'Are we talking Primrose Hill here, or Mount Everest?' I felt dizzy and breathless and my head was aching.

'It's 140 over 100,' she replied. 'And your notes say that it's been fairly steady at 110 over 70 throughout your pregnancy.'

'So what does it mean?'

'It suggests pre-eclampsia. Are your feet and hands normally this swollen?'

'No.' It was as though someone had blown them up with a bicycle pump. I winced as the nurse inserted a canula into the back of my right hand.

'We should be able to get your blood pressure down with this hypertensive medication,' she went on as she rigged up the drip. 'So don't worry.'

'What if it doesn't come down?' I asked after a moment.

'Then we'll have to deliver the baby today.'

My stomach did a flick-flack. 'By Caesarean?' I hated the idea of being cut.

'Yes,' the nurse replied, 'because they have to be quick. Now what about your partner?' she went on as she passed the electronic belt round my vast middle to check the baby's heartbeat.

'I don't have a partner.' I felt my eyes fill. 'He didn't want me to have the baby. He lives in Indonesia now.'

'Oh . . .' A look of regret crossed her face. 'Well, don't fret,' she said, stroking my arm. 'Don't fret now.' Her name badge said 'Amity' – it seemed to suit her. 'You're going to be fine and so is baby. Listen . . .' She turned up the monitor so that I could hear the watery iambics of the baby's heart. 'But you should call *someone* – in case things happen today. What about your family?' she added.

'Hopeless,' I replied shaking my head. Cassie was away for the weekend at some fashionable spa in Austria and I wouldn't want to worry Dad before it was all over.

'And is your head still hurting?'

'It's hell.'

Then the obstetrician on duty came in, introduced herself, checked my reflexes and blood pressure and went away. Fifteen minutes later she returned, checked both again, this time her expression darkening slightly.

'What is it now?' I asked her as the armband deflated with a wheezy sigh.

'Not so good,' she replied. 'It's 150 over 120.' She held up her hand. 'Do you have any double vision, Anna?'

'I'm not sure.' I'd been crying and everything was blurred. 'But my *head*,' I whimpered. 'It's such . . . agony.'

'Well, that's going to get better very soon.'

'How? Are you going to guillotine me?'

'No.' She gave me a lovely smile and pulled up a chair next to me. 'We're going to deliver the baby.'

I felt a wave of fear. 'When?'

'I'd say now's as good a time as any.'

'Oh,' I said faintly. 'I see.'

'You have pre-eclampsia,' she explained. I felt a flutter of panic. 'And the cure for that is to give birth. But we need to get you gowned up in this fetching little green number ready for theatre, OK?'

I nodded bleakly. I had never felt more alone. Amity began to help me undress and as I was taking off my shirt I heard my phone ring. She passed me my bag and I fished out the mobile with my left hand.

'Anna? Hi! I'm just ringing to ask how your exams went.'

'Oh. Fine, thanks, Sue . . . I think. I can't really remember to be honest . . . It's all a blur you see, I . . .' my voice trailed away.

'Anna – are you feeling all right?'

'Not really. In fact I'm at . . . birth's door.' I explained what was happening.

'Have you got anyone with you?'

'No.' I felt my throat constrict. 'I'm alone.'

'Would you like me to come? I've had two kids after all – plus I feel partly responsible for your being pregnant in the first place – it's the least I can do.'

I looked at the clock. It was a quarter past four. 'Well . . . I'd love that,' I replied. 'Just to have a friend with me – but you'd never get here in time.'

I heard Sue's footsteps tapping across a stone floor. 'I'm not at home. I'm at Tate Britain . . .' I heard her breathing speed up. 'With my sister. But I'm going to leave . . . for the hospital right . . . now. Chelsea and Westminster, isn't it? I'll jump in . . . a cab. I'll call you later, Lisa,' I heard her add. 'Anna's having the baby.' Then I heard her running down the steps. 'Which ward . . . are you on?' she asked, raising her voice above the roar of the traffic on the Embankment. '*TAXI!!!* Give me twenty minutes . . . tops. I'll be there.'

The lights were so dazzling as I was wheeled into the theatre a short while later that I had to shield my eyes from the glare. As I sat on the operating table, the anaesthetist explained that he would give me an epidural, for which I had to sit stone still. As I watched him fill the syringe with the anaesthetic I suddenly heard Sue's voice.

'I'm here, Anna!' I heard her call. 'I'm just being gowned up but I'll be with you in two seconds, OK?' Then the door opened and there she was, in a green gown and hat and white overshoes. She stroked my shoulder. 'You're going to be fine. This is the happiest day of your life . . .'

I nodded, then a large tear plopped on to my lap, staining the pale green almost to black. In the background the doctor, in her surgical gown and mask, was conferring with the theatre nurses as they laid out the instruments.

Sue stroked my arm as the needle for the epidural was pushed into my lower spine.

'Hold absolutely still,' said the anaesthetist quietly. I focused on the large clock on the wall, watching the second hand click forward fifteen times. 'Well done,' I heard him say.

71

'Now,' he said after five minutes or so. 'Let's see if it's working. Can you feel this cold spray?' I saw him squirt something from a small aerosol on to my shins.

'No,' I replied 'I can't.'

'What about this?' He did the same to my thigh.

'No.'

'And this?' He sprayed the top of my bump.

'I might as well be a slab of sirloin.'

'Then you're ready to go. Let's get you lying down.'

A nurse lifted my legs on to the bed, then a blue sheet was erected at mid level, shielding my lower half from view. Sue sat on a chair by my head while the scalpel went in. As she held my hand she told me all about the exhibition she'd just been to, as though she were having a nice cappuccino with me, rather than watching me being eviscerated.

'Beautiful watercolours . . .' I heard her say. 'Still lifes and landscapes . . . and some gorgeous flower paintings . . .' From time to time she'd glance nervously at the other side of the screen. 'You'd have loved it, Anna.'

'It's going very well,' the doctor said. 'Now you'll feel a little pressure . . .'

I felt an odd sensation as she rummaged around in my insides as though she were doing the washing up. 'And a little more pressure . . .' I was dimly aware of a pulling feeling. Then there was an odd, sucking sound, like a retreating wave. I looked up so see the screen being lowered, and now I saw the doctor's gloved hands raise up this . . . *alien* creature, its body the colour of raw liver, its head coated in a bluish white, its arms outflung, its tiny fingers splayed, its filmy eyes squinting into the glaring lights.

'There's your baby,' Sue said, her voice catching.

'Yes,' I heard the doctor say. 'She's here.'

'A girl . . . ?' I felt a twinge of relief.

'A *gorgeous* girl,' Sue said. 'She's *lovely*, Anna.' She squeezed my hand.

I felt tears trickle down the sides of my face. The baby opened her mouth and emitted a piercing cry; then she was whisked to one side, where I saw her being wiped, then weighed, then gently laid in a resuscitator.

I glanced at the clock. The time was five past six. But what was the date? Of course. It was the eighth of June.

I've got the peculiar feeling that I was meant *to meet you.*

It was the first anniversary of my mother's death.

FOUR

I spent three nights in hospital, the first one in the High Dependency Unit, attached to a hydra of drips and trailing wires, while Milly lay beside me in her Perspex cot, in her white hat and vest, her tiny limbs waving like windswept flowers. Round her left wrist was a little band saying 'Baby Temple'.

'Amelia Lucy Mary Temple,' I whispered to her as she lay in my arms. 'Amelia and Lucy after my two grandmothers, Mary after my mum and Temple after my family. So you're Miss Milly Temple.' I kissed the top of her head. 'Welcome to the world.'

The nights in hospital were hard, the crying of twenty or so newborns making sleep impossible. Some of the babies sounded like kittens; others – including Milly – squawked like peacocks; there was one baby who made a trumpeting sound, like a tiny elephant, while the baby in the next bay emitted a constant shivery bleat, like a chilled lamb.

During the day it was depressing watching the other mothers being visited by their husbands, having congratulatory kisses bestowed on them, then being taken home with the respect shown to triumphant Olympians. My dad collected me but it felt all wrong. Xan should be doing this,

I thought, as we walked through the revolving door with Milly in her car seat.

I e-mailed Xan three photos of her. Her features were already so identifiably his, in feminine miniature, that I thought he'd melt, but he didn't reply. But then, as if to compensate me for his coldness, a flood of gifts and flowers arrived from family and friends. Each day a beribboned parcel would turn up, containing a teddy or a toy, or a tiny pink dress.

But the best gift of all was from Dad. 'I want you to have a maternity nurse,' he'd said at the beginning of May. He'd been in London and had dropped in to see how I was.

'What's made you think of that?' I asked as I glanced up from my drawing board.

'Cassie suggested it – it seems that one of her knitting circle runs an agency that specialises in maternity nurses; I think it's a good idea.'

'It is. But at £700 a week I can't afford it.'

'I'll pay.'

I put down my pen. 'No, Dad, honestly, that's too much – and I'm sure I'll manage . . .'

'But you'll need someone to look after *you*. Please let me do this for you, Anna. It's not a luxury in your case, it's a necessity, because you have no partner to help you and no mother.'

'No, but . . .'

'And if she'd been here she'd have stayed with you and helped you and shown you what to do, wouldn't she?'

'Yes,' I agreed sadly, 'she would.'

'So I'd like to give you the next best thing. A maternity nurse – for six weeks.'

'But that would cost nearly four and a half grand.'

'But think of how often I've helped Cassie. I've always indulged her,' he added, looking out of the window. 'It must have seemed unfair.' He returned his gaze to me. 'But now

75

I'd like to do something for you. Let this be my baby present, Anna. It would make me very happy.'

'Well . . . OK, then,' I said quietly. 'Thanks.'

And so the day after I came out of hospital, Elaine arrived.

I'd already met her, two weeks before, when she'd come for her interview. She was Australian, late fifties, slim and neat, with her ash-blonde hair swept into a bun, a pair of little tortoiseshell specs strung round her neck. She radiated the kind of calm that makes you instinctively lower your voice. Within ten minutes of meeting her I knew she'd be fine.

And she was. She was friendly without being familiar. She took charge without being abrupt, swiftly establishing a sleeping and feeding routine for Milly. She moved about the house as unobtrusively as a cat.

I stayed in bed for the first three days, recovering from the surgery. But as I became more mobile Elaine showed me how to use the steriliser, how to breastfeed more effectively, how to burp Milly and bathe her tiny body – a proposition which terrified me – how to swaddle her to make her feel secure. She revealed to me the Byzantine mysteries of the baby sling and showed me how to collapse the pram. She'd cook for us both and clear up; she'd make me rest; she'd go to the local food store while Milly slept.

'How's it going with the maternity nurse?' Dad asked me over the phone a week after Elaine arrived.

'Wonderful.' I sighed. 'She's like the Angel Gabriel and Florence Nightingale rolled into one.'

As we became used to each other we talked. Elaine was from Melbourne, where she'd been a nurse. She'd been separated from her husband for just over a year.

'Last April I found a note from Don on the kitchen table,' she said quietly, as we sat under the parasol in my small courtyard garden one sunny morning in late June. Milly lay peacefully in her arms, swathed in a soft pink blanket, her eyes flickering with sleep. 'The note said that he wouldn't be back for dinner because he was leaving me for Julie – a close friend of mine.' At least Xan had only abandoned me for a job, I reflected. It seemed less humiliating. 'At first I didn't believe it,' Elaine said, 'because by cruel coincidence it was April the first. Then I phoned him and realised it was true. I learned afterwards that they'd been having an affair for six months. I'd had no idea.'

'How terrible.'

'For two months I hardly ate or slept. I wouldn't leave the house because I couldn't face people. I'd adored Don – we'd been married thirty-one years. But then I suddenly woke up one day and said, "To hell with this misery." I was fifty-six. I still had a lot of life left to live – God willing' – she knocked on the table – 'and I resolved to *live* it. My two boys were grown up so I arranged to come here.'

'Did you know anyone?'

'An old school friend who lives in Bath and my nephew, Jamie. He's been here for three years.'

I glanced at the bees buzzing about in the lavender. 'You were brave to come.'

'Maybe – though you might say that I was running away. But I knew that only a complete change of environment would save me.' She stroked Milly's outstretched hand. 'But maternity nursing suits me. I love tiny babies – I don't mind the nights because I'm a light sleeper – and it means I get to travel and meet some wonderful people. I miss Don, of course, but at least the life I've made for myself now isn't a bad one.'

'You're such a positive person,' I said. 'I should try to be more like you and stop feeling sorry for myself.'

'So . . . what about your fella?' she asked. All I'd told Elaine was that I wasn't with Milly's father. 'Not that it's any of my business,' she added, 'so excuse my Aussie directness and you don't have to answer.'

I smiled. 'I don't mind. In fact, I'd like to tell you . . .'

'How do you feel about him now?' she asked quietly, when I'd finished.

'Well . . . I feel sorry for him in many ways. The truth is he *hadn't* known me that long. It's also true that I could have taken more care not to get pregnant – I knew I was taking a huge risk that night. But something . . . strange had come over me and I just wasn't . . . myself.'

'Bereaved people never are,' Elaine said.

'So . . . I don't blame Xan for feeling angry. But at the same time he's thirty-seven, not twenty-two, and he's far from poor, so I feel he could have been bigger and better about it all. Milly's been in the world for three weeks now and he has yet to acknowledge her existence. It seems heartless,' I added bleakly.

'He's probably terrified,' Elaine said.

'How could anyone be terrified of Milly?' I murmured, stroking her head. It was as soft as swansdown.

'He's terrified of what it means. Because the minute he does acknowledge that she exists, he also has to acknowledge that he's a father and that his long "boyhood" is over. Plus he wants to punish you.'

'That's certainly true. He said he'd never forgive me.'

'But he won't always feel as he feels now. Everything will change. Because it always does.'

It wasn't that what Elaine said was ever startlingly original, but her insights were always comfortingly spot-on. And she had a gift for sympathy – an ability to relate in a thoughtful, imaginative way to other people's feelings.

She worked six days a week and had Sundays off. On these she caught an early train to Bath to stay with her friend, returning twenty-four hours later. Dad spent the first two Sundays with me, then, on the third, Cassie visited me with a number of knitted garments. 'Sorry they're a bit wonky,' she explained. There were visible mistakes on every one. 'But because we all gossip so much at Stitch 'n' Bitch – or Knit 'n' Natter as I prefer to call it – I didn't notice until it was too late and I hate undoing knitting.'

'Don't worry,' I said. 'They're . . . lovely.' I wished that she could knit her own life into some more meaningful shape.

'And this is for you.' I opened the little pink gift bag. Inside was a tub of Crème de la Mer.

'What a treat, Cassie – thanks!'

'Well, I figured you'd need a bit of luxury having just had a baby. Anyway' – she offered Milly her little finger to clasp – 'she's . . . adorable. Aren't you, darling? Yes, you *are*, sweetie. She's like Mum, isn't she?' she added quietly. And this surprised me as Cassie rarely mentions Mum – as though she can't bear to.

'She *is* a little. The mouth. And the chin.'

'And is she good?'

'As gold.'

'Feeding well?'

'Fairly champing at the tit.'

'And has *he* been in touch?' Cassie asked in her characteristically direct way.

'No,' I murmured. 'He hasn't and, to be honest, I'd rather not discuss him.'

Cassie slumped into a chair. 'I think I know why it didn't work out between you.'

'How could you possibly know?' I said wearily. 'You only met him once, for five minutes.'

'That's true – but I could tell that he was somehow . . . restless. It was as though he was poised for flight.'

'I don't see how you could have known that when I didn't,' I protested. 'Especially as I hadn't told you anything about him.'

'It was because of his footwear,' she replied.

'His what?'

'I noticed that he was wearing desert boots and they're often worn by men who travel a lot.' I stared at her. 'Plus you had hopelessly incompatible names. How could you go out with a man called Xan, when you're called Anna?' she went on. '"Xan 'n' Anna" doesn't exactly trip off the tongue, does it? Nor does "Anna 'n' Xan" – though you could have just called yourselves "Xanna", I suppose . . .' She wound her long dark hair into a thick knot and secured it with a pencil while she considered the question.

'How was your Austrian spa?' I asked, keen to change the subject.

'Interesting,' she said judiciously, 'if a little rigorous. All we got to eat were these prison rations of plain yoghurt and sourdough bread, each bit of which we had to chew seventy-five times.'

'And how much did you have to pay for this privilege?'

'Two grand all in.'

'For one weekend? Good *God*. So your work must be going well, then. What are you doing?'

'Nothing you'd approve of,' she replied cheerfully.

'Still temping?'

'Well . . . the agency hasn't got much at the moment, so to make ends meet I've started doing some evening work.'

'Of what sort?' I asked suspiciously.

'Well, it's just talking to people over the phone . . .'

'What people?'

'Male people,' she replied. She pulled the pencil out of her hair and down it fell with an almost audible *swish* . . . 'Men.'

'You talk to men on the phone? What for? Is it market research of some kind?'

'No.' She sighed. 'It's because they're rather lonely and a bit . . . sad, really . . .'

The penny dropped. 'Oh my God – you're doing telephone sex. *Please* don't tell me you're doing telephone sex,' I said, wondering, as I often do, how the same ingredients could have produced Cassie and me. It's not so much that we're like chalk and cheese, and in any case I've always thought that chalk and cheese – especially Cheshire cheese – aren't that dissimilar – from a distance. No, with us it was more a case of chalk and coal.

'Well . . . I prefer to call it "adult phone entertainment".'

'You can call it what you like, it's still . . . *sleazy*, Cassie.'

'Not really,' she said amiably. 'I only *talk* to the men after all – I call myself "Jade" – and it doesn't take that long. The average call only lasts six minutes, you know – I can knit while I do it – although some of them want to talk about some *pretty* unusual things and . . .'

'Spare me the details. I don't know how you can!' I added crossly.

'Well,' she said evenly – Cassie rarely takes offence – 'I can because I'm not a prude, and because I have a very active imagination: and to me it's all part of life's rich tapestry,' she added airily. 'More important, I can make a hundred and fifty pounds in an hour.'

In late June, Jenny got in touch and invited me over for tea on Sunday. Her little girl had been born a fortnight late, ten days before, so this was the first opportunity for us to see each other with our babies.

I fed Milly, put her in her sling with a pink sun hat on her head and set off on foot for Hesketh Gardens on the other side of the Goldhawk Road. Within a couple of minutes Milly had been lulled to sleep by my walking and by the warmth of the day, her head flopping forward like a wilting rose. Panicking that she couldn't breathe, I kept trying to tip it back, but down it would droop again, so I gently cradled it with my left hand. Wimbledon was on and as I walked along I could hear the thwack of tennis balls floating out of open windows, then bursts of loud applause, like sudden rain.

Jenny had a basement flat at the far end of her street. I went down the iron steps. A burglar alarm winked at me, the windows were cross-hatched with bars, and there were large stickers on the door with stern injunctions to deter hawkers and junk mail. There was also a large 'Neighbourhood Watch' sign.

I pressed the bell and after a moment heard a bolt being drawn back, then the turning of a key and finally the sound of the chain being taken off.

'Your security's tight,' I said as Jenny opened the door. 'It's like Fort Knox around here!'

'Well . . . the area's a little bit . . . rough. And being in a basement flat . . . alone, with a baby . . .'

'Of course – you can't be too careful.'

'Anyway.' She smiled. 'Come in. Let me see her . . .' I lifted off Milly's hat. 'She's utterly adorable.'

I felt a burst of maternal pride. 'Thanks.'

I followed Jenny down the narrow hall into the small sitting room, where a Moses basket was lying in the middle of the sofa. I peeped inside. Jenny's baby was lying on her back, her hands up, in that 'I surrender' pose that babies adopt. She had a downy covering of fair hair; her mouth was a perfect little Cupid's bow; her eyes, flickering with sleep, were large and thickly lashed. Her cheeks were a peachy pink.

'She's beautiful,' I said. 'She has the face of an angel.'

'The face of an angel,' Jenny echoed, almost sadly, I thought. In the momentary silence that followed I wondered if she was thinking about the baby's father and whether she longed for him, as I still longed for Xan.

'She looks like you,' I added.

'Do you think so?' Jenny said happily, as though I couldn't have said anything nicer.

'I do. And Grace is a lovely name.' I undid the poppers on the babysling. 'Did you call her that because she was born on a Tuesday?'

Jenny shook her head. 'I decided on it long before she was born – from the moment I knew that I was having a girl.'

'So you found out? You never said.'

'I didn't tell anyone – I wanted to keep that knowledge just for myself.'

'That's understandable – but why did you want to know?'

'Because . . . I thought it might help me bond with the baby. I wanted to begin that process as early as possible.'

'Did you have a preference?'

'No,' she replied carefully. 'But when the radiologist said it was a girl, I did feel a little relieved.'

'I felt that too,' I admitted as I settled Milly on my shoulder. 'But only because I thought that a girl might cope without a father a bit better than a boy would do.'

Jenny nodded. Then we went through the names that the other women in our class had called their babies. We'd had e-mails announcing the arrival of Louis, Jacob, Amelie, Lucas . . .

'And *Lilac*,' Jenny exclaimed, rolling her eyes.

'At least it's not Daffodil,' I pointed out.

'Or Mesembryanthemum!' She giggled. 'Katie's twins are Jonah and George.'

'Then of course there's Erasmus,' I snorted. 'Who but Citronella would inflict Erasmus Pratt-Barker-Jones on their child?'

'Poor little boy,' Jenny said. 'And her accompanying description of the birth – did you get that?'

I rolled my eyes. 'In all its gory details – as though none of us had just been through it ourselves!'

'Still, at least we don't have to see her again,' Jenny said as she went into the kitchen. 'Now, let's have some tea.'

'Can I do anything?'

'Yes – relax.'

As Jenny filled the kettle I stood by the open french windows and glanced at her patio garden; it was almost bare, with a few straggly white geraniums, some dark-pink valerian and an enormous yucca in a glazed pot.

'I'm afraid the garden's a bit of a disaster area,' Jenny called out.

'I wouldn't say that. It just needs a few more things in it.'
I squinted at the sky. 'But it's west-facing, which is good.'

'I'd like to make it nice, but I haven't a clue about gardening.'

'I could get you some plants.'

'Would you really?'

Now I glanced around the room. The walls were lined with serious-looking novels, and heavy-looking books about education and psychology: *Female Empowerment and Feminist Theory*; *What About the Boys? Issues of Masculinity in Schools*; *Cyberfeminism*; *The Gendered Self in Discourse*. There was a colourful screen print over the fireplace, a reclining nude in blue pastel on one wall, but not a single family photo, and only two or three baby cards, as though she hadn't told many people. Nor was there a hint even of the man responsible for Grace's conception.

By now I'd known Jenny for three months. I knew a bit about her childhood in Northern Ireland; I knew she had an identical twin sister who was married and lived in France; I knew about the school where Jenny had taught and the near-violence she'd endured from one or two of the more disruptive pupils. Yet when it came to her private life, Jenny remained an enigma.

'So how are you finding motherhood?' she asked as she brought in the tea.

I gently rubbed Milly's back, while she nuzzled at my neck, making little squeaking noises. 'I find it wonderful – but terrifying.'

'It *is* scary.' She set down the tray. 'The idea that another human being's entire safety, health and well-being rests in our inexperienced hands.' She lifted the lid off the pot, stirred it, then looked at me enquiringly. And I thought she was going to ask me whether I took milk or sugar. 'Do you have any regrets?' she suddenly said.

'Regrets?'

'I mean . . . about going it alone. It's not going to be easy, is it – emotionally – it's going to be hard at times . . . and lonely . . . there'll be a lot of anxiety . . .' She let the sentence drift.

Did I have any regrets? I remembered what my mum had once said – *I don't think having a child is ever a mistake . . .* – and now I could honestly say the same. 'No, I don't,' I replied. 'And you?'

'I thought I would,' she said quietly as she poured the tea. 'My greatest fear was that I wouldn't love the baby. I *needed* to,' she went on, with a flash of the strange intensity that she sometimes displays.

'But you *do* love her?'

'Oh yes.' She clapped her hand to her chest with relief. 'More than I ever imagined I would – I love her more and more each day.' She gazed at Grace. 'It's a miracle.'

'It is.' I stroked Milly's cheek. 'But although I don't for a second regret having her, at the same time I do feel . . . sad.'

'Why's that?' Jenny asked softly.

'Because Milly's this living, breathing piece of a man I loved and hoped to live with, but who doesn't love me in return, or want to live with me.' My throat ached. 'Even though I've had his child.' I felt a tear slide down my face, then seep into the corner of my mouth with a salty tang.

Jenny came and sat next to me. 'I can understand that,' she said softly, as she handed me a tissue. 'But maybe as your relationship with Milly grows you'll feel so happy that any regrets about not being with her father will fade.'

'That's what I'm hoping.' I sniffed. 'But they might actually get worse – as she becomes more like him, or starts asking me about him as she gets older. That won't be easy.'

Jenny's expression darkened. 'No.' She sighed. 'That won't be.' She passed me my tea. The mug was stamped with 'Behind Every Successful Woman Is *Herself!!*' in large pink letters. 'And have you heard from him?'

I shook my head. 'But if he does get in touch, I've decided that I will want him to see Milly – however painful it is for me. I don't feel I can deny that to either of them.'

Jenny shifted uncomfortably before returning to her chair. 'Well . . . in your situation that's probably right.'

I felt suddenly emboldened to ask her a personal question. 'Do you think you'll see Grace's dad?' Perhaps she'd softened her position since having the baby.

'No,' she replied firmly. I heard her inhale deeply, as if steadying herself. 'As I've said before, he's not on the scene . . .'

'But will he help you financially?'

'Oh no.' She seemed to shudder with distaste. 'And I wouldn't want that even if –' she looked out of the window – 'if things were . . . different.' She sipped her tea. Her mug bore the slogan 'I Think, Therefore I'm Single'. 'And how's your maternity nurse?' she went on, keen to change the subject.

'She's wonderful.' I dabbed at Milly's mouth with my muslin. 'I wish she could stay for ever.'

'But you'll be fine on your own,' Jenny said as she swatted a fly away from the Moses basket. 'Babies sleep so much that you can still get a lot done. I've been able to work quite a bit since Grace was born – I even managed to write half an essay yesterday for my counselling course.'

I put down my cup. 'But you've had some help too, I guess. From your mum?'

Jenny gave me a wintry smile. 'I wish . . .'

'Oh. I . . . thought she might be helping you.'

'Well, it would be normal to think that, but she and my dad haven't even been to see us.' Grace began to stir, so Jenny picked her up and unbuttoned her shirt.

'Are they far away then?' I asked, surprised by this confidence. Perhaps they were still in Belfast.

'No,' Jenny replied, as she began to feed Grace. 'They live just up the road, in Acton. And Grace is their first grandchild so you'd think they'd be curious, if nothing else, wouldn't you?' she added bitterly. She adjusted Grace's position and stroked her cheek to stimulate sucking, as we'd been taught to do in the class.

'So, don't you . . . get on with your parents then?' I ventured, aware that I was on thin ice.

'I used to.' She sighed. 'But they've been, well . . . disapproving, to put it mildly.'

'Because . . . you're not with Grace's dad?' I could hear the ice creak and groan.

'Sort of.' Jenny sighed again. 'It's a bit more complicated than that, to be honest.'

How? I wanted to ask. *How is it more complicated? Please tell me!*

'They're very religious,' she added, as though that explained everything. Then she changed the subject and I decided not to risk offending her by appearing more inquisitive than I already had.

As I walked home I decided that Jenny must have had an affair with a married man. Why else would her parents be so censorious? She'd had an affair with a married man and his wife had found out. I imagined a dreadful scene – the wife storming round to Jenny's flat in the early hours, hammering on the door and calling her all kinds of vile names. I imagined the neighbours throwing up their windows at the commotion; the husband scuttling home to avoid divorce. Then I imagined Jenny's parents, fire and brimstone Presbyterians, so appalled at their daughter 'falling pregnant' in this way that they'd cut her off – grandchild or not.

Mum would never have been like that, I thought as I opened my door. Nothing would have kept her from her grandchildren, however they'd come into the world. And if Mark *had* stayed with Carol and had a child with her, Mum would have mended bridges and been a wonderful grandmother. I felt the usual pang at what my mother was missing in not knowing

Milly – and what Milly was missing in not knowing her. But why, I then wondered as I undid the sling, would Jenny's ex agree to have no contact with his own child? Maybe that was the price his wife had exacted from him for not divorcing him – or maybe he was happy not to get involved. Or maybe he had no idea that Jenny had even had his baby. That was quite possible.

Perhaps Jenny was gay, I wondered – not for the first time – as I fed Milly, but cropped hair and no make-up was hardly evidence for that. Perhaps her ex was one of her pupils' fathers, I speculated, as I sat Milly up and gently burped her. That would also explain why she'd given up teaching – perhaps she'd been hauled before a disciplinary committee and sacked. Whatever Jenny's situation was, she wasn't telling. Perhaps, in her own time, she'd open up.

That night I got an e-mail from Xan: *I can see from the photos you've sent that a DNA test would be superfluous. However, I would like to send you some money. Please provide me with your bank details so that I can set up a direct debit. X.*

I stared at the 'X': when I was with Xan I saw it as a kiss – now it simply defined our fractured relationship.

I hit Reply: *Thanks but no thanks.*

The relief I felt as Elaine returned the next morning was swiftly superseded by a burst of panic at the thought that she would be leaving in less than two weeks. Her soothing presence had lulled me into such a relaxed state that I'd almost forgotten that I would soon have to work. So I had my stationery printed and got my website completed. I placed ads in two West London magazines. With Elaine's help, I finished organising my attic workroom – I'd only ever used the space for storage before. But I'd had it decorated in the spring and now the freshly painted walls were lined with gardening books, most of them my mother's. I needed to index them when I had more time, I thought, as I wiped their creased spines with a cloth.

I'd bought a big Victorian plan chest to store my drawings in, and some wooden files in which I kept the details of builders' merchants, trade nurseries, stone specialists and people who supplied water features, external lighting and wrought iron. At the far end of the room were my drawing board and my computer, and a stack of gardening magazines. Lining the walls were samples of bricks, decorative pebbles and rocks.

'So you're all ready to go,' Elaine said as she surveyed it with me.

'Not quite. I need two more things – my first commission and a contractor.'

'Why a contractor?'

'Because as a designer I won't be building walls and laying paving myself. I'll need someone to do that – but with all that's been going on I haven't had time to find anyone. I'll just have to go through the business pages and ring up a few.'

'I can help you with that,' Elaine said.

'That's all right – it won't take me long.'

'No, I mean, I know someone who might do.'

'Really? Who's that?'

'My nephew, Jamie – the one I told you about. He's a builder – very reliable and he only lives five minutes' walk away. You never know' – she shrugged – 'he might fit the bill. Would you like to meet him?'

'Well, thank you. I think I would.'

So a couple of days later we strolled over to Blythe Road, Elaine carrying Milly in the sling, so that I could talk to Jamie without waking her. She rang the bell and he opened the door.

'My sainted aunt!' He beamed. 'Come in, Elaine. Hey, what a little cutie,' he said, looking at Milly. 'Hi there.' He offered me his hand. 'I guess you're Anna.'

He was about twenty-five, an inch or two taller than me,

but heavily built, with an open face, a mop of dark-blond hair and warm brown eyes that disappeared when he smiled. He was wearing a white T-shirt with 'Olympian Landscapes' emblazoned across it in dark green. His jeans were pale with washing and frayed at the knees.

We followed him down the hall. On a side table I noticed several photos of a beautiful woman in her early to mid twenties.

'That's Thea,' Elaine explained. 'Jamie's wife.'

'She's lovely,' I said, slightly taken aback both at his being married when he seemed so young and at his wife's luminous beauty.

'Oh, Thea's gorgeous,' Elaine said. 'They only got married last summer. It was quite a wedding, right?' she added as Jamie opened the door to his office.

'It was the business, Auntie Elaine.'

'They had the reception on a boat, on the Thames.'

'How wonderful,' I said, with a pang of envy.

'We had a few tinnies, didn't we, Jamie?'

'We certainly did. Now . . . excuse the mess in here . . .' The carpet was strewn with spreadsheets and invoices that had been weighed down with a silver trophy against the breeze from the open window.

'Sorry,' he muttered as he threw it on the sofa, then cleared a bit of floor space. 'But I'm doing my VAT.' He sat down behind his small desk, which was piled high with box files saying 'Purchase Invoices', 'Sales Invoices' and 'Bank'. I noticed a cricket bat leaning in the corner. 'So, Anna,' he began, as his mobile trilled out. 'You're looking for someone to do your dirty work?'

'Well, I wouldn't put it quite like that.'

He peered at the number, then let it go to answerphone. 'Just joking.' He smiled. 'You need a contractor, right?'

I nodded. 'I need someone to build the gardens that I'm going to design. Ideally I'd like them to work with me on a regular basis so that we have a proper working partnership.'

'Well, I'm pretty busy right now . . .' His mobile rang again. He checked the screen, but didn't answer.

'What sort of things do you build?'

'Here.' He handed me his portfolio. His phone trilled out yet again and this time he took the call while I flicked through the large black ring binder. There were photos of newly constructed garages and extensions, forecourts and conservatories. 'That's great,' I heard him say. 'Just the sharp sand – no worries – I'll pick it up tomorrow . . . G'day, mate.'

'How long have you been in the business?' I asked as he snapped the phone shut. I looked at the detailed close-ups of his work.

'A bit over two years. I've got six guys on my payroll.'

'And are you qualified?'

'I did a three-year construction course back home.'

'And have you built many gardens?'

'To be quite straight with you – none.'

'That's not true,' Elaine said. 'You built your own.'

A look of surprise crossed Jamie's face. 'I'd forgotten about that.'

'You should show Anna.'

He scratched his head. 'All right.'

'He led us through the kitchen, opened the back door and we stepped outside into the large patio garden.

The ground was paved with reclaimed red brick laid in a circular pattern surrounded by Indian sandstone flags cut on the diagonal, which had the effect of lengthening the space. Along one side was a single raised flowerbed, gently curved in outline and filled with delphiniums, peonies, lupins and climbing roses, with pillows of mauve *Aubretia* tumbling over the sides.

'You built this?' I asked him as I glanced at the dining area, which was elegantly screened by a little row of pleached hornbeams.

'Built and designed it,' Elaine said.

91

'Well, I just did a few sketches,' he protested. 'But it was a right old scrap heap when we moved in six months ago – wasn't it?'

'It was an eyesore,' Elaine agreed. 'Full of junk.'

'You've done a wonderful job,' I said. 'It's a great use of the space, lovely stone and I really like your planting scheme. And this area here?' It had been left clear.

'I've left that bit free for a little sandpit, or a swing.'

'Do you have kids?'

'We're working on it.' He laughed. His mobile phone rang again. 'Hi, darling – I was just talking about you . . . wow . . . it's forty-three degrees, is it? Well, keep that lovely face of yours out of the sun, sweetheart . . . but look, honey, can I call you back in ten minutes?' I found myself envying Thea – that she was with a man who sprinkled his words to her with so many endearments.

'Is Thea away again?' Elaine asked Jamie as we went back inside. 'She works in sports PR,' she explained to me. 'So she has to travel quite a bit.'

'She's in Dubai for five days,' Jamie replied. 'One of her clients is sponsoring a yacht race there.'

'Right,' Elaine said.

I'd seen all I needed to see. I told Jamie that I'd like to work with him, when I landed my first job.

'That'd be fine,' he said, 'and we can see whether or not we're compatible.'

'Exactly. But I'll need your phone number.' He jabbed an index finger at his T-shirt. 'Oh . . .' It felt odd staring at his chest as I tapped the digits into my mobile.

He held out his hand. 'Good to meet you then, mate.'

'Er . . . yes,' I said. 'You too.'

''Bye, Auntie Elaine. Bye-bye, Princess,' he whispered to Milly, who was fast asleep under her sun hat. He gently clasped her tiny bare feet in his big, broad hands. 'You're a little darling, you are . . . Let me show you guys out.'

''Bye Jamie,' I said as we stood on the front step. 'I'll be in touch.' I noticed a Bentley Continental GT in Racing Green parked outside his flat. 'Is that yours?' I asked, nodding at it.

'I wish.' He laughed. 'It belongs to my neighbours – they're both bankers, jammy guys – that's mine.' He pointed to the blue pick-up truck parked over the road. 'Anyway, be seeing ya, ladies! G'day!'

'I liked him,' I said to Elaine as we walked back.

'Ah, Jamie's a great lad. I can say that with confidence because I've known him for all of his twenty-eight years.' So he was older than he looked.

'His garden's fantastic – I was really impressed. His building work looks sound.'

'He's a very talented sportsman too.'

'He is?'

'He was a professional cricketer.'

'Really? Is that what the trophy was for?'

'Yes – he's got loads of them.'

'Who did he play for?'

'New South Wales. He was a very good spin bowler.'

'And what brought him to the UK?'

'He played for Surrey for two seasons during the Ozzie winter and liked it here.'

'But why isn't he playing cricket now?' I asked as we skirted Brook Green. 'He's still young.'

'Because he was in a car crash six years ago and his leg got smashed up.'

'How terrible.'

'It was – not least because he'd been tipped to play for Australia. But that's why he retrained as a builder. He still plays cricket, but only for fun, with some showbiz team that raises money for kids' medical causes – which is how he met Thea. She was doing the PR for one of the charities involved and he . . . well, bowled a maiden over as you might say. But

93

you'll like working with Jamie,' she added. 'He'll never let you down.'

I called him the following week. My first commission had come through my website and, though small, it felt exhilarating just to be getting started. The clients had told me that they didn't have the budget for a 'new' garden in their house in Chiswick; they wanted to have the existing one refreshed.

When I went to see them I first asked them how they thought they wanted it to look. They said they wanted the pond taken out as they were having a baby; they also wanted to have the lawn re-laid, but that they were open to any other ideas. So I suggested that they have the raised flowerbeds removed as they were unnecessarily wide, crushing the already limited space.

'What about this?' I asked, looking at their acacia tree, which had been savagely pollarded over the years and was no more than a big stump.

'We'd love to cut it down,' the husband explained, 'especially as it takes up part of the lawn, but there's a Tree Preservation Order on it so we can't.'

'Then you could turn it into an attractive feature by growing climbers up it,' I said. 'Just treat it as a very big stake. You could have a clematis on one side – there's a new one called Ice Blue, which flowers from May to October – then on the other side you could have a rambling rose, say *Felicite Perpetue*, which is creamy white and very fragrant. And you could hang a little swing from that lower branch quite safely, and you could have a circular seat built round the base. It could look lovely.'

'What else would you do?' the wife asked.

I looked at the back of the house, which was featureless and south-facing, then inspected the patio, which had been paved with simple concrete slabs.

'We could brighten up these stones by cleaning and re-grouting them, then we could build a large arbour over the

94

patio, which would provide a shady area for eating outside, or for your baby to play under. It wouldn't cost very much. You could grow a summer jasmine over it, or a honeysuckle – there's a lovely red one called Dropmore – I've brought a few plant catalogues with me, I'll show you.'

We agreed a total budget of three thousand pounds. Jamie undertook to do the landscaping and within three days he'd started work. When I went round to the house to check its progress I found him kneeling by the newly emptied pond.

'You can hop but you can't hide,' I heard him mutter as he peered into the mud. 'Gotcha!'

'What are you doing, Jamie?'

He looked up. 'Oh hi, Anna. Catching frogs. I need to get them all out before the guys start rotovating the lawn because we don't want any casualties. Here you go, little fella . . .' He cupped his gloved hands together then dipped them into a yellow bucket. 'I think that's the lot now.'

I peered inside where a dozen or so khaki-coloured frogs were pawing uselessly at the sides. I watched them for a few seconds.

'Are you keen on frogs?' I heard Jamie ask.

'Not especially – I'm just wondering which one to kiss.'

He laughed. 'Do you need to?'

'Sometimes I think so.' I smiled. 'Anyway, what are you going to do with them?'

He heaved some old bricks into a wheelbarrow. 'I've found a foster home for them three doors down. They might have jumped along there on their own,' he said as he straightened up, 'but I didn't want to risk it. They're taking the newts too,' he added, nodding at another bucket which was full of water and weed.

I found Jamie's tender-heartedness touching – he also refused to cut back the plum tree as he'd seen some late fledglings nesting in it – and his workmanship was first-rate. He and two of his landscapers took a day to remove the raised flowerbeds, another day to rotovate the lawn and re-lay it, and a further two days to build the arbour and put a seat round the acacia tree. Then I went in with the plants. In under a week the garden had been transformed. The clients then recommended me to a friend of theirs – a young solicitor who wanted her courtyard garden completely redesigned. Things were beginning to take off.

In the meantime Elaine left – she was booked to look after a new baby in Norfolk – but promised to visit us when she was back in London. I cried for two hours after she'd gone – not just for the practical help she'd given me, but for the bond of friendship we'd formed. But I had to accept that my 'babymoon' was now over and that the 'new life' I'd started had truly begun.

FIVE

Until Milly was three months I took her everywhere with me, trying to schedule appointments to fit in with her feeds. I'd take her with me to see clients, and to the trade nursery in Chobham where I bought all my plants, and to the builders' merchant in Maida Vale where I selected decking, paving and bricks. At home she'd sleep in her Moses basket as I worked on my drawings, or I'd cradle her in my left arm, or she'd lie next to me under her Baby gym, batting at the pendant toys with her tiny hands. Sometimes it worked well, but at other times, especially when she was colicky, I'd get very little done. As she got bigger I knew I'd have to have proper child-care for her. An au pair was the only option, given my uncertain income, and I struck lucky the first time with Pavlina, who was Czech.

Pavlina was twenty-six, serious-minded, organised, quiet and hard-working. She had cared for babies before, had wonderful references and was to stay with me for nearly two years. She looked after Milly every morning while I went out on site to meet Jamie, or to client briefings. In the afternoon I'd have Milly with me in her playpen, or on her bouncy chair watching Baby Einstein or the Teletubbies while I made phone calls or did administrative jobs. If I needed additional help I'd pay Pavlina extra. She was more than happy to have the money as she was saving to buy a flat in Prague.

Then when Milly was nine months, I got the e-mail from Xan that I'd both hoped for and dreaded: *I'll be in London for five days from 25 March and would like to meet Milly. X.*

I felt as though I'd fallen down a manhole. I'd had no word from him for so long. Now, faced with the prospect of seeing him again and having my emotions churned up, a big part of me wanted to refuse. How much easier it would be if I could simply airbrush him out of the picture, as Jenny seemed to have done with her ex, but I had to put Milly's needs before my own.

I clicked on Reply. *Come on Sunday, 27, around four.* Then, my stomach in knots, I clicked on Send.

My heart was banging against my ribs when the bell rang on that afternoon. I'd hardly slept the night before, dropping off just before dawn. I checked my appearance once more in the large circular mirror at the bottom of the stairs, took a deep breath and opened the door.

I had Milly in my arms and Xan's eyes instantly lighted on her, with a blend of wonderment, recognition and guilt. Only then did he see me. As he crossed the threshold I noticed that he looked tanned, that his hair was cut short and that his temples were now stippled with grey. He tried to kiss me but I turned away, determined to project a chilly dignity. He'd called me an 'iceberg' after all.

'Would you like tea?' I asked him as I moved the buggy out of the way. 'I'm afraid I still don't have any PG Tips,' I quipped. 'I should have got some in specially.'

Xan didn't react. 'A cup of coffee would be great.' He took off his leather jacket and hung it up.

I put Milly on her play mat while I went into the kitchen. When I went back in with the tray, my hands trembling so much from the encounter that the cups rattled in their saucers,

I found Xan standing by the window, in the same spot where he'd begged me that night not to have Milly, holding her in his arms, just gazing at her.

Everything will change. Because it always does.

To my amazement Milly wasn't crying, or struggling. She was just staring at Xan, as if transfixed. Perhaps she understood in some inchoate way that she was inextricably bound to him – as I now truly realised I would be for the rest of my life.

'Hello,' Xan said to her softly. 'I guess you're wondering who I am . . . Well . . . this may sound a bit funny to you . . .' I heard his voice catch. 'But actually, sweetie, I'm your dad. Yes, that's right, darling, I am. No kidding.' Milly put one dimpled little hand on his cheek. Xan's mouth quivered for a moment but my heart didn't melt – he'd made me cry enough after all. 'She's just . . . sweet,' he whispered.

'Thanks. I think so too.' I silently congratulated myself for keeping my composure. 'So, Xan . . .' I sat down. 'Why now? Has curiosity finally got the better of you?'

'Don't be bitter, Anna,' he murmured. 'I know you think I've behaved badly . . .'

'You have behaved badly. Do you take milk?' I asked. 'It's been so long since I've seen you I'm afraid I can't remember. We had a lovely christening by the way. In case you're interested, Milly's godmother is my former PA, Sue – who, you may recall, was with me the night you and I met – and her godfather is my brother, Mark.'

'I thought you had no contact with him.'

'Very little,' I replied. 'Which is precisely why I asked him – to keep the channels open. Anyway, he did at least fly over for it. But what a pity you couldn't make it,' I added pleasantly. 'Your own daughter.'

'Please, Anna.' Xan sighed. 'Don't. I've been in such turmoil.'

'Poor you. Whereas I've been having a ball, obviously, being a working single mother.'

'Please don't punish me,' he went on. 'I want to do the right thing, but you have to understand my anger at having no say in whether or not I had a child.'

'But you did have a say,' I replied calmly. 'Because you chose to sleep with me that night and, as everyone knows, one and one sometimes makes three.'

'I've felt so terrible,' he went on. 'It's been hard to concentrate on my work – impossible at times to sleep. All I could think about was Milly.' I wondered how much he'd thought about me. 'I was paralysed – not knowing what to do. Gradually I realised that the only way I was ever going to feel better was by meeting her.' I didn't reply. 'I could have seen her in December,' he added after a moment. I looked at him. 'I was in London for three days . . .' I felt a sudden pang at the thought that he had been so close. 'I wanted to see her, but I felt . . . confused. I even walked past your house –'

'No,' I murmured. I imagined his footfall echoing on the pavement.

'But I couldn't face it, so I walked away. I'm sorry, darling,' he whispered to Milly, his voice breaking now, as he held her closer. 'I promise I'll never do that again. I'll come and see you whenever I can, my little girl.'

'And how often is that likely to be?'

He put Milly down on her play mat. 'It's hard to say. Probably no more than three times a year. I wish it could be more, but I live seven thousand miles away.'

'I'm aware of that,' I said grimly. I pushed down the plunger on the cafetière. 'But Milly needs to know you. I do think you could have replied to my e-mails about her,' I added bitterly.

'I'm . . . sorry, Anna. But I was . . . scared. That may sound strange but I was terrified.' So Elaine's analysis had been right. 'But I'll try and make it up to her from now on.'

Then Xan reached into his holdall and produced a Harrods carrier bag. Out of it came a soft, caramel-coloured teddy

100

bear with a pale mauve ribbon and a sweetly perplexed expression. Milly clutched it to her face with both hands, squeaking with delight.

'I do intend to support her,' he added as I poured his coffee. 'You've refused to let me, but I want to.'

'Well . . . now that you've met her, I don't mind. I didn't want your money.' I sighed. 'Just your involvement. But I won't deny that a little help would be welcome.'

'I've already opened an account for her – here.' He reached into his bag and handed me a statement. 'I put money in it each quarter – I'll convert it into a joint account so that you can access it – I'll send you the forms.'

'Thanks.' We stared at each other for a moment, then I looked away.

'I'm not a bastard, Anna,' he said quietly.

I struggled to suppress the longing I still felt for him – a longing that made my bones ache. 'I know you're not,' I replied. It would be so much easier if you were, I thought miserably. Then I could get over you.

'I'm sorry I behaved as I did. I hope you forgive me.'

His features began to blur as my eyes filled with tears. 'Yes,' I whispered. 'I do . . .'

He suddenly reached for my hand and I gave it to him, elated at the familiar pressure of his fingers round mine. 'Don't cry, Anna,' he said after a moment. 'Please don't.' He handed me his hanky and I pressed it to my eyes. 'Can we be friends, now?' I heard him say. 'For Milly's sake?'

Friends . . .

My chest filled with sadness. 'Of course.'

From then on Xan would reply to my e-mails. He'd send Milly presents – Indonesian dolls, and carved animals, and colourful wall hangings. He'd ring up sometimes and speak to her. Her face would light up like a firework at the word 'Daddy' and she'd burble delightedly into the phone. Her happiness was both a shard in my heart and a profound comfort. I put out a photo of him that I'd downloaded from the BBC website as I didn't have a good one of my own. For Milly's sake I needed to let bygones be bygones; so I explained that although Xan lived a long way away he would come and see us whenever he could. We watched the six o'clock news in case he was on.

Then, when Milly was almost a year, Nicole from my ante-natal class threw a first-birthday party for her son Jacob. There'd been a couple of reunions in the interim, but I hadn't been able to go.

'I hope to God Citronella won't be there,' I said to Jenny, as we pushed our buggies down Nicole's road in the May sunshine.

'She's bound to be,' Jenny said. I looked at all the flowering plants in the front gardens – azaleas, clematis, tulips and wallflowers. If Citronella were a plant, I suddenly thought, what would she be? Ivy. Insidious, hard to shake off and quietly destructive. Jenny would be a Sensitive Plant – rewarding to grow, but if you touch their leaves they fold up. Cassie would be a Venus flytrap, I reflected, seductive but dangerous. Xan would be . . . a sunflower – offering a glorious, but dismayingly short-lived display.

What would I be? I wondered, as I rang Nicole's bell. A *Dicentra spectabilis*, I realised bitterly – a Bleeding Heart.

The other mums were already in the balloon-festooned garden, sitting on plaid rugs with their wobbly offspring on their laps, or holding them up like puppets as they toddled around.

'-Jonah's been walking for two weeks now.'

'-Shall I kiss it better, darling?'

'-Erasmus walked at ten months.'

'-I'm still breastfeeding Phoebe.'

'-Good for you! I was useless at it.'

'-You should have eaten more grass!'

'He'll be going to Sweet Peas,' I heard Citronella say. My heart sank – that was the nursery school I'd put Milly down for. 'Isn't he *gorgeous*?' Citronella suddenly said to me, looking at Erasmus with smug adoration.

'Er, yes,' I said politely. *To you!* He was wearing a blue T-shirt emblazoned with 'I'm Mummy's New Man!'. He'd inherited Citronella's sturdy physique and her coppery hair.

'And did you get the invitation for Erasmus's birthday party?' she asked.

'I . . . did,' I replied, my heart sinking. 'Thanks.' I'd gasped when I'd opened it, not so much because I was surprised to be invited, but because enclosed with the invitation had been a list of acceptable gifts, with suggested retailers, like a wedding list. Jenny had told me that she'd thrown hers away. 'But I'm not sure . . . that we'll be . . . able to make it,' I floundered as I picked Milly up. 'I'm afraid I've got a client briefing that afternoon.'

'Can't your nanny bring her?' Citronella demanded.

'I don't have a nanny,' I replied. 'And my au pair takes Milly to Monkey Music on Thursday afternoons – and you love Monkey Music, don't you, darling?' Milly clapped her hands. 'But I'll let you know,' I added, hoping that would conclude the conversation.

But it was clear that Citronella wasn't done. 'Is your gardening business going well?' she asked.

'Yes, thanks,' I said, surprised at her sudden interest. I swatted away a wasp. 'It's a good time of year, of course, but I'm pretty busy.'

'I see your partner, Xan, is too,' she added slyly as she bit into a sausage roll.

'Ye-es,' I said again, profoundly regretting that I'd ever been stupid enough to mention Xan's name, let alone what he did.

'We've seen him on TV. He's awfully good,' she added as she flicked pastry flakes off her large lap.

'Hmm.' I wondered what this was leading up to. 'Is Erasmus talking yet?'

'I expect you'll be glad when he's back.'

'Oh . . . we will – especially Milly – she adores her daddy, don't you, poppet?'

'Da-da!' Milly beamed, dribbling happily.

I caught Jenny's eye. 'Well . . . I ought to circulate. Nice to see you again, Citronella,' I lied.

She daintily licked the ends of each finger with a little sucking sound. 'Funnily enough there's a piece about him in this week's *Hello!*.'

I felt as though I'd fallen down a mineshaft. 'Really? I mean . . . he did tell me but I haven't . . . bought it yet. I've been . . . busy.'

'I've got it with me,' Citronella said innocently. 'Would you like to see it?'

'Er . . . OK,' I said, my pulse racing. 'Thanks.'

Citronella shifted her vast bulk – seemingly undiminished by childbirth – and returned a minute later with the magazine. 'It's on page 112,' she said helpfully as she handed it to me. Then she began talking to Tanya on her other side. I found the page, quickly registered Xan's photo among the other foreign correspondents they were profiling, then scanned the piece, my heart pounding.

Xan Marshall, thirty-nine . . . reports for the BBC from Indonesia . . . based in Jakarta . . . former banker . . . Hong Kong . . . Suddenly, my face was aflame. *Marshall lives with his girlfriend of six months, Trisha Fox, CNN's South East Asia reporter . . . Harvard-educated Miss Fox, twenty-eight, is a rising star at CNN . . .*

I shut the magazine, my hands trembling, bile simmering at the back of my throat.

'Are you OK?' Jenny whispered.

'Did you read it?' I heard Citronella ask. 'I haven't read it myself yet,' she added innocently.

'Yes, thanks, I did.' I handed it back to her and stood up, my legs shaking. 'But Milly and I have to go now.'

'What a shame,' she said sweetly.

''Bye, Nicole,' I said. 'It's been great.'

I was so upset that I couldn't work for the rest of the day. I didn't know what hurt me most – the verification of what I knew to be inevitable, or Citronella's malice. When I'd seen Xan I'd been careful to confine the conversation strictly to Milly – it would have been too painful to know anything about his personal life.

'Of course she'd read it,' I said to Jenny when she phoned me later and I tearfully explained. 'It was all so calculated. She *is* evil.'

'She isn't,' Jenny insisted. 'You don't know what evil is, if you think that.' Why did she always have to be so nit-picking about it, I wondered crossly. 'But she's certainly odious.'

'What've I ever done to her?' I wailed. The woman wasn't just ivy – she was *poison* ivy.

'You've done nothing,' Jenny replied. 'Which only goes to show that she must be unhappy.'

'Unhappy? She's the smuggest woman on earth. She's always going on in her wretched column about how "blessed" and "fortunate" she is, and how "sad" or "brave" other people are.'

'Exactly. She has to put everyone else at a disadvantage to her. But do genuinely happy people need to do that?'

'No,' I conceded after a moment. 'They don't.'

I briefly wondered what reason Citronella might have for being discontented – banker husband not rich enough? House in Luxembourg Gardens not huge enough? – before throwing her invitation into the bin.

Over the next few days I managed to persuade myself that Citronella had done me a favour. It was A Good Thing if Xan was attached because it meant that I'd have to relinquish any lingering feelings I still had for him and view him in a different way. I even comforted myself that I'd find someone else, though I couldn't imagine this happening before Milly had left home – by which time I would be *fifty-one*. Saga material, I realised miserably.

Xan met Milly four more times before she was two. By then she was so smitten with him that she would rush to the television every time he was on and kiss it. The screen would be smudged with her little hand and lip prints, which Pavlina would dutifully rub off. She 'talked' about Xan a lot, and would 'phone' him every day – on her Postman Pat mobile or if that wasn't to hand, on my calculator, on a cowrie shell, on the bath plug, or just on the palm of her hand. Their conversations were invariably animated and I would often feel excluded. I tried not to think about Xan's girlfriend, and if I had to phone him I did so on his mobile, never on his home number. I couldn't have coped with hearing her voice.

When Milly was a bit over two, Pavlina left. She'd saved enough to put down a deposit on a flat, and wanted to return to Prague and work in the Czech tourist industry. I was sorry to see her go – she'd been even-tempered, efficient and reliable. But it wasn't until I tried to replace her that I realised quite how good she had been.

The same agency sent me four more au pairs, each of whom proved hopeless – if not downright dangerous. First there was Gabi from Bonn who got off to a good start, but then became so homesick that she left after three weeks. After that I had Natalie, who was French. I dispensed with Natalie's services after a month, not just because she was lazy and disorganised but because I caught her slathering Milly's rear end with my Crème de la Mer. Then came Lucia from Rome who'd take to her bed for a week every time she had a period; then there was Svetla from Bulgaria, whom I liked – until, in defiance of my strict instructions, she gave Milly egg. Luckily the allergic reaction that it then triggered in Milly was 'only' severe and not fatal.

I was thinking despairingly about this as I went to buy some milk one late January morning when an advert in the newsagent's window caught my eye: *I like work au pair. I kind heart. I lob kids and doogs. I startet right now. You no egrets I work for you. Bery good referencias. See you soon! Luisa . . . xx*

I was so desperate for help as I was doing my GMTV appearances every morning the following week that I called the mobile number. Luisa's spoken English was as bad as her written, but we managed to establish that she would come and see me later that day.

She had been in the UK for a month, but had worked for a family in Marbella for a year. She was twenty-three, Colombian, rather plump, but with pretty, mobile features and an appealing vivacity. My main problem would be how to communicate with her.

'I wan lairn spik Eenglish bery *good*,' she said as I sat with her in the sitting room. 'I go school eaches days. Lairn spik Eenglish bery *queek*.'

Milly was holding on to my knee, eyeing Luisa suspiciously.

'I'd like to take up your references,' I said. 'Could you tell me who to ring?'

Luisa looked at me blankly.

'Telephone?' I said. She pointed helpfully at the phone on the sideboard. 'No. Who do *I* telephone?' I jabbed my chest then made dialling and ringing gestures. 'To get a *reference* – for *you?*'

'Ah. *Referencia. Sí.* I hab *bery* good *referencia.*' She dug into the back pocket of her jeans and produced a dog-eared letter, the folds seamed with dust. It was all in Spanish, but there was a number on it.

'And when would you be able to start?' I asked her as I wrote it down. 'If we decide to go ahead?'

107

'Head?' Luisa repeated, clearly confounded.

I suddenly saw that I was wasting my time.

'Look, Luisa . . .' I said. 'You seem very nice, but I really don't think that this is going to work out, I'm awfully sorry . . .'

But then something remarkable happened. Luisa, who'd been smiling at Milly intermittently, suddenly threw out her arms: '*Venga aquí, preciosa!*'

In a flash she'd swept Milly on to her lap and was bouncing her up and down, making funny faces at her. Instead of crying or struggling to get down, Milly was laughing. Then Luisa gave Milly a great, smacking kiss on the cheek and that, somehow, was that.

I did of course take up her references. In broken English the husband said how much they had all loved Luisa and how good she'd been with their little boy, now five, and how sad they'd been when she'd left to go to London, where she felt opportunities were better.

Opportunities for what? I'd found myself wondering.

'And she seeng,' he added.

'Seeing who?'

'No, she *sing*,' he enunciated. 'Tra la la *la*. Luisa hab lobely voice. Real *lobely*.'

'Oh,' I said. 'That's nice.'

The following day Luisa moved in. She came on the bus from Shepherd's Bush, where she'd been in a flatshare. It had been a crystal clear day and there was a hard frost. She rang the bell at the appointed time – 6.30 – and beamed at me and Milly as she stood on the doorstep in her silver puffa jacket, with her small blue suitcase and her guitar.

'*Hola!*' She waved a mittened hand at Milly, who was clutching my leg.

'Hi, Luisa,' I said. 'Come in.'

'Starry starry night,' she added as she stepped inside.

'I'm sorry?'

108

She pointed behind her to the sky. 'Ees starry starry night.'

I peered outside, craning my neck. 'Oh yes,' I said. 'So it is. We don't often see the stars from here. Anyway, come in, Luisa. Welcome.'

She took off her blue bobble hat. '*Gracias.*'

Over the next few days I told myself that lots of au pairs didn't speak much English to start with – that's why they wanted to be au pairs. But I was so desperate for Luisa to learn that I told her I'd pay for her language classes as she said she didn't have any money. It would cost five hundred pounds for the six-month course. She would go to school every weekday morning, in Bayswater, while Milly was at Sweet Peas. Luisa would collect Milly at one, give her her lunch, then play with her all afternoon while I worked.

Perhaps because my expectations were so low, I found myself pleasantly surprised. Luisa was efficient around the house and kept Milly's toys and clothes in neat order; she'd do useful things without being asked. She liked cooking and was good at it, although it was usually Spanish or Colombian and I noticed that Milly was soon eschewing fish fingers and sausages, and developing a taste for chorizo and refried beans. She took the allergy problem very seriously. She always read the backs of packets and learned the word for 'egg' in a dozen languages. In one of her old copies of *Hola!* she found a recipe for an eggless cake.

I liked Luisa's Latin warmth, which I appreciated after Pavlina's cool detachment. Best of all, she seemed to adore Milly. She loved playing with her, even when off duty. She'd watch *CBeebies* with her and I'd hear them laughing their heads off at *Pingu* while I cooked supper for us all. Luisa was always cuddling Milly or giving her big noisy kisses. And I soon discovered that Luisa could, indeed, sing. The first time I heard it was about a week after she arrived. I was lying on my bed, having a quick rest. '*Starry starry night . . .*' Up it floated from the kitchen, this rich, folksy contralto.

'*Paint your palette blue and grey . . .*' Her pronunciation was a bit odd, but her voice had a purity and a huskiness that tugged at the heartstrings. '*Look out on a summer's day, with eyes that know the darkness in my soul . . .*'

It was indeed 'lobely' – so much so that I never found it annoying, not even when I was working. It invariably made me feel calm.

'This could be a lot worse,' I told myself as I drove back from Surrey with a sleeping Milly after my final farewell to the house. 'Luisa appears to love my child and takes great care of her; Milly's happy to be left with her when I have to go out. Luisa works hard and is thoughtful. What more do I want? Her English will get better in time.'

I'd already been surprised by how slow her progress had been. She had fifteen hours' tuition a week, yet I'd detected zero improvement in the three weeks that she'd been with me. Still, give it time, I thought.

'How are your English lessons going?' I asked her the evening after I'd returned from my final visit to Oxted. I put down the box containing my mother's trowel and the three gardening books I'd taken: *Flowers of Southern Italy*; *Gardeners' Latin* and *The New Small Garden* – a classic text. 'Are you working hard on your English, Luisa?' I tried again.

'Ah! *Sì*!' She nodded enthusiastically. 'Absolutamente!'

My father moved to London the next day. His flat was on the top floor of a modern apartment building on Campden Hill, overlooking Holland Park.

'What wonderful views,' I said, as I helped him arrange the furniture a couple of days later. 'I can even see the London Eye – and you've got this lovely balcony. You'll be able to watch the sunset – and you'll hear the open-air opera in the summer.'

'And the peacocks,' Dad added ruefully.

'I'll get you some nice new planters,' I said, looking at the desiccated geraniums in their cracked terracotta troughs. 'Chrome ones would look good.'

110

'Fancy moving to London at my age!' Dad sighed. I helped him unpack his books and the few paintings he'd kept. Then I saw him open another box and put his wedding photo on a side table. I'd been fourteen when I'd suddenly seen that Mum was pregnant. I've never forgotten the shock. Once, years later, when I'd had a couple of drinks, I'd jokingly mentioned it. 'Well . . . the wedding *was* a bit quick,' she'd said with a brittle laugh, and then she'd changed the subject; and I'd felt sorry for her that she should still have felt so self-conscious about it all those years on – as though anyone could have cared less.

Now, as Dad went into the kitchen, I looked at the photo again. I was slightly surprised, now I'd had a baby myself, at how visible her bump was after only two months; but on the other hand Mum was quite curvy and curvy women seem to show their pregnancies earlier than skinny Lizzies like me.

'Well, if you're OK, Dad, I'll be off.' I gathered up some stray bubble wrap and stuffed it in a bin liner. 'I told Luisa I'd be back by nine. Plus I've got to get my drawings finished for my client meeting on Saturday.'

Dad held up crossed fingers, then blew me a kiss.

The appointment was for 2 p.m. I'd agreed to see the clients on a Saturday because it was such a big commission. Jamie was due to meet me there.

I got up early so that I could go shopping for Milly. She badly needed some new T-shirts, which I usually get at the Hammersmith Marks & Spencer. So after breakfast I put her in her buggy and we got the bus to King Street. By eleven I'd found what I'd wanted and paid; then I went over to the food department and bought a few groceries. And I had just left the shop, pleased with my swift progress, when I suddenly glanced down at the buggy.

'Oh Milly,' I wailed. 'Where's your shoe?'

'Shoe gone, Mum!' Her right one was missing. 'Iss *gone*,' she repeated happily, inspecting her little stockinged foot.

'You must have kicked it off *again*. I do wish you wouldn't keep doing that, darling,' I bleated as I did a swift U-turn back into the store. 'Now we'll have to find it. Do you remember where you dropped it?'

'No,' she shouted. 'No, no, *no*!'

I began to scan the shop floor for her pink Startrite. This was just what I didn't need. I had to get home in good time so that I could get everything ready for my appointment. She'd had both shoes on when I'd bought her clothes, so she must have lost it since then.

I retraced our steps through the shop, peering at the carpet, stopping an assistant to ask if anyone had found it. While she went over to Customer Services to check I returned to the food department and asked the cashier who'd served us if anyone had handed in a little pink shoe.

'Sorry, love,' she said. 'No. But you don't want to lose that,' she tut-tutted, 'not with the price of kids' shoes these days.'

'Exactly,' I murmured. 'Thirty-five pounds.'

I glanced at my watch. It was five to twelve. It would take us half an hour to get home, then I'd have to get my stuff together and drive over to The Boltons, and the traffic was ghastly on Saturday when Chelsea were playing at home. Jamie had already phoned to warn me.

The shop assistant came up to me. 'Sorry, Madame, but nothing's been handed in.'

'Thanks for asking.' I dug into my handbag and gave her my card. 'Can I give you my number in case it turns up?'

I ran out, feeling flustered by now, and I was standing on King Street, by Curry's, trying to flag down a taxi, as I couldn't afford to waste time getting the bus, when I heard the church clock begin to strike twelve.

Bong . . . Bong . . .

All the cabs were taken – *damn*!

Suddenly I heard a shout from behind: 'Excuse me!' I turned round. 'Is this yours?' A smartly dressed man in his early forties was standing on the pavement holding Milly's shoe.

'Yes, it is . . . thank you!' I clapped my hand to my chest with relief. 'It's my daughter's.'

'Milly shoe!' Milly shouted indignantly, pointing an accusing finger at him. 'Das Milly shoe, Mum!'

The man handed it to me. 'I saw you looking for it,' he added, 'but you ran out of the shop before I could stop you.'

'You have no idea how relieved I am. Thanks *so* much.' I could have kissed him.

Bong . . .

'You're welcome.'

'It would have been a disaster if I'd lost it,' I said as I strapped it back on. 'Especially as they're new. We'd only just got them – last week, actually,' I gabbled away, disconcerted by the fact that I found him immensely attractive. 'They're a bit big, so she must have pushed it off. Anyway.' I straightened up and smiled. 'Thank you.'

'No problem. Delighted to help.' I saw him glance at my left hand. There was a momentary silence. And I was just about to say a polite goodbye when I heard him say, 'I don't suppose you'd like to have a cup of coffee, would you?' I looked at him, astounded. He'd met me less than a minute before. 'There's a nice café over there, next to the theatre, and I feel like a cappuccino and just wondered . . . if you could do with one too . . .'

'Oh . . . I don't think so,' I stuttered, embarrassed, but at the same time, yes, flattered. 'You see we've got to get going because . . . well . . .' I didn't have to explain. I didn't know the guy.

'Daddy!' Milly suddenly yelled.

'No, darling, it isn't your daddy,' I said patiently. 'It's a total stranger.'

'Iss my *dad*!' she insisted. And now I saw that she was

pointing at Curry's. I turned and looked. In the window were several flat-screen TVs, the biggest of which was tuned to *News 24*. There was Xan, looking devastating, doing a piece to camera somewhere by an ancient temple – it looked like Angkor Wat.

'Daddy!' Milly screamed again. '*Dad-dy!*' She began crying.

Bong . . . My heart sank.

'Yes, sweetie.'

Bong . . .

'Want *Daddy!*'

'I know you do, darling.' I suddenly saw a taxi and flung out my arm. 'I'm sorry,' I said to the man. 'It's very kind of you, but we've got to go now.'

Bong . . .

'I understand,' he said, as the cab drew up. He held the door open for me, while I rolled Milly's buggy in. 'Goodbye,' he said regretfully.

''Bye,' I smiled out of the open window. 'And thanks.'

As the taxi drove away, I remembered that I'd seen the man in the food department. He *had* seemed to notice me as we'd walked past, but I was so distracted, and so unused to male interest, that I'd barely registered it. Anyway, I thought as the taxi turned right, he was very attractive, he had nice manners and he'd paid me a compliment, which was rare enough, God knew. But my priority now was to get home.

'Give Milly chicken and pasta please,' I barked at Luisa as I charged into the house fifteen minutes later. 'There are some fillets in here,' I shoved the carrier bag at her. 'And she'll have peas with it.'

'No. I gib her paella,' Luisa said, as she unstrapped Milly. 'Milly lob paella.'

'All right,' I said. 'Paella. But no prawns. And no garlic – she reeked of it for days last time.'

Luisa looked at me blankly. I grabbed the Spanish dictionary I'd recently bought and which was already dismayingly well

thumbed. Garlic: *Ajo*. How did you pronounce it? 'No . . .
ajo.' I shook my head and wagged my forefinger.

'Ah. *Acccchho. Sí*,' she nodded enthusiastically. 'Just chilli.'

'No – no chilli,' I shouted as I raced upstairs. 'She doesn't
like it.'

'Want chilli!' I heard Milly shout.

I put on a pair of smart trousers, a silk shirt and suede
jacket, then ran a brush through my hair. I grabbed my briefcase and into it put the drawings I'd done of the site. Then
I kissed Milly goodbye and jumped in the car.

The traffic was dreadful and I needed most of the hour I'd
allowed to get there. I drew up at five to two. Jamie's pick-
up truck was already parked outside number 63 – like all the
houses in the exclusive Boltons it was the size of a super-
market, stucco-fronted and white.

'Hi, boss,' Jamie called out indolently as I parked by the
church.

'I'm *not* your boss,' I corrected him as he jumped down
from his truck. 'I'm not even, officially, your business partner
although we work together so much. I'm . . . your . . .'

'Haughty Culturalist,' he suggested as I locked my car door.
'I thought you were stuck up when I first met you, but then
you started to grow on me and now I think you're really
quite nice.'

'Thank you. But, as I say, I'm not your boss, and you're . . .
I don't know what you are exactly.'

'I'm the bloke who makes the earth move for you.'

'Ha! Anyway, you're looking smart.' I glanced at his navy
jacket.

'This is my best cricketing blazer. Thea insisted. She's keen
for us to get this too. Not that her job isn't going great guns
– I hardly ever see her.'

'Has she been away again?' I asked as we opened the gate.

'Yeah,' he said, rolling his eyes. 'She's been to Rome, New
York, Monaco – you name it – and she's off again tomorrow,

to Cape Town for a tennis tournament.' Poor Jamie, I thought. No wonder they still hadn't had kids. 'Anyway,' he went on as we went up the steps, 'how's Princess Milly?'

'She's fine – except that this morning she kicked off her shoe in Marks & Sparks – and I'd given up all hope of finding it when this rather attractive man came up to me holding it.'

'Ah . . .' Jamie raised his left eyebrow. 'You've been snogging frogs again, haven't you?' He often teased me about that. 'So was his name Prince Charming?'

'No . . .' I was flustered. I pressed the big brass bell. 'I have no idea what it was.'

'And did he invite you to the ball?'

'Sadly not – but funnily enough, he did ask me to have a cappuccino with him.'

'What's so funny about that? You're a nice-looking sheila.'

'Thanks. And you're a handsome Bruce.'

'Anyway, I hope you accepted,' Jamie added as he straightened his tie.

'Of course I didn't,' I said stiffly.

'Why not? Was he clutching an axe?'

'Not that I could see.'

'Was he hideous?'

'Far from it.'

'Then, in my opinion, you should have said yes.'

'My criteria are slightly more stringent than that,' I said, although, for a fleeting moment I wished I had accepted – I'd found the man very attractive; but I then dismissed my regrets to concentrate on the matter in hand. I calmed myself with a couple of deep breaths.

'I hope we get this,' I whispered.

'So what's it to be?' he whispered back. '"Contemporary Architectural"? "Lush and Wild"? or "Timeless Elegance"?'

'"Timeless Elegance",' I replied. 'It would be a great one for the portfolio – switch off your phone, will you,' I said as I turned off my own. 'Not that we're short of work.'

'That's true.'

I thought of how quickly the business had grown. We'd achieved this by being flexible. No job was too big or too small. The commissions we had done ranged from doing a few window boxes, to putting in some trellising, or laying a patio, to building a whole new garden from scratch. I got a lift from my career that distracted me from my sadness and even if I'd had a broken night with Milly I'd still wake up full of enthusiasm for the day ahead.

Suddenly the gleaming red front door was pulled back. There was Gill Edwards, slim and wiry, head to toe in casual Gucci, and standing a little way behind her in the vast hall, her husband, Martin, a big bear of a man, in brick-coloured corduroys and a blue chequered shirt. I'd heard of the Edwardses when I worked in the City – they were both known to be very tough. She was a stockbroker for Cazenove and he, at fifty, a few years her senior, was a vice-chairman of Goldman Sachs.

'Anna.' She smiled. 'Come in.'

'This is Jamie Clark of Olympian Landscapes,' I said. 'He builds all my gardens, so I thought he ought to come with me today, if that's OK.'

'It's absolutely fine.' She shook his hand. 'Hi . . .'

'These designs are lovely,' Gill said a few minutes later as she pored over my drawings in the huge yellow drawing room. I passed her the computer-generated image of what the garden would look like with all the perspectives drawn in.

'And this is the mood board.' I handed it to her husband.

'Mood board?' he repeated.

'It's a collage of photos of the proposed architectural structures, water features and decorative elements to give you a feel of the design – as well as the planting scheme.'

'We don't want too much planting,' Gill interjected. 'We both have very busy working lives – plus we spend most weekends in the country.'

117

'I've borne that in mind,' I said, wondering why anyone would spend such a fortune on their London house, only to flee from it every Friday.

We went outside, shivering a little in the early spring sunlight. For such an enormous house the garden wasn't that big – about twenty metres. It had a scrubby-looking lawn and some raised flowerbeds full of mature shrubs that were so overgrown as to give it a claustrophobic feel. Around the perimeter were some York flagstones, with a thin scattering of gravel between them, and, in the centre, some scraggly-looking box hedges – the remnants of what had once been a miniature knot garden. The whole thing was on a slight slope.

'The last people had been here fifteen years,' Gill explained. 'They'd done little to it latterly, as you can see. But as we said when you came before, we'd like the garden to be an extension of the house, largely for summer entertaining.'

I talked them through the design. The garden would be levelled and new steps built. There would be a square lawn in the centre, surrounded on three sides by clipped box balls of different sizes, to add a degree of formality. At the back would be the main focal point, a long black granite water trough with a keyhole spout. The area round the lawn would be paved with Portuguese limestone, with raised flowerbeds and huge black granite planters. The plants would be mostly low-maintenance perennials such as lavender, *Euphorbia*, peonies and *Acanthus*, supported by a number of hardy climbers and shrubs. Along the left-hand side would be a seating area, screened by four pleached limes. This part would contain a large, modern *chimenea*, flanked by two specially commissioned teak box benches in which the cushions could be stowed. There would be an irrigation system and, set into the limestone, discreet uplighting to add drama at night.

'It's very contemporary,' Gill said, 'but also classical. I like it.'

118

'Well . . .' her husband said. 'I don't like it . . .' Damn you, I thought. 'I *love* it!' I exhaled with relief. 'It has a – I don't know – a . . . a . . .'

'Timeless elegance?' Jamie suggested.

'Yes. Exactly. A timeless elegance.' I flashed Jamie a warning look.

'But would you want to remove all the existing plants?' his wife asked.

I shook my head. 'I'd keep all the ones that are going to work well with the new scheme – in this case the Moroccan broom, though I'd like to move it so that it gets more light; I'd also like to keep the *Fremontodendron* – that's the California Glory there – although we'd have to cut it back and train it properly; and the fig tree of course.'

'Do feel free to dig up the hydrangeas,' Martin said indolently.

'Absolutely not!' his wife protested. 'You know perfectly well that I love them.'

'And you know perfectly well that I loathe them, darling. Always have done.' He suddenly blasted them with an imaginary shotgun.

'Well,' I said, taken aback, 'these ones are old and rather diseased, so I was going to replace them with new ones.'

'Don't bother,' Martin insisted. 'I can't stand them – they're yucksville.' He was making gagging gestures.

'Well, I adore them,' Gill said. 'And would you cut out the histrionics, darling?'

'Hydrangeas are so . . .' He pulled an appalled face. '*Suburban.*'

'They're not,' she flung back. 'My parents had them in Poole.'

'Exactly,' he murmured.

'And let's face it, darling, you like gladioli which are completely naff.'

'That's tosh.'

119

'And as we have a whole border full of your ghastly orange gladioli in Oxfordshire, I really don't see why I shouldn't be allowed to have a few harmless hydrangeas in town. Don't you agree, Anna?'

'Erm . . . well, I like them, I must say, and the dried flower heads provide winter interest – but you're the clients so it's your call.'

Now Martin was pointing at the hydrangeas and making slashing gestures across his throat.

'Anyway,' his wife went on, rolling her eyes, 'let's discuss something less contentious – money.' She looked at me expectantly.

I took a deep breath. 'Well, this is a big project,' I said. 'With a corresponding budget.' I handed her the costings and her eyes skimmed over them to the bottom line.

'A hundred thousand?' she said, her brow pleating. That's for everything presumably.'

'Yes.'

'And your fees will be what?'

'About six per cent of that.'

'Would you do it for eighty?' she asked.

I'd been prepared for this. 'I can't,' I replied. 'Because of the stone. For eighty you'd have to have something much cheaper, like Indian sandstone. It's very attractive,' I assured them, 'but I feel that Portuguese limestone is essential, because that's what you have in your hall, and you said you wanted the garden to be an extension of the house, to flow from it, almost.'

'We do want that.'

'I could get the costs down to ninety-five thousand, although I'd have to cut a few corners.'

Martin shrugged. 'Seems a shame to spoil the ship for a hap'orth of tar.' Especially as they must be pulling in at least three million a year between them, I thought. 'And how long would it take to build? We're hoping to have a big house-warming in late June.'

'It would take about four months from beginning to end.'

Gill stood up. 'Then I guess you'd better get started.' My heart leapt. 'Is that OK, Martin?'

'That's fine – as long as there's a "no-hydrangea" clause in the contract.'

'So what happens next?' she asked me, ignoring him.

'I'll send you the paperwork,' I replied.

'And I'll draw up a quote for the materials,' said Jamie. 'If you accept it I'll need a deposit of thirty per cent so that I can start ordering everything, but you'll get itemised receipts.'

'That all sounds very satisfactory.' Mrs Edwards held out a perfectly manicured hand. 'So I guess it's a deal. Isn't it, Martin?'

He nodded. 'Looks like a deal to me.'

'That's . . . great,' I said, doing my best not to look too thrilled.

Jamie and I stayed for another hour or so, so that he could survey the site with me in more detail, taking further measurements and calculating the amount of earth that would have to be removed, as well as the elevations and the best drainage points.

When I got home I drew up the contract and as I was putting it in an envelope the phone rang. It was Joanna Silver, the vicar's wife. 'I just wanted to remind you about next Friday,' she said. My mind went blank. 'I hope you haven't forgotten.' I had. 'It's the fund-raising party for the church's new Community Outreach centre.'

'Oh, yes, of course.' I'd offered to do a Gardener's Question Time session.

'The evening kicks off at seven,' I heard her say, 'and you'll be on at eight for half an hour. I've been telling everyone about you and, I don't know whether you saw it, but I also put a photo of you in the local paper, with a few lines about the event.'

'I didn't see it, no,' I replied, feeling irritated that she hadn't

121

asked me, but at the same time pleased to have had the publicity.

'I used the photo on your website,' she went on. 'There's already quite a bit of interest. But I've also done something else which I just wanted to run by you . . .'

'Yes?'

'Which is to make the first prize in the raffle a free garden design consultation with you. I hope you don't mind.'

In fact, I did mind because I was about to be very busy and it was extremely unlikely to lead to a commission.

'That's absolutely fine,' I said.

On the Friday evening I got to the church hall early and had a glass of white wine to steady my nerves. Citronella and her husband arrived shortly after me, and were soon smiling and nodding graciously at everyone as though they were hosting the event. I wished she'd sent Erasmus to a different nursery school but fortunately his Italian nanny, Claudia, usually brought him, as Citronella was presumably too busy writing her weekly bilge.

At least the other mothers seemed nice, I thought, as I circulated, listening to the string trio hired for the evening. I didn't know any of them that well yet, as Milly had only been there a month. But I could see Annabel Goodchild by the tombola, and Nina Taszkanowski selling plants, and Michal Navon was manning the bookstall – she and her family had recently moved here from Israel – and there was that little girl Lucy's mum – she was always friendly; what was her name? Oh yes, Claire.

I chatted to the few people I knew, then I bought some toys for Milly, including an erasable Mega Sketch Magic Writer and an almost new DVD of *Beauty and the Beast*. I bought two white *Hellibores* for Jenny's garden – then I paused at the produce stand.

'How about some honey?' the woman behind the stall

asked me, tapping the lid of a jar. 'It's produced locally.' I glanced at the label, which was illustrated with a large, stripey bee with a halo over its head. Bee Good, it said.

'No thanks,' I replied. 'I'm afraid I don't really like honey.'

'Don't you?' She looked slightly horrified, as though I'd said 'I don't like giving to charity'.

'I find it too sweet,' I explained. 'But I'd love some truffles.' I then tried to buy a few raffle tickets but, to my surprise, they'd already sold out. I had another glass of wine to give me Dutch courage and glanced at my watch. It was two minutes to eight. I saw Joanna Silver waving at me from the stage, so I stepped forward and she tapped on the mike.

'And now, the highlight of the evening,' she began as the hubbub subsided. 'To those of you who don't already know her, may I introduce our local celebrity garden designer – Anna Temple . . .' She indicated me with a sweep of her hand. 'Anna – whom you may have seen on GMTV recently – has kindly agreed to answer all your horticultural queries this evening.'

There was a polite round of applause as I went up the worn wooden steps at the side on to the stage. I sat at the table and looked at the sea of faces staring up at me, and felt suddenly embarrassed and exposed. An uncomfortable silence descended, so I blew into the mike, then straightened it.

'Thanks for that, Joanna . . .' I began nervously. 'Hi, everyone. Erm – I'm not a celebrity – and I've only been designing gardens professionally for a couple of years. But all my adult life I've been a keen amateur gardener – as was my mother, from whom I learned lots of useful gardening tips, which I'd be more than happy to share with you. So all you have to do is ask me a question about your plants or trees, or your rockery, or whatever it is, and if I can answer helpfully, I will.'

There was another silence, then Joanna coughed. 'Let me

get the ball rolling,' she said. 'This is the time of year for planting baskets. Any advice as to how to make them look good?'

'Well . . .' I cleared my throat. 'When planting a hanging basket, the trick is to work from the inside out, then finally push the plants through the outside, using a potato peeler to make a space for the roots. I also recommend lining the baskets with used tea bags before adding the compost as they make a great fertiliser and also retain water.'

'How can you stop the baskets dripping so much when you water them?' Joanna added.

'By putting a few ice cubes on them instead – it also uses a lot less water in these drought-stricken days.'

'I'm not very tall,' a tiny woman in a yellow coat said. 'How can I make it easier to water my baskets?'

'You could attach a length of bamboo to the last few feet of the hose to keep it rigid.'

'Ah . . .' She nodded in an enlightened way.

A silver-haired woman to my right put up her hand. 'I do about ten pots every year,' she said. 'But I find them very heavy.'

'Then you could reduce their weight by filling the lower half with polystyrene chips, then adding the compost on top.'

A man in the front row put up his hand. 'How can I keep slugs out of my planters?'

'By smearing them with Vaseline every couple of weeks – the planters, that is, not the slugs.'

'Glad you clarified that!' someone said and tittered.

'You could also stand them in a large tray of water or, better still, lager. But please don't use slug pellets as hedgehogs tend to eat them. Another deterrent is to sprinkle the base of the plants with salt or broken eggshells. Alternatively you could keep a few toads.'

'We seem to have a lot of snails in our garden,' a man said. 'I don't know why.'

124

'Do you have any ivy?'

'Yes. Along the back fence.'

'That's the reason, then – snails love it; so unless you're very fond of it, I'd get rid of it – in any case there are so many nicer things that you could plant in its place.'

'How can I make my house plants greener?' a man at the back asked.

'By adding a drop of castor oil to the soil every six weeks. House plants also love tea – preferably warm – and their leaves enjoy a wipe down with beer.'

'How can I revive cut flowers?' a woman in a pink jacket asked.

'Just drop an aspirin into the vase – the salicylic acid comes close to the natural growth hormones found in plants. A two-pence piece will do the same thing because the copper perks them up. Add a teaspoon of bleach to stop the water going cloudy.'

'I love tulips,' her neighbour said. 'But they always flop so quickly.'

'I know – it's so disappointing,' I replied. 'But if you prick their stems, just below the head, they won't flop, because it breaks the vacuum allowing water to be drawn up.'

We then came on to the subject of weeds.

'How can you kill the weeds on a path without using chemicals?' a man asked.

'With a concoction of boiling water and salt – add about a cupful to half a bucket of water – but use a metal bucket and be careful carrying it.'

'I've got some very nice, lightweight plastic garden furniture,' a woman in the middle of the room said. 'But it's become very stained and no amount of scrubbing seems to make a difference.'

'Then make a paste of baking soda and water and rub it on – wipe it off after half an hour and the furniture will have a new lease of life.'

'Where's the best place to put a pond?' Michal Navon asked.

'In a semi-shady area,' I replied, 'because direct sunlight encourages the growth of algae.'

'We get herons coming down to ours,' a man said, 'taking our fish and frogs. We love herons, but wish they wouldn't do this.'

'Then make life tricky for them by making access to your pond more difficult. Plant shrubs right up to the edge. This will also prevent innocent passers-by such as hedgehogs from falling in.'

'Do you think bizzie lizzies are non-U?' I heard someone say. There was a ripple of laughter.

'Do I think bizzie lizzies are non-U?' I repeated. 'No. I don't – not at all. And I find the idea of being snobbish about certain flowers or plants ridiculous – but you'd be amazed at how worked up some people get. I have clients at the moment – the husband loathes hydrangeas and his wife loves them – we're still trying to resolve the issue without involving lawyers; I have other clients who argue quite viciously over whether or not to include dahlias in the planting scheme, or marigolds, or petunias.'

'Crazy . . .' someone murmured.

'I agree. There are certainly fashions in planting – and at the moment black flowers are, well, the new black. New varieties of black *Alliums*, black scabious and even black delphiniums have been cultivated, and they can add a certain dark excitement to a border. But to me, it's a question of the right plant for the right place. I've just been commissioned to do an Italian-style garden in Hampstead, so obviously I'm not going to be filling it with forget-me-nots and foxgloves, but with lavender, oleander, plumbago and with aromatic plants such as rosemary and thyme. But to go back to bizzie lizzies – I often use white ones in window boxes, or to brighten up a dark corner – so no, I don't find them socially unacceptable in any way.'

We then discussed the best way to mark plants – I suggested using white plastic knives, and a black chinagraph, which is what my mother did; I talked about how hollyhocks will grow taller if you give them beer; I was asked how to make a new lawn grow faster – by refrigerating the seeds for a couple of days before sowing them. I glanced at my watch. It was eight twenty-five.

'I grow lettuces,' a man at the back shouted, 'but the birds still get at them, despite the strings of tin foil I always put up.'

'Then lay pieces of hosepipe about a yard long among them – the birds will think they're snakes.'

Then Citronella put up her hand. 'We're fortunate enough to have a house in the country . . .' I braced myself for her brag-fest. 'It has a tennis court . . .' I tried to imagine Citronella lumbering around it and couldn't. 'But we'd like to disguise it. What would you recommend?'

'Something which doesn't drop its leaves,' I replied, forcing myself to sound polite. 'You could have a rambling rose at one end – I'd recommend 'Veilchenblau' or 'Rambling Rector' – and, at the other end, an evergreen clematis. Armandii is a particularly lovely one, with very fragrant white flowers and large glossy trefoil leaves which look almost tropical – or *Clematis montana* always gives excellent coverage.'

'We have lots of moles in our cottage in Devon,' someone else asked. 'What can we do?'

'Wherever you see a hole, stuff a rhubarb stem down it – moles loathe the stuff. You could also put a child's windmill into each molehill as they hate the vibrations from it as it whirls round.' I glanced at my watch. It was eight thirty-five. 'Well . . .' I said. And I was about to bring the session to an end when a male voice from the very back said, 'How can we make our gardens more attractive to bees?'

I looked up. The man looked familiar. Early forties. Attractive. My stomach did a flick-flack. It was the guy who'd found Milly's shoe.

'Erm . . . bees are wonderfully helpful insects to have around the garden,' I began, feeling my face heat up. 'They're great pollinators, they aren't aggressive and of course they make honey. Anyway, to answer your question, I'd recommend planting buddleia – which also attracts butterflies of course – as well as *Ceanothus*, foxgloves, *Penstemons* and anything particularly scented such as *Nicotiana*, summer jasmine, wallflowers and honeysuckle. If you have space for an elderflower they'll also love that.'

'Thank you.' He smiled.

Then Joanna stepped forward. 'Sadly we have to stop there, but that was fascinating,' she said, 'so I'd like to offer our thanks to Anna for sharing such a wealth of information with us this evening.'

There was a polite round of applause. Then I stepped off the stage, where one or two people were waiting to ask me further questions. As I answered them I became aware that the man who'd asked me about bees was standing in the background. He gave me a diffident smile.

'Hi,' I said, smiling. 'It's you . . .' He had a lovely open face, prematurely grey hair, which made him look distinguished, and large hazel eyes, which seemed almost the colour of ginger. His lips were fine and were framed by two curving lines, like brackets, which gave him an amused expression. There was a tiny, crescent-shaped scar on the bridge of his nose.

'It's nice to see you again,' he said. 'You were obviously in a tearing hurry when we met the other day.'

'I was on my way to see potential clients. I was feeling rather nervous. But . . . do you live around here?'

He shook his head. 'I used to – but I'm in St Peter's Square in Hammersmith now.'

'I know it . . .' He must be successful, I realised. It was one of the loveliest squares in west London. 'So what brings you here?'

'Well . . . I saw the piece about you in the paper yesterday and I recognised you from last Saturday and so I thought' – he shrugged – 'that I'd come along.'

'Oh. Well . . . you asked a nice question.'

'I'm afraid it was a bit staged.'

'In what way?'

'If you come and have dinner with me some time you'll see.'

'But . . . I don't know you,' I said, laughing. 'I don't even know your name.'

'It's Patrick,' he said. 'There. Now you do.'

'Attention, please, everyone!' we heard Joanna shout. 'It's now time to announce the result of the raffle and my daughter, Bella, is going to draw the winning tickets. So let's start with the third prize, which is a signed copy of David Attenborough's latest book, *The Planet Earth* – and that goes to . . .'

Bella, who looked about twelve, smiled self-consciously, revealing a mouthful of metal. Then she dipped her hand into the top hat, rummaged around for a moment and pulled out a pink cloakroom ticket. 'Number two five thixth,' she announced.

'Number 256!' Joanna repeated loudly. 'Anyone have that ticket? 256?' No one came forward. 'We'll check it after-wards,' she said, 'we have names and addresses. On to the second prize then, which is lunch for two at the River Café . . .'

Bella dipped her hand into the hat again and pulled out a blue ticket. 'It'th number one three theven,' she said, waving it about.

'Number 137,' said Joanna, her eyes scanning the crowd. 'Who's the lucky person with ticket 137?' There was silence. 'How odd,' she said after a few moments. 'Never mind – we can track them down. But now we come to our first prize, which is a free garden design consultation with Anna Temple – worth a hundred pounds. Could you draw the winning ticket, Bella, please?'

She dipped her hand into the hat for the last time and pulled out a green ticket. 'It'th number thixth!'

Patrick fumbled in his pocket and produced a strip of tickets. 'That's me!' he shouted. He grinned at me and went up to collect his prize.

'Congratulations,' I said wryly when he returned with the gold envelope.

'I'm delighted,' he replied. 'Now you'll *have* to see me again.' I smiled. 'Here.' He handed me his card. It said that his name was Patrick Gilchrist and that he was the Non-Executive Chairman of Total Technology. He opened the envelope. 'And all your details are here. So I hope you won't mind if I call you – now that I've got a valid reason to do so.'

'No,' I said. 'I won't mind at all.'

SIX

I assumed that Patrick would call me within a few days but I didn't hear from him. I was taken aback at how disappointed I felt, but at the same time, oddly, I was cheered since it at least proved that I could be interested in a man again.

The following week I bumped into Joanna Silver in the local delicatessen.

'Thanks so much for your talk,' she said as we hovered by the cheese counter. 'The evening was a huge success – oh, that large goat, please – we raised four thousand pounds. But you know that man who won first prize in the raffle?' she went on. 'Patrick Gilchrist?'

'Yes,' I said, my pulse racing slightly.

'Well, the funny thing is that when we checked the other winning tickets, those were both his numbers too.'

I stared at her. 'What an amazing coincidence.'

'No it wasn't,' she corrected me. 'Because it turned out that he'd bought nearly all of them: 460! At fifty pence each! But when I phoned him the next day he said he hadn't wanted to claim the other prizes because he didn't want to appear greedy. Wasn't that nice?'

'Very nice,' I concurred. So the only prize he'd wanted was

the consultation with me – which made it even odder that he hadn't called.

Another two weeks went by and still Patrick hadn't been in touch, and I'd just made up my mind to forget him, deciding that he must be eccentric, when I got an e-mail from him, explaining that he'd been away, but was now back and would love me to come and see his garden. As much of my working week was being spent on the Boltons project I suggested that we made it on a Friday afternoon.

Let's make it this Friday then, he e-mailed back. *At 4.30. And I hope you'll stay for a drink.*

I clicked on Reply: *If I can square it with my au pair that would be nice.*

'I'm going out now,' I explained slowly to Luisa at 3.30 on the following Friday. 'I have that meeting I told you about. Remember? But I should be back by 7.30 as I'll put Milly to bed myself. *I'll* put her to *bed*,' I repeated. I clasped my hands by my ear to indicate sleeping.

Luisa looked nonplussed. 'You go bed now?'

'No, Luisa.' I sighed. 'I *not* go bed now. I go *work* now. I back 7.30.' I wrote it down in numerals. 'Me back' – I 'walked' two fingers along the table – '7.30.' *Jesus!*

'*Ah, sí*,' she said, beaming. '*Comprendo. Las siete y treinta. Bueno.*'

'*Bueno!*' Milly echoed, looking up from her book.

'Luisa,' I said in exasperation. 'You really must work harder at your English. You've been here two months now and it's little better than it was when you arrived.'

'*Sí – iss* little better,' Luisa agreed happily.

I groaned inwardly, then bent to kiss Milly. As I did so, my eyes strayed to the picture book that she was reading. 'Where did you get this, darling? It's lovely.'

'Luisa gib to me,' she replied.

'Did you, Luisa?' I asked. 'Did you give Milly this book?'

I held it up to aid comprehension, then pointed at her, then Milly.

'*Sí.*' She shrugged. '*No, es nada* – iss nothing.'

'Well, that's . . . very kind.' I looked at the back – it had cost twelve pounds. 'Thank you. It's beautiful. 'Bye, my little darling.' I kissed Milly again.

'*Adiós, Mamá!*' she said.

As I drove over to Hammersmith I wondered what Luisa *did* all morning at her English classes. This couldn't go on. What if there were some emergency and she couldn't make herself understood?

I found a parking space in Black Lion Lane, which leads into St Peter's Square. I dabbed on some scent and checked my reflection in the driving mirror. My heart sank. My hair was a mess. Because it's so fair I don't have to have it high-lighted, but it's very fine, so it needs to be well cut. As I ran a comb through it I thought enviously of Cassie's long, lux-urious dark tresses. I was lucky if my hair made it down to my nape. Locking the car, I made a mental note to make an appointment with Sandra, my hairdresser of twelve years, then I walked round the corner and found number 36.

The house was an early-Victorian villa – smaller than the other houses, but with elegant arched windows. I went up the front steps and rang the bell.

'Anna!' Patrick was beaming at me. He looked tanned.

'Hi. You've caught the sun. Have you been somewhere hot?'

'Hotter than here. New Zealand.'

'Was it a business trip?'

'No . . .'

'Do you have family there?'

He hesitated for a moment. 'My son lives in Christchurch.'

Patrick must have been a very young father, I thought – or the boy might be on his gap year. 'What does he do?'

'He's in pre-school. He's four and a half.'

133

'Oh . . .' I murmured. I felt a wave of compassion for Patrick.

'Anyway . . .' he said, 'it's great that you're here. Will you have a cup of tea before we start?'

'No thanks – I'd prefer to crack on as there's only an hour of daylight left.'

He took his jacket off a peg, then nodded at the Nikon round my neck. 'You've brought your camera?'

'I photograph every garden I survey so that I have that early visual reference; not that you have to commission me,' I added quickly. 'It's only a consultation. You can ask me anything you like about your garden, or I could suggest ways to revamp it with a few new plants maybe, or an additional border.'

We walked through the tiled hallway into the kitchen and he opened the back door. I stepped on to the terrace and stopped in my tracks.

'It's lovely,' I said. 'And it's big.'

'Big for London – about thirty metres.'

As we walked through it I saw that it had clearly been professionally designed, using classic design principles in which the plot is divided into three parts.

The part nearest the house was terraced with brick, on which there were a number of planters filled with yellow and white hyacinths; there was a large arbour and underneath it an elegant wrought-iron table and chairs: then there was a diagonal path leading to a formal lawn, which was circular and semi-enclosed by a slightly raised border that glowed with daffodils and primulas: beyond that another diagonal path led off to the right towards the very end of the garden which looked as though it had been left artistically wild.

'You've got me here under false pretences,' I said. 'It's beautifully done.'

'Do you think so?'

'I do. There's a lot of interest – the diagonal paths confound

134

the eye so that you don't see the whole garden at once, but are led through it, gradually; the borders are well planted and attractively shaped. You have plenty of mature shrubs – these camellias are lovely – and that *Magnolia grandiflora*'s going to be fantastic. There are plants for dark places, like these lovely hellebores, there are grasses to give texture, and scented things . . .' I could smell the seductive, lily-like fragrance of the *Mahonia*. 'It must look wonderful in the summer if it's as good as this now.'

'It's not bad.'

'Did you have it done?'

'No. It was more or less like this when I bought the house.'

'It looks perfect – do you have a gardener?'

'Not at the moment. I prefer to do it myself as I have the time, and I find it therapeutic.'

'I don't know what to suggest,' I said as we neared the end. The shrubs had recently had their first prune: the grass had been mown and the edges trimmed; creamy *Narcissi* mingled with china-blue *Chianodoxa* in the crescent-shaped borders. 'We could talk about planting if you like – I could suggest a few unusual annuals that would look wonderful in the summer: I don't know whether you like zinnias – there's a beautiful lime-green one – or giant *Alliums* and there's a crimson sunflower which looks quite spectacular – oh.' I'd stopped in my tracks. There was a small pond and beyond that three gnarled old apple trees, which were just about to blossom, and underneath each one a gabled beehive. 'You keep bees?' I murmured.

'I do. But don't worry – they're still in their quiet winter mode. The odd worker pops out occasionally to do a recce – like those ones buzzing about over there – but it's still a bit early for any real activity although I think they'll start again soon – maybe next week.'

'How long have you been keeping them?'

'Since I moved here nearly two years ago. I'd been through

135

an awful break-up and needed to sweeten my life,' he added wryly as we sat on a wooden bench. 'I saw a TV programme about beekeeping and fell in love with the idea.'

'The bees must make your garden even more beautiful.'

'I certainly get more flowers because they're such good pollinators.'

'So that's why the question you asked at the church fair was staged – you knew the answer.'

'Yes. But I just wanted to . . . make myself known to you again.' He smiled. 'Plus there was a bit of self-interest at work. The more bee-friendly flowers there are in people's gardens, the better for me and my bees.'

'You bought all the raffle tickets,' I said.

'Damn . . .' He reddened, then smiled again. 'How did you know?'

'I bumped into the vicar's wife and she mentioned it.'

'Well . . . I wanted to win that first prize.'

'I'm very flattered.' I laughed. 'But it would have been far cheaper just to phone me up for a normal consultation!'

'It would – but I thought it would be more fun to do it that way. Plus I'm fond of that church as Sam – that's my little boy – was christened there. Anyway,' he said, his voice suddenly catching, 'back to the bees . . .'

'Yes . . . The bees. So . . . what do you do with the honey?'

'I sell about half to local delis and cafés. But the rest I give away to charitable events as it's only a hobby – I'm not out to make a profit.'

I remembered the pots of honey at the church fund-raiser. 'Is your honey called Bee Good?'

'It is.'

'There were a few beehives at the Chelsea Physic Garden where I did my design course – but I've never seen one in a private garden in London.'

'There are lots of them in cities. I have a friend in Manhattan who keeps a couple of hives on his roof terrace. They forage

136

for miles around, so all you need is the space for the hive itself.'

'And is it fun?'

'It's fascinating – and it keeps me calm. Now . . .' he said. 'The light's beginning to fade – let's have that drink.'

We went inside and I sat in the coral-coloured sitting room as Patrick busied himself in the kitchen. On the sideboard were a number of family photos, several of them of Sam – a beautiful little boy with large hazel eyes, like his father's. How heartbreaking for him to be so far away. I wondered why that was. Perhaps Patrick had had a fling with someone out there.

He reappeared with a tray – he had a gin and tonic, while I sipped a weak spritzer. He told me about his work – he'd started an Internet company fifteen years before, at the beginning of the technology boom.

'It specialised in payment systems for Internet shopping,' he explained as he cradled his drink. 'Then last year I got an offer I couldn't refuse from Paypal and sold it.'

'What will you do next?'

He shrugged. 'I don't know. I'm in talks with an old colleague about starting another Internet venture, but in the meantime my bees keep me busy – and sane.' He offered me an olive. 'And you? You said you'd been a garden designer for two years, so what did you do before?' I told him about my time in the City. 'And your little girl? She's what? Three?'

'In June.'

'So who's looking after her now?'

'My au pair, Luisa. Her English is appalling, but she adores Milly and vice versa.'

'And what about Milly's father?' he added slightly anxiously.

'Well . . . he's not really around. We're on good terms,' I went on, keen to make myself appear attractively positive rather than embittered and sad. 'But he works in Indonesia. He's been there for three and a half years now.'

I could see Patrick doing the maths. 'That must have been tough for you,' he said. 'And for him,' he added feelingly, 'being so far from his child.'

'It *is* hard for him,' I said. Especially now that he has a relationship with Milly, I thought. Seeing her intermittently, then having to say goodbye, must be far worse than if he'd never got to know her. 'It's very hard for Milly too. And you?' I added. 'You must find long-distance fatherhood . . . difficult, to say the least.'

He rattled the ice in his drink. 'I find it unbearable. Sam was taken to New Zealand the day after his third birthday.'

'I didn't think the law allowed ex-wives to take the children out of the country,' I said, 'let alone to the other side of the world.'

'I wasn't married to Sam's mum. I was wary of marrying her,' he went on, as if he felt he had to justify it, 'largely because I'd only known her three months when she got pregnant.'

'Were you happy about it?'

'Not at first, no – I felt trapped.'

'At least you did the decent thing and made a home with her,' I said bitterly, thinking of how Xan had failed to do that with me.

'I did make a home with her – and when Sam arrived I was thrilled. But I gave Suzie a very nice life. She didn't have to work. We lived in a big house in Brook Green. She had a nanny, a cleaner and a gardener – we took great holidays. She was very well looked after.'

'It sounds like the life of Reilly,' I said wistfully.

'I'd say it was. But it still didn't seem to be enough, because when Sam was two, I discovered that Suzie was having an affair with a guy at our tennis club. Three months later she left me, taking Sam, which was terrible enough: then a few weeks after that she dropped the bombshell that she and Sam would both be moving to New Zealand with her lover – he's a Kiwi.'

138

'But . . . couldn't it . . . be stopped?'

'God knows I tried. But as an unmarried father I had no automatic rights and she'd refused to give me a parental responsibility order. It went to court, but the judge took against me.'

'Why?'

'Oh . . . because . . . Suzie . . . lied.' Bitterness suddenly twisted Patrick's features. 'She told these blatant lies – it was shameless.' I found myself wondering what she'd lied about. 'I then appealed against the decision but lost. And I was preparing to take it to the House of Lords when her lawyer wrote to say that Suzie was four months pregnant. My solicitor advised me that in this situation the courts wouldn't want to break up her "happy family unit"' – he rolled his eyes – 'so there was no point in fighting on.'

How terrible to have his child whisked away from him – transplanted to another country, on the other side of the world – let alone for that child to be brought up by another man.

'Relations between Suzie and me then broke down to the extent that a final meeting was arranged, with a social worker present, at an office near Holborn, for me to say goodbye to Sam.' I felt tears prick the backs of my eyes. 'All I'd got was the right to phone him and write to him "occasionally", but I then negotiated a separate agreement with Suzie to be able to visit him twice a year. I'm lucky in that I can afford to do that,' he went on, 'otherwise I'd never see him. Anyway . . .' he seemed suddenly embarrassed. 'I didn't mean to talk about it. It's depressing, to put it mildly, but as there's nothing I can do about it, I just try to cope with the resentment I feel – and the stress.'

'I'm sorry,' I said quietly. I glanced at the ormulu clock on the mantelpiece. It was 7.30. 'Well . . .' I picked up my camera. 'I'd better go. It's been lovely, but I told Luisa I'd be back by now and I like to put Milly to bed myself.'

'I can understand that,' he said feelingly as we stood up. 'What bliss to be able to.'

We went into the hall. 'I'm afraid I can't think of anything to suggest for your garden,' I said. 'It's gorgeous as it is – a traditional English garden with lovely proportions, beautifully landscaped and imaginatively planted.'

'I'm still glad you've seen it,' he said, 'and I . . . hope that you'll come again.' He looked at me. 'Will you?'

'Maybe . . . it's . . . a possibility . . .' I smiled at him.

'Can I tell you something?'

I looked at him. 'Yes.'

'I saw you on the TV a few weeks ago – I never watch at breakfast time, but that morning I happened to have it on. And there you were, and I just thought you looked so . . . nice. The way you talked about plants – your passion for them – the way you said that they even have "personalities".'

'They do – they have distinct "characters". My mother taught me that.'

'What was that thing you said about Cinderella plants?'

'I was talking about snowdrops and other early spring bulbs. They're shut away, out of sight for most of the year, then in February they get the chance to go to the ball and everyone's enchanted with them. Then at the stroke of twelve they vanish into the ground and you see nothing of them. Then the following year, the fairy godmother obligingly waves her magic wand and off they go to the ball again.'

'I liked that.' Patrick smiled. 'Then I recognised you in the shop that Saturday morning and when I found the little shoe and it turned out to be your daughter's, well . . .' He shrugged. 'I felt it was fate. But you probably thought I was a bit of a weirdo,' he added with a laugh.

'No – I thought you looked rather nice: but I *was* taken aback when you asked me to have a cup of coffee.'

'But I felt I'd already met you – though you couldn't have known that. But now that we have met properly, perhaps

140

you'll come and have dinner here one evening? I'd love to talk to you again and I'm not a bad cook. You don't have to say yes now,' he added diffidently. 'You could think about it.' He kissed me on the cheek and I felt a sudden frisson of desire.

'I think I would like that, Patrick. Thanks.'

'Beast! *Beast*!' Milly exclaimed on the Monday morning. She had grabbed the DVD of *Beauty and the Beast* and was brandishing it at me. 'Want watch Beast, Mum!'

'Not now, darling,' I said. 'I know you love it, but we've got to have breakfast, haven't we, then we're going to Sweet Peas to see all your friends. So come and have your Rice Krispies.'

'Kribbies,' she repeated happily as I tipped some into her Peter Rabbit bowl. '*Leche*!'

'I'm sorry?'

'Want *leche*!'

'You mean milk?' I opened the fridge. 'I do wish you'd stop speaking Spanish, darling.'

'*Leche*!' she shouted as I poured some in. '*Más*!'

I suddenly noticed that Milly was clutching a doll. It was brand new, with a sweet, smiley face, curly red hair, a pink leopard-skin coat and shiny pink trousers.

'Darling – where did you get that?' I asked. It looked expensive.

Milly sat the doll down next to her plate. 'Luisa gib to me.'

'Oh.' Suddenly I heard a creak on the stairs and Luisa appeared. She usually leaves the house early – before Milly and I have breakfast – so I don't see her in the mornings. Milly jumped off her chair and ran to her for a hug.

'*Caramelo de buenos días*!' Luisa crooned as she picked her up and kissed her. 'I go school now, Anna.' She smiled.

'Luisa,' I said. 'Did you give Milly this doll?'

141

She nodded. '*Sí*. Iss nice.'

'It's lovely – but you really mustn't buy things for her. You bought her that book a couple of weeks ago. It's very sweet of you, but please, no more presents for her, OK? It's not as though you can afford it.'

To my surprise, Luisa blushed, as though I'd offended her.

'All I mean', I tried again, 'is that you must try and save your money, Luisa – as you're not paid very much.' She reddened again, rather oddly. 'But thank you for being so kind.'

'I go school now,' she said. She gave Milly a noisy kiss, like water going down the bath plug, then put on her small blue rucksack. She waved. 'I go school now.'

'*Hasta la vista*!' Milly said.

'So . . . tell me about your friends?' I said to Milly a little later as I walked her to Sweet Peas. She was clutching the teddy Xan had given her under her left arm. 'What are their names?'

'Erm . . .' Milly stopped to scratch her nose, then placed her right hand in mine again. 'Carna . . .'

'Yes, Carla.' The cherry trees that lined the street frothed with pink blossom.

'Phoebe . . .'

'Yes, she's very nice.'

'Erm . . . Alfie . . . *and* . . . Lily . . . *and* 'Ris . . .'

'Iris, yes. And what about Erasmus?'

'No,' Milly said firmly. 'No me gusta. Me mordeó.'

'What, darling?'

Sweet Peas is in a large Victorian house overlooking Brook Green. The morning session starts at 9.30 and parents stay for registration, where they sing a couple of songs with the children, before 'lessons' start.

As Milly and I arrived – picking our way through the usual pile-up of buggies and scooters – the other parents were hanging their children's coats and hats on the painted pegs, or helping them on with their smocks. Erasmus came in – dressed in brown corduroy knickerbockers, a miniature green Barbour and a tweed cap – as though he was about to go on a shoot. This morning, unusually, he was accompanied by his dad. I knew why. Citronella had spent the previous day's column describing how she'd sacked the nanny for stealing a gold ring of hers, an accusation that, without accompanying proof, struck me as defamatory. Claudia, Citronella had added with an odd kind of pride, had been the fifth nanny she'd sacked in a year.

'Good afternoon, hel-lo . . .' we all sang to the piano.
'Hip, hip, hip hooray!
We've come to school to work and play
and be happy all the DAY!'

'Anna?' The headmistress, Mrs Avis, approached me as I was about to leave the building. 'Could I have a word?'

'Oh. Yes. Of course.' I followed her down the brightly painted corridor to her office, my heart instinctively sinking.

'We're a little concerned about Milly,' she began as she motioned for me to sit down. 'Her speech is not all it should be. I don't know how you feel, but . . .'

'I feel it could be better,' I agreed, glancing at the huge painted rainbow on the wall.

'Milly's comprehension is fine,' I heard Mrs Avis say. 'But she's two and three-quarters so she should be able to form fairly coherent little sentences by now.'

'I know.' I looked out of the window at the colourful climbing frame with its red plastic slide. 'But I suppose children develop at different rates.'

'They do . . .' Mrs Avis steepled her fingers. 'But the thing that's bothering us is that Milly's using quite a bit of Spanish.'

'Oh dear. Does she do that here too?' Mrs Avis nodded. I sighed. 'She's picked it up from our Colombian au pair.'

'Doesn't she speak English?'

'Not much. She goes to language school for three hours every morning but seems to be a very slow learner.'

'So she speaks Spanish to Milly?'

'All the time. I have mentioned it.' I sighed. 'But I'll discuss it with her again – with Milly as interpreter. Anyway –' I stood up, relieved that the problem wasn't more serious – 'I'm glad you told me.'

Mrs Avis was still sitting down. 'But I'm afraid that's not all. I'm sorry to say that there have been a couple of biting incidents lately involving Milly.'

I sank back on to the chair. 'Milly bit someone? But she's *never* done that. She's very sweet-natured.'

'Well – let me rephrase that: she tried to bite one of the other children – twice, actually – but was stopped.'

'Who was it?' I asked.

'I can't say, because with biting or hitting our policy is not to mention any names, but to deal with it ourselves.'

'I see. Well, at least nothing really happened, as it turned out.'

'No. But the reason why I wanted to talk to you is because I have wondered whether Milly's current confusion over language is contributing to a degree of frustration which might be leading her to indulge in this sort of behaviour.'

'Maybe,' I said. 'It's possible.' Or maybe it's because she has an absentee father, I speculated miserably, and is destined for delinquency.

'I just felt that you should know.'

'Thank you.' I stood up. 'I'll do what I can to make sure that it stops.'

'It's a big problem,' I said to Dad a couple of days later. Luisa had gone swimming – I'd got her membership of my health club because they had a half-price offer on for Easter – Milly was in bed, and Dad and I were having supper. He comes round

144

two or three times a week at the moment. I don't mind, as he's lonely, he's still adjusting to London and I worry that he doesn't eat properly when he's on his own. 'Milly's never tried to bite *me*,' I went on as I helped him to some potatoes. He still hadn't had a haircut I noticed. It was well past his collar.

'Would you consider getting a new au pair?' Dad asked. I tried to imagine the house without Luisa's warm presence.

'Not unless I have to.' I gave the French dressing a shake. 'I like Luisa and Milly adores her. And she's very careful about Milly's egg allergy – so I trust her on that front. But she's going to have to learn to speak English,' I went on crossly. 'That's why she's here after all.'

'I've only ever heard her speaking Spanish,' Dad said. 'I've been amazed at how much of it Milly seems to understand.'

'So have I, but little children soak it up at that age. I hope it's good Spanish she's picking up,' I added anxiously. 'With a nice accent and everything. But what Luisa's doing at her language school I really don't know.'

'You need to find out,' Dad said as I poured him a glass of burgundy.

'I've been meaning to ring her teacher but he's only there in the mornings and I don't have his number.'

'Can't the school get it for you?'

'They don't give them out. Anyway, they've broken up for Easter until the end of next week.'

'I know how you could check what she's been doing.'

'How?'

'Easy. Just look in her exercise books.'

I helped myself to some salad. 'I suppose so . . . But she keeps them in her room and I don't like to snoop.'

'How long has she been with you, Anna?'

'Two and a half months,' I replied dismally. 'She arrived in late January.'

Dad flicked out his napkin. 'Then I think you have the right to . . . investigate. Firstly, you've paid for her course and

145

secondly, her failure to speak English is causing Milly behavioural and learning problems.'

Put like that, I was convinced. So on Good Friday, when Luisa was going to see a film with a friend, I waved her goodbye, bundled Milly off to bed, then, feeling treacherous, sped up to the third floor.

Luisa's bedroom door was shut. I gently turned the handle and pushed it open. The room was immaculately tidy – I was impressed. The bed was made, with the bedspread pulled up and the cushions arranged neatly on top. The floor was clear, apart from her guitar, which was leaning in the corner, and a pile of sheet music. I flicked through it. She'd been learning classic ballads by Nanci Griffith, Joan Armatrading, and Don McLean.

I advanced into the room, my heart pounding, one ear alert for Luisa's unexpected return. I quickly scanned the room for her blue book bag, but couldn't see it. She was so tidy that she'd left nothing out. All there was was a photo of her parents standing outside their small farmhouse in Bogotá, her hairbrush and a couple of books. On top of the wardrobe was the little blue suitcase she'd arrived with. I opened the wardrobe door. I looked among her shoes for the bag but it wasn't there, then I lifted my eyes. To my surprise the wardrobe was quite full – she must have bought some new clothes; and now I thought about it I realised that she had been looking smarter of late. There were a couple of silk shirts, a Chanel-type jacket, a navy pea-coat, which was infinitely nicer than her puffa jacket, and a glamorous-looking evening dress. I fingered the red velvet – then looked at the label: Joseph.

'How could she afford that?' I heard myself say.

I shut the wardrobe door and continued my search. I peered under the bed, but could see only her slippers. I looked under the dressing table, but her book bag wasn't there. Now I went to the chest of drawers. On top of it was the small TV, in the top drawer was just her underwear, neatly folded, then in the one below her T-shirts and trousers, and a couple of jumpers. I opened the bottom drawer and there it was – her blue rucksack. I pulled it out and as I examined its contents my heart sank. The large English textbook had hardly been opened and the two exercise books were blank, except for three or four pages of simple vocab.

'She's done nothing,' I breathed through clenched teeth. And I was just about to put the bag back, wondering how to confront her about the issue without letting on that I'd snooped, when something caught my eye – a gold biscuit tin, which had been pushed to the back of the drawer. Fury with Luisa overcame any finer feelings about respecting her privacy. I prised off the lid.

'Good *God* . . .'

Inside was a thick wad of fifty-pound notes. I did a rough count – there were about eighty of them – four thousand pounds. I put the lid back on it, my head spinning. So that explained the new clothes and the presents she'd bought for Milly. But where could she have got so much cash?

Suddenly I heard Milly cry. Heart pounding, I put the tin back where I'd found it, shut the bedroom door and ran downstairs.

'What's the matter?' I panted.

'Want poo,' she whimpered.

'Don't worry, darling.' I went to lift her out.

'No,' she protested. 'Want *Pu*.'

'I don't understand, sweetie.'

'Winnie *el Pu*! Want *music*!' Milly pointed to the end of her cot, strapped to which, I now saw, was a brand-new 'Winnie the Pooh' musical *son et lumière* box.

'Did Luisa give you this?' I asked wearily.

'*Sí*, Mummy.'

'Oh. Well . . .'

'*Música, Momia*! NOW!'

'OK . . . OK. Here we go.' I wound it up, settled Milly

147

down again, then tiptoed out as the music tinkled forth and the light box cast moving shadows on to the ceiling of Tigger, Piglet and Pooh with his pot of honey.

'Nighty night, darling,' I called out softly.

'Buenas noches, Mamaíta!' She said.

SEVEN

'Does she have a part-time job?' Cassie asked as we sat in her tiny, chintzy sitting room in Chelsea the following Tuesday evening. I'd dropped in on my way back from The Boltons to ask her advice: Cassie may lack judgement, but she's far worldlier than I am and knows the casual employment market better. 'Does she work in a bar, for instance?'

'No.'

'Would she tell you if she did?'

'She'd have no reason to conceal it.'

'She might think you'd worry that she'd be too tired to help you.'

'True, but even if she didn't tell me I'd know because she'd come back very late, reeking of booze and smoke.'

'But she must be doing *something* because she goes to college in the mornings, right.'

'Yes. Every weekday morning.' I felt a stab of annoyance that I'd paid all her fees when she had more cash than I did. I felt even more irritated about the health club, though to be fair to Luisa, she had vigorously resisted my offer to pay the subscription.

Cassie picked up her glass of champagne – it's the only thing she drinks. 'Then she looks after Milly until . . . ?'

149

'Five thirty.'

'Which just leaves nights and weekends.' She sipped her wine, then narrowed her eyes. 'Do you think she's on the game?'

I stared at her. 'No – she's not . . . like that.'

'Having met her, I'd tend to agree, but' – she raised a suggestive eyebrow – 'still waters and all that.'

'But Luisa doesn't go out a lot in the evenings; sometimes she meets a friend, but she's often at home just playing the guitar or watching her TV. I assumed she couldn't afford to go out much.'

Cassie picked up her knitting – a wedge of bubblegum-pink yarn hung off one needle. 'Bank heist?' she suggested as she looped the wool round her forefinger.

'No. And I'm sure she hasn't been mugging old ladies either – or shoplifting. Perhaps she's had a lottery win – does that pay out in cash?'

Cassie shook her head. 'Cheque. I once won five hundred pounds so I know.' She turned the needles round and began a new row. 'Maybe she's been gambling. When I was a croupier there was a nanny who made eight thousand pounds in one night from three games of blackjack with an initial stake of ten pounds.'

'I can't imagine Luisa in a casino. But she had four thousand pounds left,' I went on. 'And she must have spent at least a thousand, with the new clothes she's bought and her mobile phone bill and other things – so that's five thousand she had to start with. How could she have saved five grand in just three months on seventy pounds a week au pair's pocket money?'

'She couldn't have done. Knit one, purl one . . .' Cassie looked up. 'So, as I say, it's got to be drugs. Blast – I've dropped a stitch . . . she's from Colombia after all. What do her parents do?'

'They're . . . farmers,' I said. 'Oh.'

'That's it then – she's selling cocaine. I don't know why you hadn't thought of that.'

'Because she doesn't seem . . . the type.'

Cassie shook her head. 'It's not always easy to tell. Plus she lived in Marbella, didn't she?'

'Yes. With her last family.'

'Well, there's a lot of it over there.' I suddenly remembered the husband's remark about Luisa hoping for 'better opportunities' in London. Cassie frowned at the knitting. 'Damn – I've got the tension wrong. I'd have another little snoop if I were you.'

When I got back I asked Luisa to take Milly to the park, then I ran upstairs to her room, this time without a shred of guilt. Because if Luisa *were* selling drugs and were caught, and it somehow got into the papers, the negative publicity could ruin my business. I imagined the headlines – the tabloids would milk the GMTV connection, however slight – BREAK-FAST TELLY GARDENER IN COKE BUST! More important, if Milly were to find any and swallow them . . . I shuddered.

I quickly went through Luisa's drawers again. I opened the gold tin and saw that she'd made another £300 in just the last few days. Then I began searching for little packets of white powder. I opened the wardrobe, and checked in her pockets and shoes. I searched her guitar case and even inside her guitar, and in her CDs, and inspected her books in case any were fake. I looked in her suitcase, her jewellery box and ran my hands along the top of the pelmet, but all this produced was a little blizzard of dust.

Perhaps there was an innocent explanation? I wondered, as I pushed on the door of Head Girls, my local hairdresser, two days later. My nose wrinkled at the ammoniac aroma of bleach. Perhaps Luisa's parents, knowing that she was going to be in Europe for at least two years, had given her the cash as an emergency float. Or perhaps it was money she'd saved from her last job. In which case why, when we had discussed

151

the costs of her language course, had she given me the firm impression that she was broke? No, she'd obviously accumulated this money recently. But how?

I couldn't possibly ask her outright as she might leave, then I'd have no help – plus I didn't want her to go unless it was unavoidable. Nor was I going to accuse her of anything without proof – that would make me no better than Citronella. If Milly were a year younger, I could pretend that she'd wandered into Luisa's room and found it, but at nearly three, Milly was likely to deny that she'd done any such thing.

As I sat in the waiting area, listening to the buzz of the dryers, I picked up a copy of *I Say!* magazine and read the True Life Confessions with thrilled disgust. 'My Gran Stole My Man!'; 'My Husband Swapped Me for a Porsche!'; 'My Mum's Secret Life!'. I'm afraid I lap up such stories when I get the chance, which is usually only at the hairdresser's. I shuddered. 'My Boyfriend Was Eaten by a Shark!'

'Hi, Anna,' said Sandra. 'I haven't seen you for so long I thought you'd defected to another salon.'

'I'd never do that,' I said as I put down the magazine. 'I've just been too busy to come.'

'That's good to hear.' She put her head on one side as she assessed me. 'But you need a good trim, poppet.'

'I need a vigorous prune. Could you layer it?'

'Sure.' She weighed the hair in her hands. 'It'll give it more body.'

'That's just what it needs – it's positively anorexic.'

'It's very fine,' she corrected me as she wrapped me in a shiny black gown. 'So how've you been?' she asked as she led me past the other clients to the row of white basins.

'I've been OK, thanks. In fact, good.'

'The business is going well then?' I put my head back as she began washing my hair. 'You were great on GMTV by the way. Now I know where to stick my polyanthus!' She giggled. 'Will you be on it again?'

'Yes – in June.' I enjoyed the soothing flood of warm water on my hairline. 'They've asked me to do it every three months.'

'So how did that come about?'

'The producer phoned my old tutor for some recommendations and he kindly suggested me.'

Sandra began to work the shampoo into my scalp and I sighed with relief as my stress flooded away beneath her strong fingertips.

'So you're busy, then.'

'I am. I've got a big project on in The Boltons.'

'Very fancy . . .'

'Then I've got two small courtyard gardens to do as well.'

'Final rinse now. And how's Milly?' she asked as we walked over to the mirror.

'She's good, thanks.' I rubbed a drip of water out of my ear. 'She's just started at Sweet Peas.'

'And what about you?' Sandra asked as she combed my wet hair. 'Have you met anyone yet?' I looked into the mirror and Sandra wagged the comb at me in an admonitory manner. 'Baby or not, you've a right to a life.' Sandra, having been a single mother to her daughter Lydia, now sixteen, likes to give me the benefit of her experience as a lone parent.

'Well . . .' I hesitated for a moment, because I know that Sandra can be a gossip. On the other hand I had nothing to hide. Why shouldn't I tell her about Patrick? I reasoned. I felt myself slip into confessional mode. 'There *is* someone, actually.' I looked into the mirror. 'In fact, I've got a date tonight.'

Sandra smiled at me. 'Good.' She pulled up a section of hair, flipped the ends over the comb, then snipped across them with the tips of her scissors. 'So tell me about him.'

'Well,' I began as one of the trainees brought me a cup of coffee. 'He's polite, decent, handsome and enterprising.'

'Sounds promising.'

153

'I haven't known him that long but I like him,' I said happily.

'I'm delighted,' Sandra said as the ducktails of damp hair fell to the floor. 'So how did you meet him?' I told her about the episode with Milly's shoe. 'Very romantic,' she said approvingly. Then I told her what had happened at the church fundraiser. 'Even more romantic,' she said. 'It was fate.'

'Er, no,' I said, giggling. 'Because I then discovered that he'd manipulated fate by buying nearly all the tickets.'

'Wow! Well, he's clearly smitten – and he must be well off. What does he do?'

'Not that much at the moment – he sold his Internet company last year and is looking for a new project. He loves gardening, though,' I went on. 'So that's something we have in common. Plus he keeps bees.'

Sandra stopped cutting. 'Bees?' she echoed, looking at me in the mirror.

'Yes – he's got three hives in his garden.'

'And where does he live?'

'In St Peter's Square.'

'And he lived in Brook Green before that? In Caithness Road?'

'How do you know?' I looked at her, but this time she didn't meet my gaze.

'You're talking about Patrick Gilchrist,' she said as she carried on snipping.

'Yes,' I said. 'I am. Do you know him?'

'Not . . . well.' She combed up another section of hair. 'But I knew his ex.'

'Oh.' I wished I'd followed my instincts and kept quiet. 'How?'

'She was a customer of mine for the four years that she was with him. I still get the occasional e-mail from her. She's nice.'

'Really? To be honest I don't think it's nice to take your

154

child to live in New Zealand when the father of your child lives in the UK.'

'Well . . . it doesn't look good,' Sandra agreed. 'But then from her point of view,' she murmured. 'She had her . . . reasons . . . I don't know . . .' Her voice trailed away. 'It's none of my business.'

'Anyway,' I said, trying to wrest the conversation back to a more comfortable footing. 'I haven't known Patrick that long, but he's very attractive.'

'Oh yes,' she interrupted. 'And he's certainly charming.'

'And he's nice,' I said conclusively. 'I have a good feeling about him.'

'Could you put your head up, please?' Sandra said.

'Can you come a bit earlier so that I can show you the bees?' Patrick asked me over the phone as I walked back home. 'Say at half past five?'

'OK. I don't think it'll be a problem.'

'Bring your wellies and wear trousers, preferably in a light colour, a long-sleeved top, ditto – and whatever you do, don't wear perfume, hairspray, wool, or chew garlic. Got that?'

'Got it,' I said, disappointed not to be able to wear the slinky cashmere dress I'd had in mind. Plus I'd have to wash my hair again, because of the spray.

As I opened the front door, I heard singing.

'*Las ruedas del autobús giran i giran, giran i giran, giran i giran . . .*' Luisa and Milly were oblivious to me as I stood in the kitchen doorway. '*Las ruedas del autobús giran i giran – TODO el DÍA!! Los bebés del autobús . . .*'

'LUISA!' I yelled. They stopped singing, Milly turned round and ran up to me for a kiss.

'Hi, my little girlie! I'll be leaving at five,' I told Luisa as I put on the kettle. 'But I'll be back by ten.'

'Iss fine.'

'You look nice,' I added, with an admiring glance at her oyster-pink silk shirt. 'Is it new?'

Luisa seemed to blush. 'Yes.'

I got the milk out of the fridge. 'By the way, Luisa, I did ask you not to give Milly any more presents – the music box is lovely, but it must have cost at least twenty pounds.'

'Oh, but Milly – she see it in shop – she like it bery much. I gib it her for Easter.'

'But you really mustn't buy her things. In any case I'm sure you don't have enough money,' I added disingenuously. 'Not on seventy pounds a week.'

Luisa blushed again. 'Iss . . . OK, Anna.'

'Well, I'd like to pay you for it,' I said. 'I don't feel that it's right.'

'No, you *no* pay,' Luisa insisted. 'I *lob* Milly.' Her big brown eyes were suddenly shining. 'And it make Milly happy so *my* happy.'

'Well,' I sighed. 'That's very kind of you, but please don't buy her anything else. And if you're ever short of money I'll try and help you, OK?'

'Oh . . . but I hab enough. You bery kind at me, Anna,' she added, guiltily I thought, as I went upstairs for my shower.

When I arrived at Patrick's house he kissed me on the cheek and I felt a sudden charge at his touch. The last man I'd slept with had been Xan. In the intervening years I'd been too protective of Milly, too busy and too sad about Xan to forge a new relationship. But now, like Patrick's wintering bees, I felt ready to emerge.

'I've been inspecting the hives this afternoon,' he said as he showed me in. 'I've left the third one until now as I thought you might find it interesting to see them.'

'I would,' I said anxiously. 'As long as they don't sting me.'

'I can honestly say that not a single visitor, friend, or neighbour has ever been stung by one of my bees.'

'Have you?' I asked as we went into the kitchen.

156

'Of course – it happens maybe three or four times a year, but usually as a result of my own carelessness. Now we'll need to get togged up,' he said as he opened the back door.

On the terrace he put on some white overalls and a pair of rubber gloves into which he tucked his cuffs, then he stepped into his gumboots. 'You need to have everything well inside,' he explained, 'so they can't get into your clothing.' I gave an involuntary shudder at the thought. 'Now,' he said as I tucked my white trousers inside my green wellies and stuffed my cotton jumper into the waistband. 'I've got this half-suit for you. Here . . .' I put it on, then he passed me the beekeeper's hat. As I looked at him through the veil, I felt like a bride. He zipped it all the way round the shoulders, tucked my sleeves into my gloves, then looked at me appraisingly, turning me round to check that everything was covered. 'Good . . . you're bee-proof.' Now he put on his own hat, zipped it up, then picked up his toolbox and smoker. 'Let's go. If a bee does land on you, don't swat at it – it's only investigating.'

'What do you actually do with the hives?' I asked as we walked to the end of the garden. The *Magnolia grandiflora* was in full, waxy, pink flower, along with the *Kerria japonica* with its exuberant sprays of apricot pom-poms. The apple trees were creamy with blossom.

'At this time of year it's basic hygiene and spring cleaning – brushing out any dead bees and checking for mites or disease. I also give them a spray of sugar syrup to get them going after the winter as their store of honey has almost gone.'

He stopped by a wooden trestle table, where he stuffed the smoker with shredded paper and coarse string, then put a match to it. 'Now,' he said as the air filled with an acrid aroma. 'It's best if you sit on the bench while I open up the hives – I'll call you over when there's something to see.'

As I retreated, Patrick puffed the smoker into the entrance.
'What does that do?'

157

'It calms them because it makes them think that there's a fire somewhere, which makes them prepare to leave – but first they go and eat some honey to give them energy.'

'How odd. If I thought there was a fire in the vicinity, I don't think I'd stop to make myself a sandwich.'

'Well, bees move in mysterious ways.' Patrick now lifted off the top of the hive – it seemed to require some effort – then, with a flat steel tool, he removed the inner wooden tray. 'These trays are called supers,' he said. 'Inside them are a number of frames' – he gently prised one out with a cracking sound – 'which is where the honey's made. How are you doing over there?'

'OK,' I said anxiously. The air was vibrant with angry buzzing. 'But you've got a swarm of bees round your head.' It looked like a black halo.

'Oh – they're just a bit pissed off because I've disturbed them. Cut it out, ladies!' he said, as they flew at his veil like tiny Spitfires. 'It's only me, girls!'

'Are they female, then?'

'Yes. The drones – they're the males – make up only ten per cent of the hive and their sole job is to mate with the queen. After they've done that they're kicked out of the hive, with their wings pulled off. I know how they feel,' he added with mock bitterness.

A few bees began to fly close to my head. 'Oooooh,' I moaned as they dive-bombed my veil. 'Uuhhhh.' More and more seemed to have appeared, flying straight at me, bombarding me, buzzing angrily in my ear, crawling over my sleeves, making my flesh creep. I tried to shake them off. 'Oh God . . .' I whimpered, my pulse racing. I flapped my hand at them, but back they came. I couldn't bear it. I stood up and walked away.

'Keep STILL!' Patrick yelled. 'DON'T walk about like that! Sorry,' he added. 'I . . . didn't mean . . . to shout. But please don't make any sudden moves or they might sting you through the veil.' I decided that beekeeping wasn't for me. 'They're simply curious,' he added, soothingly now, as I tentatively sat down again, my heart still beating wildly. 'They want to know all about you – just like I do.'

I began to feel calmer. The bees, perhaps sensing this, seemed to retreat.

'Don't your neighbours mind you keeping bees next door to them?' I asked after a few moments.

'It's been fine,' he said. 'The main thing is to place the hives next to a fence or a tree so that they're forced to fly straight up when they leave. It's also important to give them a water supply' – he nodded at the pond – 'so that they don't go looking for it in other gardens. Plus I don't open the hives at weekends and I give my neighbours honey – that always goes down well on the PR front.'

'Can I confess something?'

'Yes – as long as it's not that you're seeing someone.'

'No.' I smiled. 'I'm not. But . . . the thing is I don't . . . really . . . like honey.'

He turned and looked at me. 'Why not? It's the food of the gods!'

'Because . . . I just don't. Sorry. I never have.'

'Oh dear – you might like my honey, though, if I'm not flattering myself. You could come and help me extract it later in the summer. Now, come and have a look.' I hung back for a moment. 'Come on,' he added coaxingly. 'They won't hurt you.'

I stepped forward and peered nervously into the hive. Several hundred bees crawled over a large honeycomb, buzzing loudly.

'*Apis melifera melifera*,' Patrick said. 'At home. These are the workers,' he explained. 'They flog themselves to death in three weeks, poor little things, collecting nectar from dawn to dusk.'

'How far do they go?'

159

'About three miles. Could you puff the smoker for me? They visit six hundred flowers a day. It takes a million flowers to make just one pot of honey. Now, look at those ones down there.'

I peered at the front of the hive where three or four bees were standing at the entrance, their abdomens raised, beating the air with their wings.

'What are they doing? Mooning?'

'They're sending out a scent, fanning it on to the air, to tell the other bees to rush back and help them guard the hive.'

'Don't bees dance?'

'Yes – they do a waggle dance – a shivering side-to-side motion – and the number of times it's repeated, its direction and the sound the bee makes all communicate precisely where the pollen is.'

'How brilliant.'

'Bees are. Brilliant and industrious. An example to us all.'

Now Patrick sprayed the frame with sugar syrup, slid it back into the super, then pulled out the next one. 'Ah. There she is,' he said happily. 'HM The Queen. Don't worry – you don't have to curtsy.' I peered at her. She was a good two inches long – and surrounded by attendants. 'Good,' Patrick murmured. 'She's fine. She's survived the winter and has started laying.' He lifted the frame up to the light. 'Can you see the tiny egg in each cell? At the moment she lays about two hundred a day, but by June it'll be two thousand a day.'

'How many bees will there be then?'

'About fifty thousand, up from ten thousand or so now. That's when bee activity is at its height because the nectar flow has reached its peak.'

'How many queens are there?'

'Just one in each hive. This one's Victoria – Beckham obviously – and the two others are Elizabeth –'

'Hurley?'

'Yes. And Cleopatra. They all have clipped wings so that

they don't leave the hive, which would make the bees swarm.'

'What's the appeal of beekeeping?' I asked as we walked back to the house twenty minutes later. 'Is it the thrill of harvesting your own honey?'

'No – because you only do that once a year. I think it's because it's all about working with Nature – accepting that here's something you can't control . . .'

'But . . . why would you want to?'

'What I mean is, you just have to give yourself up to Nature and . . . tune in to it. When it rains, for example, you know that the bees will come rushing back to the hive, because they hate the wet. When there's a storm approaching you hear a roar from the hives as the bees flap their wings because they're annoyed.'

'And when they're happy?'

'You just hear a nice hum. I love that gentle hum of contented bees,' he went on, as he took off his hat and overalls. 'Beekeeping's better than any therapy – it's a modern-day yoga. Whenever I'm working with them my stress just evaporates. I tell them everything,' he added as he unzipped my veil.

'Really?'

'Yes, today, for example, I told them that you were coming over.'

'What was the buzz?'

'They were delighted – especially when I said that you're a gardener. Anyway – enough hive talking – let's get this off you.' He lifted off my hat, the veil lightly brushing my skin. Then he unzipped my jacket. And as I was still standing there, close to him, he put out his hand and stroked my face. I felt a sudden charge of electricity. 'Let's have a glass of champagne . . .'

'And what's the appeal of designing gardens?' Patrick asked me as we sat at his kitchen table an hour later in the candle-light. 'The fact that gardening's become sexy? The new rock 'n' roll?'

161

'No.' I spooned up the last of my chocolate mousse. 'It's because it involves art, and architecture and horticulture and colour – and knowledge of light and soil. I love it because no two days are the same, and because I'm often outside, and because I'm designing something that will, I hope, give pleasure for years to come.'

'That must be rewarding.'

'It is. The idea that I'm able to turn some scruffy back-yard into, say, a little piece of Italy, as I've been asked to do recently in Hampstead – that's a great feeling: I love the *transformation* of garden design – and the fact that I'm making something that's going to endure.'

'The plants don't,' he pointed out as he filled the kettle.

'That's true – they've got a limited life. But the skeleton of a garden – the paths and walls and paving – will last for decades. And that's what I didn't have when I was in the City – the sense that I was doing anything that mattered, let alone that I was creating anything that would last. And with hedge funds – well, you know how it works: these people are trading in shares they don't actually own – just hedging their bets as to whether the market will rise or fall, then taking their twenty per cent cut of the huge profits. I couldn't believe they were being paid so much for working with something that doesn't even exist. I knew I had to get out and do something . . . worthwhile.'

'And now you are – with considerable success.' I thought of the garden in The Boltons – it was shaping up well. 'Now . . . would you like some mint tea?'

I shook my head. 'I ought to get back.'

'I hope I see you again,' he said as he helped me on with my coat.

I picked up my bag. 'I hope you see me again too,' I said.

'Really?'

'Yes.' I smiled at him. 'Really.'

He was staring at me. 'In that case, do you mind if I kiss you?'

162

My heart did a swallow dive. 'No. I mean – yes, I mean . . .
I don't . . . mind, actually . . . I . . .'

But Patrick's lips were already on mine. As he held me, I
enjoyed the solid, sexy feeling of his strong physique against
my own slight one, and the feel of his arms encircling me
like a hoop.

Driving home, my body humming with desire, I thought
of Xan. He'd moved on from me a long time ago and now
the moment had come, at last, for me to move on from him.
Sandra was right: I *did* have a right to a life, and a right to
try and find love – or at the very least a good partner, who'd
be a father figure to Milly. She needed that and Xan could
hardly object. For nearly four years I'd led a Cinderella existence, waiting quietly in the shadows; maybe it was now time
for me to go to the ball.

EIGHT

'That's balls,' Jamie said three weeks later as we stood in the mud and rain in the Edwardses' garden. 'You're out by a good six centimetres.'

'I'm not.' I felt a drop of water trickle down my neck. 'I measured it exactly.'

'I don't think you did, sweetheart.'

I showed him the site plan again. 'I don't know why we always have to have this argument, Jamie.'

'Because we have lots of arguments,' he said tetchily. Normally good-natured Jamie had been in a difficult, crotchety mood all day.

'We do wrangle over things,' I said, 'that's the nature of our professional relationship – but we always work it out, so let's just look at it again.' I took out the tape measure. 'Grab the other end, will you?'

'I tell you it won't work,' Jamie insisted. He pointed at the drawings. 'And we can't afford to get this wrong – not when the stone's a hundred and twenty pounds a square metre.'

'That's true.' I looked around the site. In the first two months the original hard landscaping had been removed and the ground levelled – four tons of earth had been carefully carried out of the garden. The electrician had put in the cables

164

for the lighting, a specialist plumber had installed the irrigation system and now the slabs of creamy limestone, which were lying under a tarpaulin, were due to be laid the next day.

'It's eight centimetres out,' Jamie insisted as we measured the space again. 'So the pointing gap between each slab will be too wide.'

'It won't, I tell you.'

'And I don't want to do any patching up with offcuts – people would say I was a crap builder.'

'We won't do that, but look, Jamie.' I glanced at my watch. 'The Edwards' will be home soon. They won't want to find us bickering in their garden – and I have to get back for Milly, so let's call it a day and sleep on it.'

'OK.' He sighed. 'Whatever you say.' He began to tidy the site, putting the tools in the temporary shed, covering the cement mixer with thick blue plastic sheeting and winding the electric cables back on to their spools.

'Could you give me a lift home?' I asked him as the ' housekeeper showed us out. 'My car's been playing up – it's at the garage.'

'Sure I will.'

'Are you OK, Jamie?' I asked as I sat in the passenger seat of his old pick-up truck a few minutes later.

'I'm fine,' he replied wearily. 'Never been better.' As he pulled up at a red light he ran his hand through his wet hair. 'I'm feeling just . . . wonderful.'

I stared at his profile. 'No you're not.'

We listened to the regular beat of the windscreen wipers as they thrashed to and fro. 'No.' He sighed. 'You're right – I'm not. I can't eat. I can't think . . . I can't sleep. I'm sorry I lost it a bit today, but I was up all night . . .' He lowered his forehead on to the wheel and closed his eyes for a moment.

'What's happened, Jamie?' He didn't reply. Then, to my dismay, I saw his mouth quiver. 'You can talk to me,' I added gently. 'We're not just business partners, we're friends. And if you're feeling down I'd like to try and help.'

He gripped the steering wheel tighter, lifted his head and stared through the windscreen.

'So . . . what is it?'

The light went green and he released the handbrake. 'I've got problems,' he said quietly as we moved forward.

'What sort of problems?' I asked, though I knew.

'With Thea.' His face was flushed with emotion.

'Because she's away so much?' He nodded bleakly.

I reflected on the fact that although I'd now known Jamie for two and a half years I'd only met Thea three or four times. On each occasion I'd found her friendly, but had felt that hers was the polished charm of the practised PR.

'Couldn't she get a job that would keep her in London a bit more?'

He changed up a gear. 'I've been asking her to, but she won't. In a way, I can understand why. She's only twenty-seven – she's ambitious; she loves travelling. She's riding the crest of a wave at work – and making good money – but it's no good for *us*.' I thought of the little space he'd left clear in his garden for a slide or a swing. 'I'd love a family,' he went on. 'I want to feel that I'm working for a reason. We've been married four years now. I'm just . . . *jack* of it.'

'Has she changed her mind about having kids?'

'No. Or at least she says she hasn't,' Jamie added as he turned into Havelock Road. 'But she's ruled it out for the time being. Before our wedding she said she hoped to get pregnant within eighteen months – but then she got this job at The Pitch agency and that changed everything. Anyway . . . I'm a bit distracted at the moment, to put it mildly.' He drew up outside my house.

'Will you come in and have a beer?' I asked as the engine ticked over.

'I don't know . . .'

'You could park in my space here – come in, Jamie. Please. I don't want to leave you like this.'

'OK.' He sighed as he turned off the engine. 'It's not as though there's anyone at home – and it would be nice to see Milly – I haven't seen her for a couple of weeks.'

As I put the key in the lock, I heard Milly running down the hall. 'Mum!' I gathered her up in my arms and kissed her. 'Hi, poppet! Thanks, Luisa,' I added, 'I'll take over now.'

'I go to swim, Anna.'

'Enjoy yourself then.' I wondered if that really was where she was going. 'Look, Milly,' I said, 'here's Jamie.' Milly smiled at him, then looked away, suddenly shy. 'He might read you a story.'

'Of course I'll read you a story, Princess.' He unlaced his muddy Timberlands. 'Let's look in your book box, shall we?'

I put Milly down and she ran into the sitting room. 'Caterpinnar!' she shouted. 'Want Caterpinnar, Jamie!'

As I opened the fridge I heard Jamie begin to read her *The Very Hungry Caterpillar* and, as usual, Milly wanted to race through it as quickly as possible, turning over the pages in rapid succession.

'On Saturday he ate . . . *one* piece of cake,' I heard Jamie say.

'. . . One pickle . . . one s'lami . . . one lollipop,' I heard Milly anticipate excitedly as she flicked over the pages. '. . . Hungry *any* more . . . bee-*you*-tiful *butterfly* . . . the END!' she shouted triumphantly.

'She always does that,' Jamie called out.

'I know,' I said as I opened two bottles of Stella. 'It's like watching the Reduced Shakespeare Company. She gallops through the story at ninety miles an hour.'

'Why do you think she does it?'

'Because she just loves shouting out "The End"! Don't you, poppet?'

'Let's read something else,' I heard Jamie say.

167

'Gruffano!' she yelled.

'*The Gruffalo*? Ah . . . here it is . . . OK? Are you ready, Miss Milly?'

'I ready.'

'Right . . . A mouse took a stroll through a deep, dark wood . . . a fox –'

'. . . Undergwound house,' I heard Milly say, '. . . knobbly knees . . . owl I scream . . . roasted fox . . . logpile house . . . Gruffano cwumble . . . The END! Want DBD, Mum!'

'Could you put on a DVD for Milly?' I asked Jamie. 'She'll choose one.'

'*Peter Rabbit*,' I heard her say. 'Want *Peter Rabbit*!'

I came in with the tray and Milly settled herself in her tiny yellow armchair as she watched the DVD, occasionally clapping her hand to her mouth at the drama of Peter's close shave with Mr McGregor, then turning to us with round, shocked eyes.

'Couldn't you go with Thea on these trips sometimes?' I said to Jamie as I handed him his beer.

He shook his head. 'I'm too busy. Plus it would look a bit pathetic, wouldn't it? As though I didn't trust her.'

'But you do?'

There was a slight pause. 'I always have done,' he replied carefully. He fiddled with his glass. 'But now I'm not so sure.' An uneasy feeling settled on my stomach. 'A couple of days ago I found something. I'm trying not to overreact here, but . . .' He shrugged. 'It doesn't look good.'

'Tell me.'

'Well . . .' He swallowed. 'Over the last couple of months Thea's been to South Africa three times – and she's going again in ten days. And I had some things to wash so I pulled everything out of the laundry basket and at the bottom was one of Thea's dresses. And I was just about to put it in the washing machine when I felt something in one of the pockets – a business card.' He paused. 'It was from this guy, Percy du Plessis.

168

She'd never mentioned him, but the card said that he's vice-chairman of the South African Tennis Federation. But on the back of the card he'd written that he "couldn't wait" to see her again, and was "really looking forward" to their "hot date" in May, and how he was going to give her "a damn good time", dot dot dot . . . it was incredibly suggestive.'

'Oh. Well . . .'

'You don't have to say anything consoling,' Jamie croaked. He sipped his beer. 'It's obvious what's going on.' It certainly didn't sound promising. 'But then there are so many temptations for Thea when she's abroad. She stays in five star hotels; she's invited to all these parties and receptions; she meets attractive, powerful men who probably want her – she's gorgeous after all.'

'And how is she towards you when she's at home?'

'Usually she's . . . fine,' he replied. 'She's very happy to see me again. But this last month or so she's seemed remote, so I'd begun to feel that something might be going on. Then I found this card and . . . well . . .' He shrugged. 'It obviously *is*.' His head sank into his hands. I saw Milly shoot him a perplexed but compassionate look. Then she came over to him and patted his leg, looking at him enquiringly.

'Thank you, sweetheart.' He stroked her head.

'But this guy, Percy what's-is-name, may fancy *her*,' I went on as I lifted Milly on to my lap, 'but you have no proof that she reciprocates, do you?'

'No.' He sighed. 'I don't.' He picked up Milly's Megasketch board and drew a cartoon of a cat on it, which Milly then wiped off with the lever. 'But you get a feeling about things,' Jamie went on. 'And my gut feeling about Thea is that she's changed recently, and this could well be why.' He now wrote 'Thea & Jamie' on the slate in large, curly letters. Then he pulled down the lever, released it and their names were slowly erased with a mechanical wheeze. 'If she had been unfaithful I could never get over it,' he added quietly.

169

'Don't assume anything,' I advised him. 'Just talk to her. When she's back from this trip, wait till she's recovered, then calmly show her the card and tell her how you felt when you found it. Give her an opportunity to explain it, otherwise your suspicions, which may be wrong, could destroy your relationship.'

'That's true. Thanks, Anna.' He sighed once more. 'Anyway, I'd better get back. I've lots to do. 'Bye, little Princess.' Milly put up her arms for a hug. 'And how are things going with Prince Charming?' he asked me as he put his boots back on. I'd told Jamie that I'd met Patrick again.

'It's going fine . . .' I said. 'We're still getting to know each other – I'm not going to rush things but I do . . . like him.'

'So he's a nice guy?'

'He seems to be.'

'Good,' Jamie said feelingly. 'And has Milly met him yet?'

'No. It's much too early.'

Jamie was so depressed about Thea that it would have been tactless of me to tell him how happy I was with Patrick. We'd been seeing each other for three weeks. I wasn't going to make the same mistake that I'd made with Xan, so we were taking things slowly. We'd been out to dinner and to the opera; I'd got tickets for a couple of plays. And the following weekend we were due to go away. Dad had agreed to stay in the house and look after Milly as I'd never leave an au pair in charge overnight.

'So you're going away for the weekend?' Dad had said when I'd phoned him to ask.

'Just for one night – to Cliveden.'

'Very posh. With whom?' he added, 'if you don't mind my asking.'

'With Patrick, actually. My new . . . erm . . . friend.'

'Ah,' Dad had said and I'd suddenly felt as self-conscious as a twelve-year-old off to her first disco. 'But then why shouldn't you have some fun in your life? Why shouldn't you have romance again after all you've been through? Why shouldn't you meet new, interesting . . . people . . . and enjoy their company?' he'd added vehemently.

There was an odd silence. 'So can I assume that's a yes, then?'

'Oh,' he'd said distractedly. 'Yes. And what are you doing about Luisa? Have you found out anything else?' I'd told him about her cash stash.

'I've hit a blank wall,' I replied. 'I have no proof that she came by the money dishonestly, but I still feel uneasy – as though she's hiding something.'

'And she hasn't taken anything?'

'Which she could have sold, you mean? Like my jewellery? No – I'm sure nothing's missing. And at that level I feel she's honest.'

'But at another level you don't trust her.'

'I suppose I don't.' The thought depressed me. 'But then it is more than a bit odd. Cassie thinks it could be cocaine, but I've found no trace of drugs in Luisa's room. She goes out quite a bit at the moment – to the health club she always says, though that could be a cover.'

'Then follow her.'

'That's what I want to do – but I'd need you to babysit. Could you do Monday, Dad?'

'I'm afraid I can't then, Anna. Sorry.'

'Oh. How about Tuesday?'

'Erm . . . sorry, no can do.' Dad wasn't usually busy in the evenings. He'd occasionally have dinner with friends, or at his club, but was otherwise at his flat, or with me. 'Can't you ask Cassie?' he added.

'I already have, but she says her evenings are tied up at the moment. But what about Wednesday? Could you do, say, from 5.30 until 7.30?'

I could hear Dad sucking his lower lip. 'I did have something planned.'

'What?' I couldn't help asking.

'Bridge,' he replied quickly.

'That's good – with whom?'

'The . . . Travises. Although . . . I could rearrange it – yes, for dinner instead of drinks. In fact, dinner might be better,' he mused. 'OK, then, Wednesday at 5.30 should be fine.'

'Nice haircut,' I said to Dad when he arrived.

'I needed it,' he said as he squeezed past the buggy. 'But you don't think it's too short?'

'No, it's fine.' I was hit by a whiff of citrussy aftershave.

'Are you sure?' he added anxiously. He glanced in the big circular mirror at the bottom of the stairs.

'Quite sure. It's rather youthful.'

'Really?' he said happily as he ran his left hand over his head. 'How old does it make me look?'

'Erm . . . fifty-two.'

'You're joking!'

'No,' I protested, happy to soothe his battered ego. Dad beamed at me. 'And is that a new shirt?'

'It is. My old ones were looking shabby, I suddenly noticed, so I went to Selfridges. Do you like it?'

'Mm. The purple check suits you,' I lied. 'And how's the flat looking?'

'Very good – but don't forget my new planters, will you?'

'Oh God, I'm sorry, it keeps slipping my mind. But I will get them for you soon, I promise.'

I'd already asked Luisa whether she had any plans for the evening and she'd volunteered that she was going swimming again.

''Bye,' I called out to her as she set off at a quarter to six.

''Bye, Anna.'

'*Adiós!*' Milly called out as she did a Teletubbies jigsaw at the dining-room table.

I watched from the sitting-room window to see which way she

went. Then I kissed a surprised Milly goodbye, grabbed my bag and pursued Luisa down the street. I was wearing trainers, so that my steps couldn't be heard. I followed her across Blythe Road, past Jamie's flat, clocking the Bentley Continental, then past Sweet Peas, across Brook Green, down Rowan Road and now, sure enough, Luisa crossed over Hammersmith Road and went into the W6 Health Club.

I flashed my card at the receptionist and lingered in the café for a few minutes to give Luisa time to change. Then I surreptitiously looked through the glass observation wall into the pool, where I now saw Luisa emerge from the ladies' changing room in her navy swimsuit. She showered by the jacuzzi, then dropped into the water and ploughed up and down for about half an hour before climbing out again and getting dressed. She walked past the café without noticing me, left the building and went straight back home the way she'd come.

'The coast's clear,' Dad whispered as he opened the door. 'She's gone up to her room to watch TV.'

'Oh,' I said, breathless from the exertion. 'Well, she said she was going swimming and that's exactly what she did do. But can we do this again tomorrow?'

'Well . . .'

'Please, Dad, it's important.'

'All . . . right,' he said. So we did and exactly the same thing happened – and the next night as well.

'I don't think Luisa's doing anything she shouldn't be,' I said to Patrick as we set off for Cliveden in his BMW the following afternoon. 'I followed her the last three nights and all she did was to go swimming, come back home and go upstairs to her room where she watches TV. She appears to lead a blameless life.'

'You may have to forget your suspicions, then,' Patrick said as we drove through west London. 'You can't ask her where she got the money . . .'

173

'No.'

'And you've no proof that she's done anything wrong.'

'None at all. Just this . . . odd feeling. Especially as the amount of cash she's got keeps rising.'

'Could she be keeping it for a boyfriend?'

'Possibly, though she doesn't seem to have one.'

'But she works hard, you say.'

'Very hard – and Milly adores her.'

'Then I'd leave it – good childcare's hard to find.'

'That's true.' I pressed the button to open my window.

'Please don't do that!' Patrick said, raising it again from the central controls.

His sharp tone took me aback. 'Why not?' I ventured. 'It's a warm afternoon. We're having an early heatwave.'

'But the air-conditioning's very efficient.'

'I know, but I like a bit of breeze. And I hate the feeling that I'm sealed inside a car like an insect in a jam jar.'

'*I* hate having the windows down while we're in town, though. The pollution makes me feel ill.'

'But there's very little traffic.' This felt dangerously like an argument. I found myself wondering at what point in a new relationship it was acceptable to have one.

'Here . . . I'll cool the air temperature a bit more.' Patrick fiddled with the thermostat. 'Is that better?'

'Yes,' I lied as I gazed through the glass. 'So how long will it take to get there?' I asked in an effort to lighten the atmosphere.

'Only an hour. That's why it's so good for romantic weekends.'

'Have you had many of them there, then?' I smiled as we turned on to the M4.

'Sadly not,' he replied. 'I've only been once before, with Suzie, when she was eight months pregnant. We spent most of the time arguing.'

'About what, if you don't mind my asking?'

'About marriage. She felt that I should just "get on with it", but I wanted to wait because we'd been together less than a year.'

'Well, I guess that sounds fair enough.'

'Anyway, the hotel's lovely and it's hard to believe that it's so near London, let alone Heathrow. I knew you couldn't go anywhere too far away, because of Milly.'

'That's true. Thanks for planning this, Patrick, I've been looking forward to it.'

We sped along the motorway towards Taplow and were soon driving down country lanes lush with long grass and parasols of cow parsley, with pools of bluebells in the woods on either side. We turned right on to a long drive, hedged with laurel, then came to a white fountain in the shape of a shell, beyond which loomed a huge Italianate mansion.

'Wow,' I murmured as it filled our view.

'It is a bit "wow" when you first see it. The architect was Charles Barry, who designed the Palace of Westminster.'

'All I know about Cliveden is that it was where Christine Keeler caught the eye of John Profumo in the early sixties.'

'That's all most people know, but the house has a great history. It was home to the Astors a hundred years ago and has been left very much as it was then.'

As we pulled up at the entrance, one footman opened the door while another took our bags. While the car was being valet parked, we were shown up the carved oak staircase to our room on the first floor. It was enormous, with a massive overmantel carved with heraldic figures, a huge marble bathroom and a four-poster bed with a yellow damask canopy.

'How sumptuous,' I said.

'It is – but there aren't many mod cons,' Patrick pointed out. 'No air-conditioning, for example, and no minibar, because it's run as if it were a grand country house, as though we were personal guests rather than paying punters. All the art and antiques are the original ones that were here when the Astors owned it. Let's go and explore.'

As we went downstairs again we paused to look at the dark oil paintings of George the Second and Princess Augusta, and the luminous portrait of Nancy Astor by John Singer Sargent. On the grand piano were framed photos of the Astors with Amy Johnson, Churchill and Charlie Chaplin. Then we had tea on the terrace overlooking the formal parterre that flowed into the seemingly endless expanse of rolling parkland.

'This is lovely,' I breathed. 'It's so . . . grand.'

We swam in the pretty outdoor pool, then sat in the hot tub as dusk began to descend, spotting the first stars among the twinkling lights of planes coming in and out of Heathrow. Then we went back to the room, took off our robes and swimming things, and made love for the very first time.

'I've been longing to do that,' Patrick said, lying beside me and stroking my face. 'Ever since I first saw you.'

'It's been such a long time,' I murmured as he kissed me. 'I haven't . . . since before Milly was born.'

Patrick kissed me again. 'Good.'

While he took a quick bath I phoned to say goodnight to Milly, then we dressed and went down to dinner.

'This is so . . . nice.' I sighed as we sipped our champagne cocktails in the bar. I felt my stress seep away.

'You deserve it,' Patrick said. He lifted my hand to his lips.

Over dinner he asked me a bit more about my family.

'Cassie sounds like a live wire,' he said.

'That's a rather flattering way of putting it. She's a woman of twenty-nine who behaves as though she's still a teenager.'

'So you disapprove of her?'

'No.' I put down my fork. 'I disapprove of some of the things she does. But I regard her with the same mixture of frustration and affection with which I've always regarded

176

her – I worry that she's wasting her life, that's all. She refuses to make anything of herself.'

'Is she clever?'

'She is. She's got a very good brain. She had a really expensive education,' I added resentfully as the waiter removed our plates. 'I had to make do with the local comprehensive, but my parents sent Cassie to this private day school, then to Marlborough in the sixth form.'

'Did you mind?'

'I tried not to.' I fiddled with the base of the candlestick. 'Cassie was six years younger than me so my parents had more money by then. But they justified it by saying that Cassie was so wayward that they worried she'd get into the wrong crowd if she went to the school I went to, whereas they'd never had those worries about me.'

'Because you were stable and hard-working.'

'Yes. I feel I've been punished for that though, while she's been rewarded for being irresponsible. But I could never do that,' I went on as the wine waiter replenished our glasses. 'If I had more than one child, I could never treat them differently.'

'Would you want any more children?'

I tried to imagine myself with another baby. 'It feels disloyal to Milly even to contemplate it,' I replied. 'In theory, yes, I would, and it would be good for her to have a sibling.' The waiter brought our puddings. 'But the circumstances would have to be right.'

'And the man would have to be right,' Patrick pointed out.

'Of course he would. What about you?'

'Oh I'm definitely the right man,' he replied with a smile.

I laughed. 'I meant, would you want more kids?'

'I'd love to have more,' he said. He sipped his wine. 'Having another family would help me . . . not to get over it – I never can – but to feel a little less heartbroken.'

'You shouldn't have them just to compensate you for that sadness.'

'No, you're right. It wouldn't be fair. I should only have them because I love children and have a lot to offer them, which I know I do.'

That seemed like a good answer. Then Patrick talked about Sam again – and about Suzie.

'How do you feel about her now?' I asked him.

He put down his spoon. 'I hate her,' he replied simply. 'That may sound harsh, but I can't help it. I stayed with her when she got pregnant and looked after her, and did my very best to make her happy. In return she had an affair, left me and took away from me the most precious thing in my life, my child.'

'If she'd at least stayed nearby . . .' I murmured.

'Exactly. Then my relationship with Sam could have been preserved. Instead, she chose to get involved with a man who she knew was going to return to New Zealand – to spite me, I felt.'

'Why would she want to?'

'Because I hadn't married her. She was angry about it, but by then I felt that she only wanted to marry me so she could divorce me. I simply didn't trust her.'

'You said she lied in court.'

'She did. There's no doubt about that,' he added.

'But . . . what was it she lied about?'

Patrick hesitated for a moment, then laid down his fork. 'Something . . . happened,' he began quietly. 'There was an . . . incident. I want to tell you about it, because I know that Suzie gossiped about me, misrepresenting me, doing me a lot of harm . . .' As his voice trailed away I thought of Sandra – she'd clearly had a negative take on him.

'So what was it?' I murmured.

He took a deep breath. 'I was playing with Sam,' he whispered, 'in the garden of our house in Caithness Road. He was just under two then and had reached the age where he loved to be swung round. He was begging me to do this and

178

he kept saying, "Again, Daddy! Again and again!" – and it's very hard to resist tiny children when they want something. So I did swing him round – but I made a stupid mistake. I now know that you have to pick up small children under their armpits if you're going to swing them, not by their hands or arms. But I'd never done it before so I held Sam by his arms, and I swung him round twice and his shoulder became dislocated.'

'Oh . . .'

'We rushed him straight to A and E and they put the shoulder back in, and yes, of course he was in pain for a few days afterwards, poor little boy, but you can imagine how dreadful I felt. It was totally unintentional, Anna. It was an accident, an *accident*.' His eyes were shining with tears. 'But Suzie twisted it in court.' He swallowed. 'She used it – she was utterly cynical and totally ruthless.' I noticed that the tiny scar on his nose had gone white.

I laid my hand on his arm. 'Can I tell you something, Patrick?' He looked at me. 'Years ago, that happened to my parents. They were doing "one, two, three, whee" with Mark on the beach in Cornwall. And they swung him a little too high and the same thing happened – apparently it's quite easily done with small children: they felt awful, but it was just one of those things.'

'Yes. It was just one of those things,' Patrick repeated vehemently. 'But in the private hearing we had about Suzie's plan to live in New Zealand, she suggested that I'd done it recklessly – deliberately even. At that time I was fighting her tooth and nail to stay in the country and she clearly thought that lying about it might help her case. And when my solicitor suggested that Sam should live with me, Suzie said she would never allow it, not least because of what had happened that day – as though I wasn't to be trusted.'

'What did the judge say?'

'She said that an isolated incident like that in no way proved

179

that I was an unfit parent. But, at a deeper level, I believe it made her take against me. So I felt that Suzie had besmirched my character – on top of the terrible wrong she was about to do me.'

I laid my hand on his. 'It's best not to think about it. But I'm glad you told me.'

'I love Sam with all my heart,' Patrick went on. 'But I have to control myself, because I feel so angry: I'm his father, but Suzie took him fourteen thousand miles away – as though my role in his life were worth nothing.'

'How often do you see him?'

'Oh . . .' He shook his head. 'All the time. I see him on the swings, or running around in the park, or just walking down the street with his mum, or sitting in the back of a car, gazing out of the window. Just about every little boy I see reminds me of Sam. But to answer your question, every six months. I go out to Christchurch and I stay in a guesthouse nearby for two weeks at a time, and I do my best to remind my own son who I am and how much I love him.'

'When he's older he'll be able to come and stay with you.'

'I hope so,' Patrick replied. 'Though that's a long way off. But for now I can hardly bear to think of what I'm missing out on, every single day of his life.'

'You must feel very deprived.'

'I do.'

The next morning we woke early and walked across the dew-beaded grass in the early-morning sunlight. I had my camera with me, to take photos of the flowers and architectural features for my database of pictures. As I clicked away, Patrick asked me to describe the personalities of the plants we were looking at in the beds and borders.

'What about these early poppies?' he said.

I looked at their tissue paper flowers, emerging from their bristly pods. 'My mother used to call those Gatecrashers because they're self-seeding – they just turn up. So do verbena' – I pointed to the tall bracts of mauve flowers – 'and that honesty over there and that buddleia growing in the crack in that wall. I love Gatecrashers,' I added. 'I love their spontaneity, the way they just drop in uninvited and enliven the garden party.'

'And what about those Crown Imperials?' he said.

I gazed at the huge scarlet *Fritillaria*, with their topknot of frilly foliage, on their fat, succulent stems. 'Those are Drama Queens. You can't ignore them. They're extroverted and uninhibited, like . . .'

'Red hot pokers?' he suggested.

'Exactly. Or *Acanthus*, or *Agapanthus* – or those huge *Gunneras* over there. They're real show stoppers.'

'The ones that look like giant rhubarb?'

'Yes.' Their leaves were so big that a ten-year-old child could shelter under them.

As we strolled back to the hotel for breakfast, my phone buzzed with a new text message: *Pls cll me when u can, Jx.* As it didn't sound urgent, and as Jamie and I either speak to or text each other up to twenty times a day, I decided to wait until I got home. He was probably ringing me about the Italian garden in Hampstead – he'd said he was going to look for some reclaimed marble paving.

After breakfast Patrick and I sat in the library with the newspapers. Patrick was reading the *Sunday Times* while I glanced through the *Observer* – I like their gardening section. Then I picked up the *Sunday News*, curious to see what garbage Citronella had spewed out this week. Today she was expatiating upon sibling relationships:

I'm very fortunate in that my twelve-year-old daughter, Sienna, absolutely adores her little brother, Erasmus. The reason is that right from the start, my husband and I did the sensible thing and prepared her properly for his birth.

181

So many parents don't involve the older child or children at a sufficiently early stage, but spring it on them, late in the day. But we told Sienna about the baby as soon as we knew. We took her along to all his scans, giving her an enlarged framed photo of him, in utero, at thirteen weeks and twenty weeks to put on her bedroom wall. We constantly talked to her about him and told her what a very special *and* clever *baby he was going to be, and what a lucky* girl she was. *We made up a charming story about him and read it to her every night. We took her with us to buy nursery equipment and toys for him. We even showed her the video of Erasmus's birth . . .*

'Yuck!' I exclaimed. 'How *gross!*'

Patrick looked up, startled. 'What?'

'Oh, just this Citronella Pratt, who writes for the *Sunday News.*'

'She lives in Brook Green, doesn't she?'

'She does, unfortunately. Her son's at Milly's nursery school.' I told Patrick what she'd written. He pulled an appalled face. 'What I don't understand is why she's got this column – all she does is write about her own life in an incredibly dull but boastful way.'

'I think you'll find that it's because her brother, Neil, is chief executive of the *Sunday News,*' Patrick replied, as he turned back to the paper. 'My PR people had dealings with him once.'

'I see.' I shut the paper. 'Well, that must explain it – because nothing else does.'

We had one last swim before going up to pack. Patrick finished first, then went down to reception to pay the bill, so when I'd collected my things together I sat on the padded window seat, enjoying the view for a minute or two longer. Below me, people were leaving and arriving. I heard the crunch of wheels on gravel as another luxury car drove slowly away, its roof gleaming in the midday sunshine, and now I saw a black cab pull up. The door clicked open, like the wing of a stag beetle, and a slim, attractive woman stepped out. From where I was sitting all I could see was the top of her head, but then she suddenly looked up at the front of the building. The shock lifted me on to my feet.

Thea? Why was she here? I peered at her through the window as she paid the driver. Perhaps she had some client event on, or maybe she was here with Jamie. I scanned the car park for his truck but all I could see were Mercedes, Ferraris and Rollses. And I had just decided to run down and say hi to her when I saw a smart, dark-haired man of about forty emerge from the hotel and walk towards her. He took Thea's face in his hands, kissed her on the mouth, then they walked inside, hand in hand.

'Are you all right, Anna? *Anna?*' I turned round. 'Are you OK?' Patrick asked as he stood in the open doorway. 'We ought to hit the road, otherwise we'll be late. Didn't your dad say he'd like us back by two?'

'Er . . . that's right,' I murmured. 'He did.'

'So have you got everything, then?'

'Um . . . yes – I have.'

Now, behind Patrick, I caught a glimpse of Thea and the unknown man walking along the landing, heads inclined, his arm round her waist.

'Have we got the same room?' I heard her ask. Then her companion said something and I heard her giggle.

'Are you OK, Anna?' Patrick said again. 'You're . . . staring at me.'

'Am I? Oh, sorry . . . I was . . . dreaming . . . erm . . . But yes, I'm ready to go.' Patrick stepped into the room and picked up my weekend bag. Suddenly my mobile rang. As I read the number, my heart sank. Now I understood why Jamie had texted me on a Sunday morning – he'd just found out and was in a terrible way. As I pressed the green button I struggled to compose myself.

'I'll see you downstairs,' Patrick said tactfully. I gave him a little wave.

'Anna?' I heard.

'Jamie!' I replied with neon brightness. 'Er . . . how are you?' I braced myself.

'I'm fine, Anna. Never been better.'

'Really?'

'Yes. I feel . . . great, actually – just . . . bonza.'

It took me a second or two to realise that he wasn't being ironic. 'But I wanted to tell you something,' I heard him say, 'because you gave me such good advice the other day . . .'

'Did I?' I said faintly.

'About Thea. I feel pretty silly, really – but you know that business card I found?'

'Yes?'

'The one that worried me?'

'Yes?

'The guy was called Percy du Plessis?'

'Yes?'

'Well, I'd got that completely wrong.'

'No . . .'

'Yes. Completely and utterly wrong. Are you all right, Anna?'

'What? Sorry, Jamie, I'm just a bit . . . tired.'

'Anyway, I did what you suggested and I talked to Thea about it – I didn't get the chance until last night. I even told her that I thought she was having an affair . . .'

'And what did she say?'

'Nothing. She just looked stricken. Then I showed her the card – and she burst out laughing.'

'She did?'

'She couldn't stop. Then she explained that "Percy" isn't a man –'

184

'Yes he is,' I interjected. 'I mean . . .'

'No, it's short for "Persephone", but she's always been known as "Percy". Apparently she and Thea get on like a house on fire and the flirtatious banter is just a private joke between them.'

'Are you sure?'

There was a momentary silence. 'Of course I'm sure,' Jamie replied. 'Thea wouldn't lie to me, Anna.'

'No, of course she wouldn't. Well that's . . . amazing, Jamie.'

'You sound surprised.'

'I am – I mean – well, not really *surprised*, but you seemed so sure . . . you had this gut feeling . . . but it's wonderful to know that your gut feeling was . . . wrong.'

'It was, thank God. I feel so relieved. I was distraught and I'm sorry it made me ratty with you. But it's good to know that I was worrying for nothing. And when Thea realised the mistake I'd made, she was pretty happy too.'

'Uh huh,' I said blankly, my mind still racing.

'I get a bit paranoid because she's away so much – I can't help it. Anyway, she's off to the Cape again today. I've just taken her to the airport.'

'You've just taken her to the airport?'

'Yes. Why do you keep repeating everything I say?'

'Which airport?'

'Heathrow. You know, Anna, you're sounding pretty stressed. Maybe you should go and unwind somewhere for a day or two.'

'Yes . . . maybe . . . Sorry, Jamie, as I say, I'm a bit . . . tired.'

'Anyway, I'm off to play cricket, but I wanted to thank you for your advice. It was spot on.'

'I'm glad,' I said faintly.

'So I'll see you tomorrow, then.'

''Bye.'

I sank on to the unmade bed, staring into space, then dialled reception. 'I'm trying to contact a friend of mine who's staying here,' I asked. 'Could you give me the extension for his room please?'

'What name is it, Madame?'

'Percy du Plessis.'

'Would you mind spelling that for me? I'm sorry, Madame,' she added after a moment, 'but there's no one of that name currently resident in the hotel. Can I help you with anything else?'

NINE

'Are you sure it was her?' Jenny asked me the following Saturday afternoon. She'd come round for tea with Grace, who was playing with Milly at the other end of the sitting room. I'd confided in Jenny because I needed to talk to someone about it, and because she's never met Jamie, and because I know that she's completely discreet. 'Is there any chance you could have been mistaken?'

'I saw her face, Jenny. I heard her voice.'

'And she doesn't have an identical twin – like me?'

'No, she doesn't. But I feel so awful, knowing what I do. Jamie told me that he'd just dropped her off at Heathrow.'

'So she'd obviously waited until he'd driven away, then jumped in a taxi and gone to Cliveden to meet her boyfriend. Oh dear . . .'

'I wonder who he is,' I said.

'Did you get a close look?'

'Not close enough to recognise him again, but he's likely to be someone she met on one of her trips. He probably had a stopover in London so they arranged to touch down together in Cliveden. But I heard her say, "Have we got the same room?"'

'Which means that she's obviously stayed there with him

before, which suggests that it's been going on for a while. Poor Jamie.'

I shook my head. 'What do I do?'

'Well . . .' Jenny shrugged. 'I don't think you can do anything. After all, it might just end and then, in theory, she and Jamie could carry on perfectly happily with him none the wiser – if she's lucky.'

'She looked pretty keen on him, whoever he was.'

'There's no upside for you if you tell Jamie, Anna.'

'That's true. Plus I don't think I'd actually be able to say it – I couldn't bear for him to be hurt.'

'You're very fond of him, aren't you?'

'Yes.' I thought about it for a moment. 'I am. Jamie's not just my business partner, he's my friend; he's a good, kind and utterly reliable man whom I trust, respect and like.'

'But that would all change,' Jenny said. 'Because deep down he'd never forgive you for breaking the bad news. My feeling is that he'll find out anyway,' she went on. 'His wife will slip up and he'll find out. From what I've seen as a counsellor, the unfaithful party often has some subconscious desire to be caught so that everything can be resolved and they can stop feeling guilty. But I'd try and put it from your mind for now.'

Having discussed my dilemma, we went to the other end of the room and played with the little girls. I gazed at Grace – her baby beauty had bloomed into infant loveliness. She had curly fair hair, peachy skin and large, lido-blue eyes. She no longer looked like Jenny but was presumably – though I couldn't ask – more like her father.

I gazed at Milly. She wasn't like me at all. She most closely resembled Xan and my mother – the two people who should have been so close to her, but who, in different ways, were missing from her life.

Grace was busy cooking something on Milly's toy cooker with a clattering of tiny metal saucepans. She rummaged in the box of play food, then put on the oven glove.

'Would you like to wear the apron too, Gracie?' I said.

She nodded, then turned and let me tie it on for her. 'There you are, poppet.'

Milly was playing with her doll's house. She held up one of the tiny wooden dolls, which had a purple jacket and a flouncy pink skirt. I knew what was coming. 'Thass my mummy,' she announced. She picked up another doll, with a yellow T-shirt and blue trousers. 'And thass my daddy.' She laid them in their little blue beds, side by side under the pink roof, and put their yellow duvets on, then she placed her left forefinger over her nose. 'Shhhhh!' she whispered. 'My mummy and my daddy go to sleep now.'

'I don't have a daddy,' Grace said without looking up from what she was doing.

Milly stared at her, dumbfounded, even though I knew she'd heard Grace say this before. Then she turned to me with a look of exquisite sympathy. 'Gracie don't hab a *daddy*,' she repeated, shaking her head sadly.

'But Gracie's very lucky,' Jenny went on swiftly, 'because she has lots of other people in her life – don't you, sweetie?' Grace nodded. 'You have Mummy, and you have Auntie Jackie in France and Uncle Philippe and your two little cousins, and you have Milly and Anna, and all your friends and teachers at nursery school – and you have Grandma and Grandpa too.'

'Your parents?' I asked Jenny. She nodded. 'So they've come round, then?'

'Not exactly.' She shrugged. 'They're . . . resigned. They behaved horribly,' she added without rancour, 'but I still want Grace to have a good relationship with them as they're her only grandparents.'

'She's doing better than Milly on that front, then,' I said as Milly offered me a spillage of plastic peas with a wedge of Black Forest gateau on top. 'Mmm . . . *delicious*, darling. All she's got is my dad.'

'What about Xan's parents?'

'They're elderly so they don't travel outside Spain. I got a card from them saying that Milly and I would be welcome to visit them any time, but as I'm not *with* Xan I feel it would be awkward – and it would make me feel sad to go there without him – regretting what might have been.'

'But you've got a *new* man now,' Jenny pointed out as she nibbled a vinyl croissant and a tiny tin of baked beans. 'This is yummy, Gracie.'

'Yummy in your tummy, Mummy?'

'Yes, sweetie. So how's it going with Patrick?'

'It's going . . . well. We like each other. We're attracted to each other. We have things in common.'

'That's a good start.'

'And I've been . . . lonely, Jenny. Four years is a long time not to be loved, or desired.'

'It *is* a long time,' she agreed. 'And I'm glad you've met someone. But to be honest I find the relationship I have with Grace quite fulfilling enough.'

'So you're not even . . . looking, then?'

'No. And it'll be a long time before I do,' she added quietly.

I was dying to ask Jenny why it would be such a long time, and why she never saw Grace's dad, and what it was he had done to deserve her condemnation. But Jenny had already changed the subject, as she so often does. 'So is Patrick divorced, then?' I heard her ask. I explained his situation. 'New Zealand?' she repeated. 'Poor guy.' And I thought Jenny's sympathy for Patrick odd, given that she had excluded her ex from Grace's life – but this irony, strangely, seemed lost on her. 'He must feel so angry.' I nodded. 'And does he show it?'

'Well . . .' I didn't want to say too much about Patrick's little flare-ups. 'He does get a bit stressy sometimes. But he admits that things affect him more – if people cut him up in traffic, for example, or keep him waiting on the phone he can get very wound up. But I know why he's like that,' I went on, 'so I have to be understanding.'

'You don't have to be,' Jenny cautioned.

'OK – but I want to be, because I like him. And he likes me. And knowing that a man is interested in me is such a good feeling after Xan's . . . rejection.'

'And has he met Milly?'

I shook my head. 'That's something I'm not going to rush.'

As late spring went on, the rhododendrons and azaleas were everywhere superseded by wisteria, dripping from the fronts of houses or stretched along walls, then by purple spears of lilac, then by fizzing blue *Ceanothus* and by *Philadelphus*, with their balls of fragrant white petals, which Milly and I used as confetti for her dolls' weddings – then came the roses and peonies of early summer.

Patrick and I had been spending more and more time together and I felt that the moment had come for Milly to meet him. So to begin with he'd 'bump into us' in the park and help me push her on the swings: she seemed a little suspicious at first, still convinced that he'd stolen her shoe. Then he began popping over for Sunday lunch, bringing armfuls of flowers from his garden for me and chocolate buttons for her. Then I invited him to her birthday tea.

'Iss my daddy coming?' she asked me as I put the Winnie the Pooh paper plates round the table that Friday afternoon. My heart sank. Xan's visits were so rare that I'd stopped telling Milly she would see him 'before too long' because I could no longer bear her disappointment. I didn't talk about him as much as before; and I now avoided the news, as she would invariably start to cry the second he'd disappeared from the screen.

As I sprinkled 'Happy Birthday' sequins over the tablecloth, Milly, dressed in the pale-blue fairy outfit I'd given her that morning, ran to the window, climbed on to the sofa and peered out. 'Iss my *daddy* coming?' she repeated, looking down the street in both directions as though she believed she might see him.

'No, darling,' I said, 'he's not.'

'He *is* coming,' she insisted. She waved her magic wand about. 'He *is*.'

'No, sweetie, he's very busy at the moment – but you had that birthday card from him this morning and I got an e-mail from him last night to say that he's posted you a present, so he's really thinking of you. But lots of other people are coming – Grandpa, and Jenny and Grace, and Luisa of course, and Phoebe and Carla from Sweet Peas, and Cassie, and Auntie Sue, so we'll all have a lovely time. And Jamie's going to pop in for a little while.'

'Jamie?' She ran to her book box and got out *The Gruffalo*.

'And Patrick's coming too,' I added casually. 'Is that OK?' Milly nodded slowly, as if she wasn't quite sure, but then Patrick was a new person in her life, I reasoned. It would take time for her to feel at ease with him.

Patrick had been quite nervous about meeting my family for the first time, but he and Dad seemed to hit it off – I heard them having an animated chat about e-commerce; Jamie went out of his way to be friendly, and I felt that Sue and Jenny approved. Only Cassie seemed less than impressed. She'd had too much champagne, and after the others had gone and only she and Dad were left, she'd blurted out that Patrick shouldn't have bought Milly a bike.

'Why not?' I demanded, not wanting to admit that I'd been a bit taken aback myself when I'd seen the 'Barbie' bike complete with pink helmet.

'Because he hasn't known her that long. It was too much,' Cassie went on as Milly played with the Fifi Forget-Me-Not doll that Jamie had brought her. 'He should have just got her some paints, or a puzzle. Don't you agree, Dad?'

'There's some truth in what you say,' he replied. 'But he's

obviously well off and he's keen on Anna, so he felt like buying Milly something special.'

'Exactly,' I said as I poured him more tea. 'Patrick's very generous, and if that's what he wanted to give her then it's fine by me – plus I like him, Cassie, so please don't criticise him.'

'Just my opinion.' She shrugged. She picked up her digital camera and began viewing the shots she'd taken earlier. 'That's a lovely one of Milly.'

'Let me see.' I sat down beside her on the sofa. 'Yes, it's sweet.'

'And this one of her blowing out the candles.'

I peered at the tiny screen. 'Could you e-mail them to me so I can send some to Xan?' I decided it would be more tactful to send him the ones that didn't have Patrick in the background, tempting though it was to show him that my life had moved on. 'And that's a nice one of Luisa.'

'She's lost weight,' Cassie said. 'She used to be plump.'

'That's true.' I hadn't noticed. 'It must be all the swimming – and that's good of Jenny.'

'Now *she* intrigues me,' Cassie mused. 'She's so open and friendly – you'd say that she's happy: yet at the same time she casts a long shadow, as though she's in pain.'

'Well . . .' I wasn't going to discuss Jenny with my sister. 'It's not easy being a single mum.' Milly clambered on to the sofa and put her arms round my neck. I drew her on to my lap.

'Doesn't Grace's dad help out?' I heard Cassie say.

'Erm . . . I don't think he does,' I said. 'No.'

'Gracie don't hab a daddy,' said Milly, shaking her head.

'Why not?' Cassie enquired in her characteristically direct way.

I shrugged. 'I really don't know.'

'You mean she hasn't told you?'

'No.'

'How odd to be secretive about it in this day and age. But don't you wonder about it, Anna?'

'Occasionally,' I conceded, not wanting to admit that I was *consumed* with curiosity most of the time. 'But I'd never ask her outright.'

'Why not?'

'Because if someone is choosing not to tell you something important about themselves, you have to respect that or risk losing the friendship. I like Jenny so I'm not going to pry.'

'But she might want to talk to you about it,' Cassie suggested with another swig of champagne.

'Then I can only say that she's had plenty of opportunities to do so. She clearly doesn't want to, so we just don't go there.'

This seemed to satisfy Cassie. 'There's Patrick,' she said, looking at her camera again. 'He's good-looking. I'll give him that.'

'I think so too,' I said.

'And he's very well dressed.' That was true. 'But the knot of his tie . . .'

'What about it?'

'It's too tight.'

I squinted at the photo. 'Can't say I'd noticed. Try not to be too critical, Cassie.'

'Oh, it's not a criticism.' She shrugged. 'Just an observation. And speaking of ties,' she went on, turning to Dad, 'yours is very snazzy.'

'Er . . . thanks.'

'It's Pucci, isn't it?'

'I'm not sure. I just liked the nice bright swirly pattern.' He glanced at his watch. 'It's half past six, I'd better be off.'

'Where are you going?' Cassie asked him.

'Well . . .' He blushed. 'I've . . . got things to do.'

'Like what?' she persisted as he stood up.

'Erm . . . Bridge. With the Travises. And don't forget my

new planters, will you, Anna?' he added as he stooped to kiss Milly. 'I've just thrown out the old ones so the balcony looks bare.'

'God, sorry, Dad, I've been so busy. I'll pick them up from the nursery on Tuesday and bring them over at the end of the week.'

'Thanks, darling. 'Bye, girls.' He blew us a kiss.

'I'll stay for a bit longer,' Cassie said with another sip of champagne. 'Then I'll have to go. I'm seeing Zack tonight.'

'Who's Zack?' I asked as I ate a lime jelly. 'I thought you were dating Sean.'

'Oh, I ditched him.' Men never ditch Cassie, it's always the other way round. She's very proud of the fact that she has a 'one hundred per cent dump rate'. 'Sean was a bit of a wimp,' Cassie went on casually as she cut herself a slice of the eggless birthday cake that Luisa had made. 'And when I told him it was over – get this – he broke down in tears.'

'Poor guy.'

'So I said' – she bit into the lemon icing – '"For God's sake, Sean, why don't you butch up a bit and behave like a man?"'

'I feel sorry for him,' I said quietly. Mum would be horrified, I thought. She'd tried to instil in Cassie the same values she'd instilled in me, but with zero success: Cassie had always done just as she liked.

'Easy come, easy go.' I heard her sigh. 'So now it's Zack.'

'And what are you doing workwise?' I asked, as I often do.

'Well . . . there's not much temping right now,' she said. 'So I've got an evening job. I don't mind as it means my days are free, which suits me at the moment.'

I groaned. 'I hope it's not – what was it you called it? – adult phone entertainment again.' I began to clear the table.

Cassie shook her head. 'I stopped that the day I got my old piano teacher on the line.'

195

'No!' I exclaimed. 'Mr Brown? The one who used to come to the house?'

'Yes.' Cassie pulled a disgusted face. 'It was hideous. I recognised his voice.' She shuddered at the memory. 'It totally put me off the whole thing.'

'I'm glad to hear it. But what *are* you doing at the moment?'

'I'm doing some work for a company called Decoy Ducks.'

The name rang vague bells. 'What does it do?'

'Well, it's a specialist thing, for women who are concerned about their husband's reliability, shall we say . . .'

'Oh my God, you're a honeytrap girl! Do you have to go in for these sleazy jobs, Cassie?' I asked as I took things out to the kitchen. 'You do seem to be attracted to the seamy side of life for reasons I can never quite fathom.'

'It's not really sleazy,' she protested mildly as she carried the teacups through. 'I only talk to them after all – they have to make the first move – but it's providing a very valuable service.' She opened the dishwasher. 'Last night, for example, I had to test the fidelity of this woman's fiancé – she's loaded, he's not and she wanted to be sure she wasn't about to make an expensive mistake. So I got chatting to him at this bar he goes to after work and within five minutes he had his hand on my backside – and within twenty he was offering to take me to a hotel. Dis*gusting*,' she added with a moue of disapprobation.

I almost admired Cassie's moral flexibility. 'The really disgusting thing, surely, is entrapping people,' I said as she washed the champagne glasses.

'It's not entrapment,' she protested. 'If the man doesn't want to stray, no woman will interest him. QED.'

'You know that's not true,' I said. 'Most men will take it if it's offered to them on a plate, so you're putting them in temptation's way. I don't know how you can do it,' I added. 'Plus you're wasting your life on these low-grade enterprises.'

'I don't find it hard at all,' she replied amiably. 'In fact, in human terms I find it quite fascinating – plus I can make three hundred pounds a night. As for wasting my life, well, it's my belief that no experience is wasted – low-grade or not.'

'Just my opinion,' I said.

In the meantime Jamie and I had finished the Italian garden in Hampstead. The client, Simonetta, had invited us to help her christen it so we went round there with a bottle of prosecco.

'I'm thrilled with it,' she said in her accented English as we looked at the 'before' photos and compared them with what was there now. She waved an elegantly bejewelled hand at us. 'I can imagine that I'm at home again in Calabria.'

Simonetta's garden had been a nondescript Victorian backyard, but was now exactly what she had asked for: an Italian courtyard complete with fountain, box hedging, marble paving, a small classical archway and a riot of luscious Mediterranean plants, which already looked surprisingly well established in their 'antique' pots.

'The thing about having so many of the plants in containers is that you'll be able to move them around,' I said, as I shifted a pot of rosemary nearer to the kitchen door. 'Like changing the furniture inside the house.'

'I adore the *Plumbago*,' she said, looking at its powder-blue florets. 'It's . . . *fantastico*.'

'It's tender,' I pointed out, 'but your garden's south-facing and very sheltered so it should be OK, but in winter you'll need to cover the roots.'

'I love the little olive trees,' Simonetta went on. 'And the sweet peas,' she added with an air of surprise. 'I'd always thought of them as being so English.'

'They're native to southern Italy,' I explained. 'They were introduced to Britain from there in the early eighteenth century. I learned about them when I was doing my course.'

'And thank you for including the *Asphodels*,' she enthused as she topped up my glass. 'I remember those so well from my childhood. There was another lovely flower,' she went on, shielding her eyes from the sunshine. 'I've forgotten the name, but it was tall, and *bellissima*, with an umbrella of pale-pink flowers, each one like a little *Campanella*.'

'Bell?'

'Yes. There used to be so many in the pastures in early summer. They had a strong . . . *profumo* and my mother used to dry them.'

'That could be Sicilian honey garlic,' I said. 'But I'd need to check.' I suddenly remembered my mother's old book, *Flowers of Southern Italy*. 'I'll look it up and if it's the same thing I could get some bulbs for you to plant in the autumn. If I don't get back to you within a week, send me an e-mail.'

'Sure. What other gardens are you making at the moment?' she asked as I took a few photos to put on my website.

'We've been doing a big one in The Boltons,' Jamie replied. 'The landscaping's all finished, so all we have to do now is get the plants in the ground and it's done.'

'Just in the nick of time,' I explained. 'The clients' grand house-warming party's next Saturday.'

'It's nice of them to invite us,' I said to Jamie as we carried the plants into the Edwards' garden a few days later. 'I didn't expect that. Are you going to go?'

'Maybe,' he replied as he put down a *Clematis orientalis* in its designated spot.

'It would be good PR,' I pointed out quietly. 'We might even get another commission out of it.'

'If I do come I'll bring Thea,' he said as we went out to my car again.

'You will?'

Jamie gave me an old-fashioned look. 'Of course I will, Thea's my wife.'

'I . . . know,' I stuttered as I tried to banish the image of her with her lover at Cliveden. I reached into the back of my Volvo estate and handed Jamie the Chilean flame flower. 'I thought she might be . . . away, that's all.'

'No, she'll be in London – in fact, she'll be spending more time here from now on.'

'Really?' I pulled out the star jasmine, being careful not to knock the flowers.

'Yes,' Jamie said. 'Why do you look so surprised?'

'Because . . . she's been . . . working abroad so much, that's all. But that's really good news.'

'It is. We'll be able to lead a more regular life.'

I wondered whether, despite everything, Thea was going to try to make the marriage work.

'And will you bring Patrick to the party?' I heard Jamie ask.

'No. As I say, I need to do a bit of schmoozing – plus he's giving a talk on beekeeping that night.'

The Edwards' planting took two days, most of which was spent trying to get the row of pleached lime trees through the house without damaging the newly decorated hallway. Then, when we'd finally got them outside we found that the root balls were too big for the holes, so that all took an extra morning, with Jamie doing some judicious stone-cutting. Finally all the beds had been planted, and all we had to do was fill the tall granite pots with the lime green tobacco flowers and the French lavender.

'This is the part I enjoy most,' I said. 'The planting.'

'Why?' Jamie asked. 'Because it means the project's over?'

'No. It's because although I love designing gardens, at the end of the day I just like digging away, getting the plants into the ground, then seeing them flourish. There's a huge satisfaction in that.'

'Very true.'

'And my own garden's too small to put much in it. I long to have a big herbaceous border to fill.'

'What would you put in it?'

'Oh, everything,' I replied happily. 'It would be crammed with dahlias, delphiniums, *Aquilegias*, *Astilbes*, *Achillea*, foxgloves, *Sedums*, *Euphorbia*, forget-me-nots . . . the works – there'd be something in flower all year round. And French lavender,' I added, as I looked at the extravagantly feathery tops of the purple flowers. 'I do love it. They look as though they're off to Ascot in their ridiculous headgear.'

'Not Ascot,' Jamie corrected me. 'The Notting Hill Carnival.'

I smiled. 'The limestone looks good. I told you it would fit,' I couldn't help adding.

'Yes . . .' Jamie rolled his eyes. 'You were right – I was wrong.'

'It doesn't matter – you're not usually.'

'I guess it was because I was so upset that day.'

'I know. But everything's fine now,' I said, as I looked at the completed garden.

I heard a relieved sigh. 'Yes,' Jamie said. 'Everything's fine.'

When I got back that evening, I found e-mails from Xan and from Mark, thanking me for the photos I'd sent them of Milly's birthday. How sad, I thought, that her dad and her uncle had never even met. With so few men in Milly's life I felt even more glad to be with Patrick – she'd need someone to be a father figure to her day-to-day, not just for a few hours twice a year. There was also an e-mail from Elaine, promising to visit Milly and me soon; the last message was from Simonetta, reminding me about the honey garlic.

I went up to my office and looked at my gardening books – there must have been four hundred of them, the majority my mother's. I still hadn't indexed them as I'd intended to do, so it was a matter of remembering where everything was. I ran my finger along their spines as I squinted at the titles. *Plants for Shady Places*; *The Gardens of Gertrude Jekyll*; *The Royal Horticultural Society Encyclopedia of Plants and*

Flowers . . . I looked on the shelf below. There was the book Sue had given me on Alpine flowers, then *Clematis and Climbers*; *A Short History of Trees*; *Flowers of Southern Italy*.

'Here it is,' I murmured as I pulled it out.

It was a very old-looking paperback, the pages tanned with age, the paper crisp and friable. The spine was heavily creased and as I opened the book it exuded the musty aroma of a previous era. I imagined my mother poring over the text, or examining the monochrome plates. As I turned the pages, some of which were loose, I saw that she'd pencilled a few notes in the yellowing margins: *Needs a south-facing position*; *Does well in shade*; *Not much scent*. The sight of her neat, forward-sloping handwriting brought her vividly to life, filling me with an aching regret.

'Honey garlic,' I murmured, as I turned to the index. I ran my finger down the list of names. 'Pineapple Broom, *Genista*, juniper, oleander . . .' It wasn't listed under its common name, but what was the Latin for it? I wondered. I used to know. It had come up in one of the lectures. It was 'Nectar' something, I suddenly remembered. Nectar . . . *roscordum*. That was it. *Nectaroscordum Siculum*, meaning coming from Sicily. I turned to 'N' and found the reference. As I was putting the book back, something slipped out of it and fell to the floor. At first I thought it was a couple of loose pages. Then I saw that it was a fragment of a letter, in my mother's hand, and a photograph.

The photo was an old colour snap. There was my mother – she must have been about twenty-eight – sitting on a tartan rug on a beach somewhere, on a cloudless day. She was wearing a black-and-white cheesecloth dress with cap sleeves and she looked radiantly happy. Sitting next to her on the rug was a very attractive dark-haired man of about the same age. He was dressed in a blue open-necked shirt and dark shorts. There were some plates and glasses on the rug, and a picnic basket, from which protruded an open bottle of champagne. Their heads were inclined together, with an unabashed intimacy, while his muscular-looking arm was wrapped round her waist.

I gazed at the photo, the blood pulsing in my ears, then I turned it over: *Chichester, 12 June 1977*, my mother had written. Who was this man and what was she doing with him? And who had taken this photograph? Dad? Hardly, given the way the man was holding her. Then I felt a peculiar thud in my ribcage as I remembered that Dad had spent most of that year in Brazil. And now, as I stared at the unknown man's saturnine features, I felt my whole world suddenly tilt a little on its axis.

I looked at the photo again, feeling my face suffuse with heat, then, just as quickly, go icy cold. For now I saw not just the unmistakable nature of the relationship between my mother and this man, but I recognised in his dark brown eyes, Cassie's; I recognised in his high, domed forehead her own. Like Cassie, the man had olive skin and hair that, like hers, was dark, and lustrous, and thick.

As I stared at the image things shifted in and out of vision in my mind, like a lens struggling to focus, then suddenly everything became startlingly clear.

Now, my hands trembling, I looked at the letter. It was from my mother to my father and with its many scorings and crossings out was clearly a draft of something that she had found hard to write.

Dearest Colin . . . how will I ever be able to thank you for your huge generosity of spirit . . . I know I don't deserve it . . . I blame myself . . . feel so ashamed . . . will do whatever I can to make it as easy as possible for you . . . I agree that <u>no one</u> should know . . .

I felt goosebumps raise themselves up on my arms. There was no date on the letter, but it clearly belonged with the photo.

I read it again, then flicked through the book once more in case there was anything else secreted inside it; there wasn't, but there was an inscription on the title page: *To Mary, with so many happy memories, amore a baci, Carlo, June 1977.*

'So many happy memories?' I whispered. Now I remembered the conversation I'd had with Dad four months before.

I was out there for eight months.

It must have been hard for you.

Yes . . . it was very hard.

So that was before Cassie was born?

That's . . . right. Cassie was born the following year.

On 15 March. I felt as though the air had been punched out of my lungs.

As I put the book away in my desk, I found myself wishing that Simonetta had never asked me about the honey garlic. Dad had clearly had no idea what was concealed inside *Flowers of Southern Italy*, otherwise he'd never have left it for me to take.

As I went downstairs, still feeling shaky, the phone rang. It was the producer from GMTV reminding me about the five interviews I was doing for them the following week. 'We've got all the plants you requested,' she said. 'I've booked the cab to pick you up at 6 a.m. on Monday, to give you time to arrange them as you'd like before the interview. Is that OK?'

'That's absolutely fine,' I replied automatically. But how would I be able to concentrate now?

As it was, the adrenalin rush of live TV carried me through. I arrived at the studios at 6.30, had a quick stint in make-up, then went up to the roof terrace and chatted to Penny Smith about the must-have herbaceous perennials for summer. We'd managed to talk about growing *Osteospermum*, *Rudbeckia*, lupins and *Verbascum*; then before I knew it she was thanking me, looking forward to seeing me again tomorrow when I would be talking about container planting, then neatly cueing into a piece about teenage mums.

When I got back, I took Milly to Sweet Peas. Then I phoned Dad to tell him that I was bringing over his planters.

'Your TV appearance went well,' he said as we unloaded them from the back of my car half an hour later. 'And they put up your website on the screen.'

'That's good.' I lifted out the tray of *Pelargoniums*. 'I got you these because they flower for so long, and there's white Bacopa to go in between.'

'That should look nice. Is everything OK?' he asked as I pulled out the bag of compost.

'Everything's fine. I'm just a bit tired after my early start, that's all.' We dragged the load into the lift, then Dad pressed the button and we juddered upwards. 'But Dad . . .'

'Yes.'

'There's something I need to ask you.'

He looked at me. 'That sounds ominous. What?'

'It's about . . . Brazil.'

'Brazil?' he repeated as we jerked to a halt on the tenth floor. The gunmetal-grey doors drew back with a resonant clunk.

'Yes. I'm thinking . . . of going there. With Patrick. For a holiday.'

'Really?' he said as we unloaded. 'Well, it's a long way.'

'I know, but . . . I was just wondering what's the best time to go?'

Dad gave an awkward little shrug. 'I'm not really sure . . .' He reached into his pocket for his keys.

'But you were out there for a while, weren't you?'

'That's right.'

'For eight months I think you said.'

'Ye-es,' he said as he fumbled with the lock.

'So which months were they, then?' There was an awkward silence. 'Can you remember?' My heart stopped as I waited for his reply.

He pushed on the door. 'I was there in 1977, from January

204

to August.' My heart started beating again, then sank like a stone at the implication of what he'd just said. 'But it's a huge country so it would depend where you were.'

'Of course. Well, I'll do a bit more research. So . . . from January to August,' I added casually as we carried the planters on to the balcony and began filling them. 'And did you come home at all during that time?' There was another odd little silence. 'Did you, Dad?'

'I should have done, as I had leave,' he replied. He put down his trowel. 'But I'd had malaria and was too weak to travel. By the time I'd recovered I decided just to press on with the project as by then all I wanted was to get it over with and come home. It was one of the worst periods of my life,' he added quietly as he gently twisted the plants out of their pots. 'It was far too long to be away and, well, lengthy separations are no good for a marriage really . . .' His voice trailed away.

'No. Of course not. Well, anyway, thanks.'

'Was that all you wanted to know then, Anna?' he added. I stared at him. 'Yes, Dad,' I said. 'It was.'

So that was that, I thought as I drove home. It was unequivocal. Dad was in Brazil when Cassie was conceived. I went upstairs and looked at the photo again, with a sick, see-saw feeling. Then I just sat at my desk, my head in my hands.

So Mum's marriage hadn't been as conventional as I'd thought – far from it. She'd had an affair. I felt a wave of sadness, disappointment and dismay. She'd had an affair while Dad was away and she'd got pregnant, and she'd told him – that was clear from the letter – and Dad had obviously forgiven her, because their marriage didn't end, it went on.

When a baby comes along I think you just have to . . . accept it.

I felt a sudden burst of affection for Dad. He must have loved Mum so much.

You need someone who'll always be there for you. Whatever . . .

Mum had always added that enigmatic 'whatever'. And now I knew what it meant.

But the shock I felt at my discovery was softened by the thought that at some deep level I'd always known. However different siblings may be, you can still detect some common ingredient even if it's only the line of a nose, or the curve of an eyebrow. But every single thing about Cassie – physical and psychological – was alien to me and now, at last, I knew why. And what would have made Mum and Dad decide to have another baby, more than six years after their last one?

'Oh, we just got broody again,' I now remembered her saying if anyone ever mentioned the age gap. 'Didn't we, darling?' she'd add breezily to Dad, who would just smile his gentle, non-committal smile.

I slid the photo back and hid the book in a drawer.

TEN

Over the next few days I felt a huge weariness of spirit, which translated into a physical heaviness, as though I was staggering around with a huge boulder in my arms, but couldn't find anywhere to put it down. I had an older brother who was virtually estranged, a business partner with marital problems, an ex who only sees our child twice a year, an au pair who might be selling drugs; and now I'd discovered that my sister was the result of an adulterous liaison.

To distract myself I went through my wardrobe, trying to decide what to wear to the Edwards' party. As I was pulling out shoes, Cassie phoned. I felt an initial discomfort at the sound of her voice, but that alien feeling quickly faded as familiar emotions flooded back.

'*Guess* what's happened,' she said.

'I can't,' I said as I found the pair of pistachio sling-backs I'd been looking for. 'I don't have the imaginative energy. You'll have to tell me.'

'It's about Dad.'

I straightened up. 'Is he OK?'

'Oh he's fine. But I've discovered something, well, rather astounding,' she went on.

It couldn't be as astounding as what I'd recently discovered, I reflected.

'So what about him?' I said as I reached for my green linen cocktail dress.

'Well, last night I was sitting in the bar of the Harvey Nichols Fifth Floor – in my professional capacity.'

'Is that what you call it?'

'And I was talking to this chap who I'd been sent to . . . check out.'

'Flirt with,' I corrected her. 'I hope this is all safe, by the way.'

'Oh, it's perfectly safe,' she replied, 'because Ken, my boss, was sitting only yards away with a concealed video recorder. Anyway, I suddenly glanced towards the other side of the bar and who should I see? Dad!'

I sat on the bed. 'You saw *Dad* in the Harvey Nichols bar?' That wasn't his kind of place. 'And did he see you?'

'No. For one thing it was very crowded, also he was engrossed in conversation with this . . . woman.'

'Woman?' I echoed. I glanced out of the window. 'So he was on a *date*?'

'Yes. I found it repulsive,' she added.

'Why?'

'Because the woman in question was at least thirty years younger.'

'Oh. How ghastly – for her, I mean.'

'Quite. She looked rather miserable, though he was very animated, chatting away to her nineteen to the dozen – he was wearing the Pucci tie, by the way. Then she went to the loo, so I made my excuses and followed her. And I overheard her ringing a friend. And she said she was on the most "horrendous date of her life" with this "boring old fart . . ."'

'Bloody cheek!'

'. . . who'd knocked twenty years off his age – he'd said he was fifty-two, apparently.'

208

'Fifty-two?' Oh. 'Well, that *is* a bit much – or rather, not nearly enough. But how had he lied about it?'

'Well, this is the point. From the gist of the conversation it became apparent that she'd put an ad in *The Times* personals and Dad had replied. She said that far from being the "fit, fun-loving, macho professional, 45–50" she was seeking, he was a clapped-out OAP.'

'That's very rude – Dad *is* fit, for his years.'

'She then said he'd told her that he'd answered quite a few of these ads – twenty-eight of them, to be precise.'

'Ah.' So that explained why his social life had suddenly picked up.

'Don't you find that shocking?' I heard Cassie say. 'Dad – doing *that* kind of thing at his age! He'll be *seventy* in September!'

I was incapable of being shocked at the moment, I reflected ruefully. 'No, I don't find it shocking,' I replied. 'So "moderately surprised" will have to do. You're not a prude, Cassie – look at the things *you* do – so please don't be too hard on Dad. He's been very lonely since Mum died. Good luck to him.'

'Are you all right, Anna? You're sounding a bit . . . weird.'

'I'm perfectly OK. I'm just tired.'

'But do you think I should mention it to Dad?'

I kicked the cupboard door shut. 'Absolutely *not*! If he wants to make a fool of himself with younger women, that's up to him – and it's got to be a lot more fun than Bridge with the Travises. Anyway, sorry, Cassie, but I've got to go.'

I went up to my workroom and looked at the photo of Mum with her lover again, as I have done many times since I first found it, scanning it for further clues. Seeing it had shattered my peace of mind, obliterating all other thoughts, as though someone had lobbed a brick into my brain. I needed to talk about it, but with whom? Not with Dad, I decided: it would rake up too many bitter memories for him. Not with

Cassie. I didn't want to discuss it with Patrick, as that would make me feel disloyal to my family. I wondered what, if anything, Mark knew. I composed an e-mail to him, telling him that I'd discovered something upsetting and would welcome a chat. But half an hour later I received an auto-reply, saying that he'd be out of town until 19 June.

Over the next few days I found it hard to come to terms with what I'd discovered about my mother. I struggled with the knowledge that she'd had feet of clay. I needed to process what I'd found out – with the help of a professional. I toyed with the idea of finding a shrink. I even looked up a few in *Yellow Pages* and was just about to dial one – a Dr D. Buckhurst, based in Hampstead – when I thought of Jenny. She did stress and trauma counselling. She gave very good, thoughtful advice. More important, she was completely discreet. Her lips were sealed – not just about herself, but about everyone. So I left a message on her machine, asking for an appointment as soon as possible.

'What's this for?' she asked as I arrived at her flat two days later with a bottle of champagne.

'It's because I think it's unlikely that you'll let me pay you.'

'You're right,' she said. 'I won't. But thank you.' She showed me into her large study, which doubled as her consultation room. 'So,' she said gently, as we sat in the two brown leather armchairs. 'You said you needed to talk.'

'I do,' I whispered as her sympathetic tone released in me a wave of pent-up emotion. 'I . . .' She passed me a box of tissues. I took a moment to collect myself, then explained what I'd found. I hadn't brought the photo with me – it was too personal – so I just described it.

As she listened, making the occasional pencilled note, Jenny's face betrayed not a flicker of shock or censure, just an intense, intelligent interest.

'Was your father definitely in Brazil for those eight months? With no breaks?'

210

'Definitely.'

'There's no way he might have forgotten, is there? It was thirty years ago, after all.'

'He does *The Times* crossword every day in twenty minutes. His memory is still excellent. He said he knew for sure that he came back on August the ninth, because that was his mother's birthday.'

'And is there any chance your mum might have gone out to Brazil?'

'That's a very good question,' I said. 'And I did ask him that a couple of days later as casually as I could; and he said that there had been no question of her joining him because she was looking after me and Mark – we were five and seven at the time.'

'So you believe that while your father was in Brazil all those years ago, your mother had an affair, which led to the birth of your sister.'

'Yes, that's what I now believe. Dad admitted that it had been a very unhappy time for him and that the marriage had been under strain; and it would at last explain why Cassie's so . . . different.'

'But what a huge thing to conceal.' An ice-cream van went down the road, blasting out its cheery but somehow melancholy jingle. 'And for such a long time.'

'You're telling me.' I pressed the tissue to my eyes.

'And how do you feel about Cassie now?'

I looked at the ceiling. 'I thought I'd feel differently about her – alienated and awkward – but the truth is I feel exactly the same. She's still my very annoying, feckless and frustrating sister . . . Cassie.'

Jenny nodded. 'But why do you think your parents wouldn't have told her at some stage – let alone you and your brother?'

I shrugged. 'I suppose because Dad was trying to protect Mum. He adored her. He must have adored her to have coped with what had happened – or what she'd done, rather,' I added miserably. 'And I assume he wouldn't have wanted Mark and me to know in case we thought badly of her.'

'So his aim was to protect her and to preserve the illusion of family unity.'

'Yes.'

'That's perfectly understandable, though unfortunately it entailed the deception with which you're now struggling. But who do you think might have taken the photo?'

I shrugged. 'No idea. Some passing stranger probably.'

'And where would you and Mark have been at the time?'

'Probably with Dad's mother, Granny Temple. She loved having us over. So perhaps Mum had dropped us off there while she went to meet . . . him. This Carlo . . .' I shook my head. 'I still can't believe it, Jenny. Even though I'm thirty-five and haven't exactly had a child in ideal circumstances myself.'

'What shocks you most about it?' Jenny asked gently. 'The thought that your mother had an affair? Or the fact that you'd never been told the truth – if it *is* the truth – about Cassie?'

'It's both,' I replied. 'But I'm principally shocked by the fact that my mother had . . . an affair. I can hardly say it, still less get my head round it.'

'Why not?' Jenny asked. 'A lot of women stray during their marriages. It's the stuff of life.'

'I know, but it seems so totally unlike her. My mother was so . . . proper,' I protested. 'She was always telling us how not to let ourselves down – how to behave well – when it now seems that she herself didn't always do that.'

'How do you feel about her now?'

'I feel a bit angry with her – and . . . let down.'

'Because you'd always idealised her?'

'To some degree – yes. But because she always projected this image of her marriage as being so perfect and rock-solid when it clearly can't have been. She had someone else's *baby*.'

212

'But she was a beautiful young woman then. She had two small children. Her husband went away for a long spell. Perhaps she resented him for "abandoning" the family, as she might have seen it. Plus you say that she'd married very young.'

'Yes, at twenty. It was a shotgun wedding.' So that was two lapses of judgement she'd made.

I heard the soft scrape of Jenny's pencil across her pad. 'And your dad was older than her?'

'By twelve years.'

'Which is quite a big gap. Who knows, they might have had problems before he went to Brazil. Then she's left on her own for eight months and she meets this handsome man, an Italian from what you say, about the same age as herself. And he makes her feel loved instead of lonely . . .' I thought of Mum's euphoric expression in the photo. 'Your mother was a human being, Anna.'

'I know.' I could hear the tick of a clock somewhere.

'And she probably gave you that advice because she was trying to make sure that you didn't make the mistakes that she felt she'd made.'

'That's true.' I thought of how she'd interfered in Mark's life too – with such regrettable results. 'But what I can't understand is why my dad would then have treated Cassie not with a resigned tolerance, or even resentment, but as though she were his favourite. He's always spoilt her in a way he's never spoilt me. That's what doesn't make sense.'

There was a pause. 'I'd say it does,' Jenny said.

'Why?'

'Because in order to keep his family together, he'd decided to bring up this baby as his own, despite the distress he must have felt. Your mother also wanted to keep the family together, clearly, so she agreed to go along with the deceit that Cassie was his. But that might be the very reason why he indulged Cassie.'

'What do you mean?'

'Perhaps he was so afraid that he wouldn't be *able* to love her that he went out of his way to spoil her – to get a positive reaction from her, which would help him to feel paternal towards her. Perhaps that was the only way he could cope. Because if he rejected Cassie, the illusion of family unity would be impossible and everything would fall apart.'

It's almost as though he was trying to compensate her for something.

'You could be right,' I said quietly. I stood up. 'I'm glad I've talked to you, Jenny. You have a lot of wisdom. Thank you.'

'So . . . What now?'

I heaved a deep sigh. 'I don't know.'

'One option is to try to forget about it and carry on as though nothing's happened. Do you want to do that?'

I shook my head. 'It's too big. But it's not up to me to tell Cassie the truth, is it?'

'So who is it up to?'

'My father, of course.'

The next night, as I got ready for the Edwards' party, I thought about how I might broach such an impossible subject with Dad. I'd have to choose my moment very carefully, I reflected as I put on my earrings. It might be easier to do it over the phone, or perhaps I could write him a letter; or maybe I should just get myself on the *Jerry Springer Show* and we could have it all out on there. Perhaps they'd even find Carlo, I mused as I slipped on my shoes. I imagined a punch-up between him and Dad, followed by a touching reconciliation brought about by an unexpectedly mature intervention by Cassie. The studio audience would go wild.

My reverie was broken by the sound of Luisa singing to Milly: '*Centellea, centellea, estrellita . . .*'

This was too much. I went downstairs.

214

'*Me pregunto que eres tu . . .*'

'Luisa,' I said quietly. 'The words to that song are "Twinkle twinkle little star / How I wonder what you are". Would you kindly stop singing them to Milly in Spanish? However lovely your voice, I find it intensely annoying – and would you please stop talking to her in Spanish because you are *confusing* her.' I thought of the biting incident at Sweet Peas. Then I thought of all the money Luisa had in her room: on my most recent narco-snoop I'd seen that her nest egg had grown to five grand. 'I paid for you to go to English classes,' I went on, struggling to control my tone. 'But as far as I can tell you've done no studying.'

Luisa flushed bright red. 'Am sorry, Anna.'

'And when I can get to speak to your English teacher, Mr Cox – with whom I have now left three messages – I'm going to ask him precisely what you do there.' She blenched. 'I know you go every morning,' I went on, 'but what you get up to there during those three hours is beyond my comprehension.'

'*Comprensión?*' she repeated blankly.

'*Sí. Comprensión*! Understanding! What we don't have enough of around here!'

'*Mamá, estás enfadada con Luisa?*' Milly said.

'I'm not cross with her,' I replied. '*Nada más estoy un poco frustrada.*'

Milly turned to Luisa. '*La Momia is infeliz actualmente.*'

'I am *not* unhappy,' I protested. 'I am fine, thank you very much. Anyway . . .' I took a deep breath. 'I'll see you later, Milly.' I kissed her. 'Be a good girl.'

'Soy *una chica buena!*' she protested indignantly.

'I know you are, darling,' I said

I got a cab to the party so that I could drink. As it drew up outside the house I saw a column of guests flowing up the steps and being welcomed by aproned caterers bearing trays of champagne. As I took a glass I glanced at the label – it

215

was vintage Veuve Clicquot. The Edwards' did nothing by halves.

I went through the hall, which was now hung with expensive paintings and decorated with two floral arrangements the size of telephone kiosks. The scent of stargazer lilies mingled with the cloud of expensive perfume that clung to the beautifully dressed crowd.

'-We'll be going to Sardinia again.'

'-We've got a place in Monaco.'

'-I did have a Sisley, but I sold it.'

'-The way the dollar's going . . .'

'-Will you be at the Cartier again this year?'

I stepped out of the french windows, stopped and looked down on to the garden, allowing myself to enjoy the moment. I felt my chest fill with pride. The limestone paving gleamed in the early-evening sunlight, the raised flowerbeds looked elegantly architectural and the plants within them complemented each other in terms of their colour and form. The granite water feature looked imposing; the pleached limes were neat and smart, their clipped branches beautifully intertwining, as though the four little trees had linked arms. I was relieved to see that no one was standing on the lawn – the high heels would have wrecked the new turf.

There were about a hundred people there already – I recognised a few figures from the City, a couple of politicians and one or two celebrities, who were probably private clients of Gill's. I spotted the cellist Julian Lloyd-Webber; he was talking to the actor Robert Powell, who was leaning against one of the tall granite planters.

Seeing Powell made me think of Carol Gowing, because she'd done an episode of *Holby City* in which she'd had some scenes with him. I found myself wondering what had become of her and whether Mark still thought of her, four years on, and whom, if anyone, he was with now.

'Anna!' Gill Edwards was at my elbow, in a salmon-coloured

silk shirt-dress. 'I'm thrilled you could come. So . . .' She indicated the garden with a sweep of her hand. 'What do you think? Are you pleased?'

'I am – if you are.'

'I'm delighted,' she replied. 'We're both delighted. Martin even likes the hydrangeas.' She giggled. These were not the pink mop-headed ones that he had so loathed, but a compromise variety – *Hydrangea paniculata* – which have elegant cones of white flowers. 'Now, who do you know here?'

'Just you and Martin, I think.'

She grabbed my hand. 'Then let me introduce you to some very old friends of ours – Antonia and Eduardo Morea. This is Anna Temple,' Gill said, leading me towards the couple. 'Anna is the very talented designer of this lovely garden.' I could have kissed her.

'You're the garden designer?' Antonia said. She was about sixty, elegant in a pale-pink silk trouser suit with a dove-grey pashmina.

'Yes, I am.' I tried not to gawk at the postage-stamp-sized lozenge diamond on her ring finger.

'Eduardo and I were just admiring it – it's fantastic. How long did it take to build?' I explained. 'And are you very busy at the moment?'

My heart leapt. 'Fairly busy,' I was careful to say.

'Because we live in Belsize Park and our garden really could do with a facelift, couldn't it, Eddie? Mind you,' she snorted, 'he says the same thing about me.'

'Don't be silly, darling,' he protested. 'But we could make much more of the garden, that's true. Oh, yes please,' he said as a passing waiter offered us some more champagne.

'Do you have a business card?' his wife asked me.

I'd decided in advance that handing out cards would look crass. 'I think the best thing would be to ask Gill. Or you could visit my website? My name's Anna Temple.'

Mrs Morea took a leather-bound notebook out of her clutch

bag and scribbled in it with a tiny gold pencil. 'Anna . . . Temple . . .' She smiled at me. 'I'll take a look. But I love these huge planters – and that fountain is wonderful and sounds lovely.'

'Thank you.'

'Well, we mustn't hog you,' she said. 'But I am definitely going to call you.' I smiled goodbye, knowing that she probably wouldn't, but having enjoyed our chat.

There was still no sign of Jamie as I went down the steps, but then I saw a familiar face. 'Miles!' I exclaimed. My old boss.

'Anna!' he almost shouted. 'How lovely to see you.' He clutched both my hands and kissed me warmly on the cheek. He still looked like an overgrown cherub, except that his blond curls were a little greyer than before. 'But . . . how do you know Gill and Martin?'

'They're clients of mine.'

'You mean you built this . . . ?'

'No. My wonderful landscaper, Jamie, built it. But I designed it.'

'Well, Fabia and I have just moved out to Hampshire. Now I know what you can do I'll get you to come out and see our garden – it's a two-acre wreck.'

'I'd love to,' I said. 'And how are your boys?' I asked as a caterer offered us a caviar canapé.

'They're great. The eldest will start boarding next year – I can hardly believe it. But what about your little girl?' he asked. 'Sue showed me a photo – she looks adorable.'

'Thank you.' It was strange to think that Milly had been conceived on my very last day at Arden – as though she were a leaving present from myself to myself.

'So you have a family life now too,' Miles said.

'I do. It's a bit unconventional, but I'm very happy.' I thought of Patrick. 'And Arden's performing well; I've seen some good coverage in the business pages.'

218

He shrugged. 'We all beaver away. That's how I know Gill,' he went on. 'She invests some of her private clients' money with us – she's a very canny woman. Now . . . hi, there, you two!'

A couple in their early forties had appeared at Miles's elbow. He kissed the woman on the cheek, then turned to me. 'Anna, have you met Andrew and Jane Barraclough?'

'No,' I replied, smiling at them. There was something familiar about the man, though I couldn't put my finger on what. He was very attractive; his wife, despite her expensive outfit and immaculate grooming, less so. She had a slightly pinched look, as though she were sucking on a caper.

'Andrew and I go way back,' Miles explained. 'We both worked at Deutsche Bank years ago.'

'More than I care to remember,' Andrew pointed out with a smile.

'Where do you work now?' I asked, keen to place him.

'I'm still in the City,' he replied. Then he nodded at his wife. 'Jane and I both work for Goldman Sachs. We're colleagues of Martin's.'

'So does Jane keep an eye on you, then?' Miles guffawed.

I saw Jane flinch. 'That's rather a tall order,' she said with an air of long-suffering, 'quite literally, as I'm on the fourth floor and he's on the thirty-ninth.'

Why did I have this persistent sense of déjà vu? Perhaps I'd seen him at some function or other when I worked in the Square Mile, or maybe I'd seen him on TV. We chatted amicably for a few moments then, out of the corner of my eye, I saw Jamie, with Thea. I waved and they came over, Thea in a shimmering pale-blue cocktail dress with her hair drawn back and a white gardenia tucked behind her ear. Her slender arms had a caramel gloss from all her travelling.

'Hi, Jamie!' I said. 'Hi, Thea,' I added with champagne-infused warmth. 'It's so nice to see you,' I lied. To my surprise she gave me a tight little smile, as though she felt uncomfortable in my presence. It was as though she knew that I knew – but how could she? 'This is my former boss, Miles Latimer,' I pressed on, 'and Jane and Andrew Barraclough.'

As Jamie shook hands with Andrew, a look of puzzlement crossed his face. 'We're neighbours, mate,' he said, smiling at him.

'We are?' Andrew gave him an odd, almost wary sort of look. Perhaps he'd disliked being called 'mate'. I glanced at Thea who was sipping her champagne and staring into the middle distance as though she were already bored. So much for your PR skills, I thought. I returned my gaze to Andrew, tantalised by the feeling of familiarity.

'You live in Blythe Road,' I heard Jamie say. So that was the reason. Andrew was local.

'Oh . . . yes.' Andrew nodded slowly. 'Of course. Sorry . . . er . . . ?'

'Jamie,' Jamie said amiably.

'I do recognise you now. It's . . . erm . . . seeing people out of context. Always throws one a bit, doesn't it? But . . . you're at number 32, aren't you?'

'That's right. I'm the proud owner of the battered blue pick-up.' He grinned. 'And you've got that eff-off Bentley!'

'I'm afraid so,' Andrew replied. 'We're terrible show-offs really, aren't we, darling?' He turned to his wife. 'Oh,' he said, reddening. She'd gone. How rude, I thought, to walk away in the middle of an introduction. 'I'm . . . sorry,' he muttered. 'She must . . . have . . . Anyway . . . very nice to meet you.' He gave us an apologetic smile and was gone.

'That was weird,' Jamie said to Thea and me once Miles had drifted away. 'That bloke Andrew made out he didn't know me, but I'm sure as hell he does because we pass each other in the street sometimes – they've got the big corner house. Didn't you think they were weird, darling?' he added to Thea.

220

As she sipped her champagne, a frown pleated her beautiful brow. 'Hmm . . .' she replied. 'Very odd.'

The next day was not a good one. My computer crashed and I had to call out an engineer to fix it, which took three hours; then my Broadband connection went down and I had to call him back in the early evening, and by the time it was restored I'd lost two days' worth of e-mails. Besides which I was preoccupied with working out how to have my difficult conversation with Dad. I'd mentally rehearse the phrases I might use, but the words would stick in my throat.

Dad, there's something I need to ask you.
I know it was a long time ago.
Photo of Mum with . . .
I didn't mean to upset you.
Please will you tell me the truth?

What I wanted to say seemed quite unsayable, especially after so long. Perhaps it was better to keep family secrets buried, I thought, as the days went by; then life could simply go on as before.

In the meantime I had two new commissions to get started on – a patio garden in Camden and a roof terrace in Maida Vale – and I was spending more time with Patrick. Milly remained a little diffident with him, as she tried to work out his role in our lives.

'Patrick's a friend of Mummy's,' I would tell her. 'And he's your friend too,' it suddenly occurred to me to add one day.

'No.' She shook her dark curls. 'Milly's friends is Gracie and Phoebe and Carna and Lily . . .'

'Because only other children can be your friends – is that it?'

'. . . and Luisa,' I heard her add.

'Oh.'

'And Jamie,' she concluded.

'Right. Well . . . Patrick would like to be your friend too. One day. When you know him a bit better.'

221

To his credit, Patrick hadn't put a foot wrong. He would just chat to Milly and read to her, or do painting or Playdough with her. He'd push her on the swings or gently spin her on the roundabout. He took us to Legoland one Saturday, then to the Science Museum the next weekend. If he stayed overnight, he would make sure Milly was asleep before coming upstairs, and he would always leave before she woke up. 'I feel she knows me now,' he said a few days after the Edwards' party. We were sitting in my garden, having a late breakfast. He trickled some of his own Bee Good honey on to his toast. 'I hope that gradually Milly will come to accept that I'm part of the picture,' he went on. 'But I was thinking that maybe the three of us could have a little holiday, later in the summer, then she'd see that we're, well, together in every sense.'

The thought of being 'together in every sense' made me feel suddenly happy.

'A holiday?' I repeated. I glanced at the sheaf of unopened mail in front of me – three letters, a postcard and an airmail packet with a strip of stamps with tropical birds on them. It was Milly's birthday present from Xan.

'Yes,' Patrick said. 'A holiday. Would you like that?'

I sipped my coffee. 'Very much. But where would we go?'

'How about Cornwall? There's a nice hotel I know near St Mawes. The beach is only five minutes away. We could take Milly paddling and rock-pooling.'

I had a sudden vision of Milly's net jumping with shrimps. 'That sounds like bliss. But when do you have in mind?'

'Late August? I'll be going to New Zealand again in early September.'

I batted away a wasp. 'Late August would be fine.'

'It'll be my treat.'

I reached for his hand. 'You're a very generous, nice man, Patrick, but I wouldn't hear of it.'

As he looked at the newspaper I opened the first envelope, which contained a flyer for the International Fuchsia

Convention in Stoke. In the next was an invitation to join the west London branch of the National Begonia Society. Then there was a friendly postcard from Elaine, who was looking after a baby in Scotland.

'What's this? I murmured, opening the last letter, which had a local postmark. I read it. 'It's about Milly's end-of-term concert.'

'A concert for three-year-olds?' Patrick said.

'I think they just sing a few songs, and the mums and dads come along.'

'Could I come?' he suddenly said.

'Sure,' I heard myself say, though I felt a little uneasy – it was too early. 'But it says here that the parents are expected to make the costumes! I hate dressmaking,' I wailed. 'And I'm busy.' I looked at the letter. 'When is it? July the twelfth! That's in two weeks. They could have given us more warning,' I muttered.

'What's Milly playing?'

'A Flower Fairy apparently – a forget-me-not one: the show's called *The Magic Garden*.'

'But she's got that fairy outfit you gave her. You could adapt that.'

'That's true . . . It's pale blue so all I'd have to do is make some dark-green satin leaves and tack them on to it with lots of little deeper blue flowers; maybe Cassie could knit her a blue hat. And I could make a magic wand with a blue flower on the end, instead of a star,' I added, suddenly enjoying myself now, 'and I could get her some blue ballet shoes, or dye some white ones. Not such a tall order then.' I breathed a sigh of relief.

'And what dates would suit you for Cornwall?' Patrick asked.

I reached into my bag for my diary. 'The eighteenth to the twenty-fifth?' I suggested, 'so that we avoid the bank holiday traffic?'

'The eighteenth to the twenty-fifth sounds good. I'll ring the hotel I have in mind and try to book one of their family suites.' He stood up. 'I'd better go. I've a meeting at ten. I'll ring you later, gorgeous.' He bent to kiss me and left.

Finishing my coffee, I allowed myself to project ahead, as I increasingly do these days. After two and a half months, Patrick and I were a couple. We planned our week together and compared diaries. The early uncertainties in our relationship had gone. I no longer worried that he wouldn't ring me back when I left him a message: our teeth no longer clashed when we kissed. By now we were beginning to feel that we knew each other and that our lives were converging.

I still luxuriated in the knowledge that Patrick had fallen for me and pursued me, and that he wanted me. If I stayed with him my life would be . . . nicer, I reasoned. With him I'd have stability and the chance of a proper family life. Milly would have the father figure she needed and maybe a sibling, or even two. I suddenly saw myself with three children, lined up beside me like Russian dolls.

But where would we live? In Patrick's house possibly – it was big enough, though the bees would have to go. I imagined them vacating the hives in an indignant swarm. Or we could buy a larger house in Brook Green, if Patrick could bear the memories. Or there were some nice houses in Ladbroke Grove with big gardens. I imagined myself digging a new border and filling it with flowering plants.

I put down my cup and picked up the parcel from Indonesia. I undid it and removed the prettily gift-wrapped present ready for Milly to open when she got back from school. And I was just cutting out the stamps for her to keep, when I saw that there was a postcard inside – it was of a green and black butterfly with turquoise swallowtails. Milly will love this, I thought. Then I turned it over and saw that it was for me.

Sorry Milly's present is late, Xan had written in his familiar scrawl. *I've been in East Timor for the last few days for*

Newsnight. *But this is to say that I'm definitely returning to London next month.*

'What?' I murmured.

As I told you in my last e-mail my posting here ends on 5 July so I'll be deputy editing in the newsroom until early September while they decide where to send me next. I'll be back in Stanley Sq. on 6 July and hope to start spending some time with Milly then. X.

ELEVEN

My predominant emotion was dismay. I didn't want Xan to come back now, stirring up old emotions just when I'd begun to feel happy again. Nor did I want his other half getting involved – the thought of it made me feel sick. I imagined opening the door and seeing Xan standing there with his ultra successful, no doubt fantastically attractive American girlfriend – or, quite possibly, she was his fiancée by now. I knew it was unreasonable of me to exclude her, given that I was with Patrick, but I couldn't stand the thought of another woman playing happy families with my child and my ex.

Pumped up with a kind of insane energy, I went to my computer and did something that, until now, I'd resisted doing. I Googled 'CNN + Trisha Fox'. Up popped a photo of a beautiful blonde in a flak-jacket on a palm-fringed road somewhere in the tropics. No, I did not want to meet her, I decided, as I skimmed through her terrifyingly impressive CV detailing her internship at the White House, her doctorate in International Relations from Harvard and her Emmy nomination for her 'outstanding coverage' of the Asian tsunami.

I composed a quick e-mail to Xan: *Your message about coming back to London didn't reach me as I've had computer problems and lost two days' e-mails, so this has come out of the blue. Of course you can see Milly – as much as you'd like. But I'd rather your girlfriend wasn't involved as . . . how* could I justify it without him thinking I was jealous? *. . . I feel it would be confusing for Milly and I'd like to keep things simple. I hope you understand this, A.*

I read through it, then clicked on Send.

'I'm not having it,' I muttered as I drove to Fulham to do a new site survey. 'If Xan wants to see us, he comes on his own.'

The garden I'd been asked to look at was in an old vicarage in Eden Lane, just off the North End Road. I rang the bell of the rather gloomy red-brick house and an attractive but worn-looking blonde woman of forty or so opened the door. She had a baby girl of about six months in her arms, and twin boys of about eighteen months were clamped to either leg, like koalas.

'Hi,' she said warmly. 'I'm Pippa. This is Kitty, Jack and Alfred.'

'What lovely children.' I held Kitty's outstretched hand for a moment and as I stroked her dimpled knuckles I suddenly realised how much I would like another baby; then I looked at the boys, who were peeping at me from behind their mum. 'Hi,' I said. 'I've come to see your garden. Will you show it to me?' They scooted off down the hall, holding hands.

'My husband will be down in a minute,' Pippa said as we followed them into the old-fashioned kitchen. 'I know you always like to see couples together.'

'I do, because I need to know that they're both in agreement about what's to be done and how much the budget will be.'

'I can understand that. He's just had to take a phone call – he works from home. Anyway . . .' She flung open the back door. 'This is it.'

As the twins toddled down the steps, I stared at it. 'Well . . . it needs quite a makeover.'

'It does,' she agreed. 'It's not very pretty.'

'No,' I had to agree. 'It isn't.'

It was . . . ugly. It was dark, with the dour, depressing air of a Victorian shrubbery. It consisted of a scrubby square lawn, strewn with toys and surrounded by overgrown shrubs such as *Viburnum tinus*, which has dark, dense foliage, a large rhododendron, and a *Choisya* that had grown out of control. There were also a number of trees – a large lilac, *Weigela* and a bay tree that had been allowed to get far too big, sucking out all the light. The garden was enclosed by very high red-brick walls and, despite the time of year, there was little colour, though here and there a rose or a clematis poked through the dusty leaves, a reminder that the garden had once been loved.

I began to take photos. 'The whole thing needs thinning out and lightening,' I said as one of the twins clambered on to a plastic rocking whale. I began to chat through a few ideas. 'I'd keep the lawn as big as possible,' I said, 'because of the children. But I'd probably change the shape a little, and put a path of cream stone round it to give it definition and brightness.'

'And I'd like a really nice climbing frame,' she said. 'At the moment I'm their climbing frame!'

I smiled. 'You could get a wonderful one – I've got lots of catalogues I could show you. And you could perhaps have a sandpit in that corner over there. But once some of these shrubs have been removed, you're going to have room for lots of flowering plants. I think the raised beds should be rebuilt at a lower level as they're unnecessarily high. And we could soften these walls with blue trellising and grow some pretty white climbers up it to give a feeling of light.'

'I'd like a patio area by the house, for eating out.'

'I'd also suggest that you have a seating arbour here, with box benches, so that you can stow away the kids' toys – it could have a shelf for drinks, or a row of tea lights,' I went on, as I clicked away with the camera. 'It would be a lovely place to sit with the newspaper.'

'If I ever have the time!' She laughed. I heard a step behind us. 'Here's Gerald.'

I turned. Her husband was advancing across the lawn. To my surprise he was a good fifteen years older than Pippa, with a shock of silvery grey hair and an upright bearing, as though he'd served in the forces.

'Ah, good to meet you,' he said. He gave me a firm hand-shake, then nodded at the garden. 'So what do you think?'

'I think . . . it's going to be a challenge – but I like challenges.'

He surveyed the garden, hands on hips. 'It's a crying shame, really, as it used to look an absolute picture.'

'Really?'

He nodded. 'My late wife used to do it.'

'Oh.'

'She was a marvellous gardener.'

'Uh huh.'

'But it's gone to the dogs now.'

Pippa smiled patiently. 'I'm afraid I'm not very green-fingered.'

'You don't have to be,' I said. 'And if you do commission me, I have lots of gardening books and photo files for you to look through so that we can identify the plants and shrubs that you like.'

'My first wife could grow anything,' I heard Gerald say. I felt my face go hot with embarrassment. 'I left it all to her – she didn't mind because she was so damn good at it.'

'How long have you lived here?' I asked him politely.

'Twenty-two years.'

'I see.' Poor Pippa, I thought, having to move into the house in which her deceased predecessor had lived for so long. How depressing.

'But after Ginny died five years ago, I asked my two teenage

229

girls if they wanted to move and they both said "no way" – so we decided to carry on here, didn't we, Pips?'

'Hmm,' she replied with a vague smile.

'But my first wife – she really knew about gardening. Loved her flowers – but now . . .' He shrugged.

'I'm afraid all I do is cut the grass,' Pippa said.

'With three tiny children I'm amazed you do even that,' I said, wondering why Gerald didn't do it himself, or pay a gardener. 'Anyway, you're doing the right thing, getting professional help.'

'Yes . . . she could grow anything,' I heard him mutter.

'And if you did choose to employ me,' I said, ignoring him, 'I'd transform this garden. But I'll do some basic drawings first, which will take about a week. But on the planting front I think we'd stick to perennials to keep it as low-maintenance as possible as you've obviously got your hands full Pippa,' I added pointedly.

'And what about the budget?' she asked.

'I'd have to work it out – but I can tell, just by looking at what has to be done and the amount of clearance involved, that it'll be in the region of twenty-five to thirty thousand pounds.'

'Good God!' Gerald exclaimed. 'That's what we're thinking of spending on a new kitchen.'

'Well,' I said, 'you should think of it in the same way. Your garden is another room in the house – a very important room – so you should consider spending a similar amount. And if you're happy to have a thirty-thousand-pound kitchen, why settle for a five-thousand-pound garden?'

'I can see the logic of that,' Pippa said. She transferred the baby to the other hip. 'But your ideas sound lovely, so will you go ahead and do the drawings?'

'Steady on, Pips!' Gerald barked. 'Can't we talk about this?'

'We need to have this done,' she replied softly. 'There's no

230

park nearby, so this is where the children will do most of their playing, and I'll go halves with you, as I've said.'

'Well . . .' The mention of money seemed to embarrass him. 'As long as the designs don't commit us to having it done.'

'They don't,' I assured him. 'You pay for the drawings separately and you only go ahead with the work if you want to.' I turned to Pippa. 'I'll get them to you within a week.'

You get a real insight into people's lives, doing this job, I reflected as I left. I walked up to the market on the North End Road to try and get some green satin for Milly's forget-me-not costume. I've done gardens for newly divorced women, for example, who've had to move to a smaller house; they want the garden done up to make themselves feel better, in the same way they might have cosmetic surgery, or a makeover, so they're very pernickety about how it's done. I've had clients whose arguments about the proposed design have been indicative of marital stress. I did a small garden for one couple who'd argued about everything from the type of trellising to the particular variety of *Potentilla*; when I went round a few weeks after it was finished to see how the plants were doing, it turned out that the husband had left.

With Pippa I could see what the scenario had probably been. She'd been a professional woman, approaching forty, desperate to have a family before it was too late; then she meets the recently widowed Gerald, who makes a play for her and isn't averse to the idea of more children, so she decides that he'll have to do. She has her babies as fast as she can, only then realising that she's now going to have to *live* with Gerald's bossy patrician ways and his tactless remarks about his dead wife, in a house she probably wished had been sold.

'BA-*NARN*-AS! POUND A SCOOP! BEST AVO-*CARD*-ERS! TWO FER A POUND!'

I walked around the crowded market, picking my way through the cardboard trays of scarlet apples and shiny courgettes. The wind had picked up and litter skittered along the street, wrapping itself round people's legs. I glanced up and saw a polythene bag floating through the air, like a jellyfish. I found a couple of fabric stalls, one of which had some green lining material, which would do instead of satin, then I went into a haberdasher's where I bought twenty small blue silk flowers and two yards of blue ribbon.

When I got home I read my e-mails and found a reply to mine from Xan. It simply said, *No problem. X.* I sighed with relief.

Then I opened the next message, from Mark. *I'm sorry not to have got back to you,* he'd written, *but I've been on vacation for a few days in Palm Springs. What was it you wanted to know?*

I clicked on Reply: *It's about Mum and Dad,'* I typed.

It's very sensitive. I've recently discovered that things weren't quite what they seemed with their marriage and I'd welcome the chance to talk to you, preferably over the phone, as it's far too personal – and upsetting – to put in an e-mail. Love, Anna.

A couple of hours later I received a reply:

Dear Anna,
I know what you're referring to, but I'm afraid I won't be able to help as I don't see why I should be the one to enlighten you about this when our parents should have done so years ago. I suggest, if he's willing to discuss it, that you talk to Dad. Sorry not to be more forthcoming, but as you rightly say, it's upsetting. Love to you and Milly, Mark.

As I stared at Mark's message another one pinged into my inbox. It was from Patrick, to say that he'd managed to book the hotel in Cornwall for the dates I'd suggested, but my head

232

was still in a whirl about Mark's reply – or rather, his rebuff. How long had he known what I'd only just found out? And why had he never told me?

I e-mailed Patrick back but decided not to tell him yet about Xan coming to London. Nor did I tell Milly in case something happened to prevent it – besides which I didn't want her to mention it in front of Patrick before I was ready to tell him myself.

In the meantime the weather had begun to warm up. The temperature, which had been a pleasant twenty-three degrees or so, began to rise daily into the upper twenties, then into the low thirties as the heatwave took hold.

COSTA DEL BRITAIN! screamed the newspaper headlines. 100F – AND IT'S GOING TO GET HOTTER!!

Every day we awoke to a cloudless blue sky and by ten it was almost too hot to venture outside into the retina-burning glare. The papers were full of photos of office workers stripped to their underwear in desiccating parks, of tarmac melting like molasses and of train tracks in Birmingham buckling like hairpins. A water pipe burst in Holland Park Avenue and there were shots of children joyfully dancing in and out of the spray.

On 4 July I took the drawings of the vicarage garden to show Pippa and Gerald. As I discussed the designs with them the twins splashed about in the paddling pool in their swim nappies. I wished I could get in with them and stay there all summer. It wasn't the heat so much as the humidity. Within minutes of showering I was wet with sweat and practically prostrate with fatigue.

In a few hours Xan would be boarding his plane for London, I reflected nervously, as I left Eden Lane. Yet I still hadn't told Patrick – I couldn't even explain to myself why. I decided to tell him the following day when I went to help him extract the honey. I'd agreed to this as long as I didn't have to go anywhere near the hives: apart from my reluctance to meet the bees again I didn't want to put on a protective suit in the heat . . .

'So it's honey harvest day,' I said when I arrived.

He kissed me. 'It is. I'm doing it a bit early because it's easier to extract when the weather's hot – it's also a lot easier to strain.'

'So have you got a good crop?'

'Bumper. I removed the supers this morning and judging from their weight I've got a good eighty pounds – that's twice as much as my first crop last year.'

We went into the kitchen, where Patrick had his extracting equipment all ready: an uncapping knife to remove the wax from the comb; an electric spinner, which looked like the inside of a tumble dryer; a clean bucket; a large sieve; four boxes of glass jars and a box of Bee Good labels. The frames were stacked on the table, oozing honey, its sweet, slightly medicinal fragrance permeating the warm, humid air.

'You've got the windows closed,' I said as I washed my hands. 'Can't we open them?'

'I'm afraid not,' he replied. 'Otherwise the bees will come in to reclaim their stolen honey.'

I shuddered at the thought. 'Fair enough. But how do you extract it?'

'The spinner flings it out, by centrifugal force.' He tied a white apron on to me, flicking my hair to one side and brushing a soft kiss on to the nape of my neck. 'Then the honey goes into this holding tank here . . . and then into the collection bucket here . . . which has this valve here, allowing us to bottle it.'

He put on his own apron, picked up a large serrated knife, dipped it into a bowl of hot water and began to slice the wax cappings off the first frame, exposing the cells of clear golden liquid, which sparkled in the sunlight. He did one side, flipped it over, did the same to the other side and

234

scraped the discarded wax caps into a huge saucepan to be separated later. Then he placed the uncapped honeycomb in the spinner.

'Could you do this one?' he asked, passing a frame to me.

'Sure.' I picked up a knife.

'Dip it in the hot water first,' he said. 'Then slice slowly upwards. Do it from side to side, as though you were cutting bread . . . that's right. Then scrape the discarded wax into this pan. Now turn the frame over and do the same to the other side.'

As we worked in silence I felt beads of sweat trickle into the small of my back.

'Patrick,' I said as I put the exposed frame in the extractor. 'There's something I need to tell you.'

'What's that?' he asked casually without looking at me. 'If it's that you don't like honey, I already know and have reluctantly come to terms with it.'

'No. It's that . . . Xan's coming to London.'

For a moment Patrick didn't reply, apparently engrossed in the uncapping process. 'For how long?'

'Two months.'

'Two *months*?' he repeated as he turned the frame over.

'Yes. His posting in Indonesia's ended . . .'

'I see . . .'

'So he's going to work in the newsroom until his next one starts.'

'Which will be where?' he said as he picked up another frame.

'He doesn't know. But the thing is, he wants to spend time with Milly.'

There was a pause. 'Of course he does,' Patrick said calmly. 'He's her father.'

'Which means . . . he'll be coming to the house sometimes so . . . I just wanted to tell you that now, before he arrives.'

'Well . . . Thank you for letting me know.' He began slicing

235

the new frame, keeping his head down as he concentrated on the task, still not meeting my gaze. 'You'll have to tell him that we'll be away in August.'

'Oh yes,' I said with a stab of regret. Now I wished I hadn't committed myself to Cornwall when it would mean that Milly would lose a whole week with her dad.

'So when does he arrive?' Patrick asked as he put the finished frame in the extractor.

'Erm . . . Tomorrow.'

'Oh.' He picked up another frame. 'So soon.' He lifted out a dead, sticky bee with a fork. 'How odd that you've taken so long to tell me.'

'But . . . I only knew myself a few days ago and I've been . . . busy.'

'Where will he stay? Not with you, I hope.'

'Of course not – at his flat in Notting Hill.'

'Well . . . I hope you won't . . . want to . . .' Patrick's voice trailed away. 'I think you know what I mean, Anna,' he added quietly.

'It's OK,' I murmured. 'I won't.' I removed an amputated wing. 'I don't know why you think I would.'

'Because whenever you've talked about Xan I can see that you once . . . loved him.' *Yes! I did!* I suddenly wanted to say. 'And so,' Patrick went on, 'I hope that . . .'

I shook my head. 'Our relationship ended a long time ago. Xan's with someone else – and has been for ages – and I'm with *you* now, Patrick, aren't I?'

Patrick looked at me for the first time since I'd broached the subject. His eyes were a clear amber, flecked with gold, like the honey. 'Yes,' he said softly. 'You're with me.'

TWELVE

'And I thought Jakarta was sweaty,' Xan breathed as he arrived at the house two days later. He kissed me on the cheek and his stubbled face felt moist. His sky-blue T-shirt had navy stains across the chest and back, like a Rorschach print. 'London's not meant to be like this.'

'I know,' I said as he followed me down the hall. 'We've all flopped like a bunch of wilting pansies.' Suddenly Milly came running down the stairs on her sturdy little legs. I'd only told her about Xan's arrival the day before.

'Daddy! Iss my *daddy*!' she shouted exultantly. As she threw up her arms for a hug I remembered her insistence, on her birthday, that Xan *was* coming. I wondered whether, in some preternatural way, she'd known.

'My little girl,' he breathed as he scooped her up in his arms. Then he dangled her above him, her legs kicking, their noses touching, both of them laughing. It made me feel elated, but at the same time outraged. Because if Xan had chosen to live with me – or at least stay nearby – then Milly could have cuddled him every day of her life.

'You're such a big girl now,' he exclaimed as he held her close.

'Yes,' she said. 'I getting bigger.' She expanded her hands.

'And bigger and *bigger*!' She suddenly clapped her palms to Xan's cheeks, then rubbed his five o'clock shadow with a slightly affronted expression.

'I think your dad needs a shave,' I said as Xan carried her down to the kitchen. 'What would you like?' I asked him as he put her down. 'Water? Coke? PG Tips?' I added with a smile – I wanted to keep things friendly, for Milly's sake.

'A Coke, please. Her dress looks sweet.' I'd put her in one of the batik print dresses that he'd sent her for her birthday.

'It does.' I opened the fridge. 'And it's cool. So . . .' I got out Coke for Xan and gave Milly her beaker of apple juice. 'How often will you be coming over?'

'That's largely up to you,' he replied as I handed him a glass, 'but I'd like to see her at least twice during the week – say on Mondays and Wednesdays, after work. I'll mostly be on day shifts, finishing at about six. We could play in the park.'

'We go park now, Dad,' Milly said, grabbing his hand with both hers and trying to pull him off his chair. 'Come, Dad!' she commanded. '*Come!*'

'Let Daddy have his drink first, darling,' I said as I handed it to him. 'He's very tired. You must be horribly jet-lagged,' I added.

He nodded blearily. 'I still can't get used to it despite all the travelling I've done. But I'd like to have some weekend time with Milly too,' he added. 'Maybe I could take her swimming.'

'Yes. Maybe.' I sat down. 'Thanks for being so understanding about not bringing your girlfriend here by the way. I just wanted to keep everything . . .'

'It's OK,' Xan interjected. 'You don't have to explain. In any case Trisha isn't in London.' Such had been my obsession that it hadn't occurred to me that she wouldn't have come with him. 'In fact' – he sipped his Coke – 'we've gone our separate ways.'

238

'Oh. . . . I'm sorry,' I lied as euphoria flooded my veins. 'I thought you'd be engaged by now.'

He shook his head. 'She's a lovely person, but we were growing apart. Then she was made bureau chief for CNN in Japan and I decided that I didn't want to follow her to Tokyo.'

'Why not?' curiosity prompted me to ask.

'Because the BBC doesn't keep a correspondent out there, so I would just have been a stringer. Plus Japan isn't seen as a particularly prestigious posting.'

'Then why did she go?'

'Because for her, at thirty, it's a great break. But I'm forty-one. So I have to make the right career moves otherwise I'll end up in a backwater.'

'Where will you go next?'

He opened the fridge. 'I don't know. I threw my hat into the ring for Israel,' he added as he took the ice tray out of the freezer compartment. 'And Washington.' He dropped some cubes into his Coke. 'I'll have a clearer picture next month.' He lifted his glass. 'Cheers, Anna. It's good to see you again.' He smiled. 'You look . . . well.'

'Thanks,' I said, wondering how much of a compliment 'well' was. Did 'well' mean 'pretty', or 'not too bad for your age', or 'nothing special'? Then I wondered why I was wondering when I had Patrick.

'Xan . . .' I had to tell him about Patrick. 'Xan . . .'

'Where's Milly?' he suddenly asked.

'I heard her go upstairs. I'll call her.' Then I heard her descending footfall and saw her looking at herself in the big round mirror at the bottom of the stairs.

'Look, Dad!' she said as she ran into the kitchen. She'd put on her fairy costume, which now sported green leaves and a liberal sprinkling of dainty blue flowers. 'Iss for my show!'

'What show, darling?' he asked.

'My in a show.'

239

'How lovely. When is it?' he asked me.

'Next Thursday. At her nursery school.'

'I'd like to come.'

'Oh. But . . .'

'Can I come to your show?' he asked Milly.

'*Yes*, Dad!' she shouted. She began to dance on the spot, waving her 'magic' wand about. 'You come to my show!'

'Is that all right, Anna?' Xan asked.

He was her father. How could I possibly refuse him – or Milly for that matter?

'Erm . . . that'll be fine,' I replied.

'I'm sorry,' I said to Patrick when I went to see him the following evening. 'But Milly wants him to be there.'

'Of course she does,' he said mildly as I set the table for supper. 'He's her father. It's quite understandable.'

I breathed a sigh of relief at how reasonable he was being. 'I feel bad about it,' I added, 'but I have to put Milly's feelings before my own.' I looked at the rows of honey jars, now filled, sealed and labelled, glowing in the sunlight.

'Of course you do,' Patrick agreed.

'And it would be awkward if you were both there.'

'Extremely awkward.' He tossed the salad. 'There'd be gossip.'

'Anyway I'm really sorry,' I repeated. 'I hate standing you down like this but I don't see what else I can do.'

'It's quite OK.'

'And you see I . . .'

He banged down the bowl. 'I've *said* I won't come so can we just drop it?' I stared at him. 'I'm . . . sorry,' he said quietly. He leaned against the sink. 'It's just that I feel . . . so . . .'

'It's . . . OK,' I murmured. Xan's arrival had made him feel threatened and hurt. 'I won't mention it again.'

He got a bottle of wine out of the fridge. 'Does Xan actually know about me, Anna?'

240

'Well . . .'

He looked at me in dismay. 'You mean you haven't told him yet?'

'No.'

He shook his head in bewilderment. 'Why not? He's been here for three days.'

'Well, one thing at a time. It's a little awkward.'

'Why? All you have to say is "I have a boyfriend now, Xan. His name's Patrick. It's serious."'

'I will tell him that. Tomorrow.'

'Please do.' He filled my glass. 'And when will he be seeing Milly?'

'He'll come on Mondays, Wednesdays and Sundays for a couple of hours each time. So you and I can work around that,' I added with more optimism than I felt. 'OK?'

Patrick didn't reply.

To begin with, Xan stuck to the designated times. He'd turn up at six, when Luisa went off duty; then he'd play with Milly in the house. If he took her to the park she'd invariably want me to come along as well. Her happiness at seeing us together pierced my heart.

'My mummy and my *daddy*,' she'd say, looking from one to the other of us as she walked along between us, gripping one of our hands in each of hers.

'How's it all going?' Jenny asked me over the phone a couple of days later.

'It's . . . OK . . . although . . . Actually, Jen, it *isn't* OK. It's very awkward.'

'Already? What's the problem?'

'The problem is . . . that I feel reluctant to invite Patrick round while Xan's in London. I haven't said this to him, but I think it would confuse Milly.'

'It might well,' she agreed. 'You don't want to have Xan in the house one day, then Patrick the next.'

I sank on to a chair. 'That's just what I mean. It would

241

feel strange and somehow tasteless, as though I'm juggling two men.' Which in a way I was, I reflected ruefully.

'Would you consider letting Xan take Milly to his flat?'

'I'd rather he didn't. It's much easier for him to play with her at my house because all her toys and books are here. It also means that I can keep an eye on things. What if there were some choking hazard at his place, or he gave her the wrong thing to eat – she has an egg allergy after all.'

'Then do what you're doing. If Patrick loves you he'll understand and it'll be a test for him.'

'Quite a tough one,' I pointed out.

'But it's not for that long.'

'No, it's not.' I felt a sudden dart of regret. 'That's true.'

'Then when Xan leaves you can gradually reintroduce Patrick to Milly,' I heard Jenny say. 'But you'll have to spend time with Patrick if you want to preserve your relationship with him. Plus he'll need a lot of reassurance.'

'Yes. Of course,' I replied distractedly. 'You're right.'

I am making a mess of this, I told myself as I got ready to go to Milly's show on the Thursday morning. I still hadn't told Xan about Patrick. I didn't know quite why. I'd had enough opportunities to do so. But I had to grasp the nettle or things would get messy. I got out my mobile and dialled.

'Hi, Anna,' Xan said. 'I'm glad you called. I'm just leaving. Where's Milly's school again?'

'It's on Brook Green, to the left of the Chinese church. But Xan . . .'

'Do I need a ticket?'

'No. Just say you're with me.'

'Ah . . . if only,' he said with extravagant regret.

My heart looped the loop at his flirtatious tone. 'You should be so lucky,' I teased. 'But can I just tell you . . . that . . . actually, Xan . . . I do have a boyfriend now. He's very nice – and he's sweet with Milly, and he's a hard-working, decent guy, who loves kids and he's called –'

'Jamie,' Xan interjected in a bored tone. 'I know.'

'Jamie?' I repeated. 'No. It's not Jamie. Why did you think that?'

'Because that's what Milly said.'

'What?'

'I asked her if Mummy had a special friend, who was a man, and she said Jamie.'

'Oh. Well, I don't know what you're doing asking her such an inappropriate question, but I think she's a little confused. Jamie is my business partner – he builds the gardens I design, so yes, I see a lot of him and he's great with Milly; but my boyfriend's name is Patrick.'

'Ah.'

'And I need to tell you that Patrick, Milly and I are going to Cornwall for a week in August. We'll be away from the eighteenth to the twenty-fifth.'

'Oh,' Xan said. 'I see.' There was a funny little silence. 'Then I guess I'd better come too.'

'What? No way!'

'I don't want to miss seeing Milly for a whole week, do I?'

'Xan, you've been missing seeing Milly for a whole three years.'

'But now I have the chance to make up for lost time – *TAXI!* In any case I don't know how I feel about another man taking my daughter on holiday.'

'Listen, Xan,' I hissed, 'you don't have much choice. You *left* me, remember? When I was *pregnant* – remember? I'm very happy for you to spend time with Milly, but in the circumstances you can't be too possessive.'

'Let's not fight about it now. I'll see you at the school in twenty minutes.'

I ran there, met Dad outside, then we went through the squeaky swing doors into the little hall where Mrs Avis was greeting the parents. We sat halfway to the back as the room filled up, fanning ourselves with the 'programme', a folded sheet of A4.

Suddenly Citronella appeared and plonked herself down in the middle of the front row, which the other parents had politely left free. She was accompanied by a sulky-looking girl with spiky blonde hair – the Infant Wonder Sienna, presumably. Sienna looked as though she didn't want to be there. As we waited for the show to start she was slouched in her seat, listening to her iPod, sending texts, or simply emitting loud, bored sighs.

Suddenly I saw Xan in the doorway and waved. I hoped that Citronella would turn round and see us together.

'Keep the chair next to you,' I whispered to him as he sat next to me. 'Luisa's going to be late. Dad, this is Xan: Xan, this is my father, Colin.' The two men smiled affably at each other as they shook hands across me.

'Good to meet you,' Dad said. I knew I could rely on him to be friendly, whatever he'd felt about Xan in the past.

'It's great to meet you,' Xan replied. 'I'm only sorry it hasn't happened before.' I guessed that this was his way of apologising for his belated involvement in Milly's life.

Dad nodded at the stage. 'I like the set.' A colourful backdrop of flowers and trees had been created from cardboard and crêpe paper.

A hush descended as Mrs Avis stepped forward. 'Welcome to Sweet Peas,' she announced, 'and to our performance of *The Magic Garden*, which will last approximately half an hour, after which tea will be served outside.' Then she went to the upright piano at the back of the stage and began to play Mendelssohn's 'Spring Song', over which I could hear the mosquito whine of Sienna's iPod. Citronella took a large video recorder out of her bag and began filming.

All the children trooped on 'stage' and sat on little chairs in a large semicircle, while they waited for their turn to perform. Some were dressed as daffodils or tulips; others as

244

birds. There was a fluffy 'cloud', three butterflies, two bumble-bees, a toadstool and a rather benign-looking witch. Some of the costumes were so good I thought they must have come from theatrical outfitters. Erasmus, a bee, was dressed in a stripy black-and-orange T-shirt and orange knickerbockers with a pair of gauzy wings and black deely-boppers on his head. Milly looked sweet in her forget-me-not dress: the hat that Cassie had knitted resembled a scoop of Ben and Jerry's blueberry ice cream.

As Mrs Avis thumped away on the piano, Luisa arrived, slipped into the vacant chair next to Xan and gave me a little wave.

Now all the children stood up and sang:

'The Sun has got her hat on –
Hip hip hip hooray!
The Sun has got her hat on and she's coming out to play.'

The daffodils and tulips stepped forward and lay on the floor, tightly curled, in an attitude of sleep.

Then a girl of about four, dressed entirely in yellow, with a huge 'sunburst' hat and a yellow-painted face, came to the front of the stage. 'I am the Sun,' she announced. 'And it is spring – time for all the flowers to wake up and play in my warm rays.' She then windmilled her arms at them to suggest solar radiation. 'Wake up, flowers!' she shouted. 'Please wake up!' But they lay there motionless. 'Wake *up*!' she yelled. 'Wintertime is over!' But they remained recumbent, their eyes squeezed shut. Then Mrs Avis played an introduction to the next song, and all the children rose to their feet again.

'It's springtime' they chorused.
'Time to be in the sun.
Time to wake up and grow and to have lots of fun!'

But the dormant flowers didn't move so much as a petal, apart from one of the tulips, which had the hiccups.

The Sun stepped forward. 'Oh dear,' she said to the audience. 'The spring flowers won't wake up. That's because the naughty witch has put a spell on them.'

The 'witch' stepped forward as the piano sounded again.

'I don't like the spring' she sang.
'I don't like the flowers.
So I've stopped them from growing, with my magical
    powers.'

'Please help me, little clouds!' shouted the Sun. 'Please help me wake up the flowers, with some lovely showers!'

Two little 'clouds' duly came and sprinkled some glittery 'raindrops' on them, but still they didn't stir. Then the 'birds' came and pecked at the ground, to the loud tapping of a woodblock, but still the flowers didn't move. Then the 'trees' came and stamped their 'roots' very noisily, to the beating of a drum – but to no avail. Then the bees and butterflies flitted round the stage crying and wiping their eyes.

'All the bees and butterflies are sad,' explained the Sun, 'because there are no flowers in the garden. I know,' she added. 'I'll ask the Flower Fairies to help me.'

I got a jab in the ribs from Dad and Xan as Milly and the two other Flower Fairies stood up and shuffled to the front of the stage, hand in hand.

'I'm the Primrose Flower Fairy,' said an apricot-coloured one.

'I'm the Rose Flower Fairy,' said a pink one.

'I'm the Forget-Me-Not Flower Fairy,' Milly mumbled shyly, her head on one side. I glanced at Xan. He was smiling delightedly at her and taking photos with his mobile.

As Mrs Avis played some ethereal, tinkly music, the Flower Fairies skipped round the recumbent daffodils and tulips, waving their magic wands at them. Now, with the music becoming louder, the flowers began to uncurl, then they got to their feet and began to wave their arms, twisting and turning in the 'sunshine', yawning and rubbing their eyes.

'Hurrah!' the children sang. *'The flowers have woken – at last!*
Thank you, Flower Fairies – that was fast!'

Mrs Avis struck up 'All Things Bright and Beautiful' and as the children sang it, the butterflies and bees began to flutter around the flowers. By now the small stage had become crowded and the children were competing for space. Suddenly I saw Erasmus, who was standing next to Milly, barge her. She squawked with indignation but stood her ground. He gave her another hard shove, which nearly toppled her, so she pushed him back. At which point he swiped her hat and flung it on the floor: and now, to my horror, she grabbed his bare forearm with both hands and bent her head to it, as though she were about to tackle a corn on the cob.

'*No*, Milly!' I gasped.

Citronella leapt to her feet. 'Don't you *dare*!'

'Mrs Barker-Jones!' shouted Mrs Avis. 'Kindly sit down. I will sort this out!'

But Citronella had stepped forward and was wagging her finger at Milly. 'Don't you *dare* bite him again, you horrid little girl!' Milly's face went crimson, then crumpled.

'Don't *you* dare speak to my daughter like that!' Xan shouted, standing up.

Citronella turned and looked at him with a sudden flicker of recognition. 'She was going to *bite* my child! I have proof,' she added, tapping the camera. '*And* she's tried to bite him before – hasn't she, darling?'

Erasmus nodded, then pointed at Milly. 'She try bite me.'

'*Pero él me empujó!*' Milly shouted. She retrieved her hat from the side of the stage.

'Sit down, Mrs Barker-Jones,' Mrs Avis repeated in the tone that one would use on a delinquent dog.

'She tried to bite my *son!*' Citronella spat as she returned to her seat. To my surprise, I saw Sienna snigger.

Milly stamped her foot. '*Pero él me empujó!*' she repeated.

'*What?*' said Citronella.

Luisa stood up. 'Milly say: "But he push me."'

'*Y él a menudo me muerde,*' Milly added.

'And he did bited me often,' Luisa translated.

'*El muerde a los otros niños, también!*'

'And he have bited all the other childrens!'

'That's true!' someone shouted from the back. 'He's bitten Lucy before now. She told me.'

'And Milo!' someone else yelled.

'He's bitten Alfie too!' I heard another voice say. 'Left teeth marks.'

'And Rosie,' said Annabel Goodchild. 'She was in floods.'

Citronella turned to us all, her face a mask of hostility; then she shouldered her bag, grabbed Erasmus with one hand, a giggling Sienna with the other and stormed out.

'Ladies and Gentlemen,' Mrs Avis said calmly as we heard the doors continue to swing to and fro on their creaky hinges. 'That concludes this afternoon's performance of *The Magic Garden*. Thank you for coming. I suggest we all go and have tea.'

The incident would have been quickly forgotten, had Citronella not written about it three days later.

Tony Blair's rather novel idea of identifying the next ASBO generation, even 'in utero', was much derided at the time she wrote. *I myself did not hesitate to speak out against it in this very column, but now have cause to think he may have been right. My own son has recently been victimised by a fellow pupil in his nursery school. The child in question, Milly – who sadly, if somewhat inevitably, is the offspring of a single mother – tried to bite Erasmus in full view of all the other parents at the school concert last week. Imagine my horror as . . .*

'Are you sure we can't sue?' I asked Xan, who'd come round in the afternoon to play with Milly.

He looked at the article again. 'Well, the problem is that Milly did try to bite him – albeit under severe provocation, which this Poisonella of course doesn't mention – so I very much doubt we'd have grounds. But what a miserable cow to put in Milly's name,' he added bitterly.

'She must be miserable,' I agreed. I screwed up the article and threw it in the bin. 'Now I know why Milly began biting – she probably learned it from Erasmus. I wonder why he does it? There's usually some underlying reason.' I glanced at the clock. 'Anyway, it's ten to eight – come on, Milly. Bedtime. Say 'bye to Dad. You'll see him tomorrow.'

'I'll put her to bed,' Xan said.

'Yes. Dad put me to bed,' Milly said happily.

'Oh. OK, then.'

'Read to me, Dad,' Milly commanded. 'Read *Fidgety Fish* and *Smiley Shark* and *Peter Rabbit!*'

'All right, Miss Bliss,' he said, as he followed her upstairs. 'And which one would you like first?'

It was strange seeing Xan doing the bedtime routine with Milly, for all the world as though he lived with us. I began picking up Milly's toys and books, which were strewn across the carpet. And I'd just put them all back in their boxes when there was a ring at the door. As I recognised the familiar shape through the glass panels my heart sank. 'Patrick!' I murmured, quietly panicking, as I opened the door. 'How lovely to see you,' I lied. 'But you should have phoned first.'

249

'I thought I'd do something spontaneous,' he replied evenly. He was holding a rented DVD. 'I've brought a film.' He kissed me. 'It's so nice to see you, sweetheart.' Xan chose that moment to come down the stairs.

'Xan,' I said, my entrails in knots. 'This is Patrick Gilchrist. Patrick this is Xan Marshall, Milly's dad.'

'Good to meet you,' Xan said. The two men shook hands with an air of cordial detestation. Xan turned to me. 'Milly's asleep.'

'Already?' I said with artificial brightness. 'She must have been exhausted.'

'Well, she's had a busy time with us this afternoon,' Xan said with casual provocation. By now the atmosphere was so chilly I could see my own breath. 'Anyway' – he clapped his hands together with mock joviality – 'my paternal duty's done for today.'

'Then don't let us keep you,' Patrick said pleasantly. My insides shrank at his tone. 'I've brought *The Maltese Falcon*,' he added to me, his voice quavering now as he struggled to control his emotions. 'I thought we could watch it. I'll make supper.'

'We've already eaten,' Xan said as he picked up his bag.

'But we could still see the film,' I said quickly. 'That would be . . . great. So, Xan . . .' I smiled at him. 'Thanks for coming over.'

'No need to thank me,' he said indolently. He kissed me on the cheek, letting his hand linger on my shoulder. 'See you tomorrow, then. Usual time. 'Bye.'

'Why was he still here?' Patrick asked as I shut the front door. 'I thought you said he just came for a couple of hours on Sunday afternoons. It's eight thirty.'

I sighed. 'There's no hard and fast rule. He stayed and chatted for a bit – then it was Milly's bedtime and she wanted him to read to her.'

'I don't like him going upstairs. This isn't his house.'

'No,' I said calmly. 'But it's mine. And he's Milly's father. And she asked him to put her to bed and I have no objections to that.'

'It's not on, Anna – you're with me.'

'But I didn't know that . . . you were going to drop round,' I said impotently.

Patrick stared at me. The scar on the bridge of his nose had gone white. 'So what other liberties might Xan have taken if I hadn't turned up?'

'None,' I replied wearily. 'He just wants to spend time with Milly,' I added as I went into the kitchen.

'Whom he didn't want to know about and then neglected.' Patrick slammed shut a cupboard door. '"Paternal duty" my foot!'

'I'm sorry you're upset,' I said. 'But it's very important for Milly that she sees Xan as often as possible. You, of all people, should understand that, Patrick.'

'And what's this?' Patrick asked, pointing to the fridge, on which was a large photo of Xan in a magnetic frame.

'He must have put that there for Milly. I hadn't even noticed it.'

'I wish he'd just get lost.'

'I don't!' I retorted.

'Why not?'

'Why not? Why *not*?' I repeated. I stared at him. Why not? 'Because of Milly of course.'

'Or is it because of you? You seemed very comfortable with him, Anna.'

'Don't be paranoid.' I sighed. 'I have to be friendly to Xan, Patrick, we're co-parents.'

Patrick leaned against the worktop. 'The man's only been here ten days, but it's already wrecking our relationship.'

'It isn't really,' I protested. 'We still see a lot of each other. I come over to you, don't I?'

'Yes – but you make me feel that I can't come here.'

'Well, it *is* tricky. I don't want to confuse Milly. I need her to get to know Xan.'

'But surely you also need her to get to know *me*.'

'Yes, of course. But although I'm grateful for the tact you've shown, I don't think surprise visits are a good idea.'

I began to walk out of the room, but Patrick grabbed my wrist, pulling me back. 'You're my girlfriend, Anna.' His eyes were shining with emotion. 'Why shouldn't I drop round to see my own girlfriend in her own house without having to worry that I'll find her ex making himself at home there?'

'Please let go of me, Patrick,' I said quietly.

He looked at my arm with an air of surprise, almost, then released his grip. 'I'm sorry,' he breathed. 'But I'm just so upset. I hate him being around. What man wouldn't?' My heart softened at Patrick's evident anguish. 'And what does his other half think? I don't suppose she likes it any more than I do.'

I stared at Patrick. 'Well, the thing is . . .'

'*Dad-eee,*' I heard from upstairs. I felt a surge of relief.

'Damn,' I said. 'Now we've woken her up.'

THIRTEEN

Over the next week Xan upped the ante, coming round not just on alternate days but every day now, staying well into the evening. It made life even more awkward for me, but I couldn't bring myself to limit his time with Milly.

'She adores him,' I said to Jenny. We'd met for lunch at Chez Christophe in Hammersmith Grove. 'And he's nuts about her. I've been taken aback at how much he loves just being with her.'

Jenny snapped a breadstick in half. 'He probably loves being with you too, Anna.'

'He likes being with us – *en famille*.' I found myself wondering whether Jenny ever regretted not being 'en famille' with Grace's father. 'Added to which there's now a huge element of competition with Patrick.'

'Of course there is,' Jenny said. 'From what you say, Xan's behaving in a classic territorial way, even though he doesn't really have the right to.' She poured us both some fizzy water. 'In fact, it's fairly outrageous, given his track record.'

'I guess it is. His arrival's caused havoc,' I added miserably.

'Can I be a bit tough, Anna?' Jenny said. 'It's up to you to prevent havoc by being fair to Xan, but at the same time protective of Patrick's feelings.'

I dipped a piece of bread in the olive oil. 'That's easier said than done.'

'But it sounds as though you're allowing Xan too much time with Milly.'

I flinched. 'How can a father be with his own child too much? Children *need* their fathers.' Jenny was staring at me. 'I'm sorry,' I added, 'That wasn't intended as a criticism of you.'

'I didn't take it that way,' she replied evenly. 'Of course children need their fathers – in most situations. But if you value your relationship with Patrick, you have to be firmer with Xan about how much time he spends with you.'

I shifted on my chair. 'I know. Now, whenever I see Patrick all we do is argue about Xan – it's miserable.'

Jenny shrugged. 'What do you expect? He'd just established a relationship with you, when Xan comes back, and starts monopolising you and Milly as though it's his right. It's hard for Patrick. Especially with his history.'

I picked up my menu. 'I know . . . I do think about that.'

'Be careful, Anna,' Jenny warned. 'You don't want to lose Patrick.'

'No,' I agreed quietly. 'I don't.'

'And you seemed happy with him before Xan came back?'

'I think I *was* happy. But now I'm . . . confused.'

'Because you're enjoying being with Xan again? Is that it?'

'Well . . . Yes. I suppose I am.'

It was true. I did like being with Xan. I loved going out with him and Milly – swimming at the health club, playing in the park, going to the Natural History Museum or the zoo. It felt absolutely right to be doing these things with the father of my child, but it also made me feel shabby and disloyal. And I was in the kitchen the following Sunday night, thinking about this conflict as I made chicken for Milly's supper, when the phone rang. To my surprise it was Mrs Morea, whom I'd met at the Edwards' house-warming, asking me to survey her garden.

'I'd love to,' I said, reaching for my diary. 'You're in Belsize

254

Park, aren't you?' I added as I heard Milly laughing with Xan in the sitting room. They were playing 'monsters'.

'Grrrr!' Milly squeaked.

'*Grrrrrrrrr!!*' Xan roared.

'Belsize Park's right,' Mrs Morea replied. 'We're on Eton Avenue.' I scribbled down the address. 'Could you come on Tuesday morning – say, at nine, as I have to leave by ten to have my hair done?'

I was so happy she'd called that I agreed, although nine was inconveniently early. I'd have to ask Dad to take Milly to the holiday playgroup in Hammersmith where she'd recently started. And I was just coating the chicken pieces in flour when the phone rang again; before I could rinse my hands Xan had answered it.

'Hello,' I heard him say. 'Yes. She *is* in . . . Who may I say is calling? . . . Ah. Hold on please – I'll see if she's available. It's Paddy.' He smirked as he handed me the receiver. 'And I think he's *in* one,' he added in a theatrical whisper.

'Patrick,' I said, scowling at Xan. 'Hi!'

'What's he doing picking up your phone?'

'Well, my hands were covered in flour . . .'

'I don't expect to ring you and have your bloody ex answer!'

'He was only trying to be helpful.' I sighed.

'Oh yeah!'

Xan was grinning at me, delighted with his little triumph. 'Is dinner ready yet, darling?' he yelled.

'What was that?' Patrick demanded.

'Xan . . . was just asking if Milly's supper's ready. Look, this isn't a good moment,' I added. 'I'll ring you later – and let's see each other tomorrow, OK?' I put down the phone and turned to Xan. Jenny was right. His behaviour *was* outrageous. 'Please don't do that again. I'm happy for you to come here, but you have to behave.'

'Oh . . .' Xan shrugged. 'I just like winding him up. The guy's so uptight you could drill for oil with him.'

255

'You're making him uptight – and you are not to answer my phone!'

Xan put up his hands in surrender. 'All right. No need to get in a bate.' He opened the fridge and took out a bottle of lager. 'Your Cornish holiday's going to be a blast,' he added sarcastically. 'But you know, Anna . . .' He flipped off the top.

'What?'

'Well . . . you could always cancel jolly old Cornwall and come to Spain.'

I looked at him. 'Spain?'

'Yes.' Xan reached for my hand. 'Milly could meet my parents at last. Then we could see Seville together and spend time at the coast.' He stroked my fingers. 'What do you think?'

I thought of all the times that I had longed for such an invitation.

Xan lifted my hand to his lips. 'Come with me,' he whispered. I didn't reply. 'Please. I want you and Milly to come to Spain with me.'

I blinked a couple of times, as though I was surfacing from some pleasant, but slightly disturbing dream.

'I'm sorry, Xan, but that's simply not on. You're deliberately ignoring the fact that I'm with Patrick now; and even if I weren't, why would I want to go *anywhere* with you when you'll be leaving the country again in five weeks?'

'That's quite true,' he said. 'But I've been thinking that maybe, this time, you and Milly could come too.'

On Tuesday morning I heard Luisa leave the house early to go to her language school as usual: her six-month course was about to end. To say I was disappointed with her achievements there would be an understatement.

I had a quick breakfast, then Dad arrived to look after Milly and take her to her playgroup.

'Dad!' I gasped when I opened the door. 'What happened?' His left eye was the colour of a damson and the lid was badly swollen. All I could see was a sliver of blue iris. 'What happened?' I repeated.

He came in, shaking his head. 'I had . . . an accident. Last night.'

'No you didn't,' I said. 'You've been *hit*.'

'Well . . . yes,' he conceded reluctantly. 'I've been rather . . . an idiot really.' He sighed, looking suddenly vulnerable and elderly in a way he'd never looked before. 'In fact, Anna, I've been a silly old fool . . .'

'How? What have you done?'

'I'll tell you some time – but you'll be late if you don't leave now. I'll tell Milly I fell over. Where is she?'

'Watching Andy Pandy. Milly! Grandpa's here!'

I jumped in my car, wondering who had hit Dad and why – one of his 'dates' perhaps, livid that he'd lied about his age. Rough justice if so, and for a woman she'd packed quite a punch.

I pulled down my seat belt, then turned the key in the ignition. All I got was a wheezy moan.

'Not *again*,' I wailed. I tried once more and now there was nothing, just a click. 'That bloody garage – I thought they'd fixed it.'

I glanced at my watch. It was 8.15. I rang Mrs Morea to say I'd be twenty minutes late, then I raced up to Shepherd's Bush tube.

Rattling along in the crammed compartment, I was grateful not to have to do this every day, as I used to do when I worked in the City. I'd forgotten how vile it was, especially in hot weather. My linen shirt felt wet and my newly washed hair was plastered to my head as I got off the train at Tottenham Court Road. I went up the short flight of stairs towards the Northern Line interchange feeling panicky and flustered. I'd never get to Eton Avenue before 9.45 and Mrs Morea had to leave at ten.

257

'Move along there!' a superintendent shouted as though we were cattle. 'Move along the platform!'

My head ached, and I was feeling upset about Dad and completely confused about Xan – I'd hardly slept. I was standing at a crossroads – and the choice of direction seemed tantalising but also dismaying. What if we *did* go with Xan? Suddenly the woman in front of me swung her bag over her shoulder, hitting me in the face, without even noticing what she'd done, let alone apologising. Tears of pain and frustration sprang to my eyes, blinding me as I walked along, aware only of the sharp, determined footfall of a thousand feet.

Then I heard someone playing the guitar – and singing: *From a distance the world looks blue and green – and the snow-capped mountains white.* As it drifted towards me I felt my stress levels drop and my battering heartbeat slow: *From a distance the ocean meets the stream, and the eagle takes to flight.*

I exhaled with relief as I trudged along the crowded tunnel, blinking slowly, clasping my briefcase to my side.

From a distance, there is harmony. And it echoes through the land . . . The woman's voice had a husky purity that suited Nanci Griffith's lyrics. It had the same calming effect on me as Luisa's, I now realised.

It's the voice of hope, it's the voice of peace . . . I was so grateful for its soothing influence that I opened my bag and pulled out my purse. *It's the voice of every man.*

I peered at my change as I walked along. What should I give her? A pound? No – it had to be worth at least two. She was talented.

From a distance we all have enough . . . I pulled out three pounds. *. . . and no one is in need.*

I couldn't see the busker for the sea of people, but I'd drawn level with her now and glanced down at her guitar case, which already glimmered with coins.

There are no guns, no bombs, no diseases . . . I dropped

in my three and looked up. *No hungry mouths to feed.* I felt my jaw slacken. *From a distance we are instruments . . .* It was Luisa . . . *marching in a common band . . .*

She looked away, her face crimson.

Playing songs of hope; playing songs of peace; they're the songs of everyman. God is watching us . . . she sang on as I lingered by her side, her voice faltering now. *God is watching us . . .*

And now, as I looked into her guitar case again, I understood where Luisa's money had come from and why she'd learned so little English.

God is watching us . . . I turned and walked away. *From a distance.*

I got back home at 11.30, scanned into my computer the photos I'd taken of the Moreas' garden and began to work on some preliminary designs. At ten past one I heard the key in the front door, as Luisa returned from collecting Milly from her playgroup.

'Mum! I back,' Milly shouted.

'Hi, darling,' I said as I came down the stairs. 'Did you have a nice time?' She nodded. 'Lunch is all ready.' She ran to the kitchen drawer and got out her bib. I sat her down.

Then Luisa, who had gone upstairs with her guitar, reappeared and stood in the kitchen doorway. 'Anna,' she began quietly, 'I bery sorry.'

'Could you come into the sitting room, Luisa?' She nodded. 'I'd like you to hear something.' I pressed the Play button on my answerphone. 'This man called while I was out this morning.'

'Er . . . a message for Anna Temple. This is John Cox from the Bayswater School of English. I saw Luisa redden. *I'm sorry not to have got back to you before – but I understand you wanted to know about the progress of a student*

259

by the name of Luisa Vanegas? I remember she came to a few of my classes in February. But after a week or two I no longer saw her, and because there are so many students coming and going the whole time, I assumed that she'd withdrawn from the course. I'm afraid that's all I know about her, but I hope it helps. Cheers.'

The machine beeped twice then I pressed Stop.

'I know your English isn't great, but did you understand that?' I asked her.

'Yes,' she replied quietly.

'Have you been busking every morning?' She nodded. 'From what time?'

'From 7.30 until 11.30.'

'I see. Always at Tottenham Court Road?'

'Also Oxford Circus or Bond Street. The busy stations.'

'So you must have made a lot of money, then?'

She hesitated. 'Yes.'

'I paid for you to go to English school,' I said. 'And every morning you pretended that you were going, but you weren't. You wasted my money and your time.'

She blushed again, then held out a sheaf of fifty-pound notes. 'Here are fibe hundred pounds, Anna. I always mean to gib it back to you when I leave. I bery sorry,' she added as she laid it on the table. 'I feel bery bad.' Her large brown eyes suddenly filled with tears. 'You hab been bery kind at me, Anna.'

'No, not kind *at* you, Anna. I've been kind *to* you.' Milly had come into the room and was looking from one to the other of us, aware that a serious exchange was taking place. 'And if you needed money you should have asked me,' I went on. 'I'd have helped you find a nice evening or weekend job, so that you could still learn English.'

'Oh, but I no do it for money,' she said, wiping her eyes.

'Really?'

'I bery surprise at how much money I make . . . But I only want be . . . notada . . . er . . . spotless.'

'Spotted?' I corrected her. 'You hoped that you'd be spotted?'

She nodded, then sniffed. 'A friend from Marbella, she busk in tube – violin – and she get job in string quartet. She play in Festibal Hall.'

'I see.' So these were the 'better opportunities' that Luisa had been hoping for in London.

'But I worry that if you know what I do eaches days, you be bery cross to me.'

'No, Luisa – I'd be very cross *with* you.'

'I feel *bery* bad,' she repeated tearfully.

That's why Luisa had bought Milly the presents, I now realised, out of guilt; that's why she'd seemed embarrassed when I'd suggested that she save her money; and that's why she'd lost weight and got some new clothes – in case she got an audition.

'And I worry that if you discober what I doing – you want to bag me.'

'Not bag you, Luisa. Sack you. You were worried that I'd want to sack you.'

'So . . . ?' She gazed at me dolefully.

'I'm afraid that I do.'

'I had to,' I said to Jamie the next morning as we drove to Pippa's and Gerald's house in his blue pick-up – my car had gone to the garage. 'She'd deceived me for six months. It was incredibly dishonest.'

'That's true . . .' he said as we crossed the Hammersmith Road. 'But it seems a shame as you liked her – and she's repaid you for the course. When's she leaving?'

'I've given her four weeks' notice so that she can find somewhere else.'

'Milly's going to be upset,' he said as he indicated left and slowed down.

261

I felt a pang of regret. 'I know.' And with the present instability with Xan and Patrick it was hardly an ideal time for a change of au pair. 'But I was furious with Luisa. I still am.'

'But didn't you ever see her leaving the house with her guitar?'

'No, because she always left very early so that she could catch the rush hour commuters – among whom she hoped would be a few music industry executives.'

'And she didn't busk at weekends?'

'No, because then all she'd get was shoppers and tourists – she wasn't doing it for the cash.'

'She must be good to have made so much, though.'

'She is,' I agreed as we drew into Eden Lane. 'She told me that she'd usually make eighty pounds a morning – which with her au pair money meant she was making almost five hundred pounds a week. She'd take it to the bank and change it into large notes.'

'Why didn't she deposit it?'

'Because she doesn't have an account. Her English wasn't good enough to fill in the forms and she was worried that she'd have to pay tax. But I'm going to help her open one. She wants to transfer half the money to her parents as they're rather hard up,' I said with a pang. 'Anyway, what time are your guys coming?' I asked as we drew up outside Pippa's house.

'I told them to meet me here in half an hour. But I just want to go round it with you first to check that I'm going to rip out the right things. Good, the skip's here. OK . . . jump down.'

As he parked I looked at the rotovator and chainsaws that Jamie had got in the back of the pick-up, ready to start the clearing. I rang the bell and Gerald opened the door.

'Good morning,' he said, giving us both stiff handshakes.

'This is Jamie Clark,' I said. 'He and his team will be

262

starting work this morning but I'm just going to show him what's to be removed and what's to be cut back, and then I'll come back at about three.'

We went into the kitchen where Pippa was giving the children breakfast. The table was a mess of boiled eggs, toast soldiers and scattered Rice Krispies.

'Hi!' she said, beaming at us. 'Excuse the mayhem in here.'

'It's lovely mayhem,' Jamie said. 'What little beauts.'

'Thank you.' She smiled. 'I'll take them all out when the work starts.'

'That's a good idea,' Jamie said. 'It'll be noisy as well as hazardous; and we'll be coming and going through the house with stuff to put in the skip, so we need to have these little guys out of the way.'

Gerald opened the back door.

'Streuth,' Jamie murmured as we went outside. 'I see what you mean, Anna. This is going to take two days,' he added as I showed him the trees and shrubs which were to be removed, and those which were to be cut back.

'It's such a pity that it's got like this,' Gerald said as Pippa and the children followed us outside. 'It used to look lovely.'

'Really?' Jamie said. He gently kicked a little blue football to one of the twins.

'Yes, my late wife was a fantastic gardener.' I discreetly rolled my eyes.

Jamie nodded. 'I see.'

'Oh, yes indeed, she'd never have let it get into this state.'

'Right,' Jamie said.

'She kept on top of it.'

'Great,' Jamie replied in a bored tone. 'But then she probably didn't have three tinies to look after. Gardening's very time consuming.'

'That's true, but she could grow anything. She won bronze at Chelsea in 1986 you know.'

'Terrific. Now what about that tree peony, Anna? Seems a shame to lose it.'

'We're not. We're going to move it to that corner.' I showed him the plans again.

'Right.' Jamie nodded. 'Good move.' His mobile phone rang and he flipped it open. 'Hi, Harry! You and Stefan are five minutes away? Good on you, mate. And have you got the earphones?' He stole a glance at Gerald. 'Because I'm going to need them.'

'We'll put down dust sheets in the house,' I explained to Pippa. 'But we'll need to move the table out of the hall and take down the paintings. If you show Jamie where you'd like them put, he and the boys will do it.'

I left as Harry and Stefan arrived, and got a cab home. On the way I phoned Dad to see how he was. He didn't answer, so I called his mobile.

'I'm just leaving Charing Cross Hospital,' he said. 'My GP sent me for an X-ray to make sure my cheekbone wasn't fractured.'

'And?'

'Luckily it seems to be fine. The nurse gave me painkillers and told me to rest.'

'Why don't you drop by and have a late breakfast?' I suggested. 'Then you can tell me what happened . . . if you want to . . .'

'It'll take about a month to heal,' he said half an hour later as we sat in the kitchen with the back doors open, sunlight flooding the floor.

'It does look nasty.'

'It looks awful,' Dad agreed, 'and it's embarrassing. People will think I've been brawling.'

'You haven't, have you?'

'Not exactly,' he replied balefully. 'But I've been . . .' He sighed. 'I've been awfully silly really, Anna.'

'In what way?' I asked, though I knew.

He sipped his coffee. 'Well, over the past two months or so I've been meeting a number of . . . ladies. I won't say how I met them if you don't mind.'

'That's OK.' I passed him a Danish pastry. 'But what were they like?'

'Some were very charming – none of them was interested in me,' he added quickly, 'but then I guess I'm a bit old for the dating scene.'

'I don't think so; you just need to find someone of the right age.'

'Perhaps you're right. Most of these women were far younger then me. I was flattering myself,' he added ruefully. 'But I've always bought them dinner and got them a cab home.'

I passed him a paper napkin. 'That's decent of you.' He must have spent a fortune, I thought.

'I feel it's the least I can do. They've spent the evening in my company – probably bored to tears I should think,' he went on miserably. 'An old codger like me.'

'Don't say that, Dad, you're a nice man and you're still very good-looking, black eye or not.'

He smiled. 'Anyway, two nights ago I met one of these women – in Morton's wine bar, in Berkeley Square. Her name was Tatiana.'

'Russian?'

He nodded. 'She was very glamorous – in her mid forties – but to tell you the truth, not very nice. All she talked about was how she wanted to find a man who'd buy her a flat and a Porsche. She was totally focused on it.'

'I see.'

'She said she was hungry, so we ordered dinner; and when it came to leaving she asked me to get her a cab home. When we left the bar I saw her make a quick call on her mobile phone, in Russian, and as we were walking along she said that the cab would cost twenty pounds – she lived down in Streatham

– and could I give her the money now. I was a bit surprised, but I got out my wallet,' – I suddenly knew what was coming – 'and at that very moment, this . . . leather-jacketed thug appeared from nowhere and told me to hand it over. I said I'd do no such thing. So a tussle ensued, during which, I remembered afterwards, Tatiana didn't call for help. She just leaned against the wall, arms crossed. Then I remember being punched and the wallet being wrenched out of my grasp. And as I lay on the ground I was surprised to see Tatiana and my assailant walk quickly away.'

'Poor Dad,' I said as I poured him some more coffee. 'They probably do it every night.'

'I wouldn't be surprised. It's not the physical injury,' he added, 'or the loss of my wallet – I only had a hundred pounds in it and the cards are easily cancelled. It's the thought that I'd spent the evening wining and dining this woman, trying to be charming, and all the time she was planning to *rob* me. I do find that aspect of it disheartening,' he concluded miserably.

'Did you report it to the police?'

He shook his head. 'I know I should have done, but I feel so stupid. I simply want to forget about it.' To my consternation, his eyes had suddenly filled.

'Dad,' I murmured.

'I'm sorry,' he croaked, swallowing visibly. 'But my life is not going very well. In fact, to be perfectly honest, Anna, it's . . . *shit!*' I passed him a tissue. 'I try to be stoical, but what happened last night has really shaken me. Any optimism I felt has all but gone.'

'But at least, thank God, you weren't badly hurt.'

'And I feel I've betrayed your mother's memory with my idiotic behaviour.'

'She'd understand,' I said. 'She wouldn't want you to be lonely, Dad.'

He looked into the garden, then returned his gaze to me,

his eyes still shining with emotion. 'That's the problem,' he croaked. 'I am. It's been four years now, but I still miss your mother so much.'

'I know you do.' I put my hand on his.

'We all miss her, of course. But you and Cassie are young – and busy. And the distraction of being young and busy is a huge help with grief. Mark's far away, so being at a distance must have made it easier for him – not having a memory of your mother round every corner. But it's hard being bereaved when you're old,' he added bleakly. 'Having so much time to feel sad.'

I nodded. 'But perhaps you'll meet someone else.'

'I think it's very unlikely, but would you mind if I did?'

'Well, I suppose it would be a bit hard to start with, but how could I possibly object? We all have to grasp our chances of happiness in life, Dad. And I'd hate you always to be on your own.'

'The problem is that your mother was irreplaceable.' He sighed.

'You wouldn't be replacing her. Just finding someone else to be with for this part of your life.'

'Yes.' He nodded. 'Maybe . . . We had our ups and downs, though,' he suddenly added.

'Did you?' I said disingenuously. I'd never heard Dad utter any criticism of Mum – he would have thought it disloyal – but it was as though he suddenly wanted to talk. 'Well, all couples go through bad times,' I added, 'however happy.'

He sipped his coffee. 'There were things that, well, tested us over the years. But whatever happened, we never wanted not to be married to each other.'

'Mum was devoted to you. She often told me that you were her "hardy perennial" – that you were "always there" for her. She felt so lucky.' With good reason, I reflected wryly as I sipped my orange juice.

'Even so we had our difficulties,' Dad said.

267

My heart began to pound as I saw the opportunity I'd been waiting for begin to unfold. 'It must have been very hard when you were in Brazil.'

He nodded and looked out of the window. 'It was hell. Those eight months apart nearly did end it for your mother and me.'

'I know,' I said quietly.

He turned his gaze to me. 'You don't, Anna, because I've never talked to you about it and I doubt that your mother did.'

'She didn't. Nevertheless I *do* know,' I insisted as I passed him a muffin. 'In fact, Dad, now that we're chatting, there's something I've been wanting to ask you – something very important. I don't want to make you feel any sadder, but it's been on my mind for several weeks.'

He rested his knife on his plate. 'And what's that?'

'There's . . . something I found recently and it's been tormenting me.' He gave me a quizzical look. 'It was an old photo,' I went on, 'of Mum. I found it purely by chance – it just fell out of one of the old gardening books of hers that you gave me. It was taken in 1977, when you were in Brazil.' I saw Dad stiffen slightly. 'And in this photo, Mum's sitting on a beach, in Chichester, with this . . . well, this . . .' I felt my face burn with embarrassment. 'With this . . . *man*. I hadn't a clue who he was,' I stumbled on. 'And there was this letter with the photo – a letter she'd written to you – and . . . you see the thing is . . .' My mouth had dried to the texture of blotting paper. I couldn't go on.

'Would you show it to me?' Dad said quietly.

I nodded, relieved, ran upstairs to my workroom, found the book and ran down again, my knees trembling. I opened it and handed Dad the photo first.

He reached into his top pocket for his reading glasses. 'Ah,' he said. He turned the picture over and looked at the back. 'Ah,' he repeated, frowning slightly. 'Chichester. Yes . . . June 1977 . . .'

'His name's Carlo, isn't it?' I said quietly.

'Yes.' Dad sighed. 'This is Carlo.'

'And he gave Mum this book.' Dad opened *Flowers of Southern Italy* and then read the inscription. 'With many happy memories,' he said. I stared at him, willing him to say more. 'Well . . .' He closed the book and took off his glasses. 'They *did* have many happy memories.'

'They did?' Unable to contain myself I blurted out, 'But he's just like Cassie! Or, rather, Cassie's just like him.'

'Ye-es,' Dad said, looking at it again. 'There's definitely a resemblance.' A silence followed in which all I could hear was the sound of a distant helicopter.

'He could almost be Cassie's father,' I ventured.

Dad was still looking at the photo. 'Your mother was beautiful,' he murmured.

'He really could be.' Dad didn't reply. I took a deep breath. '*Is* he her father?' I finally said.

Dad looked up at me. 'Is he what?'

'I'm sorry to ask you, Dad, but is Carlo Cassie's father?'

Dad stared at me. 'Is Carlo Cassie's father?' His neck was stained with red. 'What an extraordinary question, Anna, whatever makes you think that?'

'Well . . . the . . . likeness,' I stuttered. 'It's so striking.'

'But Anna,' Dad said, as he put down the photo, 'we all resemble a few people to whom we have no family connection. You look a little like Gwyneth Paltrow, but you're not related to her.' He looked at the photo again. 'But there is a similarity of type between Cassie and Carlo, I quite agree.'

Dad was clearly in denial. But I needed to know the truth. 'But it isn't just that Cassie looks like Carlo,' I pressed on. 'She looks nothing like you or me, or Mark.'

'That's true. But Cassie *is* like my mother, Anna. Didn't you ever see that?' I shook my head. 'She's very much like Granny Temple – when Granny was a young woman. She

269

was rather dark-complexioned too and Cassie's build is similar.'

'Oh,' I said faintly. 'It's a long time since I've seen any photos of Granny in her younger days.'

'I'll show you a few some time, then you'll see. The resemblance is unmistakable.' Dad shook his head in bewilderment, then put down the photo. 'But where did you get this idea?'

'Well, the thing is,' I struggled on. 'The thing is it isn't just the photo. I worked out that you were in Brazil when . . . erm . . . when . . . nine months before Cassie was born,' I concluded delicately. 'You were there from January to August 1977; you told me that recently.'

'That's right,' Dad said. 'I was.' A look of enlightenment suddenly crossed his face. 'So that's why you were asking me those odd questions about how long I was out there for?'

'Yes. Because if Cassie was born on the fifteenth of March 1978, and you hadn't returned from Brazil until the ninth of August 1977, then I don't see how . . . how she . . .' My skin was prickling with embarrassment.

'How she could be my child? Is that what you're saying?'

'Yes. It just didn't add up.'

'Anna,' Dad said patiently. 'It did. Very simply.'

'How?'

'Because Cassie was premature.' I stared at him. 'She was born nine weeks early – didn't you know that?'

'No. I *didn't*. You and Mum never said.'

'Well, I suppose we didn't talk about it, no; but that was because Cassie so nearly didn't survive. And your mother never talked about things that had been sad or distressing once they were over. That was always her way.'

'Nine weeks?' I shook my head. 'That's a lot . . .'

'She was tiny, Anna.' He turned up his palm and I suddenly imagined Cassie lying in it. 'She weighed two and a half pounds. She was in an incubator, with all these wires and drips, her little ribcage heaving up and down. The doctor warned us that she'd probably die, as so many premature babies did in those days. So we had her baptised in hospital, the day after she was born. We couldn't hold her, so we just stroked her and told her that we loved her . . .' He turned away.

'I'm sorry, Dad,' I whispered. 'I didn't mean to upset you. But I never knew this. The only thing Mum ever said was that we were all a "bit early".'

I saw him swallow. 'You were – that's how it was with your mother's pregnancies. Mark was a fortnight early – we had him in the airing cupboard for a while. Then you came three weeks too soon, which is why I had to deliver you because of the heavy snow we had that February. But Cassie was dangerously early – she should have been born in late May, but arrived in mid March.'

'I see,' I whispered. I imagined her tiny body, striving for life.

'I think that's why I've always spoilt her,' I heard Dad murmur. 'It's probably been bad for her, but I couldn't help it because I could never eradicate from my mind that image of her struggling to survive all those weeks. And because your mum had you and Mark to look after, I used to go to the hospital every day; I took time off work. And I'd sit outside the special unit she was in, looking at her through the glass, just willing her to hold on – to keep breathing – and, by some . . . miracle she did. So I'm afraid your calculations about her birth are quite wrong.'

'But . . . it wasn't only that,' I persisted. 'It was because you said that it was hell while you were in Brazil.'

He sighed. 'It was – the separation was so hard, for both your mother and me. She felt abandoned – she was angry about it. And when I came back in August she got pregnant straight away, even though we'd regarded our family as complete. I think she thought that if she had another baby it would be harder for me to leave again.'

'Ah.'

271

He looked at me wonderingly. 'So you thought . . . that I wasn't Cassie's father? Is that what you thought, Anna?'

'I did,' I replied quietly. 'I'd worked it all out . . .'

'Overlooking the fact that not all babies are born at forty weeks. As you've had one yourself, Anna, I'm a bit surprised at that.'

'I didn't think of it.' Now I remembered the long conversation I'd had about it with Jenny and cringed. But the fact that Carlo wasn't Cassie's father didn't mean that Mum hadn't had an affair with him. The photo suggested that she had.

'Your mother would never have been unfaithful,' I heard Dad say as though he'd caught my thoughts. 'Any more than I would have been. Carlo was just a good friend.'

'How did she know him?'

'When she left school your mother spent some time in Naples, learning Italian. Did you know that?'

'Yes – vaguely.'

'She was a paying guest with a family called the Rossis. They had a daughter of the same age, Maria.'

'I remember Mum mentioning her from time to time.'

'Maria and your mother got on very well and your mother stayed with them for three months.'

'So that explains her interest in southern Italy.'

'Yes. Anyway, Carlo was a friend of Maria's and after your mother left they all kept in touch and when I was in Brazil I remember your mother saying in one of her letters that Carlo was coming to the UK to see some play or other at Chichester – he was a successful theatre designer by then – and they arranged to meet for the day. She was delighted to see him again. I think he reminded her of a very happy time in her life when she was so very young and completely carefree.'

I looked at the snap again. 'But the way he's holding her . . .'

'Well . . .' Dad shrugged. 'He was very fond of her, but they were never . . . lovers.' I wondered how he could possibly have known that for sure. 'Your mother told me that when she first met him she did fall in love with him. But she said that Maria told her, very tactfully, that her affection was unlikely to be returned as he'd never shown much interest in girls.'

'Oh. I see . . .'

'But they remained in friendly touch over the years. He was a nice man,' Dad added. 'A very exuberant, creative man – warm and tactile – he was always laughing. I met him twice and liked him enormously.'

'He *was* a nice man?' I echoed.

'Yes. He died. In the mid eighties.'

'How sad.'

'It was. He was only forty-three. His parents said it was cancer.'

'Oh . . . But Mum never talked about him,' I said. 'I remember her mentioning Maria, but never Carlo.'

'As I said, she tended not to talk about things that made her feel sad.'

I looked out of the window. 'But this letter,' I said, picking it up. 'This threw me too.' Dad held out his hand and I gave it to him. He put on his glasses again and as he peered through the half-moon lenses I saw his expression darken.

He took off his spectacles and closed his eyes. 'If I'd known that this existed, I would have burned it with the rest of your mother's papers.'

'Is it about Carlo?'

He shook his head. 'No, it has nothing to do with him. But for some reason your mum kept it in the same place as the photo and that's obviously misled you as it's an undated draft.'

'But what's it about?' I took it from him and read it again. *I blame myself . . . feel so ashamed . . . I agree that no one should know . . .* 'What did she feel ashamed of, Dad. And what was it that no one should know?'

Dad didn't answer. Then he pinched the bridge of his nose,

273

sighing deeply. 'There *is* something I've wanted to tell you, Anna, for a very long time. It's something that will probably make you very angry, so let me apologise in advance.' I didn't reply. 'Your mother and I thought we were doing the right thing,' he went on, 'but it's clear that we mishandled things and I feel very sorry about that now.' He sipped his coffee again, sadness furrowing his brow.

'What did you mishandle?' He didn't reply. 'What is this letter about, Dad? Please will you tell me.'

He pushed away his cup. 'I will. It isn't going to be easy, so you'll have to bear with me.' He sat back, gazing into the middle distance, then folded his arms across his chest. 'Do you remember the awful row that your mum had with Mark?'

'Of course I do.'

He looked at me. 'And you know what happened?'

'Yes.' Why was Dad asking?

'Tell me, then.'

'Well, you and Mum bumped into Mark with his new girl-friend, Carol Gowing, at Glyndebourne. You both disliked her on sight and the next day Mum told Mark not to get involved with her. He and Carol then broke up, and Mark was so upset at Mum's interference that he moved to the States and has barely been in touch with us since.'

Dad nodded slowly. 'That's right. But why do you think Mark didn't just carry on seeing Carol and tell your mother to mind her own business?'

'I don't know,' I replied. 'To be honest, I was surprised he didn't. He was thirty-three – he could see whom he liked.'

'That's true. But there was a very good reason why Mum objected to Carol.'

'Which was what?'

Dad folded his hands in front of him. 'It was to do with something from your mother's past.'

'I didn't think Mum had much of a past, given that she was only twenty when she married you.'

274

Dad didn't reply. 'When she got back from Italy she began looking for work. She took a flatshare with another girl in South Kensington and started temping. This led to a secretarial job at Granada TV.'

'I never knew she'd worked there – she never mentioned it.'

'She was only twenty and was very unworldly. And there was a producer there – about ten years her senior. He was very attractive, ambitious – and married with two children.'

'And?' I said impatiently.

'He made a beeline for your mother and they began an affair. It was the first real relationship she'd had.'

'Then what a pity he was married.'

'Yes – but she was, by her own admission, very naive. She believed that this man loved her and that he was getting divorced, because that's what he'd told her.'

'Oh. Except that he wasn't, presumably?'

'No. But she saw him for about two months, believing innocently that it was a grand passion for them both. Then his wife found out and all hell broke loose, so he ended the relationship with your mum overnight. He also fixed it that she lost her job.'

'Poor Mum,' I said. 'What a shit.'

'I'm afraid that epithet describes him rather well.' Dad paused. 'His name was John Gowing.'

'Oh,' I murmured. 'I see . . .'

'It was shortly after that that I met your mother – in the Lyons Corner House on The Strand. She was sitting in the corner, on a rainy Saturday afternoon, and I asked if I could share her table because the café was crowded – and I could see that she was very distressed. So I asked her if she was all right, or if I could help her in any way.'

'Lucky Mum,' I breathed, 'having you ride to her rescue.'

Dad smiled. 'So we started talking . . .'

'Then you both fell in love,' I went on, 'got married and

had three children. Then, years later – horror of horrors – Mark meets John Gowing's daughter and falls for her . . .'

'Yes. Horror of horrors,' Dad echoed quietly.

'Poor Mum,' I breathed. 'What a shock – of all the women that Mark could have dated. I suppose she couldn't bear having all those bad memories raked up – let alone having to see Gowing again when he'd treated her so badly.'

'He did treat her badly,' Dad agreed. 'She was heartbroken. And when Mark introduced us to Carol at Glyndebourne that night your mum immediately realised the connection – not just from the name, but because she could see the resemblance to Carol's father. She was terribly shaken: and the next day she went up to town and told Mark the truth, face to face . . .'

'I understand now,' I interjected. 'If a man's really hurt you, the last thing you'd want, years later, is to be forced to have a connection with him – let alone a family one. It would be ghastly.'

'Yes, Anna, but . . .'

'What a horrible turn-up for Mum. I thought she'd simply disliked Carol because she was so much older than Mark and didn't want more children.'

Dad shook his head. 'That wasn't the issue at all. Your mother – like most mothers – just wanted her kids to be with anyone who made them happy. But . . .'

I clapped my hand to my chest. 'I'm so glad you've told me,' I said. 'I thought that Mum had been wrong to interfere, but now I can sympathise with what she did. But I wish you'd told me this before – I can't for the life of me think why you didn't.'

'Anna, I haven't . . .'

Suddenly my mobile rang. 'Sorry, Dad.' I rummaged in my bag. 'Hello?'

'Is that Milly's mother?' said a female voice.

'Yes.' I felt my heart begin to race.

'It's Lorraine from the playgroup here. Sorry to disturb you . . .'

'That's OK,' I said anxiously.

'But Milly's not well.'

I stood up, my heart banging in my ribcage. 'What are her symptoms?'

'She has a rash on her face, she's feverish and rather unhappy.'

'Has she been given any egg?' I demanded as I picked up my bag. 'In the snack break? She can't risk *any* contact with it, as I explained when we met.'

'We don't think it's that,' Lorraine said calmly. 'In any case we ask the parents to exclude egg and nuts from their kids' lunch boxes.'

'But there's an egg glaze on some types of bread, or the other children could have had egg on their hands from breakfast. It would only take a tiny bit.' I felt sick with anxiety.

'They all wash their hands before starting play.'

I scooped up my keys. 'I'm coming right now, but if she develops breathing problems you may have to give her the adrenalin shot – the Epipen's in the medical bag I gave you.'

'I've had first-aid training in dealing with allergic reactions,' Lorraine said camly, 'and I genuinely don't think it's that – I think it's chicken pox.'

I hoped she was right. 'I'm on my way.' I put down the phone. 'Sorry, Dad. Emergency. But thanks for explaining things at last.'

'But Anna . . .' He was staring at me.

'I must go – I'll call you later.' I sprinted to the minicab company in Shepherds Bush Road and within ten minutes was at the church hall. I gathered up Milly in my arms and sat her on my lap.

'Mum-*my* . . .' Milly looked floppy and flushed. But her lips weren't swollen, her eyes weren't closing up, she had no bumps on her face and her breathing wasn't laboured. But on her chest and face was a scattering of red blisters.

'I'm sure it's chicken pox,' Lorraine said.

'Have any of the other children had it?' I asked, my panic subsiding.

'We did have a little boy here last week who had, but his mother said he was definitely past the infectious stage – but he may not have been.' She looked at the other children. 'We'll soon know . . .'

'That's chicken pox,' said my GP as she examined Milly's skin under a magnifying lamp an hour later. 'It's good to get it at this age – she'll have milder symptoms. There's not much I can recommend except Calpol, Calamine lotion to prevent itching and tepid baths if she's in any discomfort. Exclude anything acidic or salty such as oranges or crisps – do not give her aspirin –'

'I never do.'

'And of course she'll need to be in isolation for at least ten days. Keep a check on her temperature.'

'I will. Thank you.' I picked Milly up, then my mobile rang again. It was Jamie. 'How's it going?' I asked.

'OK,' he replied. 'Apart from a certain person who's driving me insane.'

'I know – it's ghastly. But just ignore him.'

'Impossible. The man's such a dingbat. But what time are you coming back?'

'I can't come back today, Jamie – Milly's got chicken pox. But I'll be there tomorrow at 9 a.m.'

FOURTEEN

Milly wasn't too bad – she had a temperature and occasionally scratched at her face but seemed otherwise unbothered by her condition. Dad had offered to look after her in the morning so that I could work.

'Are you sure you don't mind?' I asked him as he arrived.

'Not at all, I'm delighted, plus I don't want people to see me with this shiner so I'm happy to be inside. Hello, Milly,' he said as she ran up to him. 'How about doing our letters this morning? Shall we do a bit of ABC?'

'Yes,' she said happily. 'Do ABCs . . .'

'Right,' I heard him say as I looked for my keys. 'So what's "A" for then, Milly? "A" is for . . . ?'

'*Agua*!'

I rolled my eyes. 'Luisa will take over at twelve. She's going to see another family this morning.'

'I see,' Dad said sadly. 'It's a shame.'

'It is, but she brought it on herself.'

'True enough.'

'Then Xan's going to come over tonight.'

'But I need to talk to you, Anna.'

'Sure, Dad. We'll chat later, OK? But I have to go now.' I kissed Milly and picked up my bag.

I went to the garage in Ravenscourt Park to collect my car, grimacing as I wrote out the cheque for a new alternator; then I drove over to Eden Lane. As I parked I saw Jamie emptying gardening debris into the skip. 'Hi, Jamie!' He gave me a thin smile. I looked at him. 'Are you OK?'

'Tip-top,' he replied. 'I'm just . . . bonza.' He didn't look it. 'How's Milly?'

'Bearing up – it's good if children can have chicken pox when they're small – they cope with it better.'

'I'll try and remember that,' he said bitterly. I hoped he'd snap out of his odd, brittle mood.

I walked into the house, ringing the doorbell, then went through to the garden and waved to Stefan and Harry. 'What a transformation,' I said.

Now that the flowerbeds were almost clear, light seemed to flood the garden; it was as though an imaginary lid had been removed. 'And where are the plants that we're going to keep?'

'They're over there,' said Jamie. 'In that corner. We've marked them all.'

Pippa appeared in the kitchen doorway with the children. 'It's great,' she said as she jiggled Kitty up and down. 'It looks twice as big now.'

Suddenly Gerald appeared at her side. 'A definite improvement,' he said as he came down the steps. He thrust his hands in his pockets. 'One can *see* the garden now. But you know it used to look such a picture when my late wife was alive. Yes, Ginny really knew her stuff. She was a fantastic gardener.'

'Gerald,' said Jamie quietly. He leaned on his spade and wiped his brow with the back of his hand. 'Can I ask you something?'

'Yes,' Gerald replied with an air of surprise.

'It's a rather personal question.'

280

Gerald looked at him suspiciously. 'What do you want to know?'

'I want to know when you had your tact bypass.'

'My what bypass?' Gerald repeated. 'What do you mean? Bypass? I've had no bypasses of any kind.'

'Then in that case could you kindly *stop* talking about your late wife?'

'Well, I'll be damned,' Gerald said.

'I've been in this garden a day and a half,' Jamie went on, 'but in that time you must have mentioned the gardening skills of your deceased spouse at least a dozen times – often in front of Pippa.'

'Yes, but . . .' I glanced at her. She'd flushed a bright red.

'I find it . . . ungentlemanly, Gerald,' Jamie went on calmly, 'if not downright rude.'

'Jamie,' I said. 'That's enough.'

'In fact,' he went on, ignoring me, 'now that I'm getting it off my chest, let me tell you that if you don't stop banging on about your dead wife in front of the gorgeous living wife you have here – with the lovely children she's given you, you lucky *lucky* man – I will not work for you any more. Because I can't stand it. Got that?'

Jamie picked up his spade and walked calmly away.

'Well . . .' Gerald expostulated. 'What rudeness!'

There was a momentary silence. 'Yes,' Pippa said quietly. 'I'm sorry, Gerald, but Jamie's quite right.'

'OK, Stefan, let's carry on,' I said breezily as Gerald went into the house, slamming the door behind him. 'I'll be back at the end of the day.'

My hands were shaking as I unlocked the car. I was pleased at one level – so much so that I could have flung my arms round Jamie and kissed him for his act of gallantry. But at a professional level I was appalled. I got into the driver's seat and rang Jamie's mobile. 'Please don't do anything like that again,' I asked him. 'I'm not sorry you said it – in fact,

281

I'm glad – but if a client is obnoxious it's better to ignore them.'

'I couldn't,' Jamie replied quietly. 'He was making me so angry I thought I'd be ill.'

'Then . . . try not to take things too much to heart.'

'I've been trying not to,' he said with a burst of mirthless laughter.

'Are you all right, Jamie?'

'I'm fine,' I heard him say. 'Never been better.'

'That's . . . good. Anyway, I'll see you later.'

I put my phone away, then looked in my diary to check the time of my appointment in Maida Vale. I suddenly saw that I'd booked to have my hair cut at eleven. I glanced in the driving mirror, wondering whether to cancel, but my hair looked thin and lank; so at five to eleven I pushed on the door of Head Girls.

'Sandra's on holiday,' said the receptionist, 'so I've booked you in with Kelly, our new stylist. She'll be with you in a few minutes.'

'That's fine.'

As usual, there was a pile of trashy women's weeklies in the waiting area, and as usual I read the lurid titles with a frisson of delighted distaste. 'I Paid for My Husband's Sex Change Op!'; 'I Shopped My Own Son to the Cops!' Good God! 'I Had Sex with My Daughter's Horse!' I picked up *I Say!* magazine. 'I Fell for My Own Brother!' Yuck. I found the relevant page, then, as I read the sub-heading, I felt my mouth turn down with disgust.

Could YOU be attracted to your own brother? Fall in love with him even? This is what happened to this week's celebrity contributor. I felt a shock of recognition as I read on. *Actress Carol Gowing, who stars in* The Midwinter Massacres, *due to be screened on Channel 5 in November, talks exclusively to* I Say! *about the forbidden relationship she had with her own brother. Some names have been changed . . .*

I glanced at the photo of Carol, in her kitchen, looking lachrymose. What an exhibitionist the woman was, writing something sordid just to get publicity for some crappy TV show she was in. Thank God Mark hadn't ended up with her, I thought as I began reading it.

'I'd been divorced for five years, and though I loved my two kids it was no fun being a lone mum. But then in the summer of 2003 my luck seemed to turn. I met this wonderful man – 'Luke' – at a party. He was tall and blond, with these ice-blue eyes that seemed to pierce my very soul. He was kind, considerate and a good listener. He was soon calling me every day and though we saw each other a lot over the next month or so, we didn't become lovers – we both knew that the relationship was too important to rush.

'This is bilge,' I muttered, wondering what it had to do with Carol's brother, whose name, I now remembered, was Peter.

I was eight years older than 'Luke'. So she made a habit of dating younger men evidently.

The age gap didn't matter to either of us, but I had to tell him that I didn't want any more kids. To my amazement Luke said that having children didn't really matter because all he cared about was being with me.

'Do you want to come through now?' I heard a voice say.
'What?' I murmured.
'I said would you like to come through, Anna? Kelly's ready for you now.'
Still clasping the magazine, I allowed the receptionist to put a black gown on me and lead me to the washbasin where Kelly was waiting.
'Put your head back, please,' she commanded. I did so but

continued to read the article, holding it aloft. My neck and arms ached but I didn't care.

Luke and I had a wonderful rapport. He was a doctor, an eye surgeon. I sat bolt upright.

'Put your head back please, Anna!'

He had just spent six months in West Africa doing cataract operations for the Sight-Savers charity. Knowing this made me find him even more attractive. Then, a month after we'd met, it was my birthday. He'd planned a surprise and told me only that I should wear something smart. When he collected me, he was wearing black tie and had a picnic basket in the back of the car. We were going to Glyndebourne to see La Bohème. *It was utterly magical and I was very happy. I couldn't know that everything was about to be destroyed.*

'Is the water OK?' I heard Kelly say.

'Yes. Yes, it's fine,' I mumbled, even though it was too hot. I returned my gaze to the magazine.

As we came out for the long interval, Luke suddenly saw his parents on the other side of the lawn. So he took me over to meet them. They were all smiles – until he introduced me to them. Suddenly the atmosphere changed. His mother seemed almost hostile to me now – yet I'd never met her before. Luke's father was also very strained, though he did at least try to make conversation.

'Would you like a nice conditioning treatment?'

'What? Er . . . no . . . thanks.'

I could see how hurt Luke was by his parents' attitude towards me. As we went back inside the auditorium he whispered to me that his mother was probably disappointed because I'd said I didn't want any more children. But that wasn't the reason for her odd behaviour, as I would soon discover.

I felt a towel go round my head.

'Over to the mirror, please,' Kelly commanded. I trailed after her in a daze, still reading. 'Just a trim is it?'

'What?' I said, wrenching my eyes away from the magazine. She looked at my reflection. 'Is it just a trim today?'

'Yes. An inch. Please keep the layers.' As she began to comb my wet hair, I read on:

The next evening Luke asked me to go his flat. He looked terrible and he didn't kiss me as he would normally have done. He told me that his mother had come to see him a few hours earlier and had told him not to get involved with me. I protested that she had no right to do that. Then he said that she'd just told him something very important – something that I also needed to know – which was that his mother had once known my father. This didn't surprise me as my father knows a great many people as he's worked in TV for forty-five years.

'Head up please, Anna!' Kelly commanded.

Luke then said that when his mother was twenty, she'd had an affair with my dad. Now I understood her objections to me. She clearly had unhappy memories of the relationship and didn't want to have a renewed association with my father, three decades later. I felt relieved that there was a rational explanation for her dislike of me. But I told Luke that it was a long time ago and that his mother should get over it for his sake. I added that she couldn't stop us being together. But Luke blurted out that she could. Bewildered, I asked him why . . .

285

'Head up, Anna!' Kelly repeated.

And he replied that the point was not just that they'd had an affair, but that he was the result of that affair . . .

I felt as though I'd been plunged into a bath of ice-water.

I stared at him in disbelief. I'd never known of my dad having any children other than me and my younger brother, Peter. I immediately rang my father and, after a few moments, he said it was true. The horror I felt was quickly replaced by a surge of relief that my relationship with Luke hadn't yet become physical. Even so I was very shocked and upset. Luke, for his part, was devastated. He said it was as though a meteor had just slammed into his life.

I felt a sudden blast of hot air as Kelly began to blow-dry my hair.

When I discussed it with my father the next day, he admitted that he wasn't proud of his affair with Luke's mother – not least because he'd been married. He said that she'd written to him, telling him that she was pregnant, but that he hadn't replied as he couldn't be sure it was true.

'Bastard!' I breathed. 'As though she'd have lied.'
'Sorry?' said Kelly.

And when he heard, not long afterwards, that she'd become engaged to someone else he'd felt that it was better to keep away. But he'd sometimes wondered whether he did have another child, so what I told him about 'Luke' came as a shock to him too . . .

I stood up. 'I've got to go.'

'But I haven't finished,' Kelly protested as I pulled off the gown.

'It's OK, I've just remembered an appointment. I'm sorry.' I opened my bag and gave her forty pounds. 'Is that enough?'

'It's too much – I'll get you your change.'

'No, please don't bother.'

'But let me dry you a bit more – I don't like you going out like this.'

But I was already halfway through the door.

'Hi,' Dad said when I got home. He was putting away the Playdough. 'Milly's having a nap – she seemed tired.' He peered at me through his good eye. 'Have you been swimming?'

'No. I've been to the hairdressers.'

'Don't they dry it for you?'

'There wasn't time as I had to leave in a hurry.' I handed him the magazine. 'Would you read this?'

'*I Say!* magazine? That's hardly my kind of thing, Anna.'

'I know. But I want you to read one particular story, this one here.' I jabbed at it with my finger. 'It's really quite startling.'

Dad gave me an odd look. 'OK.' He put on his glasses and I watched his features contract with pain as he read the piece. Then he lowered the magazine.

'Is it true?' I demanded.

'Yes.' He paused. 'It's true.'

'Well . . . thanks for telling me!'

Dad closed his eyes. 'I'd started telling you yesterday,' he croaked. 'But then you had to rush off to Milly's playgroup so I couldn't finish. Then I tried to tell you this morning, but you had to leave. I was just about to tell you the whole story, Anna.'

'Only thirty years late!' I stared at him. 'How could you

287

and Mum not have told us?' Dad didn't reply. 'And how could you and Mum not have told Mark?'

'We should have done.' He sighed. 'We made a terrible mistake.'

I sank on to a chair. 'So . . . when you first met Mum she was already pregnant?'

Dad nodded. 'I met her in the Lyons Corner House that day and we chatted, then I asked her if I might see her again. I was very attracted to her, but I was also worried about her as she'd seemed so upset. And at that second meeting she told me why she was so unhappy – because she'd had a failed romance and was eight weeks pregnant.'

'Poor Mum.'

'She was extremely distressed. Her greatest fear was that when her mother found out she'd force her to have the baby adopted. She assumed that I'd want nothing further to do with her, but by then I was falling in love. So we talked some more, and then I took a deep breath and told her that one solution would be for me to marry her.'

'She must have been . . . *gobsmacked*.'

'She was. She thought I was stark, staring mad. She said I didn't know her. I replied that although that was true, at thirty-two I knew myself and I knew that I was very drawn to her. I said that if we did marry, I'd bring up the baby as my own, but on one condition – that no one was told. I believed that would provide the most stability for us as a family, and would protect your mother from gossip. So, three weeks later, we were married in Chelsea Town Hall. All our guests knew that it was a shotgun wedding and there was the odd ribald remark, but we didn't mind as that only strengthened the impression that the baby was mine. To make the dates fit, we pretended that we'd met six weeks earlier than we had.'

Now I understood why Mum had looked more than two months pregnant in the wedding photo. By then she would have been well over three.

288

'But how weird to get married when you didn't *know* each other.'

'We didn't,' Dad agreed. 'But, as I said to her, if things didn't work out between us, at least she'd be a divorced mother, rather than an unmarried one, and her child would still have a "father".'

'But it *did* work out.'

'Miraculously – yes. Although we had our ups and downs as I say.'

'Hardly surprising, given the circumstances. But had you decided that you'd *never* tell Mark?'

Dad shrugged. 'We hadn't thought it right through. We'd talked about telling him when he was about eight. But by then we found it impossible to puncture the illusion of family unity that we'd created – especially as we'd just had Cassie, who needed special care for quite some time; so, to our shame, we kept putting it off.'

'For so long?'

'You'd be amazed at how quickly the years passed – and as time went on it got harder and harder to say. Plus we thought it might destabilise Mark at a critical time: suddenly he was taking his Eleven Plus, then he was doing "O" and "A" levels; then he was at university, then at medical school . . . We didn't want to risk upsetting him when he was working so hard, taking exam after exam, so we let the issue slide. Then he went to Africa and not long after he came back he met Carol Gowing. The rest you know.'

I sat down. 'So that's why Mark left.'

'Yes.' Dad rested his head in his hands. 'He couldn't cope. Not just with the shock of it, but with the way he'd been told – the fact that it was all mixed up with meeting Carol. He was so angry. He said he no longer knew who he was – or who *we* were. He just took everything from his bedroom, as though he'd never lived there.'

'Then he went to San Francisco.'

'Yes. He said he needed the distance. I guess he's been finding himself ever since.'

'But once Mark knew the truth, why didn't you tell Cassie and me?'

'We were going to,' Dad said. 'But then your mother suddenly died and I had enough to deal with, so yet again I put the issue to one side. And now you've found out for yourself – as I always suspected you would,' he added quietly.

I stared out of the window. 'How weird,' I murmured. 'I'd convinced myself that Cassie was my half-sibling, because she's so different from me. But all the time it was Mark . . .'

'Who's so like you . . .'

'Yes.' I looked at Dad. 'Isn't that strange?'

'Perhaps you *wanted* to believe that it was Cassie.'

'Why would I?'

'Because she's always been a bit of a thorn in your side. And so you've always focused on the dissimilarities between you rather than looking for common ground.'

I felt a wave of shame. 'I think you're probably right.'

I went to the dresser and picked up the photo again. Now I saw that there was only a general likeness between Cassie and Carlo – yet my prejudice had made me see more. And now I understood Mark's rebuffing e-mail, and Mum's prickly reaction when I'd pointed out that she'd been pregnant on her wedding day. Her embarrassment wasn't out of coyness so much as guilt at the secret she'd been hiding from her children for so long.

And then this divine-looking man came along and asked if he could share my table – and that was that!

No. 'That' wasn't just 'that'. Far from it.

'What a deception,' I murmured.

'Yes.'

'So this letter is the draft of a longer letter that Mum had sent you before you married.' Dad nodded. 'But she was so *lucky* – that *you* came along. How many men would have done what you did? No wonder she loved you so much.'

'I believe she did love me,' Dad replied. 'Partly for myself I'd like to think, but mostly because it had meant that she was able to keep her baby. But then, ironically, we lost Mark as an adult through our own misjudgement. But I hope he'll come back, Anna.' Dad looked out of the window. 'I miss my boy.'

'I think he *will* come back,' I said, 'one day.'

I didn't return to Eden Lane that afternoon; I was still so shocked at what Dad had told me that I didn't trust myself to drive. Instead, I spent the afternoon on my own, looking at my old photograph albums, reassessing the images as I gazed at Mark's face as a toddler, as a little boy, as a teenager and a young man. No one, looking at those pictures, would have guessed that he wasn't Dad's own flesh and blood.

At six, Xan came round to see Milly. He peered at me as he stepped inside. 'Are you OK, Anna? You look a little . . . distraite if you don't mind my saying so.'

'I'm fine,' I lied. 'Just a bit tired.' Xan was holding a big, inexpertly wrapped parcel. 'What've you got there?' I asked as Milly ran downstairs to greet him.

'Something to cheer Milly up.'

Milly tore off the stripy pink paper. 'A *scoo*-ter!' Her eyes were like tea plates. 'I got a scooter, Mum!'

'It's a get-well present,' Xan explained.

'Well, that's very kind of you – say thank you to Daddy, darling.'

'Thanks, Dad!'

I knew why Xan had bought it for her: because he'd discovered that Patrick had given her the bike.

'We'll have to play with it in the garden, Milly,' I explained. 'Until your chicken pox is better.'

'Are you sure you're OK, Anna?' Xan persisted. 'You look frayed at the edges.'

'I am a bit.' I said. 'It must be the heat.'

'But it's cooler now. *You* haven't got chicken pox I hope.'

'No. I had it years ago. And what about your posting? Any news yet?' He shook his head. 'I should know by next week. But I was wasn't joking about you and Milly coming with me.'

'I didn't think you were,' I replied.

'So . . . have you considered it – at least as a possibility, depending on where I'm sent, of course?'

'I have considered it, yes.'

'And?' he asked anxiously.

'It would be crazy.'

'What's crazy about a family being together?' Xan protested. 'I'd like to live with my little family. I know that now.'

'What a pity you didn't know it three years ago.'

'I wish I had,' he replied. 'Please will you think about it?'

'But I already have. And I have commitments here, Xan – professional and personal – I have family and friends . . .' I suddenly thought of Jamie. 'Milly has *her* life here and *her* friends. You're offering us this too late.'

I picked up Milly's Magic Writer and wrote *Nowhere* on the slate, then beneath it *Now here*. That's what had happened to me with Xan.

'We'll talk about it again,' I heard him say as I pulled down the eraser. 'But what shall we do with Milly this evening? We can't go to the park as she's in quarantine.'

'I thought you could play with her, then bath her and put her to bed, then Luisa will babysit for the rest of the evening.'

'Why do you need a babysitter?'

'Because I'm going out.'

'Oh.' Xan rolled his eyes. 'With Paddy I suppose.'

'With Patrick,' I corrected him. 'Yes. With my very nice, long-suffering boyfriend, Patrick. We're going to see a film.'

'How romantic,' Xan said bitterly.

'But I have to do some work before then. Milly, Dad's going to play with you for a while – OK?'

'OK!' She wheeled her scooter into the garden. 'C'mon, Dad!'

I went up to my workroom, sat at my drawing board, with the window open, working on my sketches for the Moreas' garden, hearing Milly's laughter drift upwards. The design process is so absorbing that it enabled me to blot out the shock of what I'd learned about Mark, my anger with Dad and my anxiety about his future, my disappointment with Luisa and my worries about who would replace her. As I drew and planned and measured and mentally planted, I felt all these troubles recede.

I'd been sitting there for an hour, totally distracted, when I heard the doorbell. I ran downstairs, but Xan had already got there.

My heart sank. 'Patrick?' I said, as I stood on the bottom step. 'I thought we were meeting at the cinema.'

'We were. But I need to have a word with Xan.'

'With *Xan*?' I repeated. 'About what?' He and Patrick faced each other across the threshold. 'Xan, will you kindly let Patrick in!'

Xan stepped aside, then leaned indolently against the sitting-room door.

'Why do you want to talk to Xan, Patrick?' I asked warily.

'I don't particularly want to, but I feel I have to because . . .' He pulled a letter out of his pocket. 'I got this from him today.'

I looked at Xan. 'You wrote Patrick a letter?' I murmured. 'Why?'

'Because I felt it was necessary.'

'Can I see it please?' Patrick handed it to me and my eyes skimmed the page: *Keep away from my family . . . something about you I don't trust . . . I consider your relationship with Anna inappropriate . . . I will not stand by while you . . .*

I looked at Xan. 'What are you thinking of? This is outrageous!' Milly suddenly appeared, so I lowered my voice.

293

'And how did you know where Patrick lives? I've never told you!'

Xan shrugged. 'You'd left your address book on the dining table.'

'You looked in my address book? You had no right!'

'I've had three text messages from him too,' Patrick said, 'abusive ones.'

'You're kidding,' I breathed. 'Saying what? Will you go outside, Milly darling, we won't be a minute.' She didn't move.

'Oh the same sort of thing,' Patrick replied. 'Telling me to keep away, and calling me a "smarmy bastard" and a "creep". That sort of thing.'

'Creep,' Milly repeated. I saw Patrick flinch.

'Please go into the garden,' I pleaded with Milly. I looked at Xan. 'I can't believe you'd do this. I thought you were a sophisticated, intelligent person, not some jealous maniac!'

Xan didn't reply.

To my surprise Patrick didn't get angry: he was understandably cold, but remained self-possessed. 'If I get any more mail from you Marshall, of any kind,' he said quietly, 'then you'll be hearing from my solicitor.'

'And you'll be hearing from mine,' Xan flung back. 'I'll get an injunction to keep you away.'

'This is insane, Xan,' I said. 'You've . . . lost it!'

'No, I haven't,' he protested. 'That's just it, Anna, I've *found* it. I've found my family – and we're a little unit, or we could be if Patrick would do the decent thing and . . . bugger off; so I repeat my simple request that he keep away. And I won't hear of him taking Milly on holiday. She's *my* child and I don't permit it!'

I felt my jaw slacken. 'You have no right to make such a demand! Go into the garden please, darling,' I repeated. 'Patrick's right!' I hissed as Milly finally scooted down the hall, with a puzzled glance over her shoulder. 'You

294

abandoned me when I was pregnant, Xan; you hardly saw Milly for three years, but now you've discovered that you *like* family life you're behaving like a demented lion defending its pride.'

'I suppose I do feel like that,' Xan murmured.

'But you can't come waltzing back here, playing the devoted family man, as though we're together, Xan. We're not!'

'But we could be,' he muttered. 'And I'm sure we would be if you weren't with this . . . this . . .' He jerked his thumb at Patrick.

'Patrick's done nothing to you, Xan,' I breathed. 'He's behaved tactfully – unlike you. He's shown self-control – unlike you. And if you ever write to him again you'll find I'll be less accommodating about the amount of time you have with Milly.' I picked up my bag. 'Now Patrick and I are going out. You're in charge until Luisa's back at eight. Make sure Milly brushes her teeth.' I went into the garden and kissed Milly goodbye.

I hardly slept that night, dozing off before dawn. I dreamt that Xan and Patrick were playing tug-of-war, with me and Milly as the length of rope. Then the sharp ring of the phone drilled into my subconscious. As I reached for the receiver I hoped it wasn't either of them.

'Anna?' It was Jamie. 'Are you up?'

'Yes,' I croaked. 'I mean no . . .' I glanced at my clock. It was 7.45. I could hear Milly chattering to her teddies in her cot across the landing. 'I've overslept,' I groaned. 'What's happened?'

'My pick-up's sprung an oil leak. I can't drive it.'

'Oh.' I swung my legs out of bed. 'But then it's pretty old, isn't it?' I reached for my dressing gown. 'Maybe you should get a new vehicle.'

'Yeah, maybe. A Bentley Continental perhaps. But look, I need to get another rotovator, so could you take me over to the tool hire place – it opens at nine – and then to Eden Lane?'

'Sure. My dad's arriving at 8.00 to look after Milly so I'll collect you at 8.15.' As I put down the phone I wondered why Thea couldn't have lent Jamie her car.

I rang his bell at a quarter to nine. 'Sorry I'm late,' I said. 'I had a bad night.'

'Me too,' he replied quietly. There were shadows beneath his eyes and his skin was the colour of ash. 'Come in for a mo – I'm not quite ready.'

As I stepped inside, I half expected to see Thea, or hear her moving about but the flat was very quiet.

'Has Thea left for work?' I asked as I followed Jamie down to the kitchen.

'Yes,' he replied. 'Thea's left.' He locked the back door. 'But not for work. For good.'

'I'm sorry?'

Jamie sank on to a chair, his face bloodless now with stress and fatigue. 'She's gone,' he whispered. 'And I'm feeling a bit . . .'

'Jamie,' I murmured.

He covered his eyes with his left hand. 'I feel such a mug,' he croaked. I sat down at the table with him. 'I knew that something was going on – even after she'd reassured me about this Percy guy; all my instincts told me that there *was* a problem, but I didn't want to believe it.'

'So you found something out?' He nodded. 'When?'

'The day before yesterday.'

'What . . . was it?'

Jamie heaved a profound sigh. 'A parcel arrived for Thea. It was from this fancy hotel – Cliveden.' He looked at me. 'Do you know it?'

'I've . . . heard of it.'

'And the jiffy bag had come open down one side, and something was falling out of it. So I pulled it out. It was this flimsy silk dressing gown. At first I thought it was something that Thea had bought by mail order. But then I opened it and saw that there was a compliment slip from the hotel concierge, thanking Thea for her lost property enquiry and apologising for having taken so long to return her missing garment. The message added that they trusted Thea had enjoyed her stay at the hotel on May the thirteenth and that they hoped to welcome her back here soon.'

'Oh.'

'So when Thea returned that evening I asked her whether she'd ever been to Cliveden. She said "no". So I handed her the dressing gown and the comp slip, and she went red, but wouldn't give me an explanation.'

'How did she avoid it?'

'She just refused to discuss it – even though we both knew that she was meant to be on her way to Cape Town that day.'

'You said you'd taken her to the airport.'

'I did. But I now understand why she didn't really want me to. She kept saying she didn't want to bother me and that she'd go by taxi, but I said I'd take her, no worries. Anyway, I confronted her about the dressing gown, we had a terrible row, then she put some things in a bag and left.'

'So that was two nights ago?'

'Yes. Then last night, at about 8.30, there's a banging on the door. I open it and Andrew Barraclough's wife is standing there – I have *no* idea why. Then she storms in and starts shouting at me like a lunatic, telling me to control my wife.'

'Andrew Barraclough?'

'The guy who lives over the road. The guy who acted so weird at the Edwards' party. The guy with the Bentley Continental.'

I stared at Jamie. 'Thea was having an affair with *him?*'

Jamie's head sank into his hands again. 'All the time I'd been worrying that Thea would fall for someone she'd met on one of her foreign trips. Instead she started an affair with a bloke who lived fifty yards away.' He looked up. 'So I've been bowled a googly.'

I remembered Cassie once saying that to me. All I knew was that it was a cricketing term. 'What's a googly?'

'A ball from an unexpected direction.'

'Oh.'

So *that* was why Barraclough had seemed familiar – he was the guy whom I'd half glimpsed with Thea at Cliveden. And that's why she'd seemed so strained at the Edwards' party – not because of me, but because of *him*.

'How long had it been going on?' I asked.

'Five months. It started in February. She'd got chatting to him in the butcher's.' He rolled his eyes. 'It seems it started over the free-range chicken breasts. When Jane Barraclough calmed down she said she'd known about it for a few weeks but was hoping it would fizzle out.'

'So that's why she walked away when I introduced you and Thea at the Edwards' house-warming.'

'Yes.' Jamie narrowed his eyes. 'That would make sense. She wasn't about to start making small talk with Thea.'

'And that's why Andrew pretended he didn't know you.'

'Yeah. But of course he did. He'd been screwing my wife! Anyway,' he took a deep breath, 'when Thea eventually came back last night she told me that she was sorry, but that she and Barraclough were in love and planned to be together. She packed a few more of her things and left to go and meet him somewhere.'

'But I don't understand,' I said. 'She'd agreed to cut down on her travelling so that she could spend more time with you.'

'No,' he said with a bitter little laugh. 'It was so that she could spend more time with *him*.'

'Well . . . I'm sorry,' I said impotently.

Jamie looked at me. 'But you're not surprised.'

'Well no. I can't say that I am. I did think Thea was having an affair, but' – I wasn't going to tell him what I'd seen at Cliveden – 'I didn't like to say it.'

Jamie nodded. 'It's usually the way.'

'So the last couple of days must have been hell.'

'Pretty much. That's partly why I lost it with Gerald.' He stared out of the window.

'So what are you going to do now?'

'I'm going to start proceedings.'

'And after that?'

'I don't know. But I think I may go back to Oz.'

FIFTEEN

'It's New York,' said Xan the following evening. Milly had
gone to sleep early and he said he wanted to talk to me.

'Are you happy about it?' I asked as we stood in the kitchen.

'Reasonably. I was hoping for one of the Washington jobs,
but New York's a pretty good posting.'

I began to empty the dishwasher. 'So when do you leave?'

'In three weeks.'

'Poor Milly,' I said quietly.

'Then come with me, Anna. Please. Aren't you tempted?'

I lifted out the cutlery basket. 'I have commitments here,
Xan, and a career. I've told you.'

'You could have a great career in New York.'

'Sure. Doing window boxes. Very challenging.'

'And roof terraces – some of them are huge – and the hotels
have gardens. You'd get lots of work, Anna, and I'd help you
with contacts and media coverage. We'd live in a nice part
of the city. We could go to the Hamptons in the summer –
have you ever been there?'

I flung the knives in the drawer. 'No.'

'The Hamptons are fun.' He reached for my hand and held
it in both his. 'Please come with me, Anna.'

'I . . .'

'Please,' he repeated.

'I can't.'

'You mean you won't.'

'Yes. I won't.' I lifted out the plates. 'I'm sorry.'

He looked at me reproachfully. 'Just because I told Paddy where to go?'

'No – although you behaved, frankly, like a madman.'

Xan raised both hands in mock surrender. 'OK – I accept that I shouldn't have written to him, but I couldn't stand him muscling in on my family.'

'He *wasn't*. He was just having a perfectly legitimate relationship with *me*. And as I'm single he's allowed to get to know my daughter, which he had been doing, in a wholly appropriate manner, before your unexpected return.'

Xan rolled his eyes. 'I don't . . . *like* him, Anna. There's something about him I . . . distrust.'

'That's pure prejudice. From the second you saw him you were trying to lock antlers with him like a stag in rut. And although I understand that you feel possessive about Milly, at the same time you have to curb your more primitive impulses as the fact is you chose not to live with us.'

'I see. So now you're punishing me for that.'

'No. I'm simply trying to preserve the life I've made for Milly and me.'

'But why won't you give it a try? You could easily end it with Paddy. It's not as though you're really in love with him.'

'His name's *Patrick*. And I don't want to end it, Xan. And even if I did, it wouldn't follow that I'd come with you to the States – or anywhere else for that matter. Do you want to know why?'

'Not really,' he muttered.

I shut the cupboard door. 'Well I'll tell you anyway. It's because you've always put your work first. You left me because you'd got the job in Indonesia; then you left Trisha because

301

she was going to Japan and you thought that was no good for *your* career. I felt sorry for her.'

Xan shrugged. 'She's tough. She's young. She'll be fine.'

'And now, having belatedly discovered the joys of father-hood, you say that you want to be with me again.'

'I do.'

'But only if I move to New York. So, yet again, it's about what's best for *you* – what's best for *your* life; *your* career; *your* future. It's not about what's best for Milly and me.'

'But surely being together would be best for us all.'

I stared at him. 'Not if it means traipsing around the world after you. Milly's the most important thing in my life, and I don't think that moving from country to country is going to be in her best interests and . . .'

'OK, then,' he interrupted. 'I won't go.'

I stared at him. 'What?'

'I won't go to New York.'

'I assume you're joking.'

'No. I'll turn it down and stay here. I'll take a job in the newsroom.'

'You wouldn't do that. Would you?'

'Yes, I would. If it meant that we could live together as a family.'

I saw myself standing at the crossroads again, looking both ways. 'But why would you do that, Xan?'

'Why?'

'Yes. Why would you want to wreck your career? You love what you do.'

'But I love Milly far more. I've become attached to her in a way I never imagined, and so . . .'

'Thank you,' I interrupted.

'What do you mean?'

'Exactly that. Thank you for being so honest about the fact that it's Milly you love.'

'Of course I love her.'

'And I'm very happy about that: but shouldn't this conversation also be about how much you love *me*?'

'Yes . . . of course . . . and . . . I . . . do.'

I shook my head. 'I don't think that's true. If it were, you'd have tried to make things work out. You'd have asked me to come with you to Indonesia, or you'd have stayed in London, or you'd have gone out there for a shorter time, instead of which you did an extra two years. You weren't exactly in a hurry to get back to us, were you?'

'Well, I was a different person then. If I'd had any idea how devoted I'd become to Milly, I'd . . .'

'But that's exactly my point. It's *her* you're devoted to, not me! And I want to live with a man who loves *me*, Xan, not just my child. Patrick's fond of Milly, but his main interest is in *me* and I find that very attractive.' Xan didn't reply. 'You should go to New York,' I went on. 'You'll be able to get back home quite often, and Milly and I could visit you from time to time. But for the remainder of your stay in London I'd like you to come every other day and leave by eight, so that I can get my life with Patrick back. And as he and I are going to Cornwall next Friday he needs to see a bit of Milly before then. So I'm sorry, Xan, I've been as accommodating as I could, but now it's time for you to take a step back.'

Xan's eyes were glistening. 'You're being incredibly hard, Anna.'

'I'm not. I'm sorry that you're upset, but you have no idea how much *I've* cried in the last three years – especially when Milly was born. And she can never alter the fact that there are no photos of you proudly holding her in your arms when she was a day old, or cradling her as she was christened, or showing her the lights on her first Christmas tree. You didn't *meet* her 'til she was nine months old.'

'But I explained why that was. I was . . . confused.'

'At thirty-seven? And until a month ago you'd only seen

303

Milly six times in three years. You'd spent no more than eighteen hours with her in her entire life – during most of which she's had to make do with seeing you on TV!' I slammed the dishwasher shut. 'I know you're making up for it now, Xan, but please, don't call me hard.'

Xan didn't reply. And I thought how strange it was that having been presented with the thing I'd wanted for so long – to have Xan in my life – I now knew, with sudden, startling clarity, that I no longer desired it.

'I want stability, Xan,' I said quietly. 'Not chaos. I'm not a nomad. I don't want to be – what was it? – "always packing and unpacking". I want to put down roots for my child. You and I will always be friends,' I went on. 'And we'll be co-parents 'til death do us part. But I don't want the past. I'd rather have the future, which means that our lives are not going to be intertwined.'

'The situation was driving me mad,' I said to Jenny the following afternoon. It had been her birthday the day before and I'd taken her a *Pyracantha* to plant in her garden. 'I couldn't stand the pressure from Xan and I hated feeling guilty about Patrick all the time.'

'Life will be clearer now,' she said as she pushed on the french windows. 'I think you've done the right thing.'

'I hope so; I suddenly realised how much I wanted my life to move on.'

'Perhaps you were just enjoying living out the fantasy of what might have been with Xan.'

'I probably was.' We stepped outside. 'But he's still piling on the grief,' I went on. 'He phoned me this morning, to say that he's "very unhappy" about Cornwall, and how does he know that Patrick's a safe driver? You're lucky not having these complications.'

'I don't feel lucky,' Jenny said quietly.

'I think you are. When I first got to know you I couldn't

understand why you'd chosen to be on your own. But after all the stress I've had with Xan and Patrick I can see the attraction of a simple, unattached life. I envy you,' I added.

'I really don't think I'm to be envied,' Jenny said flatly. She was in one of her negative, slightly prickly moods.

'Yes you are,' I protested as I put the plant down. 'You're attractive, independent and successful. You have a beautiful little girl. Where is Grace, by the way?'

'She's with my parents this afternoon. They've become quite devoted.' She added sourly. 'Anyway thank you for the *Pyracantha*. I love them. But where should it go?'

'Next to the passion flower?' I suggested. 'It won't matter if they grow into each other; in fact the sky-blue flowers will look lovely with the scarlet berries. I'll plant it.'

'You don't have to do that,' she protested.

'Of course I will – I've brought my trowel. Anyway, I like planting things.'

I saw Jenny's eyes glisten. 'You know, Anna, you're a very good friend.'

'Well, so are you to me. You've helped me a lot Jen.' I picked up her watering can so that I could soak the ground before planting. The heatwave had dried it to the texture of brick.

'I just wish I could help myself,' she muttered.

'What's up, Jenny? You seem a bit down today.'

'I am a bit,' she whispered.

I began to water the ground. 'Can I help?'

'I don't think so,' she replied as I knelt down and turned the earth over. 'I'm rather struggling with something at the moment.' I twisted the plant out of its pot then tweaked the roots. 'Do you want to talk about it?' I asked as I dug away. Jenny didn't reply. So I put the plant in then scraped back the soil. She wasn't going to tell me and that was fine. She was a very private person.

'It's . . . about Grace,' I heard her say. And I thought that

305

Jenny was going to tell me that Grace was having tantrums, or refusing to go to bed at the right time or put her toys away, though I found this hard to imagine as she's a sweet, co-operative little girl. 'She . . . keeps asking me about her father.'

I felt goosebumps stipple my arms at this unprompted reference to Jenny's ex. 'Well . . . it must be difficult for her,' I ventured as I pressed down the earth with my fingertips. I stood up then washed my hands at the tap.

'Yes. It's very difficult,' she agreed as we went back inside. She handed me a towel. 'Up until now I've told her that her dad's not around, so we can't see him – and she's accepted that. But lately, seeing her friends playing with *their* dads on playdates, or in the park – like she's seen Milly and Xan doing recently – has made Grace ask why she can't see her dad, and where he is.' Jenny's eyes were suddenly shimmering with tears. 'And I don't know *what* to say. Even though I've had this coming for almost four years now.'

'Well . . . is there any chance you'd change your mind about having no contact with him?'

'No,' she replied quietly. She sank onto the sofa, while I pulled up a chair at the dining table. 'He's not in our lives, Anna, and never will be.'

'He's not . . . dead, is he, Jenny?'

She shook her head. 'If that were the case, I'd have told her.'

'Does he live abroad?'

'I wish he did. But he's in London. At least he was the last time I heard.'

'So . . . couldn't you see him, then? However much you hate the idea, wouldn't it be better if there could at least be occasional contact?'

'I don't think so. Not in our situation. It's out of the question.'

'But – sorry, Jenny – why not? Is he married? Is that it?'

'No. He's not married.' She took a deep breath, then clasped her hands as if in prayer. 'He's in prison.'

'In *prison*?' I wondered what he'd done. Perhaps it was fraud, or embezzlement, or some white-collar crime of that kind. 'Was what he did serious?'

'Yes,' she said blankly. 'It was.' There was silence, then she looked out of the window. 'It was assault.'

As I flinched at the word, possible scenarios scrambled for space in my mind. Perhaps he'd got in a fight in a pub, or hit someone in a fit of road rage, or maybe he'd been at a demonstration and things had turned nasty and he'd thumped someone. 'Who did he . . . ?' I murmured.

'A woman,' Jenny replied. She was gazing into the middle distance as if in a dream. 'He assaulted a woman.'

'My God . . .' I breathed. 'But . . . *why*?'

'It was a sexual assault,' she replied. 'In fact, it was rape.'

I stared at her, astounded. The thought that Jenny's ex had raped someone was too awful. No wonder she wanted nothing to do with him. She must feel so . . . ashamed. 'So, did he . . . know this woman?'

She looked out of the window. 'No,' she said flatly. 'They'd never met. He was a complete stranger to her.'

'My God . . . And did you have any idea that he was capable of such a thing?'

'No.' She shrugged. 'I didn't. It . . . came from nowhere.'

'So how did they catch him?'

'Through DNA – and the evidence I provided.'

'You testified against him?'

'Yes.' She paused. 'I had to.' Her eyes were brimming with tears.

I passed her a tissue. 'What an ordeal.'

'It was.'

'And this poor woman – his victim – did you know her?'

'Oh yes,' she said bitterly. 'I did know her.' A tear spilled down her face. 'I *do* know her,' she emitted a tiny sob. 'Because the thing is that woman was *me*.'

My heart stopped beating. Then started again. Jenny pressed the tissue to her eyes.

'I'd always been so careful,' she wept. 'I never went anywhere alone at night; I never talked to men I didn't know, or accepted drinks from them. I never went to dodgy places or walked down deserted alleyways. I always took cabs after dark, or if I wasn't sure of my way . . .' I heard her swallow.

'When did it happen?' I asked gently.

'In 2003. I'd been to a party.' Jenny sat back and looked straight ahead into the garden, her hands clasped lightly in her lap. 'It was in Willesden and was given by colleague of mine at the school where I worked. It had been a very nice evening. And I'd booked a cab to pick me up – the car was from the minicab firm that I always used. And at about 11.30 I got the usual call on my mobile to tell me that the driver was there, and that the car was a black BMW. So I said my goodbyes and left. I walked down the steps of the house, I'd had a bit to drink; not much – maybe three glasses – but enough for me to feel relaxed. And I saw this black BMW waiting there, with its indicators on, to the left of the house, outside an off-licence. So I went up to it and looked in, and the driver, who was taking the cellophane off a pack of cigarettes, lowered the window. And I said, "Are you taking me home?"

'I realised, even as the words came out of my mouth, that that wasn't quite what I'd meant to say; so I immediately corrected myself. "Are you my minicab? For Reid? Hesketh Gardens?" The guy nodded, then he repeated "Hesketh Gardens". So I got in and we drove off. My first impression was that it was a nice car – leather seats and all that – and the driver had a pleasant, friendly manner. I'd asked him not to smoke, so he'd put the cigarettes away. I was tired, so I closed my eyes.' She closed them now and put her head back then opened them again with a sigh. 'I must have dozed off for a minute, because when I opened them I realised that we hadn't headed south towards Shepherd's Bush, as we should have done, but were going north-east past Hampstead Heath.' Her hands were clasped more tightly now, her back a little straighter. 'So I told the driver that he'd made a mistake. But he didn't reply.'

'How terrifying.'

She inhaled, slowly and deeply. 'At first I was furious, rather than afraid, because I thought that he didn't actually know where Shepherd's Bush was. So I told him to turn the car round. But he didn't. So I said, "We're going the wrong way. This is not the way!" But he looked at me in his driving mirror and he just said, very calmly, "Relax, lady." And then I realised.'

'My God . . .'

'So I got out my phone and began to punch in 999, but he twisted round and managed to grab it. So I pulled on the door handle but it was locked, as were the windows. I was hysterical by now. So I tried to attract the attention of other cars by banging on the glass and shouting, but they didn't seem to notice. So then I took off my shoe and started hitting him with it, but he suddenly turned off the main road into a side street, then right again into a small turning near a canal. We were in an industrial mews. It was deserted and in complete darkness . . .' Jenny was sitting bolt upright now, her hands clasped so tightly that her knuckles were white. 'Then he parked the car and got out. He came round to my side and unlocked the door. I thought that I'd run away, and if I couldn't do that I'd knee him in the balls, or stab him in the face with my pen. But then he reached into his jacket pocket and pulled something out. I saw it glimmer in the darkness.' Her eyes had filled. 'Then he held it to my throat . . .' Her chin was puckered with distress. 'So I begged him not to hurt me.'

'Oh *Jenny*.'

A sob escaped her. 'And all the time, I kept thinking how nice I thought he'd looked. How kind. How *angelic*, almost . . . Then it was over and he was pulling me out of the car, and I was shaking and crying. And then . . .' She looked at me, her eyes red with weeping. 'He put his arm round me. Just for a moment. It was so strange,' she added. 'That brief tenderness after such brutality. Then he started the engine and drove away. But as he pulled out of the mews I caught a glimpse of his number plate. I kept saying the number to myself, over and over. I can still remember it four years later.' She wiped her eyes. 'I'll remember it for the rest of my life.'

'Did someone find you?' I whispered. 'Help you?'

'There was no one around. He'd got my mobile, but I staggered to a phone box and dialled 999. Then came the police questioning, the statements, the medical investigations and the hospital tests . . . all negative, thank God, but waiting for the results did my head in – especially the HIV tests as those take three months. But I was in such a terrible state I barely left my flat all that time. I'd stopped work because I knew I wouldn't be able to cope psychologically with school – especially with the aggro I often got from some of those kids. I knew it would freak me out.'

'How long did it take the police to arrest him?'

'Three days.'

'Presumably your minicab company helped track him down.'

'No. They couldn't. They didn't know him.'

I looked at her blankly. 'But I thought he was a minicab driver.'

She shook her head. 'I'd made a terrible mistake. I didn't see that there were *two* black BMWs parked outside the house – one of them was my minicab, the other was . . . him. The reason he was there was because he'd just stopped at the

310

off-licence to buy cigarettes, then I approached his car, and when he realised my error he saw his opportunity . . .'

'How evil,' I murmured.

Jenny looked at me, her eyes blazing. 'Yes. The trial was five months later.' She went on after a moment. 'At Harrow Crown Court.'

'Five months seems quick.'

'They fast-tracked it.'

'Why?'

'Because . . .' Her chin quivered again. 'Because I was pregnant.'

She has the face of an angel. My insides seemed to dissolve.

'*He's* Grace's father?' I whispered.

Jenny nodded. Then her head sank to her chest.

'Good God.' I'd been too stunned by her story to make the connection. I felt my eyes fill.

Jenny gave a teary gasp then looked up. 'To begin with I thought that the stress of it all had stopped my periods. But after the second month I began to feel sick. And when I did a test and it was positive I was faced with a terrible dilemma. The options would go round and round in my head. Abortion? Adoption? Keep the baby? They all felt impossible.'

'So what made you decide to go ahead?'

'The fact that I was so full of *hatred*. I *loathed* him. He'd violated me, body and soul. And I came to realise that if I had the baby and let myself love it, perhaps this hatred wouldn't eat away at me for the rest of my life.'

Now I remembered some of the things that Jenny had said when the girls were first born.

My greatest fear was that I wouldn't love the baby – I needed to.

I love her more and more each day.

Do you have any regrets?

I thought it would help me bond . . .

Your life's about to be filled with unimaginable love.

311

'It's a miracle,' I heard Jenny say. 'Because when I look at Grace, I feel nothing but love. Yet that love came out of something that was brutal and ugly.'

I now understood why Jenny had excluded Grace's father; I understood her secrecy; I understood the elaborate security on her flat. I understood why she was so resolutely single, and why she could be moody. I understood why she had named her child 'Grace'.

'Amazing Grace,' I murmered.

'I think she is,' Jenny said, looking at the photo of Grace on the mantelpiece. 'She's my golden lining.'

'You're amazing too, Jenny. To have shown such courage.'

'I knew it was the only way to save myself.'

'But were your friends supportive?'

She looked at me. 'I didn't tell them. I felt so ashamed . . .'

'But you'd done nothing wrong.'

'I didn't want to be seen as a victim. I preferred people to think I'd had a fling and that it hadn't worked out.'

'Didn't you have a best friend you could talk to about it?'

'Not really, because my closest friend had moved to Aberdeen the year before. I told my sister Jackie, of course, but she was living in France by then with her husband. I had a lot of counselling and that helped – so much so that I decided to retrain as a counsellor myself.'

'And your parents – you said they weren't helpful.'

'Helpful?' Jenny emitted a little shriek of bitter laughter. 'They were *awful*. When they realised what I intended to do.'

'But why? You weren't at fault in any way and the baby was totally innocent.'

'Well, they're not the most broad-minded folk. They were worried that there'd be gossip about how the baby had been conceived and that this would be somehow stigmatising – I suspected that they were worrying about themselves more than me. I suppose they simply couldn't deal with it,' she went on. 'So they didn't want the physical reminder of it.

312

They urged me not to go ahead – despite being so "religious" of course,' she added contemptuously. 'Mum said I'd never get over it if I had the baby. But I believed that was the only way I *would* ever get over it. They didn't meet Grace until she was nearly two, and then only under pressure from my sister. There's a part of me that will never forgive them for that. Just as I will never forgive him.'

'And how long did he get?'

'Eight years. It was a long sentence because he'd abducted me and threatened violence – although the police never found the knife, so there was only my word against his in court about that, which added to my stress.'

'Did he plead guilty?'

Jenny gave me a wintry smile. 'No. He claimed that it was consensual. He said that I'd come up to his car and asked him if he "was going to take me home" and that he'd interpreted this as a come-on. But the jury didn't buy it; the guilty verdict was unanimous.'

'Had he ever done it before?'

'No. And the Home Office reports say that he's shown "considerable" remorse while inside. He's in Wormwood Scrubs. Less than three miles away,' she added with a shudder.

'And when will he be out?'

'He'll come up for parole next year and will automatically be released the year after that, when he's served six years.'

'Did he know you were pregnant?'

'No. I asked for the witness box to be screened so that he couldn't see me. But the jury could. So there it is,' she said quietly. 'Now you know.'

'I wish you'd told me before.'

'I sometimes wanted to. But I find it easier to bear if I say nothing about it. I'm only telling you now because I'm so anxious about what to tell Grace. I'm a counsellor, Anna, but I can't counsel myself on the most important issue of my life. Because whenever I imagine talking to Grace about it,

313

then I inevitably have an image of him, which makes me feel so angry that I can't even think, let alone find the right words. So . . .' She looked at me. 'What would you say?'

I shook my head. 'I really don't know. It would be incredibly hard. The knowledge that one's child's beginnings had been so . . .'

'Violent,' Jenny whispered.

I nodded. 'I can see how you'd want to say nothing, or invent a story.'

'Oh yes,' Jenny sighed. 'You'd do anything to conceal the truth.'

'So . . . what *would* I say? Well, you could maybe simply tell Grace that her father wasn't nice to you, so you're angry with him and you don't want to see him at the moment.'

'I *never* want to see him.'

I looked at her. 'No. Of course you don't.'

I stayed with Jenny for a while, just sitting with her, still reeling from what she'd told me, and at the thought that she'd carried this terrible secret for so long. I yearned to offer her some piece of comforting advice, but in her situation there could be no easy solutions or right answers. She was going to spend the rest of her life working it out.

What had happened to Jenny made me reflect over the next few days on the many different ways in which men can father children – within long marriages, or short relationships, or from one-night stands, or from a hate-filled encounter of the kind she had suffered, or through the clinical arrangements involved in sperm donation, or the contrived collision of gametes in IVF. I thought of the way men can become de facto fathers through adoption, or unwittingly, through a partner's deceit, or by agreeing to stand *in loco patris* to another man's child, in the way Dad had done with Mark. And of course they can become stepfathers – as Patrick would probably be to Milly one day, I thought as I got our things ready for St Mawes.

'Would you like to watch a DVD while I do the packing, darling?' I asked Milly. 'Patrick will put one on for you.'

'Of course I will,' Patrick said.

'Beast!' Milly yelled. 'Want watch Beast, Mum.'

'*Beauty and the Beast* it is, then.' Patrick put the disc into the player while I went upstairs to get everything ready. We were leaving after breakfast the following day.

Patrick had arrived with his large leather bag and with a Maisie Mouse suitcase for Milly – it was typically thoughtful of him, and she'd already filled it with her toys, crayons and books.

As I got my things out of the wardrobe I thought how lucky I was to be with someone as decent and generous as Patrick. I thought of how tolerant he'd largely been about Xan and of the self-control that he'd shown. I thought, with shame, of the way I'd often failed to protect Patrick's feelings, but of how forgiving he'd been.

Milly was looking forward to Cornwall, but couldn't understand why we were going with Patrick, not Xan.

'The reason why we're going with Patrick', I'd explained the day before, 'is because he thought it would be lovely for you to go to the seaside; and also because he's Mum's special friend, darling.'

'No. Dass Jamie,' she'd corrected me without looking up from her colouring book.

'Well, Jamie *is* a special friend of Mum's – but in a different way, because he works with Mum, doesn't he? We make . . .'

'Gardens,' she interjected happily.

'Yes. We make gardens together.' Though not for much longer, I'd thought miserably. Jamie had decided to go back to Australia once our current projects were finished. 'But Patrick is my special friend,' I tried again.

'No,' Milly had insisted. 'Dass Jamie.'

'Whatever you say,' I'd said and sighed.

As I pulled summer dresses, cardigans and jeans out of my

315

wardrobe I heard Patrick coming upstairs. 'Is everything all right down there?' I asked. 'I've just got to get Milly's things ready, then I'll make supper.'

'It's fine,' he said, bending to kiss me. 'She's being as good as gold.' He sat on the corner of the bed while I folded things into my suitcase. 'How long is it since you've had a holiday?'

I straightened up. 'A very long time. I had a week in Brittany when Milly was eighteen months and that was it. She's been rather short-changed in that department.'

'We'll take her on some lovely holidays,' Patrick said and he kissed me again. As he went downstairs I felt a warm glow at the prospect of our shared future.

I crossed the landing into Milly's room and got out her T-shirts and shorts and her socks and summer dresses and her little mac with the ladybird pattern, and her red swimsuit because, although the sea would be too cold for her to swim in, the hotel had a heated pool.

Then the phone rang. It was Cassie, wanting to talk about Dad's seventieth birthday on 9 September. 'We should throw a surprise party for him.'

'No,' I said. 'He's not in the mood. Let's just do something low-key but nice in a good local restaurant.'

'At lunchtime, presumably, so that Milly can be there.'

'Yes.'

'And how many people should we have?'

'About ten? We'll ask Dad whom he'd like to invite.'

'And we'll pay for it,' said Cassie. 'Fifty-fifty?'

'Sure. In fact, I'm happy to stump up more if you haven't got it at the moment.'

'Oh I'm fine,' Cassie replied. 'For once in my life I'm quite flush, Anna. In fact, my fortunes are about to turn.'

'Really?' I said. 'Why?'

'I can't tell you,' she said enigmatically. 'Suffice it to say that I've been working hard on a special project and my

316

enterprise is about to pay off.' As I had little faith in Cassie's 'projects' my heart sank. But before I could ask her more, she'd gone on to discuss venues for Dad's party. 'How about the Belvedere?'

'Possibly. Or Julie's. We could have a big table in the window upstairs. But we'd better get on with it,' I added. 'It's only three weeks away.'

Then Xan phoned, worrying about Milly's car seat. Had it been correctly fitted into Patrick's car? I assured him it had been and that Patrick was a sensible driver. Then he wanted to say goodnight to Milly so I took the phone down to her. Although it was only a brief call, it seemed to upset her. 'Daddy,' she said, her eyes filling, when we'd hung up.

'You'll see him very soon,' I said. 'Next week.' Shortly after which he'd be leaving for New York, I thought miserably.

'Want Dad!'

'You're going to have such a lovely time in Cornwall, poppet. I'll buy you a little fishing net. Would you like that? A pink one?'

'Yes. Want pink net, Mum. And pink bucket. And pink spade.'

'We'll catch some little pink fish,' Patrick said. 'And some pink crabs.' Milly smiled. 'And I'm sure we'll find some pink shells. Wouldn't that be nice?'

She nodded. 'Want my *dad*.'

I made her some warm milk, settled her in front of *Beauty and the Beast* again with Patrick and went back upstairs to finish her packing. As I was putting in the last of her things I heard her let out a squawk.

'Please don't do that, Milly,' Patrick gently admonished her.

'No!' I heard her yell. 'Go away!'

'Be a good girl, Milly.' Milly was obviously doing some-thing she shouldn't be doing, but it sounded as though Patrick was handling it well.

317

'Get down,' I heard him say, louder now. She must be standing on the table. 'Please get *off*, Milly.'

'Go away!' she shouted. 'My don't *like* you.'

'I know you don't mean that. Now, come on, Milly . . .' I decided to let Patrick sort out the situation. He was a father himself, after all, and I didn't want to look fussy or mistrustful. Besides which I wanted Milly to recognise him as a figure of benign authority.

'Go a-*way*!' she yelled.

'Right.' I sighed. Time to intervene. I lifted the suitcase off the bed and dragged it to the top of the stairs.

'Would you please get down, Milly,' I heard Patrick say as I began to walk down the steps. 'Now!' he commanded.

'Go *a-way*!'

'Come on, Milly,' I heard Patrick say. 'I don't want you to fall down and hurt yourself, sweetie.'

'Go A-WAAAAAAY!'

'You must do as you're told, Milly. I won't ask you again. I'm going to count to three. One . . .'

By now I was halfway down the stairs and as I came down I looked into the circular mirror at the bottom of the steps. It's positioned at a slight angle, so that it 'looks' into the kitchen and, as I stared into it, I saw Milly standing on the worktop by the microwave – she must have climbed up on a chair.

'Two . . .'

Patrick was trying to coax her down, but she wouldn't oblige, and was dancing up and down on the spot.

'Three.'

He went to lift her down, pleading having failed. He put his hands up to her chest to pick her up, but as he did so I suddenly saw Milly turn her head and bite his hand, hard. Patrick cried out in pain. I was horrified at what she'd done although I was also fleetingly aware of all the change and flux she'd had in her life recently, with Xan suddenly being

318

around so much, and then the conflict between him and Patrick, and the fact that Milly now knew that Luisa was leaving us. The past few weeks hadn't been an easy time for her. Even so, biting was unacceptable . . .

I was about to go in when I saw Patrick lift her down on to the floor. Then he yanked up her arm and brought his hand down on her bare leg with a hard, viscious slap.

The sound seemed to resonate for a split second. Then Milly threw back her head and screamed, her face pink with pain, tears starting from her eyes, her mouth a rictus of distress.

'You hit her!' I breathed. I was trembling with anger and disbelief. 'You *hit* her. Don't you *ever* hit my child!' I said as I gathered her up in my arms. 'Not ever! Do you understand? Never! *Never*!' I hardly recognised my high, keening voice.

'She bit me,' he protested. He held out his hand to show me the red mark as though expecting sympathy.

'I don't care what she did! She's *three*. She's a little child. And you don't hit little children, Patrick – especially if they're not even yours!'

I took Milly into the sitting room and she sat on my lap, sobbing, more with shock than pain I suspected, while I rocked her back and forth. As I closed my eyes I saw again, as if in slow motion, the curiously practised way in which Patrick had jerked up her arm and smacked her leg. And I suddenly knew that this was something that he'd done before.

'It's OK, darling,' I breathed. 'It's OK.'

'My arm,' Milly sobbed, clutching it. 'It hurts.'

As I kissed it better, I was aware of Patrick standing next to me. I didn't look at him.

'It was the shock,' I heard him say. Milly was still on my lap, her head pressed to my chest, emitting teary little gasps. 'I didn't want her to fall. I didn't mean to lose my temper,' he added impotently.

'You do lose it, don't you?' I said, looking at him now.

319

'Children have to be disciplined,' he murmured weakly. 'And biting's not on.'

'That's true, but you don't just . . . lash out.'

And now, in a flash, I saw another scenario, with another child – a little boy.

'I'm sorry,' Patrick said. 'I'll never do that again.'

'No,' I said quietly. 'You won't.'

Within half an hour Patrick had gone. He kept saying that he wanted to talk about the incident, but there was nothing to say. I offered to pay half the cancellation charges for the hotel but he refused.

'I think you're overreacting,' he said as he brought in Milly's car seat.

'No,' I said coldly. 'I'm not.' When he'd left I went to the kitchen cupboard, took out the jar of Bee Good honey and threw it in the bin.

Milly looked at me. 'What you doing, Mum?'

'I'm throwing away this honey. Because I don't like honey and I never have done.'

Then I turned off *Beauty and the Beast*. Milly came upstairs with me and I explained that we wouldn't be going to the seaside after all.

'Because Patrick did smack me?'

'Yes,' I said. 'That's why. Does your arm still hurt?' She rubbed it, then shook her head. 'But I'll take you to the seaside another time soon, OK?'

'And you buy me a pink net?'

'Yes.'

'And a pink bucket?'

'Yes – and a pink spade, and a pink . . . everything.'

Milly beamed. Then we lay on my bed and I read her *The Gruffalo*, which made me think of Jamie. He wouldn't have hurt Milly in a million years. And she leaned her soft little body into me, turning over the pages in the excited way she always does, racing through the story: '. . . logpile house . . .

owl-ice-cweam . . . it's a Gruffalo! . . . Terrible teeth . . . his tongue is black . . . and the nut was good – The END. Iss THE END, Mum!' she yelled.

I thought of Patrick. 'Yes Milly,' I said. 'It is.'

SIXTEEN

'How are you enjoying Cornwall?' Jenny asked the following evening when I phoned her.

'I'm not. Cornwall's been cancelled.' I explained why.

'How . . . vile,' she murmured. 'So I guess that's that then.'

'Yes. Though I feel sad about it in many ways.'

'But you'd never be able to trust him.'

'No. I wouldn't.' Each time I replayed the incident in my mind I felt sick.

'He didn't hurt her, did he?'

'No. But her arm ached for a while.'

'Do you think he'd ever done it before?'

It was totally unintentional. It was an accident. An accident . . .

'I really don't know . . .'

'Well, I'm very sorry,' Jenny went on. 'He seemed so likeable; but you said he had a lot of anger.'

'He did . . .'

Beekeeping's better than any therapy.

Keep still!

I've said I won't come!

Would you let go of me, Patrick . . .

'But I didn't realise quite how much.'

322

'Are you going to tell Xan?'

'No. And I've asked Milly not to – there's no point and he might go berserk. I just told him that I'd had a last-minute change of mind about the holiday.'

'He must be delighted.'

'He is.' I thought of how Xan had distrusted Patrick. I'd attributed it to jealousy, but he'd clearly picked up something that I'd failed to detect.

Suddenly I heard the TV blaring. 'Milly!' I called out. 'Sorry, Jen, Milly's just switched on the telly, she's always fiddling with the remote.'

'Grace does that too.'

'Please turn it off, sweetheart.' I glanced into the sitting room. It was *The X-Factor*. On the screen a thin boy in a red bobble hat was anxiously awaiting the panel's verdict. 'Andy,' Simon Cowell was saying to him. 'You have got one of the *weirdest* voices I've ever heard in my life. You are *fabulously* awful. There's no *way* I'd have you in the next round . . .'

'Turn it off, please, Milly,' I said again as I resumed my conversation with Jenny. 'Just press the red button.'

'Tom,' Simon Cowell was now saying to the next contestant. 'You're fat. You're ugly. You're discoordinated. But you *sound* great. So I'm going to say . . . "Yes".'

'Milly, would you please turn it off – or down, darling.'

'Someone else who's dreaming of a "yes",' said the presenter, 'is . . .'

'*Mira*!' I heard Milly murmur.

'. . . Luisa Vanegas from Colombia.'

'Luisa on telebision, Mum!'

'Hang on, Jenny.' I walked into the sitting room, still clutching the phone to my ear, and stared at the screen.

'Twenty-three year old Luisa is an au pair, but she dreams of stardom.' There was Luisa, sitting in the hangar-like waiting room with hundreds of other hopefuls.

323

'Luisa's on *The X-Factor*,' I gasped.

'I'll just put my TV on,' I heard Jenny say. 'Oh my God. So she is. But didn't she tell you?'

'No,' I replied. 'I haven't seen much of her lately.'

The camera panned in on her, as she waited, in her red velvet dress, sipping a cup of tea. I could tell from the length of her hair that it had been recorded in June, a couple of weeks before I found Luisa busking.

'She looks good, doesn't she?' Jenny said.

'How long have you been waiting today, Luisa?' the presenter was asking her.

'I hab been here a bery long time . . . fibe hours.'

'Well, it's your turn now, Luisa, so good luck.'

Luisa jumped up and smiled nervously at the camera. Then we saw her walk into the audition room and stand in front of the three judges.

'What are you going to sing, Luisa?' Louis Walsh asked her.

'"All the Way from America" by Joan Armatrading.'

Sharon Osbourne gave her a nod. 'So let's hear it.'

Luisa composed herself for a moment, then began to sing: *You called all the way from America, and said hang on to love, girl. But the weeks and the months and the tears passed by, and my eyes couldn't stand the strain . . .* 'She sounds fabulous,' Jenny said. *. . . of that promised love, all the way from America.*

Simon Cowell was sitting back, arms folded, his head cocked to one side.

You called all the way from America and said I'll soon be home, girl. But the weeks and the months and the tears passed by and my eyes couldn't stand the strain, of that promised love, all the way from America. All the way from America . . .

'OK, that'll do!' Simon suddenly shouted.

'Shit! He hates her,' I said. Luisa looked crestfallen.

'We've heard all we need,' Louis Walsh agreed.

'So now it's time for Simon's verdict,' said the presenter.

'Luisa' Simon began, 'That was more like "All the Way from Latin America". Your pronunciation is crap. You need to work on your English – but you have a very powerful voice. You have conviction. You *look* good . . . and I'd be happy for you to go through.'

'Thank God,' I breathed as Luisa gave him an ecstatic smile.

'You've definitely got the X-Factor, Luisa,' Louis was saying now. 'So, although I don't often agree with Simon, it's a "yes" from me too.' Luisa clapped her hands together as if in prayer.

'But will Sharon agree with them?' Said the presenter.

'Luisa,' Sharon began. 'You have an *amazing* voice.' I exhaled with relief. 'You're as good as Joan Armatrading – in fact, you're so good I wondered whether you'd got a tape recorder stuffed down your bra – yet your voice is also very distinctive. You're through.'

'How fantastic!' I heard Jenny say. Milly was beaming.

Luisa blew the judges kisses and ran out of the room, radiant with joy.

'So how are you feeling, Luisa?' the presenter asked her.

Luisa threw back her head and laughed. 'I am feeling just . . . *maravilloso*!'

'Do you want to say a quick hello to anyone while you're on air?'

'Yes,' Luisa replied. 'I would like say *hola* to my lobely English family – Anna and Milly – if they watching this.'

'This is the family you're au pair to?'

'*Sí*. Anna is a wonderful person and Milly *es una niña fantástica. Adoro a* Milly!' She blew the camera a kiss.

'*Y yo adoro a* Luisa,' Milly said.

The next morning I woke early and went downstairs to have some coffee. While the kettle boiled I picked the newspaper off the mat and saw that next door's *Sunday News* had been delivered instead of my usual *Observer*. As it was too early to swap them over I sat at the kitchen table and flicked through the *News*. There were the usual tabloid preoccupations with immigration, tax rises, speed cameras and celebrity cellulite, as well as special offers for Center Parcs.

From upstairs I heard Luisa's door open. Today was the day she was moving out: I'd been so preoccupied I hadn't thought about it until now. I felt a wave of sadness.

YOU PAY MILLIONS IN TAX TO FUND LABOUR! announced a story on page 2 of the *News*. OBESITY LINKED TO MEMORY LOSS said the headline below. DIANA – NEW EVIDENCE was the story on page 3. I turned over to page 4. SUNDAY NEWS JOURNALIST LOSES HOME IN BLAZE.

I sat bolt upright.

The Sunday News *columnist Citronella Pratt and her family escaped injury in a fire that destroyed their weekend retreat in East Sussex. The Old Rectory at Aldingly, near Hastings, was razed to the ground on Friday.*

I looked at the helpful 'before' and 'after' photos of a beautiful, rose-covered Georgian house and a huge heap of smouldering ash.

Ms Pratt, her second husband and their three-year-old son, Erasmus, had gone out for the afternoon, leaving Ms Pratt's thirteen-year-old daughter from her first marriage, Sienna, at home. The blaze is believed to have started in the little boy's bedroom, where a favourite teddy bear is thought to have caught fire . . .

I turned to Citronella's column on page 18.

On Friday our beautiful country home in East Sussex burned down. But far from being downcast I realise how

326

very fortunate I have been. Not only, first and foremost, in that none of my family suffered any injury, but also in that we lost nothing of any sentimental value: the teddy which caught fire, for example, was only Erasmus's second-favourite bear, luckily, and not his beloved Steiff, which is kept in London. I also feel fortunate in that my husband and I were in any case thinking of giving up country life as the village was not conveniently located for the new school which Sienna will start in September – a remarkable establishment for particularly spirited young people which we feel will offer our brilliant child the challenging environment she needs. So it is no sacrifice for us to give up our rural idyll so that we can get there in time for what the staff there amusingly call 'visiting hours'.

So Citronella clearly had serious problems with the not-quite-so-perfect Sienna. Maybe that's what had been eating her up. But I envied Citronella her magnificent fortitude. She could have a nuclear device dropped on her and would still find a way to portray herself as having been somehow 'fortunate'. *Fortunately I was vaporised instantly . . . which fortunately meant that I didn't leave an unpleasant stain on the Axminster . . .*

From upstairs I heard sounds of Milly stirring. But instead of coming down to find me I heard her going up to the top floor, drawn to the sound of Luisa singing:

'*So what happens now? Another suitcase in another hall. So what happens now? Take your picture off another wall . . .*'

'What you doing?' I heard Milly demand as I went upstairs.

'I packing,' Luisa replied. 'I leabe today.'

'I don't want you to go,' I heard Milly say. '*Quiero que usted permanezca.*'

'I hab to go,' Luisa replied. 'But I come back and see you, *mi caramelo.*' I heard the familiar sound of Milly's cheek being kissed.

I knocked on Luisa's door and pushed it ajar. On the floor

327

was the new red suitcase she'd recently bought. Milly was sitting in it.

'Luisa, I wish you'd told me you were going to be on *The X-Factor.*'

'I bery surprise too. I not know that they show my audition on TB.'

'Thank you for the nice things you said about Milly and me.'

'I mean it, Anna.' She took two shirts out of the cupboard. 'And I'm sorry that we've hardly spoken lately.'

'You hab been bery busy, Anna.'

'Yes . . . I've had a lot on my mind. But, do you actually have another au pair job, Luisa?'

'No,' she replied. 'I not found a family I like. So I going stay in Shepherd's Bush again with my friend.'

I looked at Milly, who was now busily taking Luisa's things out of the suitcase and stuffing them back in the drawers. I thought of how much Milly loved Luisa, and of how much she loved Xan, who was leaving in a fortnight, and of how fond she was of Jamie, who would soon be going back to Australia. It was all too much change at one time.

'Well, Luisa, I don't have a new au pair – I haven't even looked for one, to be honest, and so I just thought . . .' I sank on to the bed. 'Please don't go, Luisa,' I said. 'We've loved having you here; I'm sorry we had that falling out . . .'

'I no blame you, Anna,' Luisa said. 'I would do the same.'

'You could stay here as long as you like. We could play it by ear.'

Luisa looked at me non-comprehendingly. 'Ear?'

'*Podríamos improvisar,*' said Milly helpfully.

'So you no want me to go?' I shook my head. 'Well . . .'

Suddenly Milly wrapped her arms round Luisa's knees. '*Stay* wiz me.'

Luisa picked her up and kissed her. '*Sí.*'

*   *   *

328

So our lives settled back into some kind of routine. Luisa started at the New Horizons language school in Notting Hill, where her English quickly improved. Milly went back to Sweet Peas, and Jamie and I finished the vicarage garden.

'I love it now,' Pippa said as Jamie and I cleared up on our final day there. 'It looked so funereal before, and now it's . . . joyful.'

The garden was light and bright, the rebuilt flowerbeds filled with white and pink roses, French lavender and pale-blue cranesbill geraniums which gave it an almost Provençal air. There was a seated arbour with box benches, a dining area screened by four silvery olive trees, and in the middle of the new lawn a handsome green climbing frame with a swing and a slide.

'What does your husband think of it?' Jamie asked as he lifted Jack into the swing.

'He loves it,' Pippa replied. 'In fact,' she added with a smile, 'he says he prefers it to how it was before.'

'Well, that's some compliment,' Jamie said as he gave Louis a push. 'I'm sorry I lost it with him,' he added. 'I was having a very bad day.'

Pippa smiled, but didn't reply. 'So what are you two doing next?' she asked. 'I imagine you're very busy.'

'We're finishing a small garden in Maida Vale,' I replied. 'Then I'll start work on a big country garden in Hampshire – it belongs to my old boss. Sadly Jamie won't be working on that,' I added.

'Oh,' Pippa said. 'Why not?'

'I'm going back to Australia,' he explained.

'For how long?'

'A few months. Maybe longer. I'm not sure.'

'You mean you might not come back?'

He shrugged. 'I really don't know.'

'Well, that's a shame,' Pippa said. 'You seem to be such a good team.'

'We are,' Jamie said. 'But I need some time out. I've come to a bit of a crossroads in my life.' He lifted Jack out.

'So I'll be working with Stefan,' I said with false brightness.

'Stefan's great,' said Jamie. 'He's a very good builder.'

'He's excellent,' I agreed. But it wouldn't be the same as working with Jamie . . .

On 8 September Xan left for New York. We'd told Milly a fortnight before, to give her time to get used to the idea that he wouldn't be around so much. I've always hated airport farewells so Xan came to the house on his way to Heathrow. 'I'll be coming to see you,' he said to Milly, his voice catching. 'And maybe you and Mum will come and visit me.'

'We'll go to see Dad by aeroplane,' I said. 'Would you like that, Milly?'

She nodded.

Xan bent down to cuddle her goodbye. 'I'll see you soon, darling,' he said. His eyes had filled. 'I'll see you soon.'

'Soon, Dad,' she echoed as she put her arms round his neck. Not that soon, I thought sadly. Then we stood in the window and waved to him until his taxi was out of sight.

The following day was Dad's birthday and we'd booked to have lunch at the Belvedere as it was so close to his flat – all he'd have to do was stroll through Holland Park. Cassie came round to me in the morning to run through the short speech that the two of us were to make.

At 11.30 the doorbell rang. I wasn't expecting anyone.

'Elaine!' I exclaimed. I threw my arms round her, as I always do when I see her because she was the first person to look after my baby, so I've always felt a little emotional about her.

'I did phone a couple of times but you were out,' she said as she stepped inside. 'I've just been to see Jamie, so I thought I'd pop in to see you and Milly on my way to the tube.'

'How is Jamie?' I asked. 'Is he ok?'

'He's . . . fine. But you all look as though you're about to go out – is this a bad time for me to have come?'

'Oh, no,' I lied. 'Although . . . actually, Elaine, we *will* have to go soon as it's my dad's seventieth and we're having a lunch for him: but do stay for a few minutes – it's just so nice to see you. Did you ever meet my sister Cassie?'

'I don't think I did.' Elaine smiled. 'But I recognise you from photos and I heard a lot about you.' I made a jug of coffee while she and Cassie chatted then I finished dressing Milly. Elaine glanced at her watch. 'It's ten to twelve.' She stood up, then stroked Milly's head. 'I'll come another day when there's a bit more time, Anna. Thanks for the coffee. Great to meet you Cassie.'

'Why don't you join us for lunch?' Cassie suddenly said.

Elaine looked dumbfounded and I was a bit taken aback myself. 'I couldn't possibly do that,' she protested.

'Why not?' Cassie asked with her customary directness.

'Well,' Elaine stuttered, 'I wouldn't want to intrude – and I'm not dressed for it.'

'Of course you are. You look lovely,' Cassie added. I was touched by her warmth.

'But it's a family celebration,' Elaine said. 'Plus I've never even met your dad.'

'Oh, you don't have to worry – he's perfectly civilised,' said Cassie. 'Anyway, it's going to be very low-key, besides which one of Dad's friends had to cancel this morning, so there's a spare place.'

'Oh. But . . .'

'So that's settled then,' Cassie concluded before Elaine could raise any further objections. I was slightly surprised by her insistence – she didn't know Elaine, but Elaine, somewhat bemused, agreed. So we all walked through Holland Park in the slanting September sunshine clutching our flowers and gifts, occasionally stopping to show Milly the squirrels and black rabbits.

Our table was upstairs, by the french windows that opened on to the terrace. The Travises were already there and Bill French, whom Dad used to work with, and his wife Jane, and Dad's sister Kay, and her husband Ted. Dad seemed genuinely touched as Cassie and I made a short speech about what a great father and grandfather he was.

'And if Mum could have been here, she'd have said what a great husband you were too,' Cassie added feelingly, because she now knows the whole story about Mark.

By this stage the wine was flowing, and with all the accumulated stress of recent weeks I'd had far more to drink than I usually do.

At some point Elaine began talking about Jamie. He was leaving for Australia the following week. 'You're going to miss him, Anna,' she said.

'Miss him?' I lowered my glass. 'I don't know what I'm going to do without him.'

'Jamie is Mum's special friend,' Milly explained as she did some colouring in. She dipped her pink felt tip in my tumbler of water.

'You know, you're right, Milly,' I said. 'He *is*.' I felt a wave of sentiment wash over me. 'Jamie's the nicest, most honourable, kind, hard-working, talented and reliable man . . .'

'I remember telling you that he'd never let you down,' Elaine said.

'And you were right. He didn't let me down. Until now. I wish he wasn't going,' I added dismally. 'I'm going to miss working with him, and talking to him twenty times a day, and arguing with him, and planting things with him, and building things and driving around with him in his battered old pick-up.' I silently cursed Thea.

'Well, Jamie needs to be at home for a spell,' Elaine said. 'He's going through a lot. Plus it's five years since he's spent any time with his family.'

'Do you think he'll come back?' Cassie asked.

332

'I . . . don't know.' Then, by way of changing the subject, Elaine asked Cassie about her work.

'Oh, I do all sorts of things,' Cassie replied. 'I'm afraid Anna disapproves of most of them.'

'I disapprove of some of them,' I corrected her. 'But you're certainly enterprising, Cassie, I'll give you that.' I lifted my glass of wine to her in sisterly salute.

'Well, I have been quite enterprising recently,' she said. 'In fact . . .' She reached into her bag and pulled out a copy of *The Bookseller*.

'Why did you buy this?' I asked as she handed it to me. 'Are you going to work in publishing now? That would be a good move, Cassie. I'm all for it. It's respectable.'

'Turn to page 8,' she said.

RANDOM HOUSE SIGNS NEW TALENT said the headline.

Random House have signed up newcomer Cassie Temple in a two-book deal worth a hefty £200,000. The former croupier's debut novel, Killing Time, *will be published next May and is the first in a series of comedy thrillers featuring private investigator Delilah Swift, a one-time croupier and lingerie model, who is asked to investigate the suspicious deaths of three antique-clock dealers in London's Portobello Road . . .*

'Good on ya, Cassie!' Elaine breathed. 'This is fantastic!'

'It is,' I said. 'I had no idea you were writing anything. When did you do it?'

'Over the past three months,' she replied. 'I was working in the evenings – as you know – but my days were mostly free. And one day this character, Delilah Swift, just popped into my head, so I started to write about her. And when I'd done a few chapters I showed them to a girl at Stitch 'n' Bitch who works for a literary agency, and she liked it and bingo! So now I'm a writer.'

'You never cease to amaze me,' I said.

Now Dad came to sit at our end of the table so that Cassie could tell him some more about the book. So I moved round and made small talk with the Travises, who are very nice if not terribly exciting; and Milly was playing with her Fifi doll Forget Me Not under the table; and now Cassie was talking to Uncle David and Auntie Glenda, and Elaine was talking to Dad. I overheard fragments of their conversation as they realised that the reason they hadn't met before was because Dad had always visited me on a Sunday, which was Elaine's day off. Then she was telling him about being a maternity nurse – how much she loves tiny babies . . . that she's a light sleeper . . . that she'd got divorced a year before but feels life is full of promise . . . Then Milly fell asleep on my lap and the party began to break up, and Cassie and I thanked everyone for coming. I looked at Dad but he was still chatting to Elaine as though they'd known each other for years. As I glanced at them, noticing now the air of unforced intimacy between them, their heads inclined towards each other, I wondered if Cassie was thinking what I was thinking; then I realised that of course she was, because that was precisely why she'd invited Elaine. By now it was four o'clock and the restaurant was empty except for the very patient maître d', and Dad and Elaine, who were still sitting there engrossed, as we left.

EPILOGUE

Five months later, Dad and Elaine are still sitting in the very same spot at the same table, in the same room upstairs in the Belvedere. Their heads are still inclined together and they are still laughing and chatting, but today they are wearing different clothes. Dad looks handsome in a grey suit and pale-blue tie – which is not snazzy at all – and Elaine is wearing a silk dress of the same pale-blue with her ash-blonde hair swept up in a french pleat and dressed with a white camellia. She looks radiant, as all brides do. She and Dad smile as the official photographer snaps away. Milly, in her pale-blue silk dress, is so excited that she has eaten nothing all day. It is the first time that she has been a bridesmaid and, as I look at Mark, who has come over for the wedding with his fiancé Marilyn, I find myself hoping that she may get the chance to be one again before long.

Mark is once more just . . . Mark. He loves his life in San Francisco. He loves his wife-to-be. But he loves us too, he says, and Dad's wedding has provided the perfect opportunity for him to do what he says he's been wanting to do for a very long time – come home.

'I didn't know how to,' he confides as we sit side by side on the top table. 'And then Dad's wedding invitation arrived and Marilyn said I *had* to come back and spend some proper time with my family. So . . .' He shrugs.

'I've missed you,' I say. 'But at least now I understand.'

Mark squeezes my hand. 'I've missed you. I was so angry, for so long. But I see things differently now.' He looks at Dad. 'And I know that the man who brought me up is my father.'

Now the cake is brought in, and Dad puts his hand over Elaine's as they cut it and everyone claps. Then he makes a short speech about what a happy Valentine's Day this is, and what a wonderful person Elaine is and how he could not have known what a favour, ultimately, he was to do himself when he hired her to be my maternity nurse. Cassie shouts out that it was her idea, thank you! Dad laughs and blows her a kiss.

As the waiters charge our glasses I reflect again on the fact that my maternity nurse has just become my stepmother and Milly's step-grandmother. The thought makes me feel happy.

'So you and I are now related by marriage,' Jamie says with a smile. 'I hope this doesn't mean I have to start calling your dad "Uncle Colin".'

Jamie is wearing a dark suit with a white corsage in one lapel and one of Milly's Little Mermaid stickers on the other. She is sitting next to him, soliciting his help with a picture she is drawing. As she passes him some crayons she tells him that her dad's coming soon. Xan missed her so much that he has recently relinquished New York for Brussels so that he can see Milly every other weekend. Now, even though I'm on my own, I feel no painful longing for Xan. We simply co-operate as parents and friends.

Then the speeches are over and we all raise our glasses to Dad and Elaine. Over the wedding cake and coffee the conversation becomes more general. Everyone is interested in Cassie's forthcoming book.

When I first read *Killing Time* with its eccentric, but

amusing plot involving honey-trap girls, casinos and purveyors of telephone sex, I saw the truth of something Cassie had once said – that 'no experience is ever wasted, low-grade or not'. Especially if it is your destiny to become a writer, as it was clearly Cassie's I now see. As I'd finished the last page of the manuscript I'd realised how judgemental I had been. Cassie was just living her own life, in her own way; and out of all her odd, seemingly unconnected experiences she has forged a clever and very entertaining book.

'Well, I hab been terrifically lucky,' I hear Luisa say to Uncle Ted. 'The standard on *The X-Factor* was so high that I didn't think I stood a snowball in hell's chance of getting to the final: you could hab knocked me down with a feather when I did. I was gobsmacked to get down to the last three. No, I don't hab a recording contract yet – in my dreams! But I hab a few auditions in a couple of weeks. Oh, I'm awfully sorry, but I think I'm needed.'

Now the tables are pushed back for the cabaret, and Luisa steps forward and does a set. She sings 'Starry Starry Night', which reminds me of when she first came to live with us. Then she sings 'Another Suitcase in Another Hall', and then the beautiful 'From a Distance'. She closes with 'Do You Know Where You're Going To?' and I realise that it isn't always a bad thing if you don't. Cassie didn't know where she was going, but seems to be winding up in a good place anyway. I decide to ease up a bit and go with the flow.

Then the dancing starts and Jamie is dancing with Milly, spinning her round, and I'm dancing with Dad, and Mark is dancing with Elaine.

Then Dad taps him on the back and the two men burst into laughter.

'It's so nice that Mark's here,' I say to Jamie as we return to the table.

'Is it nice that I'm here too?' Jamie asks.

'It's wonderful,' I say. 'I wasn't sure that you'd come back.'

'Well, I missed London – and you.'

'Hence all the texts and e-mails?'

He nods. 'I didn't like not talking to you. I'd become used to it. So I wanted to keep in touch. And then I had to come back for Elaine's wedding, didn't I?'

'So are you going to stay?' I ask, aware that my pulse is racing a little.

'Yes,' Jamie says. 'I'm going to stay. I don't suppose there's any chance of a job with you is there?' he asks with another sip of champagne.

'I think there's a very good chance,' I reply.

'It's your birthday tomorrow,' he suddenly says.

'Yes, its is. I'll be thirty-seven,' I add with a grimace.

'An old lady! I've got a little present for you.'

'Really?' I hold out my hand.

'I'll give it to you tomorrow. I'll come over for breakfast – OK?'

'OK.'

The next morning I wake up, slightly hung-over but happy. At ten I hear the doorbell ring and Milly thunders downstairs.

'Iss Jamie!' she yells as she peers through the coloured glass. She runs to her book box and comes back with *Cinderella*, *The Snail and the Whale* and *Monkey Puzzle*.

'Happy birthday Anna,' Jamie says. He smiles his familiar, crinkly-eyed smile.

Luisa is still in bed, but has left flowers on the dining table, and one of her eggless cakes which we have with coffee.

'OK, then,' I say. 'I can't wait any longer. So what have you got me?'

'Close your eyes.' Jamie says. 'And hold out your hands.'

I do, and I feel something very light land in them. I look.

338

In my cupped palms is a packet of seeds with a picture of some delicate purple flowers.

'*Aquilegia*?' I murmur. 'How lovely.' Jamie then hands me another packet with a photo of some feathery white plumes.

'*Astilbes*?' I say. 'I love them.'

'I know you do.' Now he gives me a packet of sky-blue delphiniums, then some pale pink foxglove seeds, then some lemony lupins, then some crimson *Sedums*, then bitter orange *Euphorbia*. All the things I adore and all, I can't help noticing, hardy perennials.

'Last one.' Jamie hands me some tomato seeds. 'Sorry,' he says with a grin, taking them back, 'those ones are mine.' He replaces them with a packet of periwinkle-blue forget-me-nots.

'I love forget-me-nots,' I say. 'They were my mother's favourite. But Jamie . . .' I start laughing. 'There's just one problem with this present. My garden's tiny.'

'No worries. I've already thought about that.' Now he hands me an envelope. Inside is a certificate from the West London Horticultural and Allotments Society. It is a rental agreement for the number 27 allotment in Duke's Meadows, Chiswick – and it is in my name.

'You're giving me an *allotment*?'

He nods. 'It's just up the road.' He stands up. 'Come on then.'

'What? Now?'

'Yes. Now.' He replies. 'Why not?'

So we put on our coats and I put on the green wellies that were my leaving present from Arden, and Jamie helps Milly on with her ladybird boots and we get in his car and drive to Chiswick.

'When did you get it?' I ask as we park. It is cold and our breath is visible in the crisp morning air.

'I put your name down for it last June,' he says as he helps Milly out of her seat.

I look at him. 'Last June?' Our feet crunch over a damp, gravel path.

'When we were filling the planters in the Edwards' garden. And you said that you wished you had a big herbaceous border to fill. You said it with such longing, and so I thought I'd get you one. Ah, number 27 – here we are.'

The plot is big – about thirty feet square, and the soil is hillocked with tufts of damp grass. In the corner there is a small, slightly derelict looking summer house.

'You got me this last *June*?' I feel a lump come into my throat at Jamie's kindness and I think how much my mother would have liked him.

'I went on the waiting list,' he explains. 'And when I got back from Australia last week the certificate had arrived.'

'What an amazing present,' I murmur. 'You've given me a garden.'

'That's exactly what I wanted to do. To give you a garden that you could plant to your heart's content.'

I have a sudden vision of the entire plot ablaze with colourful blooms. I rattle the seeds in my pocket. 'Well this is the right time to sow.'

'It is. You could grow sweet peas too,' Jamie muses, 'and vegetables. You could have runner beans, leeks and Swiss chard. You could have your own little Harvest Festival.'

I smile at the idea, but am also dismayed. 'It's wonderful, Jamie,' I say. 'And I love the idea. But it's going to be so much work.'

'Yes,' he says matter-of-factly. 'It will be.' My heart sinks. 'But you won't have to do it on your own.' He reaches for my hand. 'I'll help you.' I feel a wave of relief mingled with a kind of euphoria. 'I thought we could do it together; and we could bring over a couple of deckchairs to sit in when we've finished, and a bottle of wine on summer evenings. And Milly could have a little patch to grow things on. Would you like that Milly? You could grow some sunflowers.' She is busy looking under a stone and doesn't reply. 'I thought that we could sow and grow together,' Jamie says.

'Grow *together*,' Milly suddenly echoes.

'Yes,' I say with a smile at Jamie. 'I think we probably will.'

BIBLIOGRAPHY

The following books provided very helpful background during the course of my research.

Plant Personalities by Carol Klein; Cassel Illustrated
Superhints for Gardeners by The Lady Wardington; Michael Joseph
Gardener's Latin by Bill Neal; Robert Hale
Beekeeping for Dummies by Howland Blackiston; Wiley Publishing Inc.
The City Gardener by Matt James; HarperCollins